Ace, King, Knave

Maria McCann is the author of *As Meat Loves Salt* (Fourth Estate, 2001) which was an *Economist* Book of the Year and *The Wilding* (Faber, 2010) which was longlisted for the Orange Prize and chosen for the Richard and Judy Book Club. She has also contributed to various anthologies, most recently to *Why Willows Weep* (2011) and *Beacons* (2013).

ACE, KING, KNAVE

Maria McCann

FABER & FABER

First published in this edition in 2013
by Faber and Faber Limited
Bloomsbury House,
74–77 Great Russell Street,
London WC1B 3DA
This export paperback published in 2013

Typeset by Faber and Faber Ltd
Printed and bound by CPI Group (UK) Ltd, Croydon CR0 4YY

A CIP record for this book
is available from the British Library

ISBN 978–0–571–29759–7

2 4 6 8 10 9 7 5 3 1

To all those who, in the words of Louis MacNeice,
'were born and grew up in a fix'

Note on Language

This novel contains some eighteenth-century terms that may be unfamiliar, including both the occasional French expression beloved by elegant speakers and also the more vital slang of the poor and the criminal fraternity. I hope that in most cases the sense is sufficiently clear from the context and that no dictionary is required. For convenience, and for those who like to know if they've got it right, there is a glossary at the end of the book.

I

Provided they are accompanied at all times by Rixam, and on no account venture further than the shallows, Papa has given permission for Mr Zedland to take Sophia boating on the Statue Lake.

Clutching her gown with one hand, Sophia is helped on board. Rixam is about to follow her when Zedland pushes off from the jetty, leaving him stranded.

Sophia laughs at the accident. 'Wait there, Rixam.'

Zedland turns the boat round and pulls away with Rixam in full view. When they are some twenty feet from the jetty Sophia, making the best of a bad job, calls over to the servant, 'If you wait, Rixam, Papa will be quite satisfied.'

The man has no option but to wait, though his unspoken *I think not* is plainly legible in his stance.

'We should perhaps go back for him,' Sophia murmurs.

'He would be *de trop*.'

The lake's steely surface beats back to them the blue fire of August. The oarblades trail molten drops, the dimples and swirls they create flattened by the oppressive heat. Waterbirds call from the reeds; flying insects cross their bows, coming (Sophia thinks) a great way from the grass and plants where they have their homes. Zedland's hands, firm on the oars, slide back and forth with practised ease.

Associating it as she does with sailors and fishermen, Sophia finds this competence disconcerting. Possibly Zedland divines her unease, since he announces, 'Though a thorough gentleman, my father was something of an eccentric. He had no time for Latin and Greek, preferring that I should excel in riding, rowing and firing a pistol.'

'And leading a set in the dance? For you do excel at it.'

Zedland shrugs and smiles. Sophia feels her own smile rise to meet his, reflecting it as the reeds are reflected, upside down, on the brilliant surface of the lake.

'Is there good angling here?'

'I believe so. Would you like a servant to come out with you?'

'My hope was that *you* might. A lady with rod and parasol, a charming picture! You needn't soil your hands, you know. Titus will manage the bait.'

'I can't always understand Titus,' says Sophia, and blushes, for the boy was given her by Zedland. Too late, she recalls the good old English proverb concerning the mouths of gift horses. Perhaps, though, it is precisely a question of Titus's mouth: his lips are too large, she believes, and impede his speech. Papa disapproves of this present of Zedland's and wished the boy to be sent back, but since Zedland and Sophia are so soon to be married he contents himself with grumbling. Titus will go with them to Sophia's new home in Essex, and will cease to trouble Papa. He is still young and, Zedland insists, very capable of learning. With opportunities to hear the conversation of educated persons, Titus will surely improve.

The surface of the lake closes almost as soon as they glide over it. Sophia fancies that to Rixam, doggedly watching from the bank, boat and occupants must appear as a doubled creature, capable of turning topsy-turvy without coming to harm. Heat-haze rising off the water melts her grey satin robe into the surrounding air, and Sophia herself is incense dissolving before the sacred image that is Mr Zedland. How much more beautiful are dark eyes, she thinks, than blue. Blue eyes have been shamefully overpraised. How he gazes about him —

Zedland has shipped oars. 'Pray, where are the statues?'

'There are none. I wish Papa would give the lake some other name. That one is quite ridiculous.'

2

'Were there not statues in the past?'

'My great-grandfather found a marble cupid buried in the mud near the jetty. Since then it's been the Statue Lake. Of course, everybody asks, "Where are the statues?"'

'Then I'm *à la mode*,' he says, evidently amused. 'But why should it displease you?'

She searches his expression for a sign that she may open her mind to him. Zedland's mouth curls up in a teasing smile. It is hardly a reassurance and yet Sophia is unable to hold out against it.

'What I mean,' she begins falteringly, 'is that "Statue Lake" sounds as if we wished to pretend to . . .'

'To — ?'

'Well. One gentleman asked if we intended to erect copies of the sculptures at Bath.'

'What would it matter if you did?' asks Zedland.

Sophia shakes her head.

'You dislike them, perhaps? But why should you? Consider how much our modern elegance owes to their inspiration.'

'They are very well – where they are.'

'That is a lady's reason, I suppose.'

She is conscious of appearing at a disadvantage. 'Perhaps it's an oddity in me, but I confess I dislike this endless copying. We're not Romans but English. I find such fakery dishonest, and the works it produces worthless.'

During the later part of this speech she glimpses in Zedland's obsidian eyes a curious look: a not altogether friendly look. Then it is gone. He takes up the oars again and propels the boat smoothly towards the centre of the lake.

The deck is bound up in a silk handkerchief. Betsy-Ann Shiner wipes her hands with cologne, unwraps the handkerchief, spreads it out and examines it for holes before turning her attention to the cards themselves.

Even to a woman as fly at Betsy-Ann, thoroughly acquainted with this line of goods, these are a novelty. Each card is divided diagonally, corner to corner, combining two pictures in one: a dancing lady on the top left, and on the bottom right, upside down, a marching soldier. Betsy-Ann fans out the deck: a gay assembly. She turns the fan upside down, shakes it and spreads it again, and now she holds an army in her hand.

Very pretty!

She turns over the fan and counts the cards. The deck is ranged in order, every card present – no soldier wounded, nor lady indisposed. Is pretty *all* they are, or have they something more to offer? Damned if she can see it. They reveal themselves directly you handle them; they can't be dealt without the trick becoming plain, and are consequently of no use to sharps.

'Where'd you find these?' she demands of the boy standing before her.

'Off a coster's cart.' He grins. 'Reckon he was fencing, too.'

Betsy-Ann glares. 'I don't *fence*, I buy second-hand goods. On that understanding we can do business.'

The boy mumbles something.

'All right, then. Your coster wants to sell, does he?'

A nod.

'I daresay he does, but they're no use to me, sweetheart. Say a penny.'

'He won't let them go for that.'

'Won't he?' She hefts them expertly from palm to palm and then, seeing the boy impressed, holds her hands wide apart and springs the entire deck from the right to the left, the cards arcing, forming a momentary bridge in the air.

'Penny-ha'penny,' she says, slapping down the deck onto the handkerchief, '*and* the wiper, and *that* only 'cause I like the look of your face.'

'The wiper's silk,' the boy complains.

'Take it or leave it.'

When he has pocketed his money and gone, she binds up the cards again in the handkerchief and lays them by.

It is almost noon: a hot, airless day. Betsy-Ann keeps the window closed and the gaps plugged with rags. As she says, better your own smell than someone else's; better the stale breath of one jordan under the bed than the arsehole belch of outside, where slops lie baking on the cobbles. There's a courtyard at the back of here, with a necessary house, but not everybody in the street enjoys that convenience and the maidservants, little slatterns some of them, won't always take the trouble of carrying a full pot downstairs. Betsy-Ann stands and rubs at the glass, cleaning a space in the dust. She sees the boy's figure dwindle along the street, hopping and skipping as it crosses a blemish in the pane.

The deck ought not to stay here. She takes it to the chimney-cupboard, where she presses on a protruding nail. The back of the cupboard opens out into a cubbyhole fitted out with shelves and hangers, and with ropes suspended from the ceiling: her secret place, her Eye. The name is a precaution in case she's ever brought before the Beak. With one of these, you can swear as innocent as the day: *I've no more, my Lord, than I could put into my eye.* This is a large Eye, a dry Eye, a dark and deceptive Eye. Inside she keeps a tub of umbrellas, picked up from the stands inside shops on rainy days. A teapot in the corner contains watches;

5

a wooden box, children's tops and other toys. Here are ribbons, needles, thimbles, a hoard of rings laid away inside a cracked cup and an entire drawer of mufflers, wipers and gloves: silk, cotton, linen, wool, silk, lacy, embroidered. Betsy-Ann sells on these goods, sometimes to trusted visitors, sometimes by loading them on a cart fitted with hidden compartments and carrying them to another district. Thimbles, ribbons and suchlike can be sold as quickly as she likes, but no wiper ever leaves these premises until she has unpicked the embroidery.

Groping under the stuffs lying in the drawer, she fishes up a box of soft green leather, holds it to her nose and inhales. Attar of roses. It hasn't faded so very much, not yet. Her breath comes quickly as she lifts the lid on its contents: white satin shoes, fresh and unworn. Betsy-Ann takes one of the shoes and presses it to her cheek, then feels inside the toe. There they are, the earrings of black pearl. Entangled with them is a hoop of gold, finished with a coral heart. She slides it onto her finger, takes it off and studies the inscription inside it.

It's only a fawney, he said, and smiled. She said, *What's that writing?*

Betsy-Ann pushes earrings and fawney back into the shoe and hides everything away again at the bottom of the drawer, beneath the piles of wipers.

From one of the ropes attached to the ceiling hangs a deep basket. She winds it down and inspects the contents: small bottles of gin, intended for display on the upper layer of her cart. She beds down the strange deck among the gin bottles, perhaps as a tribute to their shared power of illusion, and takes up another from a nearby shelf: the Tarocco.

3

'Peter is party to a plan,' Sophia says. Titus looks blankly at her; she points at her mouth and then at his to indicate that he should repeat her words. 'Peter is party to a plan.'

'Feeter iss farty to a flan.'

'Party.'

'Farty.'

Were this an English boy, she would suspect him of vulgar insolence as well as the coarsest possible language, but his eyes, that seem to be all pupil, show only perplexity and distress.

Is it possible that he is deaf? If so, it must be a very particular kind of deafness. He pronounces *m* and *n* without difficulty, so why should he not distinguish between *f* and *p*?

'Titus, listen!' She tugs on his ear. 'P-p-p-p-p-p-p! Party!'

'F-f-f-f-f-f —'

'Stop!' Sophia cries. If they are all so difficult to school, she wonders that the *ton* should find them desirable as servants. Apart, of course, from the saving in wages; but persons of quality need hardly fret about that.

The boy's mouth is trembling.

'We'll try again another day,' she tells him, ringing the bell for the housekeeper. 'Wait here.'

Mrs Hooton appears and makes a point of not looking at Titus.

'Mrs Hooton, kindly take Titus to your room and keep him with you an hour or two, conversing with him as you carry out your work. Pray correct his pronunciation.' Mrs Hooton nods with no great show of enthusiasm. 'Titus, go with Mrs Hooton, listen carefully to her and endeavour to reproduce the sounds of a native English speaker.'

Panic flares in his face: he has not understood.

'Go with Mrs Hooton,' she repeats, betrayed into gesturing like a fishwife. 'Go away.'

When they have left the room Sophia flings herself down in a chair. How can she rid herself of the boy without offending Zedland? Titus is intolerable; he will bring her into ridicule wherever she goes. What is she to do?

She could leave him at home, of course, but how can he be made a contented servant, when he cannot be fitted into the servants' world? If his age is what Zedland says it is, he will never be tall and substantial enough for a footman, even supposing one could find just such another and make up a matching pair. It is a great pity: two coal-black men in cream-coloured livery would look exceedingly well. But (*revenons à nos moutons*) there is nothing to be done with this particular black. Even in the stables he would be the butt of the other lads. Sophia has never witnessed the cruelties that underlings inflict upon one another but she is aware that they take place. Papa was right on this occasion, as on so many others: when he offered to decline Zedland's gift on her behalf, she should have agreed.

Perhaps when they are married her husband will come to understand that Titus is unsuitable. With this thought comes an inner prompting to rise and examine herself in the glass. Sophia could not explain the origin of this impulse, which is as irresistible as it is trivial. Though not vain, she now carries out such inspections several times a day, a habit which took hold around the time when Mr Zedland first began to pay court.

This morning she perceives a young lady of the middle height, narrow-laced and graceful in her posture. She is thankful that from her earliest years she was trained to carry herself well. The restrictions she found so unbearable as a child have become second nature and whenever she sees some bumpkin girl waddling along, jaw poked out in front, back humped and elbows thrusting, Sophia is filled with an agreeable sense of superiority. A gentlewoman's very shoulders convey composure, the essence of breeding. Such an elegant female can take comfort in the knowledge that, while not listed among the first in Beauty's golden book, she is of goodly report in that of Beauty's sister, Grace. As for her natural advantages, she has fair ringlets, a white skin, blue eyes. She is not pockmarked or coarse-featured and is neither fat nor thin. On the debit side, it must be admitted that a gentleman once described her, when he thought she could not overhear, as a 'blank'. Nobody has ever written sonnets to her features, which are so mild as to border upon dullness. Sophia, who can bear witness to the power of bewitching eyes, knows that she cannot pretend to such attractions.

She reads aloud with pleasing expression, has a good French accent, sings in tune, plays the harpsichord, can make correct sketches in pencil, is in health, is kind to the poor and considerate towards the servants. She is considered a satisfactory young woman by those judges whose opinions count for most, namely those who know her well. She is her parents' sole heir, with a modest fortune of her own and more to follow on that terrible day when Papa and Mama are no more. She takes no pleasure in anticipating this future wealth; on the contrary, she tries to forget that such a day must come.

In short, her character is virtuous and refined, her father's offer honest and plain, her person elegant. All this shall be Mr Zedland's portion.

What will he lay down to match it?

Here Sophia's breast begins to rise and fall, her blood to beat up into those blank cheeks.

She has heard the term *worship* used to describe some preference of man for woman, or woman for man, but always in such a way as to imply that the tenderness thus referred to was a frivolous, perhaps immoral, connection. Now, however, she herself has arrived at a condition for which there can be no other expression. Zedland's manners, so different from those of her rustic neighbours, seem the attributes of a god. It is true that his skin is a little brown, but an olive complexion has a charm of its own, and as for his hands – so long and fine – Sophia would be surprised if any gentleman in the whole of her native county could match them. The truth of the matter is that Zedland is Sophia's maiden passion, the only man whose flesh has ever spoken to hers. It murmurs and wheedles all the time she is with him, until she scarcely knows how to breathe.

Her one instinctive defence has been to conceal her fevered condition both from him and from her parents, who believe hers to be a union recommended by reason. Since childhood she has been accustomed to their 'Sophy is rational' – high praise for a girl – and could not bear them to witness her infatuated.

How can the dim creature peering out of the looking-glass be worthy of *Mr Zedland*, whose very voice makes Sophia squirm with unspeakable sensations, as though a child were already kicking in her belly? His eyes, deep and dark (their whites so clear as to be tinged with blue), are the bewitching orbs with which she forlornly compares her own, and sees how very unenslaving they are. Yesterday, when he proposed taking her out in the boat and Papa consented, Sophia actually shook to think of the coming *tête-à-tête* and when her suitor pulled away, marooning poor Rixam, her mouth grew dry. After this initial wickedness, however, Zedland acted quite correctly. He spoke of his own love for Sophia and his wish that his domestic arrangements might please her; yet he smiled on her so long, gazing into her all the while, that she was persuaded he had fathomed her entire secret, penetrated right to her soul and seen his image enshrined there, with herself thrown at his feet.

It is of course natural and proper for a young lady to feel

love for her intended. But what is love? Sophia thinks, in those fleeting moments when she is able to think at all. Is this what is meant – this *cruelty*? For as they sat, seemingly balanced, in the boat, each reflecting the other, she knew that they were not balanced at all, that Zedland's strength rendered her powerless, that he could make her do anything, and that if he did not understand this now, he very soon would. Again she examines her person in the mirror. How calm and controlled that reflected image! How dignified!

My Dear Sophia,

I trust this finds you and your esteemed parents well. For my part, I am fully recovered from the chill of which I told you, free of bottles and boluses and master of my own time. The last of the papers being now come from Essex, I propose to bring them with me on my next visit to Buller. That is, on the sixteenth or seventeenth of this month.

How it grieves me that my beloved parents cannot share our joy on that day which is to witness our entry together into perfect happiness! For perfect, my Sophia, I am convinced it must be. Where two persons, as well matched as we, are surrounded by universal goodwill and cemented by mutual tenderness, happiness must be the inevitable outcome. For proof of that you need look no further than your own dear father and mother, whom I may soon address, with the warmest affection, as my own.

I must now come to something less agreeable. I trust you will not be too disappointed when I tell you that my agent has not purchased the silks, &c., as agreed. There were none of the best quality to be had at the price we had allowed, London being so very expensive just now. On consideration it appears to me that

you might buy as good at Bath, where you may consult your
own choice entirely and have them made up while we are there

Sophia clutches the letter, almost crumpling it.

'What is it, darling?' Her mother's gentle voice invites confidences. 'He hasn't taken a turn for the worse, I hope?'

'No, no, Mama, he's quite well now, but the most provoking news! He's neglected to act for us – he says I can buy the stuffs in Bath and have them run up on the spot.'

'He has a great deal of business to attend to,' is Mrs Buller's comment. 'Still, you must have your trousseau.'

'You didn't wish him to buy the stuffs,' Sophia admits with shame.

'No, indeed. We should never have consented, only he made such a point of the superior choice and quality. I must say,' Mama sniffs, 'we were very open-handed with him. Enough, I would've thought, even for London prices.'

This is Sophia's first disagreement with Mr Zedland (although the man himself does not know it yet) and her courage fails her at once. 'Perhaps it won't matter so much, in the end? What do you think, Mama – could the things be made at Bath?'

But Mama says, 'Of all men, he *ought* to understand. His own tailoring is so very elegant, and everyone knows how much time that takes. I shall write to him.'

'Oh, Mama, you won't quarrel with him, will you?'

'Don't you know me better than that, child? Let me see the letter.'

Though the greater part of the contents remain unread, Sophia hands it over without hesitation. Mr Zedland never descends to 'warm expressions'; his communications might be read by the Archbishop of Canterbury himself.

'He hasn't bought the mare either,' her mother murmurs. 'Quite right, since it appears she was lame – but to fancy you can be married out of a mantua-maker's! No, no, that must all be finished with before your honeymoon.' Mama folds the letter up briskly and hands it back to Sophia. 'You shall see what I write.'

Sophia hugs her – 'Thank you, darling Mama!' – before going off to read the remainder of her letter in private.

It is partly her own reaction that she wishes to hide, since she finds his letters strangely disappointing. Could it be their very correctness which is so lacking in charm? Uniformly polite, they breathe chaste love and dutiful affection, when what she craves is some hint that he thinks of their approaching wedding as she does, with mingled desire and terror. Sophia reflects bleakly that the coming ordeal may be all her own, men's lives and bodies (her mother has explained) being differently constructed from those of women, so that the act which bathes a husband in voluptuous sensations may pain his wife, though as Mama said, 'it will soon pass off'. (Sophia turned scarlet on being told this; it was the fault of the words *voluptuous sensations*, which themselves brought about curious stirrings she would be puzzled to describe to Mama.) It seems that Nature has allotted Mr Zedland the lion's share of happiness in the marital embrace: should he not be correspondingly more eager to lay claim to it than his yearning, yet shrinking, bride?

Sophia has more cause to shrink than most. Since childhood she has been troubled by a 'little weakness', as Mama insists upon calling it; according to Mama, such weaknesses are not uncommon in the gentle sex and Mr Zedland, as a loving husband, will soon accommodate himself to a flaw which can in no way be traced to any vice. It is plain, however, that Mama is not quite so easy on this head as she wishes to appear, since a few months ago she wrote to a celebrated physician residing at Bath. Dr Brunt's reply, when it came, was encouraging: though one could not undertake with absolute confidence to cure the condition, patients often responded well to simple, practical measures and those who did not, even those of Sophia's age, might still grow out of it. He wrote that he had a particular interest in such cases, and it had long been his opinion that parents should endeavour to treat their afflicted children with tenderness, striving to discover and remove any little sorrow or suffering that might weigh upon their spirits. It was imperative that no beatings or other punishments should be used or even threatened, and that all should be done to foster a romping, carefree disposition. Such a course of action, faithfully adhered to, not infrequently brought about everything that was desired; patience was essential, however, as several weeks might pass before any improvement could be detected. Marriage itself, if happy, might well effect such a change, but it was (he had underlined the words) *desirable for the happiness of all parties that the utmost frankness should be employed towards the bridegroom.*

The good doctor added that he must not be understood to be accusing either Papa or Mama. It sometimes happened that cheerful young people, guided by the most loving parents, were afflicted by reason of an innate weakness in the body. For these, also, treatment might do much. He respectfully submitted details of a regimen which, if scrupulously followed, would reduce the symptoms or even do away with them altogether.

Sophia assured Mama that she had no secret sorrows and that nothing distressed her save the condition itself. They therefore pinned their hopes on Dr Brunt's regimen. At table Sophia takes as little salt, or salted food, as may be; she shuns dishes swimming in any kind of sauce or gravy, takes no liquid after eight o'clock, and is careful to visit the necessary house frequently before retiring to bed. She has made considerable progress this way, and hopes she may make more.

In her chamber she unfolds the letter and reads:

The little mare I told you of has had a fall and now limps

intolerably. Paterson tells me she will hardly recover within a
month. It is a pity, as I am persuaded you would have taken to
her, but since I had not closed the bargain when she fell I have
instead purchased a hunter, a real beauty. I am now seeking
another mount for you; Paterson knows of a quiet grey

Sophia sighs. She understands that female happiness depends upon attracting a protector who takes just such pains as these to secure her comfort. And yet . . . an ardent *billet-doux*, a forbidden familiarity, would comfort her more than any amount of such household stuff. What is more, she finds it difficult to reconcile Zedland's glamorous person and intimate, teasing manner with his prosaic outpourings on paper. Her parents, however, seem quite satisfied. Possibly she is the only person to perceive him thus – and this because of what older people call 'youth and innocence'. Perhaps, after all, these different aspects of Mr Zedland are perfectly reconcilable, and the mixture a proven recipe for married bliss?

In the meantime she has domestic concerns of her own. She rings the bell and asks the servant to send Titus to her, to see if he has made any progress in curbing his defective speech.

4

Betsy-Ann, says Sam Shiner, 'talks like a sheep'.

She knows what he means. She burrs instead of chopping her words short, the way folk do here. And why should she? She once learned to read — learned some of the letters, at any rate — and she reckons that when the letter R was made, it was made to be used. When she first took up with Sam he sometimes mocked her way of speaking. When she protested, he said it was nothing more than merriment, no harm done, but the Corinthian never used to mock her for it and that was another difference between the two men.

These days she's given up most of her country words, though she can't take the taste of them out of her mouth. She's up to every lay in Romeville — the Deuce himself couldn't fool Betsy-Ann Shiner — but she still talks like a sheep.

Let Sam laugh, he doesn't know everything. Look at the way he talks about the Corinthian, with his, 'Hartry taught her everything she knows,' when all the time it was the other way round. As far as that goes, she *made* Ned Hartry. She can't play the public tables, but she was brought up to the cards and it was to Hartry, the Corinthian, that she gave up her secrets.

All but one or two: she always keeps something back for herself. Once a man's drained you dry he starts looking round for a full hogshead, and that's when *you* start missing that little bit you should've kept back. Is Sam looking round, then? He's been going out a lot, lately, and not giving her straight answers.

Fine thing that'd be, when she's only just got used to him. She didn't take to Sam at all, at first, on account of how he came by her. Not that she could stand off from him, O no!

Those first few weeks she was constantly put in mind of the old song:

> *Sometime I am a butcher bold*
> *And then I feel fat ware, Sir.*
> *And if the flank be fleshed well*
> *I take no farther care, Sir,*
> *But in I thrust my slaughtering-knife*
> *Up to the haft with speed, Sir*

— and didn't he just! Another woman might've been put to the squeal but Betsy-Ann wouldn't give him the satisfaction.

That apart, he's not so bad. She goes by his name, as if they were legally spliced. The Corinthian never laughed at her speech but he never called her Mrs Hartry, either. For all that, she sees him in her dream. It's always the same dream. He sits down to the card table with Sam and winks at her, and this time he sweeps the board.

'Ever seen books like these?' She fans the strange playing-cards under Sam's nose.

He grunts. 'Shams?'

'No.' She upends them, turning the soldiers to ladies. 'That's all the trick there is.'

Sam laughs. 'Well, if there's another, you're the mort to find it out.'

'Am I?' she says. 'Seems to me there's a lot I don't find out.'

He's been back a day now and still not told her where he went. Something bad is coming: Betsy-Ann can feel it.

'I've made bubble and squeak,' she says.

Sam clicks his tongue. 'Curse me, I forgot.' He goes to the door and bellows, 'Liz!'

Elizabeth Jane Williams, a creeping crone who occupies a cupboard on the ground floor, is heard wheezing her way upstairs. She haunts the staircase in the hope of errands and obliges everybody in the building, though being such a tortoise, she can never earn much by it. The nearest gin shop is two doors away, which makes her just tolerable for deliveries.

'Get us some lightning. A quart of the Royal Cream,' Sam tells her, handing over an empty jug.

When Liz is gone, Betsy-Ann says, 'Royal Cream? Flush, aren't we?'

'You needn't have any.' He avoids her eyes; he's working up to something. 'Harry said he might step over.'

And there it is, the bad thing. She knows now where he's been, and what he's been doing, this last fortnight. She thought as much: there's a dirty smell on him.

'You saw Harry today?'

'Any reason I shouldn't?'

'Course not. Only I never thought you was fond.'

Betsy-Ann herself isn't fond, though she was born Betsy-Ann Blore and Harry Blore is her own blood brother.

'I ran into him up by the Haymarket. He was —'

Betsy-Ann turns on him, jabbing her finger towards her face. 'Them's my *eyes,* Samuel Shiner! You've been out with him, haven't you? After we agreed —'

'Blunt's blunt.' Sam's talking seriously now, no longer fencing with her. 'Somebody has to bring it in.'

Since he doesn't like to be reminded, she forces herself not to look at his maimed hand as she says, 'Don't I make enough for us? We got two chambers here, a snug little ken —'

'I'm not being kept by a mort.'

'That shows your manly spirit, Sammy. But what about me? I won't know where – what you've been touching.'

'It's trade!'

'Coming from *them* into our bed.' For the life of her she can't stop her voice quivering; it's a relief when she hears Liz toiling up the stairs. Betsy-Ann watches Sam take the jug and pay her off, then listens to the old woman creeping down again before repeating, 'Coming from them into our bed, Sam! Turns me funny just to think of it.'

She sets out cups but he does not pour the drink. Instead he says, 'Think what? That I'm kissing them – squeezing their bubbies? Eh? You got a mind like a midden!'

It does look that way, Betsy-Ann has to admit. She tries another tack. 'Tell us one thing, though, Sam. How was it? Was you boozed up?'

'What d'you think, we'd do it cold?'

'They talk about Tom Ball – eh?'

'One thing, you said.'

'Tom Ball. The Flash Kiddey.'

He clicks his tongue. 'Who's Tom Ball, in the name of Christ?'

'You've got his situation, you might say.'

She takes the gin from him and pours, humming one of her tunes. There's no end to them, and she knows words to every one. She hands Sam a cupful and watches him swallow.

'Well,' he says at last. 'What manner of cove was he?'

'Dimber – a regular heart-breaker. And knew it. Anyway, they was lying up, two days' drinking time on account of the moon, then suddenly there's cloud, so it's off we go, drunk as kings. They've just got a large on the cart and they're going for another, right next door it is, so they chuck the soil from the second grave into the first. Then they get the signal, Davey's spied the patrol, so they toddle quick. They're away and sitting on the cart and Pete Hindmarsh – you met Pete?'

Sam nods.

'Pete says, "Where's the kiddey?"'

She pauses.

'Get on with it, girl. Where was he?'

'Where d'you think!' she spits. 'They'd buried him.'

'Never!' He flaps his hand at her. 'Who told you —'

'Harry. Harry told me.' She watches that sink in. 'He was lying drunk in there and they covered him over.'

'So – what then?'

'Well.' Betsy-Ann shrugs. 'They couldn't hang about.'

'Didn't they go back?'

'Couldn't, could they? Not once the patrol was there. You should hear Harry tell it, he laughs fit to choke.'

Sam downs the last of his cup without looking at her.

She says, 'And you'll trust Harry after that?'

'I never trusted Harry.'

She pours him another flash, and one for herself. After a while he's looking more cheerful so they go into the next room, leaving the bubble and squeak for later, and lie down together on the bed. When Blore arrives to discuss business, he has to hammer to make himself heard and Betsy-Ann goes to the door with her stays unlaced and her hair hanging down.

Ask anyone who knows him to describe Harry Blore and one of the first words out of his mouth will be 'heavy'. Betsy-Ann is a tall, strong woman; Blore is a tall, strong, thickset man, sallow and with a pungent stale smell about him. Some say it comes of his trade, some that it's his by nature. There's also a whiff of the bare-knuckle fighter he once was: the solidity of a man not easily put down, the ferocious gaze, the broken nose that gives him his blunted profile.

Acting the quality again, thinks Betsy-Ann, eyeing his shabby laced coat. She smiles, gestures to him to come in and pushes the gin towards him. Blore ignores the cup set ready and helps himself from the lip of the jug.

He looks her up and down. 'You'll wear the cove flat at this rate. Tell him I'm here.'

'Thought you'd come to see your beloved sis.' Pulling a face once she has turned her back, Betsy-Ann goes out of the room. In the bedchamber, Sam is wriggling into his breeches.

'No need to break your neck,' she whispers. 'And not a word of what I said.'

'Don't nag me, we're not spliced.'

'No, thank God!'

He goes into the other room and Betsy-Ann tidies herself. When she emerges from the chamber the two men are huddled together. She puts on her bonnet and cloak and leaves them to it.

5

When the clock chimes three, Papa and Scrope are still shut up in the library, scrutinising Mr Zedland's papers.

'Poor William!' says Mama without looking up from her netting. 'He detests such business. Thank Heaven Scrope can be trusted.'

'Is something out of order, Mama?' Sophia asks with a little clutch of dread.

'Nothing that need concern you, my love. Papa wishes to be quite clear upon certain matters, that is all.'

'You said, *thank Heaven*.'

'Bless the child, how fretful it is! What I said had no reference to Mr Zedland – I was speaking of lawyers. Most of them are a rascally set, but Papa has every confidence in Scrope.'

Her daughter is not entirely reassured. Mr Zedland, heir to Wixham, sole offspring of deceased Essex gentry, brought forward all of his legal documents months ago and is now Sophia's acknowledged intended. Why, then, should Scrope have been summoned at all?

'Will Papa tell us about it afterwards?'

'It's only a matter of figures, my dear. Let the gentlemen take care of it. *You* should be engaged in something more amusing. How's that blackbird of yours? Have you taught him to sing?'

Seeing herself blocked, Sophia obediently banishes fear from her face, if not from her heart. 'He's tolerable,' she says. 'Should you like to hear him?'

Titus stands before the two women, his feet planted far apart as if to repel an assault.

'Now, Titus,' Sophia announces with a glance towards her mother, 'repeat after me. Peter Piper picked a peck of pickled pepper!'

'Feeter Piper picked a peck of fpickled peffer. Pepper.'

'You see how improved he is, Mama?'

'Indeed.' Mama smiles, not at the slave but at Sophia who has trained him so well.

The boy clasps his hands in front of him. Until recently his complexion was a dull grey, as if scoured with ashes. Sophia thought he might be sickly, perhaps pining for his native sun. An apothecary was consulted and suggested that Titus's skin should be massaged with butter. He was duly given an allowance for the purpose, since which time he has returned to his original deep brown shade.

'I know a bank,' Sophia prompts.

Titus begins to recite, 'I know a bank where the wild thyme blows,' with the careful, expressionless enunciation of someone who has memorised a rigmarole. Though he still confuses *f* and *p* whenever he is flustered, and pronounces 'weed' as 'wade', there can be no doubt that he has made progress.

'It's extraordinary, my dear, how much patience you've shown with the little beast,' Mama says when Titus has finished. 'A few more weeks and he'll be fit to go out in public. Don't you think?'

Though his face gives not a flicker of recognition, Fortunate has understood the word *beast*. All day long the imperatives and insults of English wash over him; though rarely able to frame a reply, he interprets for himself more than anyone suspects. Nor is he surprised that the old one has called him an animal. He is accustomed to being addressed as Blackbird and Monkey-Boy, names as stale as the sagging face of this woman with her eyes like dirty water, her ruined teeth and her body that hardly moves all day. A memory surfaces: his mother as a young woman, in a brightly patterned wrapper, laughing and gesturing to his aunts, all of them tall and strong and graceful. These Englishwomen walk stiffly, like very old people, their skin as pale as the bellies of fishes. The younger one's mouth does not sag, but one can see that they are mother and daughter. They have the same deformed nostrils, as if a god decided at their birth to pinch the breath out of them.

Why has Dog Eye brought him here? He was happier in their rooms in the city, learning to play dice, than he has been at any time since he was taken from his home.

His home! Home is now this country of savage manners, where the people carry weapons with them and are ever ready to take offence. Their women stare at Dog Eye without shame, as if they had never been taught better, and everybody pretends not to notice. To the English, Dog Eye must seem beautiful – to Fortunate, all these people look much the same – since the inferior women in the kitchen, who behave in front of Fortunate as if he were deaf, speak laughingly of his master's eyes, and laugh. It is true that they are unusually large, clear and bright. Fortunate once had a hunting dog with just such a luminous gaze.

'Dog Eye,' he says softly to himself in his own language.

The younger woman pounces. 'What was that?'

At the sound of her scratchy voice Fortunate starts and his English deserts him.

'What did you say?' the woman demands.

He cannot answer. His face is hot with humiliation. The older one says something and now he cannot even understand.

6

Betsy-Ann is lying tucked up with her brother. The bedding has a warm, earthy smell, like the potatoes her mother brought back from the field. The farmer made the women turn out their pockets, but Mam knew a trick worth two of that and had put three big potatoes down the front of her stays. Betsy-Ann sees them come tumbling out onto the grass, the children snatching at them and then the bucket over the fire, boiling up a mess of potatoes and bread and milk. Her mother's tanned, stringy hand stirring the broth with a wooden spoon, her fingernails rimmed with clay.

She wakes hungry, Sam snoring beside her. By the time she came home, supperless, Harry had eaten her share of the bubble and squeak. Sam most likely offered it from spite, but trust Harry to take advantage. Perhaps, she thinks, he still suffers the hunger of childhood, like Betsy-Ann herself. It never goes off, even now.

Keshlie hung about the edges of her dreams last night, prowling and whingeing outside the tent. Whenever she appears she's always some way off, never in the warm earth-smelling shelter with the rest of them. Betsy-Ann saw her walking over the field, wearing a little gown of cornflower-blue, her curls dangling down her back. The Corinthian came along and gave her a piece of sugar to suck.

Betsy-Ann tries to sink back to sleep. Sam's snoring doesn't bother her, but hunger continues to nag until she knows she has to get up. Painstakingly, so as not to wake him, she rolls out of bed and feels her way to the door. In the next room she gropes about in the food cupboard and lays hand on the heel of a loaf and a dish of pickled cucumber. That will have to do.

She draws the tattered curtain for light and sits at the table mopping up cucumber and vinegar with her hunk of bread. The street is quiet tonight, just the occasional shout from neighbouring yards. Moonlight spills into the room, picking out a corner of the table, the back of a chair. Harry and Sam work by darkmans: the sky's too bright for their line of work, too bright for any of the canting crew, so Sam must wait at home.

Behind doors is another story. Behind doors you can do what you like. The Corinthian told her how in St James's, fine ladies dance without a care in the world. Turn the pack that is Romeville upside down, and there's the other side: high toby men arming and setting out for Hounslow Heath, flats coaxed into flash houses, resurrectionists shrinking like vermin from the light.

Far off in the city smoke surges up, rolling in crimson-bellied swags towards the east. Somewhere there is pain, people running about, but from here the fire is a rose warming itself in the moonlight and Betsy-Ann sits dreamily admiring it. She has heard of bloods who set houses afire for pleasure. She herself would never be so wicked, but she understands the temptation.

Strange to dream of Keshlie with the Corinthian. Awake, Betsy-Ann hates to remember her, because of what she turned into. In dreams Keshlie's true face comes back, a pale flower amid the dark twinings of her hair. Betsy-Ann's not what you'd call dimber, not precisely: she was behind the door when they handed out sweetness but Keshlie got enough for both sisters. She wonders if Keshlie might not have been her sister's true name. What, then? Catharine? Keziah? She grew up calling her Keshlie, never questioned it. Now there's nobody to ask but Harry, and he won't know. He doesn't care about such things.

'How are the togs?' Sam asks. 'Will I pass?'

Betsy-Ann turns her head away.

'Come on, girl. Cleave to me a bit.'

Reluctantly she confronts him. Clad in a threadbare blue coat and breeches, he holds his hat before him with one hand and scratches under his arm with the other.

'I see you got plenty of active citizens,' Betsy-Ann observes. 'Come free with the shirt, did they?'

'Forget them. This is life and death.'

'Think I don't know that? Go on, then.'

Sam arranges himself in a respectful attitude. 'I've come for my aunt, Madam, so I can bury her from my home.'

'What's your name?'

'William Cliffe. My aunt, God rest her soul, was Joanna Jane Barlow.'

'That poor old woman!' Betsy-Ann frowns. 'I don't recall you ever visiting your aunt, William.'

He hesitates.

'Buck up, Sam, I'm losing faith in you.'

'Ma and her fell out. We was forbidden to visit. Me, I always liked the old lady, never wished her any harm.' He seems to choke at the last word and buries his face in one of Betsy-Ann's stolen handkerchiefs.

'Come in quicker next time. And don't overdo the wiper.'

'I wouldn't want her shamed by a parish funeral.'

'That's a good tune. They'll like that one, the tight-arsed bastards.'

They run through the lay several times, adding questions until Betsy-Ann can think of no more.

Sam claps her on the shoulder. 'Reckon I'm better now.'

'*I* never felt worse.' Betsy-Ann goes to the cupboard and takes out the gin. 'Have a flash?'

Sam hesitates. 'They'll smell it.'

'Nothing wrong there, you've been toasting the dear departed. You can't do the thing without, Sammy.'

'No.' He reaches for the cup she has poured him and swallows it in one. 'I don't mind telling you, girl, I don't like this bob.'

'Nobody does, Sam. That's why you napped it.' She puts her arm around his shoulders. 'Why don't you go to bed? I'll tell Harry you was sick. You'll get off this once.'

Sam shakes his head. 'Promise me, though. If anything goes wrong, I mean anything – you won't let Harry take me, will you?'

Betsy-Ann withdraws her arm. 'After all I've said, you're asking me that? Seems to me *I* should be asking *you*.'

When he's gone she paces up and down before the window. Over there is where the fire was, the other night: she wonders who lived in that house and if they're living still. A stink of bad pork, and Harry levering up the coffin lid: no, no. She fights that off, but now come pictures of a woman and child huddled under gaping rafters, open to rain and hail. Their ken's most likely been stripped by fire priggers – 'O Madam, I'll convey your goods to safety' – and everything not burnt or prigged now sodden and filthy, the mattress, if they had one, burst open and buried in fallen plaster.

Betsy-Ann knows what it is to sleep under rain. There's a lot worse off than us, Sammy, and yet . . .

She stops pacing and sits down next to the jug of gin.

These days, Shiner smells as foul as Harry Blore. It's in his duds, in his skin: a mixture of the sweat off the crew themselves (Shiner was a dry man but now he sweats like a sponge, that's the fear for you) and the corruption they work in. He looked so sick when he started, she let him talk; now she can't forget what he said. You have to get them fresh, no market for them else, but they're not always lying alone. Some cribs are packed – to get one, you have to move the others. Then sometimes the one you want turns out to be a drowning, or left too long before it went in the ground.

She insists on washing the shirts, breeches, anything she can tear off his back; she does more scrubbing than a laundrymaid. She believes she'd know a resurrectionist among the evillest-stinking crowd in Romeville, know him blindfold among a thousand.

The stink pays, she's not denying it, but they could do without. During a single day on the Oxford Road she sold seventeen bottles of lightning, a diamond fawney and two shawls: not once has she failed to make the rent. Why don't men listen to women? *You need a long spoon to dine with Harry* – her very words, and all she got for them was a shrug. The Flash Kiddey, for all his knowing airs, was just such an unsuspecting daisy. Sam's begun to know his man, though. It makes him sweat worse than before.

Such fine talk, when she passed into Sam's keeping. Honour, obligation. She was helpless against all that, led away like a turkey. And then the pair of them shook down together, more or less. She wasn't happy, never happy. But settled, you might say. Her wings well clipped.

Sam's clipped too, come to think of it. That butchered hand of his, his luck sheared away with his finger.

For weeks now she's felt change in the air, like the first pinch of autumn, and a queer sort of restlessness: her wing feathers, you might say, growing back.

She goes to her concealed cupboard and lifts down the deck of cards. On top lies Pam, the Knave of Clubs. Her lucky man, though it's not often she has the chance of a hand at Loo. First she shuffles keeping Pam always on top; next she slips him from top to bottom, bottom to top, twenty times without pause; then she picks out sections of the pack and holds them concealed and ready while seeming to shuffle in the ordinary way. All this is done without looking at the cards. Instead, Betsy-Ann sings one of her mother's songs, smiling and wagging her head about, as a substitute for the chatter of company. Your hands have to seem the last thing on your mind, their movements natural as breathing.

Her fingers, that were stiff from lack of practice, are now warming up. The flick and slither of the cards bring back memories: O, for the Corinthian! She and Corinthian Ned would sit for hours shuffling and dealing, Betsy sitting judge and jury on him: loosen your thumb, you looked at the books, you stopped your talk as you came to the ace, do it again, again. They drank throughout; he got every move off pat, drunk or sober.

'Show me how to plant them,' he begged.

'How many hands?'

'Say six, with you and me.'

She showed him and with painful care he stacked the deck. Betsy-Ann snatched it up, shuffled and dealt the hands. He took up his: all aces and royalty.

'What did the rest get?'

'Have a look.'

He turned them over. Deuces, trays, fours: a dog's portion. He looked up in wonder. Betsy-Ann fell in love all over again at the sight of Ned Hartry's innocence: you saw what he might have been in a better world.

'Well,' she said, 'you saw me shuffle?'

He nodded. Betsy nodded too, and then mockingly changed to shaking her head.

'What you *saw* was my hands. This time, watch the books. See where they go.' With slow, exaggerated movements, she went again through the sham.

'You're not shifting them,' he said at last. 'It only looks like it. Could another sharp tell?'

She laughed. 'What's the use of sharps playing sharps?'

For days he practised shamming the shuffle. Then came righting the books when somebody else has shuffled, so as to restore your preferred order, and digging a fingernail into the side of the pack, and forcing, and palming.

'You're a prodigy,' Hartry said to her as they lay in bed one afternoon.

She had to ask him what a prodigy was.

'A she-gamester. A marvel.'

'That's nothing, Ned. Only my upbringing.'

He pulled up her nightgown and softly, very softly, closed his teeth on her titty; he wasn't shy of the marvel, not he. That was *his* upbringing. She wondered how many hands had stroked the skin of his back, as she was doing now, to make him so practised and cunning: a 'man of spirit' who had served a long apprenticeship between women's legs.

'Knave of Hearts,' she said. The words excited her. A king had a queen, and duties, but a knave only ever had mistresses; he was slippery and dangerous, like the cards themselves.

Betsy-Ann sighs. One thing she'd stake her life on: Ned's not standing at a door begging some old woman's bones. He was elegant down to his fingertips, fingertips perfect for the trade. Not even he, though, learnt her best trick, because she never taught him. Perhaps if she had, things would've gone differently between him and Shiner, and Betsy-Ann wouldn't be bedding down each night between sheets that smell more and more like graveclothes.

But then, Ned might have got the thing to perfection, put on his hat and bid her farewell. He had it in him to do that.

7

Specks of sunlight flash in the weave of the sack as the man beneath him strides along. From time to time a stumble sends his bound knees into the man's belly. His mouth is packed with the same coarse stuff and the jolting, the jerking, the man's dirty smell, his own tied hands, all put him in terror of vomiting: if he does so, he will choke, unable to make a sound or move a finger to help himself.

From time to time he hears a woman's voice, low but harsh. Though they are not his people, he understands something of their language. Once, she shouts out in rage: the child she carries has wet itself. Without taking Fortunate from his shoulder, the man halts. There are yells, and the gasping of the woman, and muffled cries from the other child, which must also be tied in a sack.

The man shifts Fortunate on his shoulder and walks on. The child's whimper goes with them. Where Fortunate's body is pressed against that of the kidnapper the heat is unbearable: he is baking, his insides congealing like meat in a pot. The man must feel it too, since the bag is so wet. Then the air becomes fresher and Fortunate can hear the movement of branches. The man moves more unevenly, sighing as if in pain. He lays Fortunate down, still in the sack, and sits beside him. The sparks caught in the weave of the sack change from gold to green and there is a sound of someone drinking.

The woman screams. The man leaps up and Fortunate hears them both running away, smashing through the bush. He strains to call to them, beg them to come back, to untie him, but all he can do is grunt. Something more terrible than the kidnappers is here: the breathing of a huge beast, coming closer. In despair he beats at the ground with his head, weeping, and now he knows he is going to be sick —

He wakes in a thin, spent, morning. English morning is spent before it begins. He knows where he is without opening his eyes, by the chill on his cheeks and the constriction of the bedclothes. It is this, perhaps, that made him dream of the sack.

Wakings are never joyous here, with those thin brown birds crying on the rooftops. Englishmen are proud of their marvellous inventions. They are indeed inventive, perhaps because they have been given so little in the way of nature. At this moment, however, Fortunate is relieved to see from his window a sky the colour of steel. He kicks at the sheets, letting the heat and stink of the sack drop away from him. Even now he can feel his body thrash inside it, waiting to be made prey, but as the seconds pass and the familiar dreariness reasserts itself – there is his cup of beer on the sill – his breathing slows.

The dream was perhaps an omen: he will be kidnapped again. In Annapolis there was a slave freed by one white man and given papers, only to be captured by more whites as he went about his business. His papers were torn in pieces and they shipped him to another place.

Might it be that the true dream was lost in waking? Suppose he had slept all the way through. A friend might have come and untied him and the child, and taken them back to their homes.

His gaze falls again on the cup of beer. No: *that* is solid and real, and his village is now the dream. He has travelled too far, passing through the hands of too many masters, for even his brothers to find him.

8

Bath is both better and worse than Sophia imagined. The architecture is certainly magnificent, so imposing as to inspire awe: at the New Hospital she stands staring upwards, admiring the purity of its lines. Above, clouds race away from her over the roof, making it appear that the façade is leaning forward. Knowing it for an illusion, Sophia half-closes her eyes and permits herself a frisson: she is about to be crushed beneath its stones.

'It appears you are a convert to the classical,' murmurs Edmund.

'A convert?'

'You said you disliked copies. Fakery, I think you called them.'

'Did I?' Sophia cannot remember any such conversation; so much has happened of late.

'Properly considered, of course, everything in life is a copy,' her husband remarks. 'Take a common sparrow, for example: the very spit, as they say,' his eyes sparkle playfully at this vulgar term, 'of its parents.'

'What of human beings? *We* are not so easily coined.'

'We men and women make a sad blunder of our copying, taking our nose from Great-Grandmama, our hands from Papa, and so on. A hotchpotch of styles without taste or discrimination.'

She does not care whether he talks sense or nonsense, since all is done to amuse her. Walking in sunlight, glanced at by fashionable strollers, the acknowledged choice of this adorable husband, Sophia is in her earthly paradise and in some danger, not of falling masonry, but of fainting away from sheer bliss.

Her happiness, however, has not blinded her to the less savoury aspects of Bath: the crush of the assemblies and bathing places and the manners, if one can dignify them by such a name, of some of the inhabitants. Edmund wished to take their honeymoon here so that he might attend to some urgent business before continuing to London; though Sophia's one desire is to oblige him, she had no notion, until now, of the promiscuity of the place. Impossible for a lady of any delicacy to immerse herself in the baths, sousing in a pickle of diseases next to hags whose protruding bones would qualify them as painters' studies for Death at the Feast. Figures yet more repulsive, infected with racking coughs and open sores, crowd in on each side and worst of all are the blades who strut alongside the waters, quizzing any lady possessed of personal attractions. Some of these go so far as to pass *remarks*; Sophia has heard that one of them was thrown into the water, fully clothed, for his temerity.

Altogether the baths present a disgusting spectacle, one that offends the nose as painfully as the eyes. She had imagined a pageant of health and beauty, of Apollos and Aphrodites, and blushes every time she recalls her folly, thankful that at least she did not confide these *niaiseries* to her husband.

There is much to be thankful for, much to enjoy. The weather is tolerably fine, and the Zedlands have bright and airy lodgings. Though Mr Derrick, the Master of Ceremonies, cannot be termed a handsome man (being as he is, carroty, undersized and undistinguished), he is remarkably civil and attentive to the needs of the ladies, among whom he has got up a regular cabal; to the ladies, indeed, he is said to owe his election. The 'Little King of Bath', as he is called (the title 'King of Bath', without the diminutive, being reserved for the late lamented Beau Nash) has persuaded Sophia to subscribe to the reading room, where she has made the acquaintance of Mrs Chase, a gentlewoman from Oxford. Mr Chase, like Edmund, must attend to his affairs, so the two ladies are often to be seen strolling about the town together, admiring the fashions. Sophia is glad to have a particular friend, or as near to one as Bath can provide. Though she attends the balls and suppers – which here rank almost as a species of religious observance – she finds them wanting, with too much heat, crush and stink for perfect enjoyment. Indeed, if the truth be told, her most sincere pleasure in such gatherings is occasioned by the admiring glances Edmund draws wherever he goes.

'Who was the lady who opened the dance on Tuesday night?' she asks Mrs Chase during one of their walks. 'I thought her elegance remarkable.'

'I didn't catch her name, any more than you. Some baroness from Prussia, I believe.' Mrs Chase makes so little effort to conceal her yawn that it is almost rudeness. '*Entre nous*, don't you find minuets tedious? One couple creeping in circles while everyone else has to wait. And I'm afraid I can't agree with you. I found nothing remarkable in her.'

'Not for a young girl, perhaps, but for an elderly lady she was so light and elegant! I admire anyone who excels at the minuet. As a girl I was praised for holding myself well, but the despair of my dancing-master – he once said I should pray never to be first in company, for I could never open a ball.'

'An insolence for which *I* should have boxed his ears,' declares Mrs Chase. 'Shall we take a stroll along by the Circus?' They turn into Gay Street and Mrs Chase continues, 'The minuet is undoubtedly an ordeal. When I remember my first time! My word!'

'It's not so much the dance itself as the scrutiny of the company.'

'Quite. One may perform correctly with the dancing-master and then make a horrid bungle in public. And then, one is holding up the contredanses, and everybody knows how much the young people love those. Some of them barely sit down all evening.'

'They give themselves excellent appetites. I myself saw a young man put away so much ham at the supper-table, I quite feared for his health.'

'Mr Zedland dances extremely well, does he not?'

'I only wish I were equal to him.'

'Nonsense! You're quite *comme il faut*. And another thing, have you noticed how Mr Derrick manages his partners?'

'Manages?'

'When he leads a lady to open the ball, he inclines his person ever so slightly in the desired direction, in case she should be unsure. He does the same with his eyes. Watch him and you'll see what I mean.'

'He has certainly an expressive glance,' says Sophia, thinking of the first time she and Edmund met with Mr Derrick. The Irishman's eyebrows positively leapt up at the sight of her husband, as if he had sighted an old acquaintance. She remarked on it later to Edmund, who laughed and said it was such ingratiating habits that made Derrick the pet of all the women. 'But I'm not sure I should care to be helped. It throws doubt on the lady's breeding, and before all the company.'

'O, he's much subtler than that! I pride myself upon being observant, but I'd watched him several times before I noticed. And you must know, if he offends he can always find a way of flattering.'

'You mean in verse. Mr Derrick is a poet, is he not?'

'Hum! Every Irishman fancies himself a poet.'

'You're not of his opinion, then.'

'I don't know anyone that is. He's yet to find a patron. Nash, now – Nash stuck to his business, he minded his suppers and his card tables. Try as he may, Mr Derrick will never measure up to *him*.'

'One hears so much about the Beau. I wish I could've met him – though of course Mr Derrick fulfils his duties very well.'

'No comparison between the two. Nash had extraordinary spirit – if, that is, we speak of him in his heyday. He grew quite disgusting towards the end of his life.'

'Disgusting?'

'Well – shabby, you know. He was dreadfully old and impoverished.'

Sophia is gazing about her at the many elegances of Gay Street when Mrs Chase passes this verdict. 'What, after such fame! And after doing so much for the town?'

'Ah, but you see, he was an inveterate gamester! Such people can't be helped.' Mrs Chase lowers her voice. 'They say the Papjoy has gone to live in a hollow tree.'

'The Papjoy — ?'

'His mistress.'

'Mistress?' Having always heard Beau Nash spoken of as a pattern of good breeding, Sophia is taken aback. 'I thought he was infirm and elderly.'

'The lady was neither. Not a third of his age, I should think.'

'But how could she live in a tree? The meanest necessities – her gown, even — ? No,' Sophia shakes her head, 'I find that very hard to believe.'

Mrs Chase shrugs. 'She can never have been a creature of any refinement. Still, to be reduced to that! One can only thank Heaven that our husbands are a steadier sort of men.'

Sophia does indeed thank Heaven for her husband. This is the month of honey and, despite all the entertainments of Bath, she is happiest when the two of them are shut up in their lodgings together. Mama was right: the wedding night was not something she would care to go through again, but dear Edmund, though evidently filled with the 'voluptuous sensations' of which Mama had spoken, was so inexpressibly tender afterwards that Sophia, recalling it days later, feels her eyes stung by tears.

They had dismissed the maid. Having kept herself thirsty since afternoon and made frequent visits to the privy, Sophia felt safe from the possibility of accident but trembled nevertheless when

Edmund climbed into bed beside her saying, 'Man and wife! Nothing between us now, my sweet!'

She had not thought they would take off their nightgowns. She glanced shyly at his dark, agile body, uncertain what was permitted her and still less certain that her own flesh could accommodate his.

'Pray don't be afraid,' he whispered. 'You're not, are you?'

She dared not say how afraid. He seemed as if he would lift her chin and kiss her but she hid her face in his neck. They lay clinging while Edmund caressed her so delightfully that Sophia could not hold still in the bed, and then he kissed her, and again began to caress, *in a bolder way*, and finally rolled her onto her back.

It was every bit as terrible as she had feared. At the dreadful moment when she understood that he was not going to withdraw again, but would press further and further in, she could not repress an animal whimper. Afterwards he spoke of the delight she had given him and his regret that, ever since our first parents were obliged to quit Eden, a bride's joy must be mingled with this little hurt, for which, however, he loved her all the more since it proved she belonged to him alone.

'Had I stopped, my darling,' (a kiss) 'it would all be to do again.' (Another kiss.) 'This was kinder, it was indeed, and with time you will find it so. Every woman finds it so.'

She was comforted to hear him speak so like Mama, still more to find, after two days, that the pain 'went off' just as he and Mama had promised. Not until some time later did she begin to wonder how her husband could pronounce so confidently upon such a topic. But then Mama herself had presumably voiced what was common knowledge, and men, having so much freedom in comparison with women, and better schooling, must necessarily learn a great deal more.

The happy couple sit side by side in Mr and Mrs Chase's apartment, admiring its situation whilst partaking of what Edmund somewhat inelegantly refers to as a 'damper' of sandwiches and madeira.

'Bath society is not of the most refined,' says Mrs Chase. '*Entre nous* we can all agree upon that. But I assure you my health has benefited immensely, *immensely*. Public entertainments one can dispense with, after all. Like-minded friends', she smiles at Sophia, 'are all I require for perfect contentment.'

Mr Chase, less easily contented, is eager to make up a card table. 'Come, Zedland,' he urges, 'be a sport. We shan't play deep.'

Edmund's smile sends waves of delicious weakness through Sophia. 'I'm afraid you must excuse me. As a boy I was fond of cards but I never developed the taste for gaming —'

'Don't call it that!' Mr Chase rallies him. 'Low stakes, between friends, in the company of the ladies?'

'I believe ladies game. But you mistake me. I would censure no man's pleasures. I was only going to observe that gaming bores me and so, dear fellow, it was out of the purest selfishness that I declined.'

Mrs Chase looks pained. 'Pray don't press our guest, my dear.'

Her husband says, 'Forgive me, I had no intention of pressing,' but it is plain that he is in a huff. There is a distinct awkwardness until Sophia declares herself willing to play, should her husband have no objection.

'There! We can have a very satisfactory game with three,' says Mrs Chase. 'Mr Zedland may look on, or read the paper, as he pleases.'

But Edmund now stands pulling on his fingers. 'I have no desire to be unsociable. I may play a hand or two.'

'That's the spirit,' says Chase. Sophia thinks he may regret his enthusiasm when Edmund, asked to shuffle, bungles it so badly as to drop several cards to the carpet. He has to sweep them up, laughing with embarrassment, before the game can begin.

Mr Chase wins the first trick, Mrs Chase the second. The third goes back to Mr Chase, the fourth and fifth to Sophia.

'Bravo!' exclaims Mrs Chase. 'Sophia will win at this rate.'

The next trick goes to Edmund, the one after that to Sophia.

'*You* could've had that, Edmund!' she cries before she can stop herself.

'I think not, my love; I'd only a tray.'

'So you did,' says Sophia, whose love will not let her expose him, but Mr Chase is less delicate.

'She means that you laid a queen on a deuce last time. That queen, Sir, was thrown away.'

'I know, in principle, how the thing should be done,' Edmund admits, looking down at the table. 'But I find such limited pleasure in the game that my concentration leaves much to be desired.'

'Possibly the case is vice versa: there must be an intelligent interest before pleasure can follow,' Mr Chase suggests, and Edmund's eyes take on the hard, shiny look of polished jet.

The game continues.

'Mr Chase, you wicked man!' his wife teases. Indeed, it seems Mr Chase is a player of some skill, for the other three cannot match him. Sophia deals, then Mr Chase, then Mrs Chase. Edmund, who has won only two tricks, seems half asleep.

Mrs Chase yawns. 'What do you think, Sophia, is low play not tedious? What do you say to doubling the stake? It may possibly wake up Mr Zedland.'

Sophia is taken aback. Of the last four tricks, Mr Chase won three and Mrs Chase one: in these circumstances her hostess's proposal strikes her as downright uncivil.

'Treble it,' Edmund replies before she can gather her wits. Sophia turns to him in dismay but he refuses to meet her eye.

'Treble it is, then,' says Mrs Chase.

Edmund takes up the cards and again drops some of them.

Sophia sees the King of Spades flip over in the air; Edmund snatches up the card and jams it into the middle of the deck.

The cards are dealt, not without a great deal of fumbling. Unreservedly as Sophia adores her husband, she feels a twinge of humiliation, not unmixed with dread: perhaps his father should have taught him cards rather than rowing. She picks up her hand to find the King of Spades in the middle of it, flanked by the King of Hearts, the Ace of Clubs and the Ace of Diamonds.

'Thank you, Lord,' she prays and at once blushes since God surely disapproves. She was able to convince herself that low play was nothing, a mere friendly amusement, but *this* is indubitably Gaming. She is disappointed in Edmund, who must have taken more madeira than is good for him since he looks ready to drop forward onto the table. The Chases, too, appear to regard him with some unease.

Sophia wins the next three tricks and Edmund the two after that.

In the next round, with Sophia dealing, each player wins a trick apart from Edmund, who wins two. The Chases shuffle and deal: honours are equal. Edmund again shuffles awkwardly, apologising for his ineptitude and reshuffling several times to make up for it.

Sophia gapes at her hand. She has again received the King of Spades, this time flanked by the King, Queen and Ace of Clubs and the Ace of Hearts. Blinking with disbelief and a sense of unmerited good fortune, she goes on to win four tricks in a row. The remaining tricks are won by Edmund. The Chases appear to have had no cards worth holding.

From now on, the wind of good fortune sets in one quarter of the compass: Sophia's. Kings and Queens flock to feed from her hand, Aces rarely desert her courts and the tricks mount at her side of the table.

'My love, you have scourged the rest of the company until we stagger and bleed,' says Edmund at last. 'In common kindness to the other players I must now whisk you away to our lodgings.'

'Pray do not go,' Mrs Chase murmurs with ill-concealed relief.

'I fear we must. Forgive me, Madam,' (he turns to Mrs Chase with a smile that brings Sophia, figuratively, to kneel at his feet once again) 'if I am such a domestic tyrant as to bring away my wife, but you know how it is with these newly married people. They cannot be long from home.'

Mrs Chase can only smirk.

'Will you settle now?' Edmund asks carelessly.

Mr Chase cannot apologise enough. He has not the wherewithal; he never intended to play so deep this afternoon; will Mr Zedland take a note until Mr Chase can visit his banker tomorrow?

'Whenever you choose to take your revenge,' says Edmund. 'No notes between friends,' and he waves away the offer.

As they make their way along Borough Walls Edmund hums to himself: some rustic air. Sophia, looking up at his elegant profile, sickens with love. She has long pardoned his ineptitude in shuffling the cards.

'The trees are beginning to turn,' she says.

'I beg your pardon?'

'The trees. They're beginning to turn.'

Edmund says, 'I prefer autumn to summer. Smoke and fruit in the air, and blue mist – in the country, that is.'

'You talk like a poet. You look like a poet.'

He laughs. 'More than Derrick, at any rate.'

'My love,' Sophia says, 'you won't play again, will you?'

'Of course not. I only consented in order to be civil.'

She touches his arm. 'But if they asked? Would you not wish to be civil then?'

He seems extremely amused. 'You little goose!' he says. 'They won't ask us again.'

'Why ever not?' While Sophia no longer likes Mrs Chase as well as she did, the rupture of a friendship is always distressing. She feels as if a layer of love and respect has been torn away from her, as if she stands before the world a little more naked than she did this morning. 'Have we offended them? Have *I*?'

'They dislike your beginner's luck.'

'But I couldn't help that! Besides,' she clutches at straws, 'I'm not a beginner. I've played before.'

'Brides are beginners in all they do.' He pinches her cheek. 'Forget Mrs Chase. She's a false friend.'

'Is she really? I liked her.'

'Then you have learnt something,' says Edmund.

9

Betsy-Ann turns up an alleyway and emerges into a court. The houses are taller here and of recent construction, though already smutted by the smoky air of the city. Down another alley, its walls plastered and painted from the time when it led to a respectable house but now greasy from bodies pressed up against the plaster, dancing the old buttock ball. A girl passing in the opposite direction smirks at Betsy-Ann as if to say, 'I know where you're bound.'

Same place as you come from, my dear.

You never know what you'll meet up with in this passageway. She can hear the Corinthian now, in his cups:

Oh, the leafy lane, the sweet retreat, where having stepped from turd to turd, the grateful cull may at last feast his ogles on this palace of pleasure, this mountain of monosyllables . . .

'Monosyllables?' Betsy-Ann asked. 'What's a monosyllable?'
'*The* monosyllable. A woman's commodity.'
'Commodity?'
She'd never heard so many fancy words for the thing.

She rounds a corner to find a man half fallen, crouching on one knee, and is past him before he has time to grab. He looks as if he wants to come after her but he's too drunk to heave himself off the ground. No companions: been shook of everything he carried, most likely, and doesn't know it yet.

The bells are chiming eleven. A bright morning, but it's dusk down here. She looks up to the sky and feels dizzy to see the roofs so far above. There's a smell of frying sausages and from a window, high up in the wall, someone is shaking out a cloth.

There, at the end of the alley: a brick archway, the underside painted red, and set into it, the smaller deeper entrance to the seraglio, their combined appearance putting Betsy-Ann in mind, as ever, of the monosyllable. She's not the only one to have had this fancy: though it's safer to enter Kitty's establishment through the front door, some culls prefer to approach it from this side, risking dirt and criminal company, perhaps because it's less visible, perhaps because they relish brushing shoulders with blackguards. Among these the place is known, far and wide, as the Cunt in the Wall, and as if to live up to its name, it stinks. She knows why: the cullies piss before going in, right here on the steps. The familiar stale odour brings back a rush of sensations: fear, disgust and a strange, warped sense of loss, not for this place but for what she once had here.

More men are approaching along the alley. That decides the thing for her: she raps on the door.

A blowen peers out from behind a chain. 'What's your business, mort?'

'Say it's one of her old girls.'

The door closes again. She waits, breathing through her mouth; the men have stopped to chat with some woman encountered in the alleyway.

The blowen returns to unchain the door and admit Betsy-Ann to a parlour where there are elegant papered walls and paintings. She remembers the paintings: scenes of whoring, mostly, and one of meadows. When she lived here, Betsy-Ann used to wonder at the meadows. The Mother's grand project was to improve the panney from a common brothel to a seraglio in the continental style, in hopes of drawing in a wealthier clientele. That might account for it.

She's led past a couple of bullybacks playing at dice, their cudgels propped between their knees. She'd forgotten the bullybacks. There'll be more of them, a warning to the wilder sort, stationed near the front door. Skirting round their tables, the blowen leads Betsy-Ann towards a sofa where a woman waits.

What the devil — ? The Mother's twice the woman she used to be, her robes filling the entire sofa without benefit of company. The blue-black hair for which she was famed, and which she still wears unpowdered, lies rough and dusty-looking on her head, as if it doesn't belong there: could it be a wig? *Kitty Hartry*, bald of the pox? Serve her right, Betsy-Ann silently exults: serve her right! The eyes, though: the eyes haven't changed. Or have they? For the Mother says nothing and remains peering at Betsy-Ann as if unsure who stands before her.

'Don't you know me, Mother?'

'Fetch a light,' Kitty says. The girl leaps to obey. When the lamp is brought over Betsy-Ann notices the puffiness of the young face and throat: another one by the look of it, not yet fifteen and peppered already.

'You've seen me many a time,' Betsy-Ann says, taking the lamp and holding it up to her own face. The woman has recognised her now. Betsy-Ann watches her pretend to search for a name.

'The tinker,' she says at last. 'Keshlie.'

'Betsy-Ann. Keshlie was my sister.'

'So she was,' says the Mother. 'You'll take a flash of lightning with me, Betsy-Ann.' She gestures and the blowen fetches a tray from a nearby sideboard.

What's served to the culls – the ones that stick to lightning, and won't stand for ratafia – is an evil brew costing four times the going rate. The whores themselves drink better. Betsy-Ann needs that flash to keep her up; she has a hard time of it, sitting opposite the Mother, whose flesh, glistening with sweat in this muggy weather, rises and spreads like proving dough. Harry wouldn't need to lever up the lid of this one. It would burst off of its own accord, and the corpse within would spill —

47

'You'll know me again,' the woman remarks.

So she can see that much. Betsy-Ann says, 'You're the picture of prosperity.'

'A tub of guts is what you mean. It keeps a-growing on me. I tried the starving, and the purging.' With a faint grunt, the Mother leans forward as if to confide a secret. 'There's culls that like it.'

'That's only to be expected, a woman of your fame,' Betsy-Ann says. She would give anything to know if the hair is a wig.

'I'm still in *Harris's List*.'

'Naturally you are.'

'*For the connoisseur of fat, a stupendous figure with dairy-works to smother a Hercules*, is how he puts it.'

She sounds as if she's pored over the words so often as to get them by heart. Most likely she wrote them herself, since nothing goes into *Harris's* that isn't paid for.

'I take it trade's brisk, then.' Betsy-Ann could just as well answer her own question. From the parlour within she can hear singing, and shouting, and screams of laughter: all the sounds of gay company.

The Mother's smile is vicious. 'Wondering if there's still a space for you?'

'No, just wanted to know if you was still here.'

'I'm not intending to die yet.'

'And to hear news of old friends.'

Ah, says the woman's face, *now we come to it.* 'Not much in that line,' she says. 'But aren't you spliced? I heard you was.'

'I'm Mrs Samuel Shiner now.'

'His autem mort?'

'Good as.'

She clinks her glass against Betsy-Ann's. 'To the well wearing of your muff.'

As a rule, lightning brings on laughter or tears: Betsy-Ann is caught between the two as she surveys the grinning creature before her. It seems only a day or two since she last looked on Kitty Hartry, Mother of the House, who at forty was still in demand with sportsmen of every shade and trade: whipping culls, debauched schoolboys, men of spirit, queer culls, flash kiddeys, cracksmen, toby men and the occasional gent. Even now, her eyes might be half blinded but they haven't dimmed. The sight of them glittering in the bloated face makes Betsy-Ann's throat tighten. Ned's have just that brilliance: black diamonds. She wonders who'll be first to bring up his name.

Kitty says, 'You're rubbing along all right, eh?'

As if she cares. Betsy-Ann shrugs. 'Not so bad.'

'That all you can say for him? Can't be a patch on Ned, then.'

Knave of Hearts. Betsy-Ann could strangle the old bitch.

'Dimber cove, our Ned,' the Mother goes on. 'Girls fighting over him before he was old enough to do the deed. You'd have wed him, eh?'

Folk have been murdered for less. Betsy-Ann clenches her fists and says, 'Sure enough.'

'Ah, but he wouldn't wed *you*.'

He's kinder than you are, thinks Betsy-Ann. Might've turned out a marrying man, even, if you'd raised him away from here. Though in that case, Betsy-Ann would never have met him.

'You know where he's gone?'

The Mother shakes her swollen head. 'Comes and goes. He knows this place is always here.'

More's the pity.

'If you see him,' Betsy-Ann says as appealingly as she knows how, 'will you tell him to come and see us? Me and Sam.'

'Oh, me and Sam! Sam, especially,' the Mother drawls. She'll say nothing of the sort to Ned, they both know that; also that Betsy-Ann came here desperate for a glimpse of him.

'Since we've always been such good friends,' the Mother adds. 'That all you come for? Eh?'

Until this moment, Betsy-Ann has sensed a change in the Mother, a change in more than appearance, but has been unable to say where it lies. With that *eh?* she knows: it's in her talk. Kitty no longer tries to sound like the Quality. Her voice has a natural milk-and-honey sweetness – like her stupendous dairyworks, it was celebrated in *Harris's* – and not so long ago she purred away in it like a woman of breeding, or tried to. Now she's let all that go, and talks like what she is.

'I wanted to see you, Mother. You was always good to Keshlie.'

Should her sister's ghost hear that lie, Betsy-Ann can only hope she'll forgive. Good to Keshlie! The best you can say about the Mother and Keshlie is that she didn't gnaw the girl's bones. Still Betsy-Ann holds on, unable, even now, to quit the Corinth, since any minute he might walk through the door.

'Dimber little thing was Keshlie. She keeping well?'

'Still dead.' It is out of Betsy-Ann's mouth before she can stop herself.

The Mother puts a hand to her heart. 'God have mercy on us, of what?'

'You don't remember?'

The woman looks Betsy-Ann straight in the eye, just as she used to when her sight was perfect, and says, 'A shame, a crying shame.'

'Shame on them that did it, *I* say.'

'Isn't that the truth?' the Mother sighs. 'At least she had a shelter here in her time of trouble.'

Betsy-Ann nearly cracks, at that. But remembering the bully-backs sitting with their cudgels, she chokes out a civil farewell to Kitty Hartry and comes out of the panney into the damp dusk of the alleyway.

She's been a fool, on a fool's errand. She knew that's what it was, but she came anyway. That's how bad things have got.

10

To Fortunate Bath seems a wretched place, worse even than Buller where he lived with Mrs Sophia and her parents, for there were plenty of servants at Buller and they were not always unkind to him. For him, Bath is a city not of sociability but of loneliness. And then —

In Milsom Street, walking behind the master and mistress, he glimpses a brown-skinned man in livery, strolling unaccompanied on the other side of the way.

'Dog Eye,' he says in his own language.

Dog Eye turns on him. *'Master*, Titus.'

When they lived together in Romeville (another word he is forbidden to use) the name 'Dog Eye' made his master laugh. Everything must change now because of this miserable ghost, this ugly new wife.

'If you would be so kind,' Fortunate says, gesturing towards the brown-skinned man. The wife is pulling stupid faces but Dog Eye sees the thing at once and nods. By the time the woman can say, 'My dear —' Fortunate is already gone, skipping over the stones towards the liveried man. He studies the stranger from behind as he approaches and a little mouse of disappointment gnaws at his heart: this person has an alien shape, an unfamiliar walk. Most likely he is not the brother Fortunate hoped to find. He may even be an enemy.

Someone nearby points at the two of them walking together, and calls out a jest or insult. The man he is following turns and looks at him in surprise.

Fortunate stammers, 'Greetings. I hope you are well today, and that your family is also well.'

The man says something in English.

'I don't understand you,' says Fortunate.

Something more, and now the man speaks with a kind of scorn. It is no use. He turns back, dragging his feet, to where the master and mistress are waiting.

Sophia and Edmund are seated in the morning room. The fire is lit, giving a cheerful air, and on the spotlessly appointed table sit chocolate, coffee, eggs and buns. This ritual of breakfast should flood Sophia's soul with deep wifely joy and would doubtless do so, were she not quarrelling with her husband.

'You really mustn't ask me to dispose of him in Bath,' Edmund says. 'He'll be better placed in London.'

'There are respectable families here.'

'Indeed there are. But my love, only consider. Servants have their societies, as we do, and in Town there are clubs for such as he. Here is nothing of the sort. You saw how pitifully he ran after that other blackfellow.'

'He should have stayed with us.'

'Into every life a little joy must come,' says her husband. 'They have feelings, like Englishmen.'

'You believe me to be unkind, Edmund, is that it?' Sophia feels tears start to her eyes. The weakness humiliates her, but is beyond her control. At the merest hint that Edmund might consider her less than perfect, she finds herself on the point of dissolving, just as she would dissolve, as a child, when reproved by Papa.

He spreads his hands in a gesture of denial. 'Not at all, my dear, I would simply —'

'How many boys in his position draw wages? And yet he's dis-contented!'

'Has he said so?'

'There's something about him. A sulkiness. Imagine how he would be if he had nights off, and subscribed to societies! Papa says it's a cruelty to bring them here. Mixing with freeborn English servants only makes them envious.'

'Papa's thoughts do him credit, as always, but I can perhaps claim greater experience. House slaves require patience at first.'

'I know that, Edmund! Our people at home will witness that I have always been considerate of their needs, provided those needs were legitimate.'

'Of course. You are the most indulgent of mistresses, to them and to me.'

Sophia sees that he wants to kiss her into quietness but she is too far gone for that; she must have her way or feel herself unloved. At the same time, she is hot with shame. Tearful, bickering, demanding proofs of affection: this is scarcely how she pictured herself as a spouse. There was a time when she looked forward to the wifely pleasure of submitting her will to Mr Zedland's, but then she never imagined he would be like *this*.

'Then you'll place an advertisement?'

'Once we get to London. Not before.'

Since they came to Bath Edmund has shown an occasional propensity to strike up acquaintance with persons lacking manners and education, in defiance of the distaste expressed by his spouse. She has ruefully accepted this tendency to *dabble in the mud*, as she expresses it to herself, but that he should side with a servant, no, *slave* against her is something new and alarming.

'To hear you talk,' she mutters, 'anyone might think you cared more for this boy than for your wife.'

'I don't propose to set up Titus as a mistress,' he says, as if to laugh it off.

'But what of *my* feelings, Edmund? Is it not mortifying to have one's servant run away in the street? There are perfectly good arrangements here. I'm told there's a bureau where —'

'I've agreed to be rid of him!' her husband exclaims. 'So far you've carried the day. Now be wise.' He snatches up *Pope's Bath Chronicle* from the table and erects it as a screen between them.

The air of comfort that formerly invested the room has fled. The large window, fresh paintwork and tasteful green-and-gold paper no longer lap her in their protective elegance; sorrow and anger have invaded her sanctuary, and perhaps just a *soupçon* of fear. Edmund is a gentleman, yes, but first and foremost a man, and a man likes to be master. He has always behaved with gentleness towards her (apart from *that time*) but in his last speech he distinctly raised his voice and she does not at all care for 'be wise', which smacks of Bluebeard.

On the table between them lies a silver chocolate pot. Sophia takes it and pours for both.

'Will you have a Sally Lunn? I'm told they make an excellent breakfast, and these are fresh.'

The *Chronicle* quivers as he turns a page. She has never known him sulk before, and the tears she has so far resisted begin to slide down her nose. She tries to dab them away with her handkerchief while she is screened from his sight but a sniffle betrays her.

Edmund lowers the paper in order to peer at her. 'What folly!' he exclaims. 'All I wish is to treat the boy with common humanity.'

'You threatened me.'

'I did no such thing.'

'You said to be wise.' As if to prove that she is not, she now cries as heartily as a child, and brings on a fit of the hiccups. Sighing, Edmund lays down the paper, comes to Sophia and puts his hands on her shoulders.

'Your pretty eyes are all puffed up.' She closes them; he bends to kiss their swollen lids. 'As if I would threaten you! My sole aim in acquiring Titus was your amusement and pleasure. We'll leave him at home in future, and directly we get to London you can be rid of him.'

As soon as he says this, she realises how much of her anger has been made up of humiliation. Titus hidden is infinitely more bearable than Titus on the streets of Bath. Her husband puts his arms around her and draws her to him. 'Is it a bargain?'

A run of hiccups prevents Sophia from answering in words. She nods.

'Very well,' says Edmund, releasing her. 'We have now gone the customary number of rounds and honour is satisfied. Let us shake hands like sportsmen and have done with it.'

'Oh,' she gasps between spasms, 'don't make us boxers! We're lovers!'

'You wish to fight it again under lovers' rules?' He sits down and stretches lazily in the chair. 'Very well. After breakfast I shall issue a formal challenge. You shall be made to feel the extent of my powers.'

Sophia's insides seem to be dropping away. She has not so much as hinted to Edmund concerning the ability of certain expressions (*voluptuous sensations, made to feel my powers*) to demolish her defences and yet he hits upon them with surprising frequency, almost as if he guessed their impact.

'We're pretty well matched for obstinacy, if it comes to that,' he observes, helping himself to a Sally Lunn. 'I was shamefully spoilt as a boy. But I flatter myself it has stood me in good stead.'

Sophia hiccups.

'I know a cure for that, too,' adds Edmund.

11

Something disagreeable occurred this morning. After browsing in an establishment offering the sweetest imaginable stuffs for gowns, Sophia had left the premises and was meditating upon the price of Honiton lace when she became conscious of someone calling after her: 'Mrs Zedland! Ma'am!'

It was the shop's boy. She waited as he came puffing up, carrying her knotting-bag, which she now realised she had left behind on the counter. Having only recently taken to the fashion of carrying one, she had not even missed it, and as she rewarded the boy with a penny (he knuckled his forehead in rather an oafish fashion; perhaps he had not been long employed there) Sophia was sobered to think how easily the bag might have been lost, containing as it did her door key and a letter from Mama bearing her address in Bath. A thief possessed of this one little item would have everything he needed, entirely as a result of her carelessness.

However, all was well that ended well. She tucked the bag under her arm and was wondering if she should visit the subscription library when she became aware of a person strolling alongside her. He was emphatically a *person*, this stroller: nobody would ever have mistaken him for a gentleman. She slowed down, only to find that he did likewise and had every appearance of intending to strike up conversation.

Accustomed as she was to visiting the poor of her parish, Sophia had yet to see anyone as degraded as this individual. His hair – smothered in stale powder – was arranged in an affected manner, his coat ill-fitting and not over-clean and his manner of eyeing her offensive in the extreme. She had, of course, been long enough in Bath to know that living there entailed exposure to people so vulgar as to imagine a respectable woman might be 'picked up' on the public pavement. It was a common enough nuisance: one that could sometimes be resolved with tact and at other times required a degree of plain speaking. There was as yet no cause for distress. She was walking along a fashionable street, with people of taste and breeding all around.

She resolved first of all to try if she could rid herself of the creature by her own efforts. Increasing the speed of her walk, she pointedly transferred the bag from her right arm to her left, away from him. He was not to be dislodged, however, and continued to walk alongside her until they reached a less crowded section of pavement. He had, it seemed, been waiting for that. Before they came up with the next strolling group of ladies and gentlemen, he addressed her, saying, 'Zedland?' He seemed to find the name amusing. 'What's the bite?'

At least, that is what Sophia thought he said. The only thing she could have sworn to was her own name, which she now real-ised he had heard from the shopkeeper's boy.

'Rum dell,' the man said, appraising her from head to foot. 'Rum duds. Take a flash wimmee?'

What language was this: Dutch? German?

'Go away, Sir. I have no rum.'

'Talks Zedland, too!' the man exclaimed in what seemed to be admiration. 'Gives it out real pretty.' This last, though broken and debased, was undeniably something like English: perhaps he was a strolling lunatic? Seeing a lady and gentleman approach, Sophia waved to them and cried, 'If you please, be so kind as to walk with me and deliver me from this . . .' She gestured and the gentleman at once stepped forward, eager to assist. But it seemed the man was not mad after all, or could at least distinguish what was said, for he turned, crossed to an alleyway and was gone.

Over the tea table she attempts to impress upon her husband the peculiarly unsettling nature of this encounter.

'*Rum*, he said. As if he craved drink.'

'How very extraordinary,' says Edmund.

The fire is smoking into the room. She must speak to the landlady about it.

'If you could have heard his laughter! Exactly like a lunatic.'

'No doubt he was one. Now, shall we —'

'He said I *talked Zedland*.'

Edmund looks grave. 'Titus has his uses, you see. Perhaps, after all, you had better not walk without him.'

'I'd prefer to walk with you,' Sophia says. 'When you talked of settling your affairs in Bath, I had no notion they would occupy you to such an extent.'

'That's not quite fair, is it, my love? I'm never entirely away.'

'No, but you're never entirely here. It's always business. If not morning, then afternoon, and if not afternoon, then evening.'

Edmund puts down his teacup. 'Let us suppose this – reprobate, madman, what you will – wanders about Bath and latches onto any lady not under male protection. A nasty, scurvy fellow, no doubt – had I been there, I'd have taught him his manners. But only consider, love. Should I neglect important business, that may affect us for years to come, for fear of his approaching you?'

Yes, Sophia longs to reply, though restrained by a sense of the ridiculous.

Sophy is rational.

Seeing he has gained his point, her husband half-smiles. 'I should've explained to you earlier, my dear, and then I believe you would see matters as I do. My father, God rest his soul, was too generous – he'd lend to anyone in need. Most of his debtors behaved honourably but with others,' he shrugs, 'it was the old story. One family even left the district in order to evade him. He died still trying to call them to account.'

'And this is your business?'

'These very debtors are here, taking the waters, imposing upon others by giving themselves out as people of fashion. I therefore intend —'

'Did you explain all this to Papa?' asks Sophia, puzzled. 'The debts, I mean?'

'Yes indeed. We went through the notes of hand together.'

'He never mentioned them.'

'Why should he? I persuaded him of my determination to resolve the matter once and for all. You see now why I was set upon Bath for our wedding trip. Here I can exert pressure. Once returned to Essex, I am no longer a matter of urgency and must, I imagine, yield place to other creditors.'

'But why press your claims in person?' she cannot help asking. 'Couldn't you send an agent? Or take them to law?'

'You don't understand these things,' he says shortly. 'Law costs money. This has to be tried first.'

'Edmund – I'm not an idiot. I know that one must pay to go to law.'

'I'm glad to hear it.'

'But surely you could employ an agent? It must give a bad impression, if you appear unable to afford one.'

'Have you ever dunned for debt?'

'No, but —'

'In that case, you'll oblige me by not meddling.'

Sophia bites back an angry reply. It strikes her that Edmund is looking seedy. There are mauve shadows beneath his eyes and even a suspicion of beard on his cheeks.

'You seem a little unwell,' she ventures.

'True, I'm not plump currant.'

'Plump currant' is one of his inelegant expressions. With her husband's permission, Sophia often corrects these; it is a lady's prerogative and duty to soften down a husband's bearishness and polish his manners but at present she is not in a polishing mood.

'I hope you're not sickening for something, Edmund.'

'It's only lack of sleep. Killerton invited me to a game.' But you cannot play, thinks Sophia. You came to bed very late. And you stank of tobacco and brandy, so it's small wonder you're not . . . plump currant. 'We indulged somewhat unwisely, I confess. You may now spare me the sermon.'

Has he lost money? Is that what has brought on this ill temper? She cannot ask him and instead attempts a joke: 'Some wives might have suspected you with a lady.'

He studies her and grins. 'You mean you did suspect me. After what you put me through, can you honestly think I'd have strength in reserve for another woman?'

Sophia feels the shock through every fibre of her frame.

'You're speaking to your *wife*, Edmund. Do you imagine I'm accustomed to comparing men or calculating their . . . abilities?'

For an instant she glimpses the cold expression that has frightened her in the past, but when he speaks it is with amusement. 'It was but a rally, my dear. The wife's part is to laugh and let the poor fool fancy himself a wit.' He takes her hand. 'Come, shall we talk like practical people? Your easiest way to discourage these prowling wolves is to reinstate Titus. Never mind his English. What matters is that you are seen to be accompanied.'

'Perhaps,' she murmurs, reluctant to give way. Edmund smiles: what a smile! One would think she had just righted every wrong he had ever undergone. Emboldened, Sophia continues: 'And you, Edmund? You won't continue with business every day that we're here?'

'I expect to bring matters to a prompt conclusion. Does that content you?'

'Yes, if you will walk out with me afterwards,' she says humbly. She rings the bell for the maid to take away the tea things.

'Mind you tell her about that damn chimney,' says Edmund, rising and leaving the room.

The maid is slow in arriving. Sophia sits drumming her fingers, then leaps up, seizes the *Bath Chronicle* from the table and holds it in front of the flames to encourage them upwards. Smoke at last begins to flow up the chimney instead of out into the room, but no sooner has the fire started to draw in earnest than the paper 'catches' and she is forced to let it go.

12

As the weather grows colder, Sam Shiner comes home more and more drunk. Betsy-Ann knows how *that* song goes: lying about in Harry's lodging with the rest of the crew, soaking up nantz. Not that she grudges him a drop or two; even Harry can't do it without. Once they're past caring it's off to the crib, dig up the merchandise, cart it to where it's needed. Harry insists on payment in darby, no promises or notes of hand, they're fly to all that, and then with each man's share burning holes in his pocket it's lush, lush, lush, anything to forget. Sam's rarely in a condition to fetch himself home. Betsy-Ann goes to sleep without him, but she keeps a candle burning, just in case, and gets up if she hears his key. As she helps him peel off that terrible coat of his, she's hit by the nantz. He sucks on that bloody nantz like a kid on a titty: it's on his breath, it's the glaze over his eyes. Under the coat he's wet to the bone, his shirt sometimes soaked with rain but always with sweat. Christ, how he sweats. She pictures the booze boiling up in his belly and squeezing itself out through his skin. His coat is mouldy; when she hangs it up over the fire it breathes death through their two little rooms, their cups and plates, their bed.

The death carried in on that coat has spread through everything. Sam hardly eats, but he's developed a pale, greasy fatness like a maggot. His brain's dead, his mouth's dead (devil a word does she get out of him, these days), his prick's been dead a fortnight at least. Try resurrecting that, Sam Shiner!

Tonight he's out again. Hail tattles on the window; she wonders if the ground will be soft enough for working. All the more time to drink. The hail drums more loudly. A wonder if he doesn't come home with pock-holes bored in his face.

She's pulled the covers off the bed and brought them over to where she's lying by the fire. They never had such a blaze when she was a kinchin. Ma would light a fire in a bucket, ash or birch if they were lucky; it was hard to get the good firewood and keep it dry. Here in Romeville it's coal, nothing but coal. The smoke's foul, a stinking yellow-grey, but it makes a brisk fire and Betsy-Ann makes bold to order plenty. She can afford to: she shakes Sam of his blunt while he's still boozed up, not all of it, just enough to go unnoticed. It makes up for the nights when he doesn't come home. Then in the morning she asks for her cut in the usual way.

She lies down, lays her head on one side and gazes into the fire's depths.

Sheer folly, on nights like this, to think of the panney, but she can't help herself. She has everything laid up in store, sour pickles and sweet plums; she preserves it, cherishes it, deep in her mind where Sam can't see, and she has a little taste each night before she goes to sleep.

Tonight she's tasting the sour: her coming to Romeville. For all its sourness, it's a common tale, common as sparrows: herself, Mam and Keshlie, huddled round a cold hearth.

Mam hung down her head. 'I should never have sold the horse.'

Betsy-Ann was silent. This was what came of trusting in Harry, in the fine bragging letter he'd paid someone to write. They should join him in Romeville, such a life! Aye, and such fools as they'd been, to follow on. Harry was to make all their fortunes: Mam talked of nothing else.

Now she never mentioned Harry's name.

'The pain's worse,' she said. 'God help us if it's the wolf. If it's the wolf, it's the end of me.' She kept on about the wolf until Betsy-Ann went out for gin and made her drink it. At last Mam got into the bed, which was for one person, and went off into a sleep. Her girls got in on either side of her. The sisters were used to sleeping close.

Betsy-Ann woke to find her mother cold beside her. She rose in the dark, pulled the sheets over Mam's head and sat by her an hour or two, letting Keshlie sleep on. It was strange sitting there, not crying. People always cried, but Betsy-Ann felt hollow and numb. She wondered did she love Mam enough. When her sister finally woke, Betsy-Ann lifted her out of the bed saying Mam was tired and needed her rest. After a while, though, Keshlie wanted to be talking to Mam, and like the little fool she was, must go tugging at the sheets behind Betsy-Ann's back. She wept and wailed enough for two but still Betsy-Ann couldn't cry. She pulled back the sheet and lifted Mam's shift.

'What are you doing, our Betsy?' Keshlie asked.

Mam's titties were meagre and sagging: men liked what they called 'pouting bubbies', and smacked their lips when they spoke of them, but women of Betsy-Ann's acquaintance were rarely plump enough for pouting bubbies. She knew the wolf came first from the sides and gnawed its way in from there. You could feel it under the skin. Timidly, she touched Mam in the armpit.

'Don't,' Keshlie said.

'I want to know was it the wolf.'

'You're nasty.'

Cold spread from Mam's skin into her hands. Shaking, Betsy-Ann pulled the shift down again to cover everything. What did it matter, after all? Mam was just as dead. She took Keshlie by the hand and set out to walk to Harry's lodging.

'I'd a share in the horse and cart,' Harry said, standing in the doorway. Betsy-Ann tried to see round him but he shifted to block her view.

'There's nothing left, Harry! We paid two months in advance, I told you.'

'I know what you told me.'

Betsy-Ann wondered if he had a woman hidden in his rooms.

64

She said, 'We was done brown, first on the horse and then on the rent.'

'More fool you.'

'And Mam, what can we do with her? You have to help, she's your mam same as ours.'

'Never mind her. She's not eating anything. Your business is how *you're* going to feed.'

'I don't know,' Betsy-Ann said. 'How will we?'

Harry rolled his eyes as if he couldn't believe she needed telling. 'Strapping wench like you, Betsy, and new in town? Sovereign a time.'

'Gold!' Keshlie breathed.

Betsy-Ann pictured her sister, whose frail limbs and pale, heart-shaped face made her seem younger than her twelve years, standing in line with the whores. The ones in Harry's street looked ready to do it for a shilling.

'No, no,' she said to Keshlie. 'It's very bad work.'

Harry sniffed. 'Wish I could make my way as easy. If you don't like it, go and dig turnips.'

'Wait,' Betsy-Ann pleaded. 'I was thinking. I can be your second, can't I? John Mucklow's sister does for him in the ring, I'll do the same.'

'I don't want any second. I'm sick of pugilism. Finished with it.'

She stared at him. 'How are you living, then?'

He began to close the door on them. Betsy-Ann flung her weight against the boards, wailing, 'What about Mam? I don't know anybody,' but she was no match for Harry. She heard him drive home the bolt on the other side.

Some friends of his came, when it was dark, and loaded the corpse onto a cart. Keshlie lay face down on the bed, refusing to speak, as Mam was wheeled away.

The night was terrible. Betsy-Ann dreamed she was buried alive, yet at the same time floating in the air, watching from above: she saw Keshlie and Harry stamping down the earth over her. She woke sweating and whimpering with relief, until she remembered they had lost Mam.

'Get up,' she said to Keshlie as soon as it was light. 'Let me comb your hair.'

They put on their best duds, ancient and flittered by the standards of the women prowling the pavements, and went to a street of respectable-looking houses. To face after face she told the story of coming to Romeville and of her mother dying, leaving them to earn their keep.

Again Betsy sees the servants turning them away, the ones who did it kindly (one woman pressed a coin into her hand) and the ones who tossed their heads and said things like, 'That's my eye, Betty Martin!' before clapping the door to.

They came to a house where a pretty young maid opened to them. She looked at each and said yes, her mistress might care to take them on: would they wait?

The maid went inside to enquire. Betsy-Ann winked at Keshlie, who looked as if she might cry. In a few minutes they were taken to a room where a lady, very genteelly dressed, was standing before a fire and gazing down her nose as if she suffered from melancholy. Betsy-Ann never discovered who this lady was; she never saw her again. The lady said she had no need of more servants, but it so happened she had a visitor in the house who might be able to use them. She sent the maid out and in a short time the visitor came into the room. Betsy-Ann could have cried out at the sight of her: she was clad in soft white stuff as if her robe had been cut from a cloud, with sparkling little stars embroidered on it. Pearls dangled from her ears, spilled over her bosom and twined in ropes around her wrists, but the lady herself was not inferior to what she wore: her soft, golden skin had a delicate surface that shamed the pearls. Betsy-Ann had once been taken inside a big house and she thought the lady's face, with its liquid eyes, was like a face she had seen in a painting there. Keshlie put her hand into Betsy-Ann's and the two girls stood dumb with admiration. Seeing this, the lady smiled.

'You did well to consider me,' she told her friend, in a voice even softer than her robe. She turned to the sisters. 'I hear you're seeking places.'

'If you please, Ma'am, maids.' Betsy-Ann curtseyed, pulling down Keshlie's hand to make sure she did likewise.

'And where's your mother?'

'She's dead, Ma'am.'

Keshlie's face puckered. Betsy-Ann squeezed her sister's fingers more tightly.

'No father?'

'He's long gone,' Betsy-Ann said. This seemed to be the right answer since the lady bent down to study the pair of them. She was even more beautiful, close to: Betsy-Ann stared fascinated at the tiny curls nestling against her neck.

'Are you good morts?'

Betsy-Ann hesitated.

'Girls,' put in the other lady. 'Are you good girls – obedient?'

Betsy-Ann nodded.

'Speak up. How old is the little one?'

'She's twelve. Older than she looks.'

'A brace of roses,' said the beauty to her friend, with a flick of the eyebrows that Betsy-Ann would only understand when it was too late. She turned from one lady to the other, afraid that in her ignorance she might lose their chance.

'What can you do?'

'Fruit-picking, Madam. Farm work.' The vision in white smiled. 'And the books.'

'You can read?'

'No. I tell fortunes and – do tricks.'

'Novelty is always in demand,' said the lovely one, looking them up and down. 'It takes a stout wench to be a maid. Your sister could never do it.'

'But *I* could, Madam,' pleaded Betsy-Ann.

'You're a fine big piece,' said the lady. 'But what a pity, my child, to dim your bright eyes with weariness! What say I look after you, and bring you up to be useful and industrious? Should you like that?'

'Oh, yes!' they chorused, Betsy-Ann adding, 'If you please, Madam.'

'Then it's a bargain,' said the lady, spitting in her hand like a man and holding it out for them to shake. 'Mind, you've promised now,' she said when both Betsy-Ann and Keshlie had done so. The other lady rang a bell and the maid reappeared. 'Wait in the kitchen with Nelly here,' said Kitty Hartry, 'until I'm ready to go home.'

She took them in her private carriage to a large, solid house. At the back of it lay the alleyway, and the brick arch with the stinking flagstones beneath, but they were not to know that when they arrived.

13

To the tune of The Sweeper Boy

My sister's gone to walk the roads
The roads of London Town, Sir,
And there she's met a wicked man
And he has brought her down, Sir.

She was not gone but half a day
But half a day in town, Sir,
He took her pure white shift away
And sold it for a pound, Sir.

And now my sister's lying sick
She's lying sick to die, Sir,
The only one that pays her mind
And gives her bread is I, Sir.

Could I but go to London roads
And find him in his bed, Sir,
Then up and at him I would go
And leave him there for dead, Sir.

And they could hang me high as high
Until my life was gone, Sir,
I'd never drop a single tear
Nor grieve for what I'd done, Sir.

14

Only this morning Sophia made the acquaintance of a sociable lady who stood fair to replace the treacherous Mrs Chase, and was invited to call on her tomorrow. Mama's last letter, too, hinted that she might make the journey and pay a visit to her precious lamb. Now all this budding happiness is to be roughly stripped from the vine.

'I thought you wanted to leave the place,' Edmund protests, pacing back and forth through the drawing room.

'I did, but don't you see how intolerable this is? You don't tell me anything!'

'What is there to tell, my love? Surely the maid can pack up your things before midnight?'

'Yes, if I supervise her, but why such haste? We can pack at leisure, leave in a couple of days, and not have the discomfort of sleeping in the coach. And Mrs Mallory will think me so rude if I don't take leave —'

'What's Mrs Mallory to you?' Edmund rolls his eyes. 'Two days ago you'd never heard of her. Christ, is there a woman in England who knows her own mind?'

'Please don't blaspheme, Edmund.'

'Well, is there? Only yesterday you were whining to go to London.'

'Because I'm always alone here,' Sophia protests. 'If you talked more to me, told me things —'

'But I am telling you.'

'I mean ask me. Converse with me. It's not right, Edmund. Papa wouldn't behave like this to Mama. He'd never be so – so peremptory.'

'Peremptory, *Papa*?' he mocks. 'He wouldn't dare. A guinea on it, he only rogered her once and that was the night they got you!'

Few things are more shocking to a woman than the revelation of contempt where she thought to find only love. Sophia covers her hand with her mouth so as not to be sick on the sitting-room floor: as a child she sometimes vomited when frightened, and frightened she certainly is. She breathes deeply, striving for control, and by the time she has recovered herself Edmund's face is wiped clear of disdain. In its place has come not repentance, but something like wariness.

'You really mustn't keep comparing me with Papa.' His voice has softened but to Sophia, still quivering from his gibe at her parents, his manner conveys only frigidity. 'No husband would like it.'

'Then don't speak of him so disrespectfully. No daughter would like it.'

She has never before answered back in this spiteful, mocking manner to him or anyone else. What has rendered her capable, where has it come from? She can only suppose that indignation conquered fear.

'You mistake me,' says Edmund, calm and poisonous. 'I meant only that your father isn't the pattern for all men.'

'No. Only for gentlemen.'

He groans. 'Very well, I spoke hastily, but you can be so trying, my sweet! After weeks of wanting to leave — ! As for Papa, he's an excellent fellow, that I'll admit. That he's a trifle countrified, not quite the thing, I think even *you* might admit.'

'As a young man, he made the Grand Tour,' she retorts.

He laughs. 'Then the public deserves to be better informed of his adventures, for nobody would ever guess.'

Sophia spends the next few minutes crying, recovering and crying again, quite unable to turn her mind to the business of packing.

By the time she is fit to instruct the maid, Edmund has shut himself away in his closet, from which headquarters Titus occasionally issues, returning with brandy and other comforts. The message is clear: since my wife declines to take care of me, I shall take good care of myself.

His wife lets him have his head; she has no desire to speak with him and a great deal to order and put away. The maid is hunted out of her room upstairs and pressed into service. Together they pack up Sophia's honeymoon: her trousseau, her books and knick-knacks, her visiting cards and invitations and letters from home.

'Madam,' the maid says as she folds Sophia's best lawn nightgown, the embroidering of which took a month, 'may I speak?'

'Yes?' She waits, but the maid appears to be having second thoughts. 'Well?'

' I hope you won't be angry, Madam.'

So far Sophia has paid little attention to this girl: an underdeveloped, mousy creature, competent enough but not a servant one would seek to promote. Now she detects agitation, even distress, and concludes, 'You've broken something.'

'No, Madam, indeed. It concerns Mr Zedland.'

For the second time that day Sophia is struck dumb, seeing the maid on her back, her gown rucked up and, plunging between her knees, Edmund. His hair falls forward as he . . . Sophia can see the thing as if she were present, or rather, she can see it from every angle. *Feel the extent of my powers.* She shakes her head to fling off the disgusting picture and stares at the girl. How fresh and pretty she is. Not mousy at all, now that one comes to look. Why did Sophia never observe this before? Amorousness drugged her, that is why: she breathed Edmund, dreamed Edmund. Other females may have been drugged likewise.

The maid says, 'I couldn't sleep at night if I didn't – only I was afraid you'd be angry —'

72

Edmund himself would be hard put to it to find words so irresistible.

'You must tell me.' Her voice is brittle. She would prefer to show herself calm and strong, but brittle must suffice.

'You know where the Master goes each morning,' the maid begins. Though phrased as a statement, it is also a question. A mistress, thinks Sophia. Not this girl. Some other woman – one who has been smiling in Sophia's face all week? Mrs Mallory? She is aware of each wincing beat of her shrivelled, crippled heart as she says, 'He's dunning for debts.' A voice from a past existence murmurs that these are their private concerns, hers and her beloved Mr Zedland's. She is exposing them to a hired hand. But then, what does it matter? They won't see the maid again, any more than Mrs Mallory, or the Chases, or anyone in Bath if Sophia can help it.

The girl's face clouds over as if she anticipated some other answer.

'He duns in person,' Sophia adds. 'I often scold him for what I consider an ill-bred eccentricity.'

A stab of pain follows as she realises that out of pure habit, she is smiling. Never again will she enjoy that privilege, the smug confidence of the indulged darling: *Edmund adores me and, great fierce thing that he is, submits tamely to my scolding.* She has shrunk, since this morning, to a wretched imitation of her former self.

'I suppose, then, Madam, he goes from that to the tables.'

'Mr Zedland doesn't game.'

The maid bites her lip. Sophia's stomach lurches but she rallies, feeling herself on solid ground as she says, 'I assure you, my husband can barely deal.'

'O, *Madam*,' says the maid, the two words full and trembling with disaster.

'Sit down.' Sophia pushes the girl onto the bed. 'Has he had a loss? Gambled, gambled away my . . .' Her numb, drying tongue will not frame the word *fortune*.

'No, not a loss, Madam.' Sophia half sobs, half gasps with relief. 'But he's bankrupted an heir. Everybody's talking of it but I thought, from your, your *disagreement* with Mr Zedland, that you hadn't heard.'

'Everybody — ? What heir?' Look at me, thinks Sophia, look at me: the whole of Bath talking, and I'm reduced to pumping the maid for gossip! Her cheeks blaze as it dawns on her that the girl must have heard their quarrel through the ceiling. The quarrels and *tendresses* of her honeymoon have been not private but public.

'A young gent, only just come to Bath. I don't know his name. Mr Zedland's made a bubble of him.'

'A bubble?'

'Ruined him, Madam.'

The girl is sparing her. It means more than that, she realises: it means *cheated*. Sophia feels like a man who, riding up to his castle, sees it suddenly crumble and slide into the sea. There is nothing to be said. The two women stand gazing on one another, each with her hand to her mouth, but again Sophia rallies.

'This is some foolish rumour,' she says. 'More likely Mr Zedland himself has had a loss, if indeed he made one of the party. He has neither time nor taste for sitting at card tables.'

'I wouldn't know anything of that, Madam. Only I've heard he – is sometimes there.'

'But from whom, child?'

The maid looks pleadingly into her eyes. 'I can't tell you, Madam, unless you promise not to speak to his master or mistress about it.'

'Whose master or mistress?'

'Will you promise, Madam? Otherwise, he'd lose his place, and that would be a poor return for his kindness.'

And mine, says her face. Sophia wants to tell this officious girl that servants do not extract promises from their superiors. But what does it matter now? If what she says is true, their disgrace so dwarfs this irregularity as to render it invisible.

'Very well, I promise.'

'Then it's Mr Southern, Madam, the manservant next door. He guessed you didn't know, and he asked if there was some way I could warn you.'

Sophia has now sunk almost as far as she conceives it possible to sink. Strange servants, not even part of her establishment, pity her and manage her affairs among themselves. Worse, the humiliation must be swallowed down if she wishes to learn more.

'But how does *he* know?'

'They had a great many callers today. He says it was constantly spoken of.'

'Is he trustworthy, this Southern? An honest man?'

'O yes, Madam, known for it.'

He is superior in that, it seems, to Sophia's husband. Probably everybody in the street, down to the very chimney-sweepers, knows what Edmund did not see fit to tell his wife. She sinks down onto the bed and crams the coverlet into her mouth.

15

Trussed in a sackcloth apron, his sleeves rolled up, Fortunate is learning how to wash silver. The maid drops soft soap into a basin of water, stirring with her fingers until the soap vanishes. Then she shows him how to wet the cloth, wring it out and wipe it inside the rim of the bowl, always following the edge: round and round and round.

'Don't go across, like this,' she says, moving the cloth from side to side. 'Tell me when you've done that one and I'll have a look.'

It is slow work. The bowl has blackened: from sitting in the air, the maid says. He has to wipe many times before its edges begin to gleam.

Why do they care so much for a metal that grows foul, just from being in the air? Perhaps because it is pale and sickly, like themselves. Gold is more glorious. They have a coin here they call a guinea, after the land of gold.

Some of the pieces – the ones she has kept away from him – rise like the smooth heads of waves, breaking not into foam but into flowers and birds and knots of polished metal. Though he knows how costly they are, he finds no beauty in them: neither in the silver itself nor in the twirling, scooping shapes these people love to bend it into. Once or twice, seeing it highly polished, set with jewels and gleaming in candlelight, he has glimpsed something of silver's ghostly power over them. But gold rivals the sun.

'Let's have a look,' says the maid behind him. She takes the bowl and holds it close to her eyes. 'Not bad. Not too much tarnish on these. Do the rest of the bowls, but mind you go round.'

He nods. He wonders if she is going blind, to hold the thing so close. The first time he saw a man wearing spectacles, he thought some enemy had put them on him. Then the man took them off and polished them and Fortunate understood they were like the instruments used on the ship, intended to help the eyes.

The man with the spectacles was Mr Watson.

His hand continues smoothing the cloth around the bowl but his mind is far away in Romeville, where he stands behind Mr Watson at a table covered in green cloth. The room is hot from many candles and Mr Watson ill at ease: Fortunate, who has come to know the signs, observes the flush spreading up his neck and a few strands of hair beginning to curl beneath the edges of his perruque. When the master looks so heated, it is best to keep back. Fortunate knows that from experience.

All the men around the table, including Mr Watson, are holding cards, and several have small heaps of coin before them.

Though Fortunate can tell from the master's flushed skin that this is an unlucky night, he has little sense of the games played. He has stood for many hours at Mr Watson's house in Maryland, holding trays of drinks and watching money pass across the tables, but nobody thought to explain the uses of the cards to him, any more than they would explain them to any other article of furniture. During the voyage from Maryland to here he again observed play, this time that of the sailors, but still without understanding. Still, to watch was pleasure enough. To walk about, too: to go wherever Mr Watson sent him, instead of suffocating below. Seeing him clad in livery, the white people behaved themselves differently towards him, some even seeming friendly. They showed him various contrivances of the ship and would have made a player of him had Mr Watson not spoken to them, saying that Fortunate had no money of his own, was forbidden to game, and that he, Watson, would not cover his debts. Though Fortunate made sure to look sorry before the men, he was secretly glad. The sailors were noisy and unpredictable in play and on one occasion a man punched another to the deck.

In Romeville, in the room full of golden statues and mirrors and lights, there is no shouting and no anger, except in that sweating neck.

The table has gone very quiet. Not long ago they were laughing and passing round a wine-flagon. That has all stopped in an instant. Then the man opposite flips down a card as if he does not care for it and a roar goes up from the others. The man who laid the card smiles towards Mr Watson.

'Damn you, Sir,' Mr Watson says, shifting in his chair. Fortunate shrinks back but when Mr Watson snaps his fingers he is forced to move forward to his master's side. Mr Watson places his hand in the small of Fortunate's back and shoves so that the edge of the table catches Fortunate in the belly.

The men grin to see him squeezed up against the table edge. One of them says the word *blackbird*.

'He speaks no English,' Mr Watson says. Fortunate is surprised, since his master knows he can speak a little.

The man opposite Mr Watson says something: his voice is soft. One of the other players, still grinning, addresses this other man and seems to put a question. The man shakes his head.

Then Mr Watson rises without warning, pushing back the chair. He throws his cards and some money onto the green cloth and hurries away. Fortunate makes to follow him. Mr Watson turns and catches him a blow across the face that sends him staggering back against the table.

The men cry out. One of them takes hold of Fortunate by the arm and makes signs that he should sit down; when Fortunate tries to struggle free and follow his master, the man pushes him into Mr Watson's chair and holds him there. Fortunate twists himself to look over his shoulder, afraid that Mr Watson will punish him for not following and for the insolence of sitting where Mr Watson should be. He manages to bring out the word *master*.

Someone says, *English*.

The man holding him turns a little so that Fortunate can see Mr Watson is gone. He goes limp in the chair, unsure what to do. Perhaps his master is coming back and has told the men to keep him there.

A glass of wine is put in front of him. The man on his right indicates that he is to take it and drink. It occurs to Fortunate that perhaps they mean to poison him on the orders of Mr Watson who is angry with him for some reason. He shakes his head. The man on his right takes the glass himself and drinks from it, then holds out the rest to Fortunate.

Fortunate sucks up a little sour-tasting wine on his tongue.

The man opposite also has a glass of wine, which he raises towards Fortunate before drinking. Fortunate knows the meaning of this: friendship. They are mocking him. But then the man drinks to him again, and looks kindly. He points to Fortunate's glass and gestures that he should also drink some more.

He does so but it is so unpleasant that he can scarcely swallow. Seeing this, the men burst out laughing.

'Master,' says the man opposite. He is pointing not in the direction of Mr Watson, but to himself. Fortunate looks at him more closely now. He is a young man with a full mouth, very red, and eyes glittering with wine. He seems a good-natured person, but Fortunate knows better than to trust in the kindliness of a white face.

'Master,' the man says again. He takes one of the gold pieces from the table and puts it in Fortunate's other hand, then makes a joke which causes the others to smile. Putting down the wine, Fortunate turns again to see if Mr Watson is coming back, but there is no sign of him. It is true, then. He has been passed from one man to the other. He slips the gold coin into his pocket and the men laugh, seeing it.

'At that time —' he says to himself.

'Jabbering again?' The maid's hand is on his shoulder. 'Is that

79

as far as you've got? It's to be packed up within the hour!' He moves the cloth faster. 'This one's clean enough,' the maid says, taking the bowl from him in order to dry it. 'Do that one.'

Betsy-Ann is practising two things together: her shuffle and one of Mam's songs:

> *He came by the mountain*
> *He came by the valley*
> *O he came full twenty mile*
> *For to be with his dearie*

So he spurred his prad, thinks Betsy-Ann, breaking off as she drops a card and blends it back into the deck. Or else he was a great walker and snoring the minute he climbed into bed, and his dearie rogered by the cove next door.

Some of the songs are stupid when you stop to think of the words, but she loves the music and the stupid words she keeps for Mam's sake. Most of them she's got off by heart; there's the odd one where she knows she's lost a verse, lost two, lost the start. If she could write – properly, not just a few letters of her ABC – she could keep everything better.

She nearly learned once, came close as spitting. Queer how it happened. A fingerpost came to this street to preach, all the usual gammon: faggots bound for the fires of hell, sinners on the broad way that leads to destruction. He should've known they'd pelt him for his trouble. His kind were never liked and the weather was so bitter that when he went on about Hell and its flames you could see folk were fairly longing to get there; failing that, they'd settle for a blazing hearth and some drink. They held back, though, since he had a boxful of Bibles. The fool gave them out and looked pleased that everyone was grabbing at them, for lighting the fire (supposing they had coal) or wiping their arses on. Betsy-Ann, standing near the front, managed to lay hand on one of the things just before his stock ran out and the filth began to fly. As the man was scurrying off without his hat, she ran alongside and said, 'Will you teach me to read it, Sir?'

That knocked him back, she thinks, smiling. He wasn't in such a trusting mood after what'd just happened to him, so he looked her up and down, trying to see if she was honest, then said his wife taught persons wishing to improve themselves, every evening bar Sunday, and gave her the place and time. 'Will you remember it?' he asked.

Betsy-Ann's head could hold more than that. 'Is it free, Sir?'

'Free,' said the fingerpost, pulling away from her in his hurry to escape being scragged.

She went the next night. St Something's: it was an autem. She'd never been partial to autems. This one was so vast she could hardly see the ceiling, and crammed with statues, the biggest of a wench suckling a kinchin-cove, her hair tied up in a clout. There were other wenches with their eyes rolled up, hands on their hearts, and bearded men, all of them wrapped in bedsheets.

The whole place was deadly cold, much colder than the rooms Betsy-Ann shared with Shiner. She wondered what would bring folk in there, except possibly the candelabra dangling above her like a huge brass spider. A neat bit of work; she'd once fenced one just like it.

The fingerpost's mort peeked out from a room at the back and as soon as she saw Betsy-Ann, came to her and steered her inside. Fair enough: it wasn't friendly to wander about pricing the furniture and besides there was a tiny fire in there, struggling in the icy air. The mort wasn't as game as her man, you could see that straight off from her sour way of twitching her nostrils, but she held up a piece of paper with letters on it, A, B, C, and they chanted it out together. The other scholars were all men, with Betsy-Ann the only female. At the back sat a huge cove like the Champion of All England, hands like a bear's paws, covering his slate with an army of pot hooks and walking sticks.

'Have you ever been to school?' the mort said.

What a green question! It annoyed Betsy-Ann, so she said, 'Only the pushing academy.'

A couple of them hooted at this but the mort didn't seem to know what a pushing academy was. She pointed at a paper pinned on the wall, with lines of these same walking sticks, and said Betsy-Ann was to copy them, it would prepare her for proper writing. So Betsy-Ann sat down with her slate. She was only five sticks in when she nearly choked on a foul hogo. She was looking round for a killed rat, when the man on her left happened to turn in her direction. He had no nose at all; he'd got the Covent Garden Ague so bad he should've been in pickle, not sitting here spoiling a slate. She turned her face away. This autem mort must have bottom, after all, if she could sit with that every night. No wonder she pinched up her phiz.

When the mort came to look at Betsy-Ann's slate, she seemed surprised. 'Surely you *have* done this before?'

'No indeed, Ma'am.'

'You have remarkable dexterity,' the woman said. 'Your hands, I mean. You are – precise.' Betsy-Ann wanted to giggle. It was the books, of course, all the shuffling and forcing, but that wasn't a thing to brag of here.

'Here, since you're a quick study. Try ABC.' The mort pointed to another paper pinned on the wall.

Betsy-Ann set to work, breathing through her mouth and only occasionally taking a little whiff through her nostrils to see if the hogo was as bad as she remembered. Now here was a thing, she thought: people who found a stink often couldn't leave it alone but must keep coming back and exclaiming again, and she was as bad as any. But when she set herself in earnest to copy the letters, they were so strange and interesting that she forgot Poxy Pete. A was a fine looking thing, standing like a monument with one leg on each side. That made it the first letter, the Upright Man of the crew. B sounded like bubbies and looked like them too: pouting bubbies. C was a curl of hair in a barber's bowl, and D a slice off an apple. E was like nothing, nor F, nor G. H was dimber, straight-limbed, sworn brother to A.

The mort even came to sit beside her, right in the thick of the hogo, and told her the name of each letter and the sound it made. Some of them she still remembers: R, for example. That's how she knows there's a *rrr* sound at the end of soldier and sailor, just the way she says it. Not sheep talk, Sam Shiner. Writing talk.

The mort wrote out ABC on a paper for her to take home and practise. 'Next time,' she said smiling, 'I'll teach you to write your name.'

Sam wouldn't let her go. He said he didn't like her hanging round autem bawlers. Any minute now they'd have her repenting, and turning him in.

'You'll get not a penny out of them,' he said, 'unless you pay 'em a pound first.'

Betsy-Ann thought that was true of most people; the only difference was that autem bawlers talked about love and charity while they were shaking you down. Look at the men she'd known in the seraglio, demanding buckets of drink and the prettiest mort in the house. They'd order her to do any number of disgusting things, enough to turn your stomach, and after she'd gone through with all that, they'd decline to settle. Kitty was fly to their sort, though: she once told Betsy-Ann that when gaming, these same cullies staked hundreds on the turn of a card and paid up, game as you like, because they were dealing with other *gentlemen.*

Later, when Betsy-Ann took up with the Corinthian, he confirmed every word of it.

His mother didn't stand for such gammon. Any cull who tried it got a sound milling from the bullybacks and was never admitted again – never, even after he'd cleared himself, in case he should take it into his head to return with rough friends. A little note on perfumed paper, offering to enlighten his family as to his habits, sometimes greased the way, especially if his father was a pious old moneybags who might cut him out of the will. Every girl of Kitty's made it her business to coax such intelligence out of her culls and have it written in Kitty's book. That might be worth ten guineas to her, should the information ever be used.

Even if the rogues paid up and never came back, there were always new cheats. Romeville was full of them as a dog of fleas. Still, this fingerpost and his mort seemed harmless. They'd asked nothing that could set her up for a touch.

She said, 'But Sammy, you can read.'

'And write too. What of it?'

'And the Corinthian can read and write, can't he? Don't make him a flat.'

'God rot your Corinthian,' said Sam.

'*My* Corinthian? What's up, Sammy? I thought you and him was trusty.'

'Never mind him. He's gone. It's you and me, now.'

For weeks afterwards she thought about going back to the autem, sitting down to her slate, until so much time had passed that Betsy-Ann would've been ashamed to explain herself and anyway, the autem mort probably thought she'd toddled or died. In those days Sam still had all his fingers. Had Betsy-Ann known he was about to lose one, she'd have gone back no matter what. She'd be far on in reading and writing by now.

84

The Curse of Scotland flies out from the deck and skids across the table. Betsy-Ann's growing tired and cack-handed. She shuffles again and sings:

> *She kissed him and lay with him*
> *Down in the valley*
> *And then said the young maid*
> *O when shall we marry?*

To hell with Johnny and his true love. Let's have something more like it. She digs a fingernail into the deck to mark the position of the ace and begins slowly, carefully to plant the books.

> *Moll of the Wood went to the fair*
> *To see what pleasure and pastime was there.*
> *She met with the drummer, he being just come,*
> *She learned to beat on his rum-a-dum-dum.*

Pleasure and pastime! Give her a sporting cull that'll lay down a bit of cash, not a Darling Johnny who tastes the goods and runs for the mountains at the first whiff of trouble. She moves the books faster: three shuffles and she has them lined up. Ace, king, knave.

Knave of Hearts.

It's no use, she can't settle. Betsy-Ann lays down the cards and goes to the window where the sky shows iron-grey. The starved sapling rooted in the gutter of the house opposite is bent over to one side, like a schoolboy about to take a whopping.

This is what she dreamed of, all the time she was with Kitty: a ken of her own, nothing too fancy, just an upstairs pair with a stout lock on the door. Upstairs is more private, and not so hard on the windows: it's months since these were last starred by a stone. The sash frames are stuffed tight with rag and the place is snug. What a joy, then, to have a hearth of her own with an un-blocked chimney! There's a bucketful of coal standing ready and a pan of lightning, with sugar and cloves, warming before the fire. Mrs Samuel Shiner should be like a cat in catnip, shouldn't she?

Instead of which she's like a bitch with the itch. She goes to the cupboard and opens up the inner door. No. Close it. No, have a look, there's nobody to know.

She finds and opens the white leather box. O, the sweet satin shoes, embroidered fit for a duchess! She looks down at her feet: Betsy-Ann has a big foot for a woman. The shoes were made to her size, but if she once puts them on, they'll stretch and lose their freshness. Better keep them as they are.

The ring, though; she might wear that. If Sam asks, one of the kinchin-coves brought it in. Her finger slides snug inside the gold band and the coral heart sits so pretty, so innocent. A child's ring. *A pretty fam deserves a pretty fawney.* One time, the hand was sweet as the ring, on the large side but soft-skinned, a graceful shape. Her fingers are coarsening with all those shirts she scrubs for Sam. She should've worn this before, just put it on as if it was nothing. He wouldn't have known.

She takes an earring, black pearls and gold, and tries its wire in one of her lobes. It's some time since she last wore any and the hole is shrunken. She licks a finger, moistens the skin and pushes hard. Like something else: lick, push, in you go. Somebody should write a song about it: *The Goldsmith's Prentice and His Lass.*

> *O no, my dear prentice, this never will do*
> *Your wire is too thick, it cannot go through.*
> *My sweet, said the prentice, Pray leave it to me . . .*

She'd like to make a rhyme with *key* but can't be bothered. The inside of her ear-lobe feels enormous as she tries to guide the ear-ring through it from front to back; she imagines corridors inside there, dead-ends of flesh glowing with pain, red like your hands when you cup them round a lantern. She won't give up. She closes her eyes and twiddles until the earring is in place. Seen in the mirror, the throbbing labyrinths she has been probing are nothing, just a slice of skin. The other earring passes through without trouble.

Betsy-Ann admires herself. You're not so bad, mort. Your eyes and those pearls. Pleasure and pastime. She's still young enough. If she moved the stock out of here, on the quiet, she could set up elsewhere.

And what of Sam, working with Harry Blore?

She takes a deep breath. Harry won't seek her out and if Sam carries on like this, he'll be in no condition to. She could set up afresh. Betsy-Ann stands motionless, picturing it.

16

Their shameful flight from Bath is the most abominable journey Sophia has ever undergone or – she earnestly prays – ever will. Before they are five miles out of the city, a storm breaks. The coach is buffeted about by wind, the rain finds its way inside and soaks into their clothing and at one point the accursed thing founders in a miry lane so that she is flung forward and hurts her hand and everybody, including Sophia, has to get down and break off branches to put under the wheels. Throughout this operation Titus wails like a damned soul and is savagely commanded, by Edmund, to 'cheese it', an expression his wife will not condescend to correct.

After this misfortune they continue on their way, Sophia's pelisse and gown plastered with mud as far as her knees. Each time she shifts position – which, since the coach is insufficiently cushioned, is often – she must struggle against the wet garments swaddling her legs. For all his impatience in directing Titus, Edmund insists on the boy sharing the coach with them rather than sitting with the coachman. This reduces the space available for stretching out, and at times her discomfort is so intolerable that Sophia gives way to a few wretched and unprofitable tears. Her husband sits opposite, arms crossed and his hat pulled over his face. It is impossible to tell whether he is sleeping or merely shamming.

It seems an eternity (how she feels the force of that hackneyed expression!) before they stop at the Blue Ball for refreshments. Though barely awake, the landlord rakes up the fire, plies the bellows with zest and invites the couple to settle themselves at a table nearby while Titus and the coachman are taken into the kitchen.

Edmund orders an adequate but not extravagant breakfast. Sophia, on the watch, detects no inclination towards lavish spending: perhaps his 'bubble' is, after all, nothing but rumour.

But why, in that case, this furious dash to London? Has he suffered a loss, as she first imagined? Or is it that he has no intention of sharing out his gains? This last thought is more discomfiting than any amount of damp and dirty clothing. Not because she covets the spoils, whether honestly or dishonestly won – and if there does exist a young fool who has been *bubbled*, Sophia would gladly restore every penny – but to come by a fortune, and keep one's wife in the dark . . . ! What, then, will he do with it?

Ah, but he may not be in possession of his winnings. What has she been imagining? Even the stupidest young coxcomb does not bring with him to the tables his disposable lands, farms, horses, mortgages, everything in short that is not entailed to keep it out of the clutches of gamesters. Most likely Edmund has a note of hand. He is not yet the caterpillar gorging on another man's sustenance, only the egg shortly to hatch into one.

'Edmund,' she says.

He turns towards her and as he does so, the landlord brings a lamp to the table where the Zedlands are seated. The light falls upon her husband's elegant features and Sophia starts: he is pale and haggard, hardly the exultant victor. She is touched, despite everything, with an unwilling pity; she had intended to confront him with the business of the ruined heir, but all she can find it in her to say is, 'You look exhausted, love.'

'No doubt you are more so,' says Edmund, civilly enough, 'and I'm sorry for it.'

He appears to have come out of his sulk. Sophia is encouraged. 'Shall we take a chamber and have our things dried? Wet clothing is so bad for the health.'

Edmund checks that the landlord is out of earshot before replying, 'We shouldn't stay too long. Some innkeepers are in league.'

'With who?'

'Tobies.'

'Tobies — ?'

'Is that what I said?' He seems amused. 'I'm tired – I talk nonsense. I meant to say that the longer we stay here, the greater the risk of meeting with uninvited company on the road.'

'Very well.' She cannot refrain from adding, 'Would we not have been safer travelling the next day? There are always people going to London. Perhaps some of them will put up here, if we wait a day or two, and then we can all go on together.'

'They won't come this way,' says Edmund. 'We've branched off from the high road.'

'Then we must tell the coachman to go back.'

He shakes his head. 'We left it on my instructions.'

Perhaps through lack of sleep, Sophia seems to see her own life, once just such a straight and open road, buckle and twist before running off crazily into a forest. Where will it come to an end?

'Husband,' she says at last. 'I came away from Bath without leave-taking or explanation, just as you wished. Now you have gained your point, would it not be better if you were quite open with me?'

'Ah,' says Edmund. His expression is a curious one, part pity, part satire; at least, so Sophia interprets it. She is careful to keep her voice steady and reassuring as she pushes on: 'My dear, your own good sense must prompt you to frankness.'

'At this precise moment, Sophia, it prompts me to sleep.'

'And *I* wish you to sleep. Soundly, without cares. All I ask, as your loving wife' – at this instant she scarcely feels the love of which she speaks, but let that stand – 'is to share your burdens.'

He flashes her a bitter little smile. 'You think so now. I believe most wives are glad to be spared the trouble.'

'But try me, dear. Try me.'

'I have affairs, Sophia, in which I must depend entirely on myself. Were you more experienced in the ways of men, you'd understand that.'

'Certainly,' says Sophia, summoning her courage, 'I shouldn't wish to keep bad company, or to be corrupted. I shouldn't wish these things for you, either, Edmund, and if you were in some scrape, in some debt, I hope I might be your rock in time of need —'

'You are that already.'

'But you tell me nothing!' she cries. 'How am I to support you – to be your wife?'

'You've done well enough until now.' He lays a hand over hers. 'And I flatter myself you find me to your taste.'

'Yes, but I wish to be your companion in *everything*, Edmund. There's more to marriage than bedding together.'

'Is there? You may open your thoughts to me as much as you wish, and yet never be married. There's a deal of cant talked about esteem, and so on. The rights conferred by marriage are of two kinds, the physical and the fiscal.'

Sophia stares at him, wondering if he can possibly mean what he says. 'I can't believe, Edmund, that you would ever hold such a view. It distresses me that you can propose it, even in jest.'

He yawns. 'Then you must blame the laws of England. When did you last see two persons marry, merely in order to converse? What did we vow in church? With my body I thee worship, with all my wordly goods I thee endow.'

'But there are also other vows —'

'Imagine us unwed, chaste and respectable. We may walk and talk together, we may even share out our property in common and still be respectable, provided the world is convinced that I never fish your pond.'

'*Fish my pond?*' She snatches her hand away from his. 'You speak like a libertine addressing – an unfortunate.'

'Is that so?' He bursts out laughing and then, with a wink and an attempt at wit deeply repugnant to Sophia, demands, 'Pray, which of us has purchased the other?'

Despite everything she can do, her face reddens and puckers

and her eyes brim. She strives to overcome it, as a man might, for Sophia knows better than to trust to tears. As a child, she learned that a crystal drop trickling down a pretty face could melt the hearts of adults, but alas! the pretty face was not hers: Sophia is of the tribe of the red-faced, snot-nosed blubberers. She saw the difference between her treatment and that meted out to her cousin Hetty, and understanding it, despaired. Now, weak and ugly before this beautiful man, she suffers as acutely as she did then.

'My aim was to amuse, not to wound,' Edmund says with an edge of impatience. 'You are too sensitive, you are indeed.' He again touches one of her hands, stroking the back of it, while Sophia's fingers lie unmoving under his. Plainly he forgot his company, but the thought brings no comfort, for where could he have imagined himself to be? A tear escapes and drops onto the inn table.

'Come,' he urges, still stroking. 'Since you're a married lady, as you keep telling me, you need not be so very prudish. Shall we talk in earnest?' Sophia wipes her eyes and nods. 'We will shortly be in London. If you allow me to go about my business without prying, we may yet shake down well.'

'But why must you be so secretive? Why do you speak of *your* business, not *our* business?'

'I mean simply that the husband has his concerns, and the wife hers, and each contributes to the common good. Surely your papa doesn't meddle in the kitchen?'

'Nor does Mama,' she corrects him in some indignation. 'We keep a cook.'

'Of course,' says Edmund, looking nettled. 'But the principle, you know —'

'Naturally Papa and Mama have their own affairs. But they've never kept things from one another.'

'You may depend upon it that they have.'

'No, never,' Sophia insists, the tears drying in her eyes at the memory of their happiness. 'A good wife is her husband's staunchest ally, his truest friend. If you don't think so, why did you —'

'Marry? How can you ask? It was because I found you irresistible.' Again he touches her, this time with a hand on each of her upper arms. 'Not desire intimacy? I was quite unable to rest, to sleep,' his face is getting closer and closer to hers, his thumbs just brushing the sides of her breasts, 'until I'd made myself your slave and your king.'

He reaches for his pocket, his hand skimming her as if by accident, and with a handkerchief dabs at her swollen eyelids.

Sophia sits motionless. In this precise fashion, during their courtship, he occasionally touched, or nearly touched, her bosom, or sometimes her neck: always with the lightest touch, in such a way that it appeared quite unintentional, a touch of which a lady could scarcely complain without appearing to protest too much. She recalls those orderly lists of objects to be ordered, purchased and repaired that filled his letters during that time. Was she herself entered in some private catalogue of his, some list in his brain, to be acquired if a price could be agreed?

But this is not the worst, not at all the worst. Possibly she herself never figured as an item on his list of desirables; it was a good marriage he desired, rather than Sophia. *Now* he speaks of hunger, of being her slave, but where was all his hunger *then*?

She remembers her own well enough, how longing for him threatened to overwhelm her: she was a fever patient craving water. Is it possible that he discerned that thirst and played on it, taking advantage of her naïvety to increase it by means that a more experienced woman would have laughed at? She can hardly bear to think so, yet she can hardly think otherwise. Those eminently proper letters: were they, then, composed for the eyes of her parents? He rated their wit no more highly than that, and (she thinks with a pang) he was right: the Bullers were quite satisfied with his productions. *Tête-à-tête* with Sophia, he had a fine time of it, laying on expertly with whip and spur until she was hard put to it to govern her feelings, but he never allowed himself to lapse into coarseness.

He has grown more careless since.

'Perhaps you were right,' Edmund murmurs, breaking away from her as the food is brought in. 'Perhaps we could take a chamber.' His voice softens, taking on the only kind of intimacy he will permit. 'Should you like that?'

Sophia hesitates, understanding his purpose. She is to be contented, reduced, stupefied. How despicable, and how easy to acquiesce! Her body is as unquestioningly wedded to Edmund as he could wish, and the prospect of dry garments a powerful additional temptation.

She resists nevertheless. 'I think *you* were right, love. We shouldn't lose time.'

Her husband's unprotesting nod only causes her a further pang.

The bread is hard, the chocolate tasteless and thin, but they devour both without complaint. Edmund caresses Sophia with his eyes; after the tempers of last night and the sulks of this morning, he is coquettish as a woman. It is hard to remain angry with a husband who gazes adoringly on his wife's crumpled, inflamed features, particularly when that wife has just refused his amorous advances. Sophia feels her resistance softening like the bread she has dipped into her chocolate. This, and no other, is the man she has married. She can take only what he has to give, and must accept that his gifts are such shallow, impermanent ones as he might bestow on any woman: beauty, and the butterfly ability of bestowing pleasure. Are there women who would be delighted with such a spouse? If so, Sophia is not one of them; but she must learn to 'shake down', as Edmund puts it, relinquishing her hopes of a husband who would also be a trusted friend at her side. How strange! As an unmarried girl she imagined that it all came about quite naturally, once a woman had the ring upon her finger.

17

Sam Shiner's ma used to run a Puss & Mew. He's told Betsy-Ann about this contraption more than once but tonight, since Harry Blore has come to sup with them, she must hear it again.

'The old man knocked it up out of crates and sacking,' Sam explains. 'She'd stand inside.' He laughs, to encourage Blore to do likewise. Betsy-Ann also laughs as she turns the beefsteaks, nicely floured and seasoned, in the pan. Her brother is like a bear, inclined to show his teeth when hungry.

'Inside? What for?' asks Blore.

Sam lays his finger alongside his nose. 'You get your bucket of lightning and your measure,' he imitates someone doling out liquid, 'and wait till someone comes up. They can't see your face behind the frame and they never say *geneva* or *lightning* or nothing, only *puss*, and you go *mew*.'

'Why's that?' asks Betsy-Ann, seeing Harry at a loss. Her brother can be chuckle-headed but he hates showing it in company; it's better for her health, and Sam's, if she helps him out on the sly.

'Nothing to swear to, Betsy.' He turns back to Harry. 'There's a drawer in the frame, see, open both ends. The cull hears the mew, puts in a penny. Ma takes it out her end, puts a flash in its place. He's under the sacking, he drinks up and he's on his way. Nothing wrong here, nothing but a cove looking for his poor old cat.'

Blore lifts his glass with a dirty grin. 'Freedom forever.'

'Freedom forever,' echoes Sam, and clinks with him. Betsy-Ann, crouching by the fire, raises her glass but takes no more than a sip as the steaks are just fit to be taken off and laid in the dish. Christ, if she should burn them now! Her hand slippery on the frying-pan handle, she lays the meat atop the onions and potatoes already prepared, and pours the juice over.

'Something smells good,' says Sam. Blore says nothing, but then she knows better than to expect compliments from him.

'Was she ever nabbed?' Betsy-Ann asks so that he can come to the next part.

'You had to watch for noses. One day she's on her pitch and a mort comes in. *Puss*, she says. My ma goes *mew*, takes the penny and hands over the dram. Next thing she knows the bitch starts screaming – This woman's selling gin! This woman's selling gin! – Ma didn't know what to do with herself.'

'Toddle,' suggests Blore.

'Can't, not in the frame. She can't get it off, neither, not quick enough, and she's pissing herself for fear. Next thing she hears another shout – A nose! There's a nose here! – and a sort of rushing noise, and then a screaming, terrible, like a scalded child, and people running. Then it all goes quiet. Nobody's laid a hand on her. She unbuckles, climbs out. First thing she notices is the street. All empty.'

'Empty! Fancy that!' Betsy-Ann comes in on cue.

'Next thing there's this noise behind her. She looks round and sees a mort, must've been *the* mort, in the road.'

'Dead?'

'No, but all over blood, and crawling.'

Blore grunts. 'Weren't the Excise with her?'

'If they were, the mob saw them off. My ma made herself scarce, I can tell you. She left the Puss & Mew standing with the lightning still in it, and the woman, dragging herself along, crying, Don't leave me!'

'They should've scragged the bitch. Her and all noses.' Blore pours himself another glass, brimming, and downs it in one.

Betsy-Ann wonders why the woman thought Sam's ma would stay with her. Perhaps when you're dying you don't know who you're talking to, or you forget you're a nose. Or you don't care because anybody's better than the company on the other side of that door.

Harry's *should've scragged the bitch* gets on her nerves. He puts it about that he's a regular trusty Trojan; for herself, she'd trust Old Harry himself before Harry Blore. Sam claims not to, either, but he doesn't always act according.

At last the food is on the table. There are the beefsteaks nicely smoking in their dish, bread, butter, wine, stewed mushrooms, buttered cabbage, some cheese and pickled salmon and an almond pudding (fetched in by Liz this morning from the pastrycook's). It's a mystery to Betsy-Ann why the men are eating with her. As a rule Harry conducts his business in his own ken, along with the rest of the crew. She's already asked Sam what the rig is but he won't tell her; he just says, 'Never trouble yourself,' and laughs.

'Here's to greatness,' says her brother. He's forever making toasts, these days: Betsy-Ann wonders when he took up the trick.

The talk dies down as the three of them settle to the meal. The men eat noisily, Blore in particular: he half-chews his food with an open mouth and then swills it down his throat with wine. Betsy-Ann's never prided herself on her refinement, never been in a position to, but she hates that *squish, squish*, like a bloody cow on the cud. She turns her face away, towards the fire. Brisk and clear it is, just the thing for beefsteaks. She draws comfort from its snapping flames, from the plump coal-sack in the corner and from the Eye whose contents Blore has never seen. There is also, under a floorboard unknown even to Shiner, a stash of darby, sweetly conveyed from his pockets whenever he comes home drunk as David's sow. Lately this stash has been growing apace. Betsy-Ann often thinks of it as she goes about her daily round and is filled with a pleasurable sense of virtuous enterprise, the independence of the true-born Briton.

The beef is tender, rich and savoury. Harry would as soon

think of flying as of giving her a word of praise, but he can't hide the satisfaction in his face. Sam's winking and smacking of his lips doesn't count, since it's only done to cry up the food for Harry's benefit. She's been busy all day and could really go at her portion, could tear at it, but for the fact that every so often she becomes aware of the hogo in the room. When Blore arrived she made sure that the fire was up and the place snug, and asked him to take his coat off. She laid the coat in the corner of the room, as far from herself as could be, but even there it makes itself known. Then there's the foulness of their shirts and trousers, and even their skin. She doesn't notice it as much as she used to, and that bothers her: does it mean she's begun to stink likewise? Sam and Betsy, a pair of corpses lying side by side.

So far, however, this looks like a good night, even allowing for Harry. Sam's taking just the right amount of drink: with luck he'll get to bed peaceable but limp, which is how she likes him best.

In fairness, she thinks, Sam was never Mr Lushington, no more than Ned Hartry. No sharp can afford to be. It's the resurrection business that's turned him lushy. At moments like this she feels sorry for Sam. Things haven't turned out right for him, either. But then, happening to look up, she sees the greasy blond hair stuck to his skull – the fashion of leaving off the periwig doesn't suit him – and remembers how stubborn he can be, about her learning to write, and about more important things. She offered to stand banker, but he *would* go in with Harry. Ned would've shaken hands on it. He understood what she was capable of, what she was worth.

'Sing us a song, our Betsy,' says Harry Blore. 'Sing *The Merry Maiden*.'

Betsy-Ann is startled. The drink's surely knocked him back; he said 'Our Betsy' just as he used to when they were kinchins. As for *The Merry Maiden*, it's not worth singing.

'Go on, Betsy-Ann,' says Sam, nodding.

If Harry said, 'Down on your back, Sis, and throw your gown over your head,' Sam'd probably nod in just that way. And hold her arms while he was at it.

'I forget the words.'

'Go on, it'll come to you.'

Betsy-Anne clears her throat.

> *It was a merry maiden,*
> *A maiden, a maiden,*
> *It was a merry maiden,*
> *In a garden so fine.*
> *Now which of you young men,*
> *You young men, you young men,*
> *Now which of you young men,*
> *Will take me for his own?*
> *O shall it be the sailor,*
> *The sailor, the sailor,*
> *O shall it be the sailor,*
> *With his eyes so blue?*
> *Or shall it be the soldier,*
> *The soldier, the soldier,*
> *O shall it be the soldier,*
> *Whose heart is so true?*
> *My father is . . .*

'Lord! What was the father at . . . ?'

Blore says, 'A-reaping.'

> *My father is a-reaping,*
> *A-reaping, a-reaping,*
> *My father is a-reaping,*
> *To bring in the wheat.*
> *My mother is a-spinning,*

a-spinning, a-spinning,
My mother is a-spinning,
So fine and so neat.
Up steps a bold young lover
A lover, a lover,
Up steps a bold young lover,
And his heart was on fire.
'Sweet maiden I must have you,
Must have you, must have you,
Sweet maiden I must have you,
To be my valentine.'
'Then I am yours forever,
Forever, forever,
Then I am yours forever,
My lover so dear.
And we will be a-wedded,
A-wedded, a-wedded,
And we will be a-wedded
All in the coming year.'

'Well,' says Sam, 'what a bite for the soldier and the sailor!' and they all laugh, even Blore.

'That's bold young lovers for you,' says Betsy-Ann. She's always detested this feeble-minded song, which is only fit for simpkins. That Harry Blore can relish it is the eighth wonder of the world.

Blore looks pleased with himself. 'Aye, he'd be one of the canting crew, that spark.'

Betsy-Ann very nearly says, 'Not a resurrectionist, at any rate,' but stops herself in time. 'Always glad to oblige you, Brother. Will you have some more drink?'

Naturally he will. Betsy-Ann pours for all of them, and sets the almond pudding on the table. She's concocting a wicked little ditty in her head:

Oh I am a grave-robber,
grave-robber, grave-robber,
Oh I am a grave-robber,
I stink the livelong day.
And when I take my coat off,
my coat off, my coat off,
And when I take my coat off,
The girls all run away . . .

'What's that?' says Sam as she sits down again. He's pointing at her precious coral heart.

'You can see what it is,' says Betsy-Ann.

'I mean, where'd you get it?'

'Where d'you think? Here, Harry.' She passes her brother the biggest share of pudding and serves Sam, too, before continuing, 'Why shouldn't I keep something back for myself? It's only the once.'

'But if somebody —'

'It was taken in the country. I'm not so green as all that.'

Nor is Sam, it seems. 'Let's have a look, then.'

She extends her hand over the table but that's not enough; he pulls the fawney off her finger so he can see inside the band. Betsy-Ann fidgets. Blore, already halfway through his portion, is eyeing what remains in the dish.

Sam hands it back. 'Too fine for a bitch booby.'

Betsy-Ann forces a laugh. 'Watch your tongue, Sam Shiner.'

'You was never a bitch booby,' Harry growls. 'Different-blooded.'

'A daisy, then.'

''Twas I that made you, eh? Brought you to Romeville, set you on your feet.'

'Me and Keshlie,' hints Betsy-Ann. She's already on dangerous ground with Sam and now she's asking for trouble with Harry, yet she can't stop; she feels compelled to go on, see how many lies he'll come out with.

'Aye, Keshlie too.'

'And Mam,' says Betsy-Ann, a woman bent on self-destruction.

Harry doesn't answer this, but he half-closes his eyes in a maudlin smile as if to say, *Bless 'em.*

Christ, what a liar he is! He's come to believe his own lies. Betsy-Ann sees herself catch hold of the frying pan and bring it down on the back of his neck, knowing all the time she would never dare. Supposing she came at him from behind and gave it all her strength, it still might not finish him, and if he got on his feet again, that'd be the end of Betsy-Ann Blore.

'What was Keshlie's proper name?' she asks. 'Was it Catharine?'

'Just Keshlie.' She can tell that he's surprised, and not sure of himself. But a man always has an answer for a woman, so as not to be put down.

The pudding dish is empty and the wine all drunk up. They are about to start again on the lightning when Sam says, 'Now, girl, Harry and me have got private business.'

Betsy-Ann starts. 'Private from me?'

'From you. Here,' he pulls out a handful of coins, 'go to Laxey's and I'll come for you later.'

'Don't trouble yourself,' says Betsy-Ann, taking the money and rising from her place so abruptly that the chair scrapes along the floor. 'I'll go to the fair, see what pleasure and pastime is there.'

'There's no fair now,' says Blore, his speech slurring.

'Anywhere there's a fire, then,' says Betsy-Ann. 'Seeing as I'm not allowed to sit by my own.'

Once there was a skylight at the top of the stairwell, until a prigger let himself in by it. Since then it's been boarded up, and the lodgers have to feel their way along the stairs. Betsy-Ann runs her palm along the banister, seeking the join in the wood that signals her arrival at the first floor. She steps off the last stair, turns to take the second flight, and shrieks as something brushes her shoulder. It's only Liz, lurking as usual, wanting company, complaining of how the house-painter's wife in the downstairs back has bilked her of a penny, but Betsy-Ann hasn't the stomach for it now. She continues downstairs and steps out into the street.

After the companionable fug indoors, the night wind bites at her neck and ankles. Pulling her cloak more tightly about her, she crosses the street towards the alleyway opposite, the one leading into the courtyard of Laxey's. They will be on the watch to see her depart, so Betsy-Ann obligingly disappears into its shadows.

Once inside the alleyway, she counts to twenty before turning back to study the upstairs window.

Shiner and Blore are still at table, Blore's hard, florid face appearing almost soft in the candlelight. She watches, fascinated, as Sam holds up clenched fists. Her brother's laughing now, well on his way to the quarrelsome stage. But what's the joke? None of it makes sense.

The window is inviting: like a jewel hanging there in the dark, with the gleam of fire and candle behind it. Not as fine as some places she's peeped inside, but cosy. By rights she should be up there with them. He's never told her to quit the ken before. It wasn't sporting of you, Sammy. Not sporting at all.

No sooner is she through the door of Laxey's than she hears a woman cry, 'Betsy, girl!' from a corner.

She sees nothing at first but a bonnet and shawl. Coming closer, she can make out a meagre figure and, under the bonnet, hair the colour of carrots.

'Selina? Is that you, my dear?'

'Who else? And Betsy-Ann Blore, as I live and breathe!'

'I'm Mrs Shiner now,' says Betsy-Ann, smiling.

Selina raises her glass. 'To the well wearing of your muff. You'll take a flash with me?'

'With pleasure. How's your luck these days?'

'Not so very good, if truth be told,' says Selina, moving along the bench to make room. She lifts a candle from the table, holds it to her face and opens wide to show a mouth full of black saliva.

'You've been in the Lock again?' asks Betsy-Ann, keeping her voice down.

Selina shakes her head. 'I tried.'

'They won't have you?'

'The one on the door knew me from last time. She says, You know the rules. So that was that.'

'Who's treating you, then?'

'A prentice. He's put me in a terrible sal. Spitting coal.' Betsy-Ann shudders. 'And Kitty's let me go. Till I'm cured, she *says*, but she won't take me back. She wants young ones.'

Selina's gin is almost finished so Betsy-Ann calls for more.

'Did Kitty pay for the sweating, Lina?'

Selina shakes her head. 'A thankless bitch is Kitty.'

'You've been worth a fortune to her. A mort like you.'

'Not everybody had my abilities.'

'She should get you a proper doctor, not some boy who don't know his business. He's given you too much.'

'That's my opinion, but what can I do?' She bends towards Betsy-Ann and whispers. 'When I was sweated, it came out at my fingertips.'

Betsy-Ann makes a disgusted noise.

'You were lucky that way, never got poxed,' her friend says.

'Oh, but I did.'

'Your little friend was very bad with it, as I recall. Katy.'

'Aye, well,' says Betsy-Ann, not bothering to correct her since Lina's version is more bearable than the truth.

'Poor lamb. What became of her?'

'Died, Lina. Died.'

The gin is brought. They fill their cups, Betsy-Ann downing hers in one. The circles of candlelight dotted here and there glow sweetly and a woman sitting nearby, who keeps flinging her head back in shrill laughter, seems the type of innocent enjoyment, angelic, as the wine and gin Betsy-Ann has downed mingle in her guts, combining against her. She slides the coral ring off her hand.

'Here, Lina. Look at this.'

Selina takes it, tries it. 'Lord! Big fingers you got.'

'The inside.' She pushes the candle towards her friend. 'Look there, hold it in the light. *Pamphile to his prodigy*, it says.'

'Can you read, then?'

'I was told. Pamphile to his prodigy.'

Selina giggles. 'What's his prodigy?'

'Not what you think. A marvel.'

'Pamphile? Like the card?'

'It means *loved by everybody*. He said it was Greek.'

'Oh, a student, is it? I never cared for students.'

'Not even Ned Hartry?'

'It's from Ned?' Selina's laughter sprays over the table. 'Loved by everybody? Isn't that just his cheek! Not that it isn't a rum piece,' she adds hastily, seeing Betsy-Ann's expression, 'what with the little heart —'

'I've been stupid, Lina. I had this fawney shut up in a box. The other day I take it out and put it on, and straight away my old man asks to look at it.'

'What old man?'

'Sam Shiner. He and Ned were trusties, once.'

'And you're wearing Ned's ring!' cries Selina. 'What's got into your head?'

'Maggots,' says Betsy-Ann.

A fiddler nearby starts up a skirling, screeching reel and folk dance about the floor. There's a black, a freed slave she supposes, jigging away opposite a pale, bedraggled mort, the two of them fairly eating each other up with their eyes. They say that touching a blackbird brings good luck. If Betsy-Ann is any judge of dancing, that mort'll be fairly showered with it before long.

It is two hours before he comes, but when he does, Sam is brisk. Nodding to Selina, he pulls Betsy-Ann up by her elbow as if she were too lushy to rise on her own feet. She shakes him off, glaring, and straightens her clothes before following him out into the street where the cold again attacks her, so that she misses the foul-smelling warmth of the public house.

'Nice to know I'm to be let home,' sniffs Betsy-Ann, 'now you've finished that important business of yours. Perhaps you're planning on overthrowing the House of Hanover, or was it the Pope of Rome?'

'Easy, girl. You've had enough.'

'On what you gave me? I could drink it again.'

Sam laughs. He's sobered up since she last saw him: not so good at bedtime.

'Still keeping your shitty little secret, eh, Sammy?'

'You'll find out in good time.'

'O, no! *I'm* not trusty.'

'Course you are. Only I've sworn not to tell.'

Is it revenge, paying her out for the coral heart? Any gamester knows Pamphile. Not so hard, after that, to guess who Pamphile might be.

It's not a name you'd ever call Sam. As she glances across at him now, even 'Shiner' seems too good for his dim, perspiring presence. Nevertheless, when he and the Corinthian played out their game, it was Sam that won in the end. He has a long memory, has Sam, and very sharp eyes.

18

The house is not at all what Sophia expected. True, it is tolerably papered throughout, the windows are snug and the chimneys, if the cook is to be believed, recently brushed, but the rooms have a frowzy, dingy air. Still, scrubbing the place down should not be too onerous – there is a cistern which, she is assured, receives a regular supply of piped water – and the sour-smelling kitchen is at least spacious, with an 'area' below the front pavement. Sophia is puzzled by a round metal plate in this pavement, just outside the front door.

'It's the entrance to the dungeon,' says Edmund.

'I beg your pardon?'

'The coal hole, my love. The coal merchant tips his wares directly into the cellar instead of carrying them through the house.'

Sophia is quite charmed by this contrivance. 'How convenient!'

He laughs. 'Especially for the merchant, who can thus cheat us with impunity.'

There is a necessary house at the end of a small flagstoned yard and the yard, strangely enough, not unpleasant, for which mercy Sophia is thankful. In Bath she heard a great deal from Mrs Chase, before that false friend was unmasked by Edmund, about certain disagreeables inseparable from London life.

Now she looks forlornly around the dining room. They left Bath at such short notice that there was no opportunity to notify the servants. As a result, there is dust on the furniture though not, Sophia notices, any lack of warmth in the principal rooms. Evidently the staff did not stint themselves during their master's absence. Papa and Mama would have remarked upon this at once and called those responsible to account, but despite his joke about the coal merchant Edmund seems not to perceive, or perhaps not to resent it.

Even the best servants take advantage, unless the Mistress exerts herself.

Just for tonight one of the maids, accompanied by Titus, is despatched to fetch dinner from a neighbouring inn. It is a slack and wasteful way of proceeding. Sophia will be up and about early tomorrow morning, eager to talk with the cook and put things upon an orderly footing.

The boiled beef brought back by Eliza is tainted with something like the essence of old chimneys. Sophia fancies that if she had ever taken it upon herself to chew cinders, they might have something of this flavour.

'The beef smells most peculiar, Edmund,' she says. 'Burnt.'

'Burnt? Do you think so?' murmurs Edmund, eating with relish.

'Well – not precisely.' That is the extraordinary thing: the meat does not appear dried or singed. When the maid comes to remove the plates, Sophia questions her: 'Did you see the cooking vessels at the inn? Were they quite clean?'

'If you please, Madam, I did and they were,' says Eliza.

'The beef had a disagreeable taint.'

'Ladies new to London often find the food disagreeable, at first.'

'Why should that be? Beef is beef.'

'It's the garden things, Madam. The smoke gets in them, you see, and tastes everything. At least, so they say. I don't notice, myself.'

Of course, Sophia thinks. Soot-encrusted vegetables in the pot, transferring their delightful fragrance to the meat.

'You'll get used to it,' says Edmund, dabbing at his mouth. 'I hope you find the house more to your liking?'

'It all seems quite . . .'

'Quite what?'

She who hesitates is lost. 'Proper.'

Comfortable she is sure it is not: so gloomy and grimy (rather like the meat) and about half as big as she imagined. Why, any thriving tradesman who aspired to rent such a dwelling might readily gratify his wishes. But then, as she reminds herself, such people are very much on the rise these days, some of them achieving an income comparable to a gentleman's, and Edmund does not rent but owns the place outright.

'It takes time to get used to a house,' she continues, gaining conviction, 'and to decorate,' but here she falters again, since she had understood, as had her parents, that her new home was already prepared to receive a bride. As Mama put it: Mr Bachelor Bird, when he goes a-courting, decks his nest.

'If you'll allow me a free hand,' Sophia says at last, 'I'm told I have some excellent notions. Mama is forever consulting me.'

New paint, new gilding! Competent craftsmen, intelligently directed, could freshen this house to the point where Sophia might walk through it with pleasure, taking an honest pride in how her woman's eye had made the very best of everything and rendered it, if not distinguished, still a temple of domestic happiness, good sense and good taste.

'You could wave a magic wand over it, I'm sure,' says Edmund. 'Unfortunately we have no time to engage workmen, but next year you shall paint and paper to your heart's delight.'

Sophia blinks.

'Reassure yourself, however, that there's no such problem at home. *There* you may employ yourself throughout the winter, and transform the place to a fairy palace, if you please.'

'At home? Do you refer to Wixham?'

'Where else?'

'Are we leaving for the country so soon?'

'But my love, surely you understood that? I've business in London, after which —' He shrugs.

'Business!' exclaims Sophia. Really, she might have married one of those craftsmen of whom she was just now thinking. If, that is, Edmund is speaking the truth.

'Yes, business.' There is an edge to his voice. 'Need I explain again?'

'Not to me, Edmund. I've heard quite enough about dunning, thank you.'

'And yet you don't understand me. To repeat: my father left certain affairs in disarray —'

'Dunning.'

'Have the goodness to hear me out. He invested money in the City. Consequently, I must visit bankers and lawyers here. Do you call that dunning?'

'Not precisely,' she admits. 'Only I hoped we might —'

'Lord, Sophia, don't you see how greatly to your advantage this is? How could I be better employed, at the very beginning of our life together, than in trying to make all clear, plain and regular?'

Sophia is silenced. The only answer she could honestly make, she does not dare: *I do not believe you. Though you talk glibly of plain and regular, you yourself are neither.*

'We shall have to practise economy nevertheless,' Edmund adds. 'By retiring to the country we may retrench on a great many expenses.'

'And are we to return before the end of the Season?'

'Perhaps,' says Edmund in a tone she has come to dread.

'It was agreed upon. You promised —'

A maid enters to put coal upon the fire. Sophia waits, palpitating, for her to leave. At last, after a puffing on the bellows which raises clouds of sooty dust and causes both husband and wife to shrink away from the hearth, the fire revives and the wretched girl takes herself off to the nether regions.

'*Edmund*,' says Sophia as the door closes behind her.

'You're on me like a pack of hounds,' exclaims Edmund. 'Barely an hour since we arrived and already you're discontented. I take you from a poxy lake with one statue, first to Bath and now to London, but nothing pleases.'

Sophia flushes. 'I didn't mean to appear ungracious.'

'You have a most happy knack, then, and achieve it without effort.'

'I admire the house, I do indeed.'

'Then what need of decoration?'

He is inviting her to bicker about that, rather than his mysterious business. In cowardly, wifely fashion, she accepts the invitation.

'No absolute need, perhaps. I always understood it was usual upon marriage.'

'I don't dispute it. At Wixham you shall exercise your bride's prerogative to the full and next year, when we have guests *here*, you shall do the same, and can choose from the newest patterns. Until then, it's just a waste of my money.'

'Our money.'

'I'm too tired for this, Sophia. I shall take a bath and I suggest you do likewise.' He rings for a servant. 'It may calm your nerves.'

Having made do all her life with a china bowl and jug, Sophia does not find the prospect of a hip-bath particularly calming and is nervous of the one she glimpsed in the bedroom. Now she listens to the tramp, tramp of the maid carrying hot water upstairs. Hot water! Cold, bracing baths are agreed to be beneficial but Edmund risks enervation of the system, to say nothing of scalds: servants are such careless creatures.

At the same time, it must be said that she is tempted. Bathing is said to cure fleas and she is sure there was an infestation of the vile creatures in the coach. Nor is she free of them, even now: at least one of the nipping, itching horrors is trapped beneath her stays. She struggles to scratch at it, pushing her hand down as far as it will go. The stays pinch her uncommonly tight this evening; Sophia could shake herself with discomfort and frustration. Perhaps it would be wise, after all, to follow her husband's example.

She so longed to be mistress of her own household. When first she saw the bedchamber, her disappointment at the shabby furnishings was intense, but then she thought: perhaps it's just as well, I can choose for myself. She pictured blue wallpaper with scrolling flowers, perhaps new wine-coloured curtains, a hundred charming refinements, the neglected house blooming beneath her womanly touch, and now they are not to stay here over the winter! Whatever Edmund may choose to signify by it, Sophia has come to hate the very sound of the word *business*.

When Edmund is in bed and the hip-bath refilled, Sophia undresses, catching the maid in a discreet surveillance of her abdomen. Her entire body is a little swollen and her bosom so tender as to be painful, but not for any reason the maid may imagine. These signs, along with her tight stays, are familiar ones: her flowers are due.

The tub is not so bad. Rendered tolerably comfortable by towels draped over its metal edges, it forms a prospect at once more private and more wholesome than the disease-ridden pools of Bath. How gratifying to picture the fleas, that meant to make a meal of her, being drowned instead in the perfumed water – to feel her muscles unknotting themselves in the warmth. The indulgence of a warm bath is surely permissible after such a long cold journey as hers.

She dozes.

When she opens her eyes there is something like smoke twining through the water, a wisp of crimson that breaks up as she moves her thighs in the tub. She asks the maid to bring clean rags and bandages and, once dried, binds herself carefully before going in to Edmund, who is already asleep.

Thank you, thank you, she prays to the Almighty as she pulls back the sheets. *That it is now and not in the coach.*

While the coach would doubtless have been torture, the bed is quite trying enough. A dull, dragging pain in her back compels her to roll this way and that until Edmund half-wakes to demand, in a sullen murmur, what the devil she would be at. At last, having heard a church bell strike two, she gets off, only to dream that she is roaming an elegant but unfamiliar square, holding a small child by the hand and with the most pressing need for the necessary house. The child is a perverse little brat; it holds back, whining, as Sophia toils up and down, knocking on house doors that never open, searching even sheds and outhouses in her desperate need for a privy. The square shifts and alters under her gaze: now it contains a garden with ornamental yews and box hedges. She drags the heavy, pouting child into a green walk and there, right in the middle of the way, stands a necessary house, but when she enters, it is unspeakably filthy and the wall at the back has missing bricks through which men's faces peer and jeer: she cannot use it. At last, barely able to walk, she spies a bush behind which she can stand. Nobody is near; even the tormenting child has wandered off and disappeared. Sophia plants her feet wide apart beneath her gown and lets go. At once the most delicious ache pierces between her legs and spreads up into her belly, growing to an intensity in which she cannot hold back but feels compelled to pull up the front of her clothing and display herself, throwing back her head in glorious, overpowering release. Looking down again, she finds Edmund standing before her, his finger a key in the lock of her body. He squirms the finger into her, tickling, unbearably tickling. 'I flatter myself you don't despise me,' he whispers. An obscure fear flickers in Sophia, an ominous sense of impending disaster. She tries to push him away but finds herself unable to move. As he continues to toy with her the tickling sensation mounts, grows exquisite, voluptuous, irresistible as the clawing of an itch.

She wakes, still in its poignant grip, and holds herself very still. A faint, whistling snore tells her that Edmund sleeps on, for the moment undisturbed and unaware. Sick with dread, Sophia slides her hand down to the mattress.

It has happened, the shameful thing.

She is still not emptied out. She drags herself over the wet bedding, her damp nightgown clinging to her thighs, and squats over the jerry in a state of horror and confusion so appalling that even Mrs Chase might pity her. The bandage between her legs drips into the jerry. Until this minute she had forgotten all that. Is she bloody? Is the bed — ?

Edmund has stopped snoring. She clenches herself so tightly that her teeth ache, but to no avail; he surfaces from his sleep and begins to take notice.

'What's the matter?' he murmurs. 'Are you ill?'

So carefully has she managed, up to now, that he has never even known her rise in the night. She whispers, 'The jerry. Go to sleep.'

But he rolls over, turning towards her. 'I'm awake now,' he says. 'Come on, give us a sight of Miss Laycock.' Curtain-rings jangle: he's feeling outside the bedcurtains for the candle.

'Not now,' she hisses. 'Go to sleep.'

It is too late. She hears him fidgeting in the bed, and then a sudden intake of breath.

'What the — ? In Christ's name, Sophy, what's this?'

'I'm so sorry, Edmund.'

Sophia crouches, fumbling. At last the sodden wadding between her legs drops away into the jerry. She gropes in the bedside table for fresh rags.

Her husband's voice assails her from the bed: 'Why didn't you get the pot?'

'I didn't wake. It's my time, you see, that makes it worse.' She shivers as she knots the ends of the rags together.

There is a silence. Then Edmund says, 'It'll stink infernally to-morrow.'

19

At Mr Watson's house in Maryland, Fortunate was beaten whenever he made a mistake.

Mrs Dog Eye sometimes looks as if she wishes to do the same. The woman is impossible to please, forever calling her husband into the room and then asking Fortunate to repeat certain words, after which she wails, wrings her hands and rushes out in tears. Dog Eye stands by as if in sorrow, but then after the wife has gone he claps Fortunate on the shoulder, asks him to say 'part, prig and puck' and laughs heartily when he does so, which makes no more sense than crying. Between these two it is difficult to know how to live.

Still, the house is more spacious than the rooms he and Dog Eye lived in before the marriage. Fortunate has a bedchamber to himself, where before he had always to share. The privacy he now enjoys is useful, because one of his tasks is to take up any letters newly arrived or waiting to be taken. Such letters should be put into his pocket and, if possible, taken directly to Dog Eye in the room where he reads over his business papers. Should Dog Eye be in company with someone else, Fortunate goes away and waits in his own chamber, for nobody is to see him carrying the letters, nor must Fortunate speak to the wife about it.

Now that they have been in the house a fortnight, he has letters to carry almost every day. Dog Eye takes them and looks at the writing on the outside. Fortunate once asked the meaning of a small thing which often appears on these letters. Dog Eye laughed and said that for men, it was a sure sign of trouble. Fortunate understood that this was some kind of joke, so one day he showed a letter to the cook, who can read a little, and who told him that the word was *Mrs*.

He is not too unhappy. He is used by now to loneliness, to looking on at others' lives. He finds comfort in the brass tap in the
scullery, shaped like the head of a bird. There are such things in
his own country, but here it is a kind of secret beauty, for only servants see it, and it seems to Fortunate that of all of them, he alone
appreciates the kindness of a tap with a bird's head where a bare
spout would suffice. Apart from his love of Dog Eye, his life is all
bound up in things. He treasures the pink carpet in the drawing
room, with its pattern of flowers, and the view of a neighbour's
herb-garden visible from the window at the top of the stairs.

One of his most beloved objects lives in Dog Eye's private
room: a small round table, its top made up of different coloured
marbles so cool and smooth that Fortunate can rarely resist the
temptation to spread out his hands upon them. His palms, polished by contact with the marble, come away chilled and smooth,
leaving ghost-hands of mist that linger briefly on the stone. While
Fortunate does this, Dog Eye reads letters to, or from, his wife
and seals them up again, stamping the seals with gold rings he
keeps in his desk. He then returns the letters to Fortunate, who
replaces them when he can do so unseen. He is proud to be trusted
with this duty and admires Dog Eye's deft, swift movements as he
heats the wax and handles his little rings, repairing the torn seals.

One morning, he has just pocketed a letter to take to his master
when he turns to find *Mrs* herself standing watching him. The
woman steps forward, her fingers an eagle's talons. Fortunate puts
his own hand over his pocket to protect the letter nestling within.

'What have you there?'

He manages to say, 'Nothing.' If only Dog Eye were present,
to explain to her! Doesn't she understand that the man must first
look at these things?

'Give it here,' the woman orders. He still keeps his hand over
his pocket, so she slaps him hard across the face: one, two. She
will have to explain this to Dog Eye. She has disgraced herself.

Handing over the letter, Fortunate lowers his eyes, watering from the force of the blows, so as not to witness her shame.

'This is private, private!' she hisses, one talon resting on the *Mrs*. She shakes the letter under his nose. 'How *dare* you!'

Fortunate cannot find the words with which to reply. He cannot say he made a mistake, for he did not. The woman throws down the letters which are not *Mrs* on the table and, clutching the one she has stolen, runs with it along the hallway and up the stairs.

My dearest daughter,

Your last found us happy and well and we are glad to know that you and Edmund are likewise. I was a little concerned to hear that you had left the Baths. Papa, of course, told me not to fret – you know how foolish your old mama can be where her darling is concerned – and insisted there was nothing to worry about, merely a change of plan. He went so far as to scold me, but I could not be at ease until I heard more from you.

I hope you now see, as I do, how wise I was in raising you to understand a woman's duty. You grew up in the knowledge that Papa must constantly occupy himself with the business of the estate, and were thus prepared for your present situation. I always say that nobody can understand the obligations of a gentleman who has not tried to live up to them. Persons who pass their days in idleness can have no notion of this but you and I have married men of quite another stamp: they have always some scheme, some object of charity or some project of improvement in hand, and are forever occupied. Few women are blessed with husbands of such an industrious character, and when we consider what a hazard every woman runs in the marriage-lottery, I am sure we should cheerfully resign ourselves to any little inconveniences. And to show that I can practise what I preach, I do

*not complain that I was unable to visit my chick before her hus-
band whisked her off to London. We shall not be long parted,
my love. I will be sure to come to you when a certain happy
event approaches, if not before.*

*I hope, my darling girl, that you will not take it amiss if I
own to some disappointment that your address is not a more
fashionable one. I understood, as did Papa, that Mr Zedland's
town house lay a little nearer to St James. This is what we expected for you, but I find, from your Aunt Phoebe's map of
London, that you are rather on the way to Marylebone.
(Phoebe insisted on bringing the map to show me: plus ça
change!)*

*Still, a London house of three storeys is well enough. I was
only in London once in my life, when I went to stay with Con-
stantia, God rest her soul, but that was out of the Season, and
besides, Town was not nearly so brilliant or elegant as they say
it is nowadays. Who has called upon you, my love? Have you
returned any visits? You must send me a regular bulletin of all
your outings and entertainments.*

*Most of our affairs, alas, are very small beer. However, every
dog has his day and every woman some news of real import,
once in a while, so here is mine: your cousin Hetty is to be married by private licence to Mr Josiah Letcher of Cheltenham Spa
– you will remember that Hetty has known this gentleman for
several months now and both parties wish to dispense with the
usual long engagement. Between boasting of Hetty's brilliant
match and complaining that the ceremony is to be a simple one,
your Aunt Phoebe is grown quite intolerable. As for Hetty herself, she laughs and says she wonders how she will bear being
called Mrs Letcher. Her Josiah has a fortune of £5,000 per an-
num and though not in his first youth is polite, mannerly and
not an ill-looking man, so entre nous, I think she will bear it
very well.*

Though it is tedious to be obliged constantly to exclaim at her good fortune, I am of course delighted for Hetty. She is, and always was, far more agreeable than her mother. You may imagine, however, how Phoebe crows over me. Even when we were girls, the most beautiful doll, the most charming robes, must always be hers, and now it is the same with daughters! All day prattling of Hetty's intended and scarcely a word to spare for your marriage – it is extremely provoking. But there. Hardly a girl in the county will marry as well as Hetty, to be sure, but if you, my love, are content with your bargain I have nothing more to wish for. And I am as sure as I can be of anything, Sophy, that you are content and will continue to be so. You were raised to surmount any little difficulty (you understand me) and a wife can come with no better recommendation.

Now for the small beer! Mary-Ann cannot work from a pain in her back, which has gained on her to the point where she is fit for nothing but lying down. Had it been Sarah we might have suspected idleness, but Mary-Ann is such a good creature that we consulted Dr Chesse directly. He says she will not be well these four weeks. It is extremely trying but the poor girl cries out at the least movement, so there is nothing to be done but wait. Chesse thinks of cupping her. As if this were not enough, Rixam has been called home to his grandmother's deathbed. I hinted at the great inconvenience to us but he said the old lady had raised him and he must not refuse. Your papa says that is quite right, but your papa does not concern himself with the management of servants. We make shift to rub along without Rixam, and have a daily girl standing in for Mary-Ann.

As you can imagine, we are all at sixes and sevens, but when we are back on our feet I intend to paper the breakfast room in silver and blue, or silver and salmon. Which do you think would go better? You have such elegant taste in these things.

Papa asks me to send his love. He says I am like all women, a

great tattler, and insists I convey his compliments to Edmund as
follows: 'Hearty greetings to Yedmund,' if you please! He means
to tease me by sending such a rustic salutation, but we women
are not to be had so easily, and I am sure my daughter will not
fail me but will know how best to trim and turn it according to
the London fashion.

    Your loving
    Mama

Sophia lays the letter on the bedside table and sits unmoving beside the bed. She seems to hear her mother's sprightly, rallying tones but today not even a letter from Mama can raise her spirits.

Never, even in the face of such provocation, could she have imagined herself lashing out at a servant. The second blow was the more shameful of the two; the first resulted from a spontaneous eruption of feeling, but in striking the second, though she was still carried along by her indignation, there was an instant during which she knew what she would do before she did it. To find the boy in possession of what was hers, to witness that peculiar manner of his, and that wretched feint as he tried to cover up the letters, was intolerable, yet none of this can excuse her.

She does not imagine she has done him lasting injury. A gentlewoman is delicate and who knows what these blackfellows do in Africa? They are tough and stubborn: it is said that they eat one another. No, she has not inflicted any serious hurt on Titus. More shameful, infinitely more shameful, is the hurt she has done herself.

Sophia has always held the lowest opinion of those mistresses who, presuming upon their social superiority, conduct themselves in such a way as to nullify it. Whether it takes the form of assaulting the staff or engaging them in amorous intrigue, it invariably degrades all those concerned. While in the Pump Room at Bath, she happened to overhear some talk of a woman of quality infatuated with her footman. The talk was of a decidedly masculine nature: a great many coarse and suggestive terms were employed and Sophia hurried away, sickened that a lady could so forget herself as to furnish gossip to the likes of these.

To compound the matter, it is now clear to Sophia that Titus was acting on Edmund's instructions, which means she has assaulted him for carrying out his duties. As a child she accidentally kicked a little pug bitch that followed her everywhere, and broke its foreleg. The dog had to be destroyed; Sophia mourned it for weeks. As Mama pointed out, it was a lesson in the folly of not governing one's body. This is another.

Worst of all, it would appear that Edmund has been intercepting Mama's letters, though she cannot conceive why he should. Their correspondence is as innocent as water; indeed, she has never hesitated to leave her letters, once opened, lying about where Edmund might pick them up. True, in this one there is Mama's hint of 'any little difficulty', but that is quite inoffensive, surely? Particularly if its true significance is understood, for Sophia knows that Mama alluded principally to her 'weakness'.

It would be of no use, thinks Sophia, for her mother to visit now. Now is too late.

A week ago, she would have come up here with her letter and read it stretched out on top of the bedcovers. Today the coverings have been pulled back and folded over the bottom of the bed, exposing the mattress in its black-and-white ticking.

The ticking is stained and gives off a peculiar mixed odour, one familiar to Sophia since childhood. Cologne has been rubbed into it, and orris, and cinnamon, despite which fragrant ingredients there rises from the mattress stuffing a fishy staleness, faintly but unmistakably suggestive of the pavement around a tavern in high summer.

The first time it happened Edmund behaved with consideration. True, he swore upon discovering the wet sheets and talked vulgarly of stinks, but on perceiving the acuteness of her distress he softened and put his arms around her. He said such things might happen to anyone once in a while; her initiation into wifehood, and then the arrival of her flowers, had most likely done the damage, and if she took care next month it need never worry her again. He stroked her hair, like a kind husband, while Sophia trembled.

But her body's sluices, forced open by the weight and press of water, cannot now be closed. Since then it has happened twice more, and last night Edmund was not kind; quite the contrary. He called her a 'bog-house' and other names too painful to be recollected. Under this provocation, Sophia too became contrary and her eyes remained as dry as her nightgown was wet. Edmund pulled away to the far side of the mattress, dragging most of the bedding with him, while for the rest of the night Sophia lay rigid, uncaressed and uncomforted.

At breakfast this morning Edmund appeared haggard, decidedly *not plump currant*. Though similarly jaded, Sophia had spent the sleepless hours in thinking matters over, and now drew up her forces.

'Edmund,' she began, seeing him withdraw behind his morning newspaper, 'may we not discuss this?'

His voice was disdainful. 'To what purpose? The thing is evidently beyond your control.'

'Indeed it is, yet I'd do anything to cure it. Surely you understand that.'

Edmund snapped the paper out, spreading it wide, his knuckles presenting themselves to her like those of a pugilist. Tentatively, Sophia reached out to touch them. 'Edmund, please don't sulk. It's unworthy of a gentleman.'

'Do you consider yourself a gentlewoman?' murmured Edmund,

flipping over a page. 'Your habits would shame a tuppenny bunter.'

Sophia withdrew her hand. 'I'm at least sufficiently refined not to be acquainted with blunters, whoever they may be.'

'Permit me to enlighten you. *Bunters* are depraved creatures so low most men won't touch them, but even they keep a dry bed.'

Sophia fired up. 'How dare you mention me in the same breath as those women! I'm not depraved, I've a weakness, an *affliction*. You knew all this before we married.'

Edmund lowered the paper, his eyes so hard and dark that they resembled knobs of polished jet pushed into the flesh of his head. He surveyed her at length before saying,

'Knew?'

Sophia's cheeks, neck and bosom grew hot, her hands icy. Her entire body seemed about to disintegrate but she managed, by clinging to the chair-arms, to hold herself upright. 'Yes, indeed,' she insisted. 'You were informed by Papa.'

He stared at her in frank, if hostile, astonishment. 'Is that what he told you?'

Sophia put a cold hand to her throat to soothe the flaming skin there. She was quite unable to speak.

20

God Rot Samuel Shiner

She'll have it stitched on a sampler, one of these days, and pinned over the mantelpiece. It's now over a week since Betsy-Ann last clapped eyes on her keeper, if she can still call Sam that. Devil a penny has she had from him since then; she's keeping herself. Even though his absence means she no longer has to share his bed, she feels the insult.

The night he brought her back from Laxey's, he was at it directly they got under the quilt, poking and poking, veins on his temples standing out so much she could see them even by candle-light. Betsy-Ann pictured herself taking a pin and pricking one of them – he was so far gone in rut, she wondered if he'd even feel it. The drink made him a slow finisher, though, and she was sore by the time he got there.

Now, remembering that sudden urge to prick the veins, she shudders. Where did it come from? It seems to Betsy-Ann that Sam's nastiness is seeping into her: the nightmares she has! Never in her life has she dreamt such things, not even during those first days at Kitty's. She wasn't capable, but she is now. Last night she dreamt she saw the crew lever up a coffin lid. Underneath was a crumbling heap of soil that crept and rippled as if full of worms. 'Far gone in corruption,' said Sam, and she realised that the soil was a woman's body, and the ripple in it an unborn babe, still living. A tiny, wizened face, like a monkey's, poked out of the heap. Someone cried, 'A turnip-baby!' and the crew sliced it out of her with their spades. Betsy-Ann woke sweating fit to beat Sam himself, fit to beat Old Scratch. No, she doesn't miss sharing a bed.

She'd just like to know he's still alive. Ten to one he is – sitting in a flash house, calling for nantz, most likely – but sometimes it's the long odds that come up, and Sam's in very bad company. She's warned him about Harry, how if you anger him he sometimes smiles but keeps score, all the same.

Well. She did what she could. A new day awaits, there's profit to be made. She goes to the Eye and unhooks a rope, lowering a closed basket. There they are, the little darlings: her measures for dispensing cheer to the needy. On the floor beneath them stands a covered bucket, brimful of England's cheapest.

They say the poor have only two joys, fucking and drink, and in Betsy-Ann's opinion drink is kinder comfort. Kitty Hartry might dispute that, but *her* dealings are with people who can pay for pleasure and want it stronger and stronger. What the poor want, mostly, is to be knocked senseless.

Betsy-Ann fills some bottles, takes another basket and lays the precious store within. She spreads a white cloth over them and arranges on the cloth some biscuits she purchased this morning from the pastrycook's, cut in halves, then lays another cloth over the biscuits and closes the basket lid. Lastly she takes a plain gold ring from a nearby pot and slips it onto her wedding finger.

She gropes her way down the unlit stairwell, expecting to find Liz lying in wait – the old woman haunts these blasted stairs, she'll get kicked down them one day – but Liz must have other business, for Betsy-Ann reaches the ground floor unmolested and steps out into the autumn day.

There's a small, high, dirty sun that would do some good if it could only get through the smoke. Down here the air is thick, a clinging web of familiar scents: stale, yeasty gusts from the doors of public houses, hot bread, piss and worse drying beneath chamber windows, mould from dank basements, horse dung, folk lighting their fires, and on the pavement a sour, bright star of vomit.

Betsy-Ann is on her way to the New Buildings.

Even when you're as partial to your own ken as she is to hers, and have plenty set by, it does no harm to stick your head out once in a while. You get a sense of how the world wags, how everything keeps bustling on. Today, however, she has business in hand. Lina told her of a pawnbroker near the New Buildings, a man of discretion. She intends, if she gets that far, to pay him a visit.

Coming through Covent Garden, she sells two half-biscuits and three bottles of lightning. In Long Acre a blowen approaches, strikes up talk and then pulls from the front of her stays a length of cream-coloured silk, for which she wants three shillings.

'Say one,' suggests Betsy-Ann.

The blowen shakes her head. 'This sells at four shillings the yard. There's two yards at least.'

'Two then,' Betsy-Ann wheedles. 'As a favour to you.'

'Look here, Mrs Betsy.' The girl spreads out the stuff on the basket top, smoothing out the creases. 'Not a hole or a mark.'

Betsy-Ann fingers its glossy surface. 'Two.'

'Three.'

Betsy-Ann shrugs. In a pet, the girl snatches up the silk and marches away.

'Like your impudence,' Betsy-Ann says under her breath. She waits to see if the girl will think better of it, but no, the striding figure turns into another street and is lost to view.

She forgets the silk directly she enters the piazza, a place which never fails to arouse in Betsy-Ann a bittersweet ache, joy and sadness mixed. From here she can see the windows – *her* windows, where she was first put into keeping by the Corinthian. Behind them lie three elegant rooms, so fondly remembered that whenever she passes the building she feels she might walk up there and take possession again.

Those rooms, like their mistress, were fitted out in style.

Betsy-Ann, who not so long ago had been living in a wagon, eating potatoes and cowering whenever the farmer appeared, now had a maid of her own and a different gown for each day of the week. When it was too wet and dirty to go out, or when the Corinthian stayed night after night at the tables, she'd ask herself: should the farmer appear, wouldn't he be struck dumb? What could his wife, that bullying bitch, find to say to her now? There were darker days still, when the weather might be fine but she was plagued with the memory of Kitty's place, and of Keshlie, when the answer to those questions would come to her in Mam's voice: *They'd know what to say, all right, and it'd be WHORE.* The only way to stifle that voice was to stand before one of Ned's presents: a fine looking-glass from Venice, the edges bevelled so as to glitter like gems. There she would go and turn about, admiring herself in her new gowns.

He was an unexpected gift, so it was fitting that she first clapped eyes on him at Christmas.

The season of goodwill was always something of a lean time in Kitty's establishment. Wives and mistresses alike demanded tributes, resulting in a general scarcity of the readies. Debauched students went home to be dull with Papa and Mama. Families had visits to make, hypocrisies to keep up, and there was also the occasional fit of repentance: a good few married men fell away each December, only to return, hammering on the door, by February.

Until they did, the inhabitants of the Cunt in the Wall might find themselves free for hours at a time. The least popular girls were put out to grass, the prettiest and the specialists kept on hand, for if a Person of Quality should arrive unexpectedly, *quel dommage* (as Kitty said) if he should find the house lacking in refinement. The girls would sit talking, curling their hair and trying out the new fashions in face-paint, wondering what the coming year would bring.

It was during this flat period that *Harris's List* came into its own, providing the man of pleasure with reading matter to tickle his appetite until he could escape back into the sporting life. As soon as a girl was 'finished' in the tricks of her trade, Kitty had her entered in *Harris's*, paying over the odds for a good account of her livestock. Betsy-Ann was listed along with the rest; when her report first came out, she asked another girl, Catharine, what was written of her.

'*A fine tall girl whose dark eyes languish sensual fire,*' read Catharine. '*Miss Bl—re well knows how to render youth free and happy.*'

'Miss who?'

'Miss – you, you ninny, they miss some of the letters out – O, never mind. *She is of the gypsy nation —*'

At this Betsy-Ann laughed aloud. 'No gypsy would think so.'

'Now, Miss! You told me you had a cart and you were gypsies.'

Betsy-Ann shook her head. 'We *knew* some gypsies. We worked the fairs —'

'Listen! *Trained up from girlhood in the amorous arts freely practised among that passionate and uninhibited race.*'

Here Betsy-Ann exclaimed, 'He knows nothing of gypsies either,' to which her companion replied, 'That may be, my dear, but Mr Derrick thoroughly understands his trade.'

'Derrick? I thought it was a Mr Harris?'

'It's named for Jack Harris, but it's Derrick who writes it. You must've seen him, little carroty Irishman, comes and shuts himself away with Kitty. Now listen . . .

Newly finished and polished by Mrs H—try, so as to excel in the most exacting disciplines of pleasure. She has considerable natural advantages in that field, for in her case the path to bliss is indeed strait and narrow. The gate of life is firm and exquisitely

deep and shaded by the most profuse vegetation. Fortunate in-
deed the eager lover who knocks and is admitted here.

She adores a hard rider, and is a connoisseuse of lusty young
fellows.

'What gammon!' said Betsy-Ann when her friend had explained
connoisseuse to her. 'I'd gladly drown the lot of them.'

'No favourite, then?' Catharine lowered her voice, in case Kitty
should happen to walk by. 'You're not looking for a protector?'

'Spinks offered,' said Betsy-Ann, 'but I wouldn't trust myself
alone in a house with him.'

'Nor I, to be sure. Got any Jews?'

'One or two. Why?'

'They're kind keepers.' Catharine nodded. 'Try for one of
them.'

When she saw him he was sprawled on a sofa between two of
the girls, whispering to each while one of them popped comfits
into his mouth. Betsy-Ann, just returned from her fourth bout
of the day, seated herself nearby so that she could watch the
thing unfold. While she had no love for any of the male visitors,
she approved the stranger's manners. He seemed more refined
than your usual cully; he was perhaps heir to some respectable
merchant, or a lively sprig from a God-fearing family who had
resolved to taste pleasure as his peers did. He might even be one
of the agreeable Jewish keepers recommended by Catharine. She
wanted to hear what he was saying but she could hardly cut in:
by the rules of the establishment he was the rightful prey of her
two colleagues. But then the young man rose, shook hands with
the whores without having so much as fumbled them, and went
away into Kitty's private room. Betsy-Ann hurried at once to the
sofa.

'What's wrong, is he poxed?'

The girls hooted. 'He'd be the first that ever bothered to tell us,' said one.

'Then what's the matter, why's he talking to the Mother?'

'She's *his* mother,' said the girl. 'His darling mama.'

'You mean that's the Corinthian?'

Betsy-Ann had naturally heard the talk, passed on from woman to woman over the years. The Corinthian was Kitty's only son, said to be the offspring of a nobleman though nobody knew for sure. As a young child he had wandered about the more decorous and public areas of the seraglio, but never when there was company; Kitty had made sure of that, by promising that any girl who broke the rule would have her head shaved and be turned naked into the street.

The pretty, prattling little fellow had become everybody's darling. When he was sent away to school, he departed laden with gilt gingerbread and wet from the tears of the more sentimental harlots. He came back with newly curious eyes, his schoolfellows having perhaps enlightened him as to the nature of his mother's business, but he continued to chatter with her girls in an easy, sociable manner, possibly too sociable for his mother's tastes. He was a gent by nature, said the whores, but that could not satisfy Kitty, who left nothing to chance. It was rumoured that she'd intrigued, caballed and blackmailed until she got him to the university, where he mixed with boys far above him socially, boys whose fathers' money jingled in his pockets. It was there, perhaps, that he picked up his nickname. He rejoiced in it, and the whores rejoiced with him. The Age had spawned Corinthians in plenty, but theirs was *the* Corinthian, Corinthian double-dyed: a man of pleasure, born and bred in a Corinth.

At the time of Betsy-Ann's first sighting him, he was but lately returned from the Continent to find all the whores who had chucked his chin quite vanished away, worn out by what Kitty referred to, when the more refined culls were present, as *the mysteries of Venus*. Ned Hartry looked about and found himself a young man among young women.

'He's like quality,' said Betsy-Ann.

'He never pays,' said the girl with the comfits. 'It's his mama's house, what's hers is his.' She grinned. 'Dimber cove, though, ain't he?'

'Except his hair,' the other girl said. 'I don't care for this new-fangled fashion, neither wig nor powder.'

'But a fine colour,' Betsy-Ann said, thinking it would be a pity to powder such hair: like dulling a raven's wing.

'True,' the girl agreed. 'I'd treat him anyway.'

The dimber cove did not ask her to treat him, or Betsy-Ann either. His choice was Jeanne DuPont, an elegant green-eyed blonde who always dressed in watered grey silk. Betsy-Ann was forced to admit that it suited her delicate beauty and made her skin appear as if washed with silver: a very taking look. At least once a day Ned would come through the room where they sat to receive visitors, go straight to the girl and bow to her. She would curtsey and allow him to lead her upstairs to the mirrored boudoir on the first floor.

His choice gave rise to furious gossip among the whores. Jeanne was wayward and wilful, so unbiddable at times that it was said Kitty would gladly have banished her. That she did not, was down to the custom Jeanne brought to the house. Of all the women there, Mademoiselle DuPont was most frequently asked for by name; she was something of a celebrity, with a number of loyal followers.

Her secret lay in her history. Before coming under Kitty's control she had worked for the famous Mrs Hayes, who supplied nuns to Sir Francis Dashwood at Medmenham. Gentlemen who had 'made her acquaintance' at Dashwood's club still sought her out; though dwindling in number, they were highly profitable, being wealthier than most of the cullies that called on Mother Hartry. There were others, less distinguished but far more numerous, whose pride it flattered to ride where My Lord had ridden before them, a privilege for which they paid – O, they paid! And so Kitty held on to her, watching greedily for the day when Jeanne's attractions would wane and she could be replaced with someone younger, fresher, of a more docile turn.

'Weren't you ever afraid?' Betsy-Ann had once asked when talk had turned to the Hellfire Club.

Jeanne gave a supercilious little laugh – 'Afraid?' – but Betsy-Ann was too curious to take the snub. 'I heard they murder,' she persisted. 'And eat the bodies. And conjure up devils.'

'It's play, you bitch booby, nothing but play – Dashwood's letch is to fuck in a monk's habit and drink champagne from your quim, that's all. These men! They can't occupy themselves, they must always be playing.'

'Not always,' put in Catharine, who had been a governess and would read a newspaper whenever she could find one. 'He's a man of parts. He was Chancellor once, and he —'

'I'm surprised he could sober up long enough,' Jeanne retorted. 'And his friend Sandwich, he's another – all sultans and slave girls.' Here she glanced at Betsy-Ann, who, having never heard of Sandwich, feigned envy, since this seemed to be what was required. Jeanne giggled. 'Harems, yes, but nobody wants to play eunuch! Though there was a creature at Medmenham dressed sometimes as a man, sometimes as a woman. It gave fencing lessons in petticoats. We had a wager: he or she?'

'And which was it?'

Jeanne shrugged. 'We'll have to wait till it dies.'

Having made herself ill by constant fuddling in her Hellfire days, she had a disgust of drink and was the only one in the house never to touch it. With those culls who preferred the Sex drunk, she acted drunkenness to perfection. With others, her demure speech and gestures made her a favourite: the most pitiful and disgusting acts, calmly, steadily, *smilingly* performed, could be made to seem almost respectable. There was a certain duke, for example, who made use of her perhaps once a month. To nobody else in the house had he ever named his desires, but in her boudoir, lying outstretched on a leather sheet, he was able to whisper them, whereupon Jeanne promptly hiked up her robe, squatted over his face and pissed.

The duke, murmuring 'My cruel defiler' as he pressed gold coins into the fanny of Mlle DuPont, perhaps thought he was paying her to keep his secret. But Jeanne preferred treachery to discretion and her sharp, sober memory was mercilessly clear.

'How much does he put in?'

'As much as I can take. He's pissing it away.'

The girls roared with laughter.

Lately she had been bragging of Ned's amorous nature – 'It's in the blood' – and as the door closed behind the two of them, some of her sisters smirked knowingly. They waited for Jeanne to reveal his particular letches, but in vain. This was Kitty's son, after all.

Betsy-Ann, who had cared nothing for any man alive, now began to suffer. In fancy she explored with her fingers, with lips and tongue, the gloss of his neck, the firmness of his belly, the silken skin of his prick. She tasted the sweat and oil of his flesh. She rode astride him and felt him arch up beneath her. At the end of each day she lay in darkness, hand jabbing between her legs, clenching her teeth for Dimber Ned.

The New Buildings have a fresh, clean look, a neat and squared-off air. No doubt about it, Romeville is a fine city, and also what she once heard it called by some drunken cully: *the Great Beast.* Under its elegant skin it swells like plague, burying entire fields in stone and brick, gobbling up the dreary little farms where girls claw in the earth with their bare hands. Here are shops with rings and bracelets, silk and china. Let the farms go, who cares for them? Not the girls!

So Marylebone is the coming thing, and Marylebone's New Buildings are rising in the world, rising on a tide of lust, for riches, for pleasure. Builders speculate and their houses are taken by women setting up in trade. Gold flows, molten, from street to street. Lina knows of a woman here who lives alone, keeps her own carriage and answers to no one. That's the style in the New Buildings: not such a good place for anyone down on her luck, but Betsy-Ann sees them, as she sees them everywhere. Some signal their trade by the usual twitching up of the gown while others, bolder or more desperate, move towards any man who hesitates.

She watches a kiddey trying to make his choice. He ignores a mannish girl who pulls him by the arm and instead sidles up to a well-dressed stroller, but it seems she is beyond his purse, for after a few words she continues on her way. At last he strikes the bargain with a plump, lecherous-looking blonde and the pair of them disappear down some steps.

Along the same pavements trudge poor but respectable morts, shamming blind and deaf. Betsy-Ann watches these, too, and fears for them. Not a few of Kitty's nuns started out like Betsy-Ann herself: innocent, until life knocked them into the mud and held them there.

A girl comes to ask if she has hot pastries to sell and goes away with a bottle of lightning. Another does the same. A third arrives, buys half a biscuit and lingers.

'How's trade today, my darling?' asks Betsy-Ann.

The girl says there's none to be had. Englishmen have gone limp in the prick. Betsy-Ann studies this girl: bloated face, pink, streaming eyes, no wonder the culls keep off. She says, 'Bad times for honest whores.'

'Isn't that God's truth?' says the girl. 'Every rag off my back is at Uncle's.'

'Then I hope you got plenty for it, sweetheart.'

The girl snorts. 'Sixpence for a shawl of French lace.'

'They're all the same, God rot them. But it only takes one honest friend to set a woman up, eh? Who knows, perhaps you'll be lucky today.'

'Not I. Been too long on the town.' The whore gives a rueful smile. 'Look at me,' she spreads her arms like a bird about to take wing, 'I cost five guineas a night, once.'

You must've been a fine piece in those days, thinks Betsy-Ann. On impulse she pulls out a bottle and presses it into the whore's hand. 'Where's your Uncle, sweetheart? It so happens an Uncle is what I'm looking for.'

'Through the gardens along there, by the horse trough,' says the girl, staring at the unexpected gift.

The lane is partly swallowed up by the New Buildings, its walls already crumbling to brick dust. She's at the right place: here are the brass balls, dusty and dented where someone has tried to knock them down.

Nobody loves Uncle.

The doorbell clangs as she enters and Betsy-Ann shivers: it's colder inside the shop than outside. Before her is a counter and fixed to the counter-top a metal grille that stretches all the way to the ceiling. Through it she can see shelves holding dusty boxes, velvet bags and heaps of papers. In the far corner, away from these, crouches an unlit stove.

The Uncle comes scurrying from his lair in the back room like a spider sensing a quiver in its web. His head is bound up in a turban, his face shrivelled, his jaws fallen in. If this is the man who gave sixpence for French lace, he should look fatter on his profits. Without a word of greeting, he mounts a stool behind the counter and unlatches a small window in the grille.

'Pledge or redeem?'

'To pledge, Sir, if you please.' She slips a wedding ring off her finger, passes it over and watches him examine it. His hand, seen through the grille, appears divided off into tiny squares of veined, purplish skin.

'Half a crown.'

'I can't take that, Sir. My man would kill me.'

He glances up at her with the weariness of one who has heard it all. 'Then go elsewhere.'

'Say two-and-ninepence, Sir, and it's yours.'

'Half a crown.'

'For a gold ring, Sir! It'll sell for —'

'I've told you —'

'I can't redeem it – it'll be yours to keep.'

The Uncle weighs the ring on a pair of scales. Betsy-Ann waits in silence. At last he slides it to one side before pushing some coins and a ticket towards her.

'God bless you, Sir! And I've something else.'

He has to get the best of a cough before he can say, 'Well? Pass it over.'

'It isn't here, Sir, not now. But my mother. She's poorly, Sir.' The man stares, unsmiling. 'I'll have things of hers, only the property won't come all at once, what with her will and her lodgings, see? I'll be fetching it over weeks, could be months.'

She can tell the exact moment he takes her meaning: his eyelids droop as if to mask the greed beneath.

'Bring whatever you have,' he says. 'I'll give you a price.'

As she begins the walk home Betsy-Ann mulls over the Marylebone Uncle. There was a moment, there in the shop, when she thought he was about to refuse her dying mother's property, but he's fly to the game, that much was plain. Still, a queer cove and no mistake, to sit and shiver with his face bound up when he could buy himself a bucketful of coals.

His price wasn't so bad, considering. Her usual man might have raised her three shillings, but he's too close to home: she's not having her bits and pieces in his window for Sam to see, not likely! With the new Uncle, she's not fouling her own nest. Fouling: that's a laugh, when you think about it. The first thing she does with the bed, when Sam goes off for a few days, is strip the sheets – a mort that's slept under sacking, on muddy ground, and still she can't bear them.

But now – she steps out faster – she's made her first move, now! Shifted some stock, and more to come, and Sam doesn't know, and won't know. She could skip with glee. The day will come, she's making it come. O the fine day that'll be, singing *Samuel Shiner, fare thee well.*

And what a to-do, to get away from him! When Sam got chivvied, his sharping brethren parted company with him as smoothly as Sam's finger parted from his hand. No hard words, no reproaches, that's how it is with men. Who'd be a woman? A woman's tied up, every which way. She's heard some Newgate jailers turn pimp: for a consideration, a visitor can enjoy any female in their wards. From time to time Betsy-Ann's thoughts return to those poor bitches. She sees them lying in darkness, listening for the sound of the key.

She strolls more slowly now, her toes rubbed raw. As a girl she tramped everywhere barefoot, with the result that her feet spread. Shoes pinch her cruelly but in Romeville you're nobody without them: even the most wretched drabs try to show a neat shoe and stocking. At least shoes keep you dry. She remembers Mam, in a distracted moment, stepping backwards off the cart into a country road where cattle had gone by, churning the earth. She cursed and lifted her gown to reveal feet and ankles shod in shining, stinking boots of mud.

She's still thinking about Mam when she's startled by a warning cry from behind. She steps away as the horses rattle past and sees the carriage with its whip-happy driver come to a stop some yards ahead, outside a house with fashionable iron railings. A black boy jumps down and runs to the front door while the driver, dismounting, helps out a feeble-looking blonde piece who stands gazing about as if unsure whether she's in England. The blonde taps her foot, waiting for someone still fussing in the carriage. At last her cull joins her on the pavement. She has just laid her fingers on his arm when the front door of the house opens. The cull turns for an instant in Betsy-Ann's direction before speaking to someone inside.

Betsy-Ann smothers a cry.

He's unhappy. That much can be seen at once: something beaten and angry in the way he holds himself. Even as she notices this, he straightens up and lifts his head. In that movement she sees something of the Corinthian that was.

How can she pass the pair of them? She can neither walk towards him nor move away. She stares fascinated at her rival, often imagined, now right there on the pavement. And how does *she* earn her bread, Betsy-Ann marvels, when many a better one goes hungry?

But now the mort seems to wake up. She looks about her, glancing at Betsy-Ann much as she might observe a scrap of rag blown about the road.

Is it her stance that warns Betsy-Ann – the set of her narrow shoulders? Or is it something else: her air of dull satisfaction, the air of one who expects to be served? Betsy-Ann gasps. This is no Cyprian. She's his autem mort. Ned, laughing Ned, spliced! And to this creature, pale and gluey as a gob of phlegm . . . that blank little phiz of hers, as if the midwife tried to scrub her out at birth. Yet there she stands, her fingers on his arm.

It seems that Betsy-Ann is at last walking forwards. Either that, or the street is flowing past her like a river, bringing in its wake carriage, driver, horse, paving slabs and the elegant couple about to enter the house.

When she is almost upon them he turns round again. This time there's no mistaking: he sees her. He says nothing but calmly hands his autem mort, if that's what she is, up the steps. The blonde's eyes, pale, discreet, flicker in Betsy-Ann's direction for a second before she passes into the house and is visible only as the glimmer of a gown in the darkness of the interior. Betsy-Ann allows herself to stop and peer inside, frantic to see more, but the black returns with a maidservant. The two of them bustle to the carriage where the maid begins to load the boy with parcels.

Betsy-Ann hurries away, her belly pitching about like a boat on the high seas. Married, Ned! She must be very rich. Catch him tying himself down otherwise: the Corinthian, that could have any —

Her face puckers as the truth hits her: not anybody. Any *whore*.

She's cold now. She wishes she'd never seen him, standing there with that bitch clutching his sleeve. What does *she* know about him, about —

Someone's running behind her, alongside her. She turns her head away, but he falls into step.

'Betsy! Don't pretend you don't know me.'

'Ha!' says Betsy-Ann, facing him. 'Who's ashamed to know who?'

'You know I couldn't,' he says softly, taking her hand and smuggling a coin into it. Without looking at the coin, Betsy-Ann holds out her arm, opens her fingers and lets it drop. A guinea rolls across the pavement.

'What a sulky child it is!' exclaims Ned.

She hadn't bargained on a guinea. It's a lot to throw away. She wishes she could run back and take it up, but pride forbids. It seems Ned is as proud as she, so on they go, leaving the money to be found by someone else.

'The Prodigy's looking well.' He again tries to take her by the hand.

Aye! Better than that piece of yours, thinks Betsy-Ann, flinging away from him. She says, 'Let us be thankful for small mercies.'

'Very high, though, ain't she? Too grand to take a present from an old friend.'

'I've no call for presents from,' she allows the pause to develop, 'strangers. Not even' – another pause – 'gentry.'

He whistles. 'Lord! I see there's money in the resurrection trade.'

'In the buttock business, too, they say.' She walks faster. '*I* know a bitch, got fat as a Dutchman on it.'

'How's Sam? Out all hours of the night, eh Betsy?'

His legs are too long, her feet too hot and painful. Betsy-Ann gives up the walking contest and stands facing him. Though she is tall for a woman, the Corinthian is taller. She can still refuse to look up, however, staring instead at one of his buttonholes.

'You can go back,' she says. 'I won't come this way again.'

'But sweet girl, why ever shouldn't you?'

Because if you thought I intended to pay a call, you'd shite yourself.

She says, 'Because I don't choose.'

'There was a time when you liked my company.'

'I did, but then you lost at cards.'

'The heaviest loss I ever suffered.' He bends his knees like a frog, drolly lowering himself until their faces are level. Betsy-Ann is amused despite herself but then she remembers something he once said: *where women are concerned, laughter's as good as wine.* She keeps a stony face, arms folded against her chest.

'Straight in to the kill, is our Neddy.'

He wobbles, drops to one knee, puts a hand to the pavement and laughs in earnest. Unable to resist any longer, she gazes down at him. He has fresh lines around his mouth and mauve patches under his eyes. The eyes themselves are the same. That's all that need be said of them. He gets to his feet, saying, 'Ah, Betsy! You're still a match for me.'

Betsy-Ann motions with her head. 'You've a match back there, I believe.'

He doesn't move. He's waiting for some sign, but she refuses to smile and he is forced to get up at last.

'Punt's,' he says. 'Tonight. Failing that, tomorrow night.'

Betsy-Ann looks away.

'I'll wait, Betsy.'

'As you please.'

'You won't give me the meeting? Why not? Tucked up with Shiner?' She does not reply. 'You'll have a better time with me.' His finger just brushes her cheek, then the gentry-cove is walking back to his house.

21

Here comes Edmund, scuttling along, pushing his way through the crowd: does he imagine he has fooled her? He *shook* when he saw that woman; she felt the spasm, mastered directly but still perceptible beneath her hand.

At once Sophia half-turned, on her guard. From the corner of her eye she spied a motionless female figure some yards away on the pavement. One glance told her enough. The creature was hard-featured but tall and striking, possessed of a certain degraded attractiveness.

Though Edmund is almost at the house now, his wife continues to stand at the bedchamber window, absently examining an almond-shaped flaw in the glass. The strange female carried a basket of some sort. If one were to judge kindly, one might describe her as a costermonger, perhaps. Whatever she is, it seems she is also an acquaintance of Edmund's, of a kind not too difficult to guess. It appears he has told her where his, no, *their* new home is situated. The insolence of the wretch, tripping by, peering into the windows! – spying on *me*, Sophia thinks. She reaches up to the shutters and pulls them across.

Downstairs the front door clicks. He must think her deaf. From this very window she watched him stride off in pursuit. Now he is returned, he will doubtless hurry to her as if to prove he has been within walls all this time – yes, here he comes, panting up the stairs. Sophia moves to the toilet table and pretends to examine her hair.

'My dear,' says Edmund, peering round the door, 'I hope I don't disturb you.'

'Not at all.' She is surprised to be able to throw such a congenial note into her voice. 'What is it?'

'An infernal nuisance. I've business with – why in the devil's name are the shutters like that?'

He enters the room and crosses to the bell-pull.

'Pray don't ring, Edmund, I myself closed them.'

'What on earth for?'

'To adjust my stockings. Gracious, how you puff! Are you well?'

'Perfectly well. I've business with —'

'Forgive my interrupting, my dear, but you're quite out of breath. If this is the result of climbing the stairs we must call in Dr Peck. You would not wish to have a consumption, I think.'

His eyes glint.

Sophia returns him a wifely, benevolent smile. 'I myself can climb the stairs without discomfort, Edmund, and you know how tightly I lace. Pray listen to me for once.'

'Yes, yes! Let him Peck me by all means. But listen, my love, I forgot to tell you I am to be at the coffee-house tonight and to-morrow night.'

'I hope you will not, though,' says Sophia. 'You can bring your friends here, surely? I should very much like to meet them.'

'I wouldn't call Hallett a friend – a tedious fellow. I should be sorry to thrust his company on *you*,' says Edmund, as solicitously as if he had not compared her to a tuppenny – what was it?

'But Edmund, consider the dirt. You're too careless of your health. One risks infection in coffee-houses and jelly-houses.'

She gazes innocently at her lord and master. During their early days here, meeting him coming out of such an establishment, she had implored him to retrace his steps and accompany her inside so that she, too, might sample the jellies. Edmund refused with an emphasis that at once roused her suspicions. She did not enter the jelly-house, and just as well; she has since learned that such establishments are a favourite haunt of degraded women.

'This isn't the season for plague,' says Edmund.

'There are other contagions.'

'If they can be avoided by staying out of coffee-houses, Madam, *you* are quite safe, but am I never to go abroad? That would be absurd.'

'Of course you may,' protests Sophia. 'But I might equally ask, what of me? I'm forever alone here.'

Edmund groans. 'That again! Well, you must bicker with me later. I haven't time for it now.' He moves towards the door.

'Pray wait, Edmund, you're always rushing off somewhere! I've something to ask you. Why should Titus take up Mama's letter?'

He does not hesitate. 'I'm afraid I can't help you, my dear. I saw no letter.'

'Perhaps not, and yet there was one. The boy had it in his pocket.'

'And forgot to bring it you?' Edmund tuts. 'He's begun to slack. I shall have a word.' Having outfoxed her on the matter of the letter, he again makes for the door.

'Thank you,' says Sophia. 'O, and Edmund?'

Her husband turns with a fixed smile.

'I understand that just before we came to London, you had a lucky evening at the tables.'

The smile dissolves. 'Pray who —'

'I heard from a neighbour in Bath.'

'Some time ago, then,' says Edmund, as if Sophia, rather than he himself, must offer excuses for not having previously mentioned it.

'I wished to leave matters to your own judgement. As your wife, I naturally thought you would tell me. When you saw fit.'

Edmund appears to consider a moment before he sighs, closes the door and throws himself into one of the chairs.

'I suppose I'm to blame,' he says, crossing his right ankle over

145

his thigh and glancing down at his stocking where a speck of dirt has dried on the calf. Edmund scrapes at it with a fingernail. He is consulting with himself as to what he should say: Sophia knows this as surely as if she could cut a hole in his brain and look inside. She observes his pallor and the heightened brilliance of his eyes. How unjust it is, she thinks, that his failings do nothing to render him less beautiful.

At last he is finished with the soiled stocking. 'You're aware that I'm not in the habit of gaming. I consider it a frittering away of a man's goods along with his peace of mind.' Sophia waits, outwardly patient, while he runs through his rigmarole. 'The thing is, Sophy, I ran into an old friend. I couldn't take coffee with him just then, or my man would've given me the slip, so he suggested I get my business over with, then accompany him to the tables.'

'Could you not tell *him* how much you dislike it?'

'You don't understand how it is. At school, Thompson behaved towards me with the greatest kindness.'

'Then you could not refuse?'

'No,' he says gently. 'And we played very low.'

'You did well,' says Sophia, wondering what is coming next.

'A married man has no business to do otherwise. At any rate, in comes a drunken whelp bent upon making an exhibition of himself. Seeing us play low, he began abusing us to the company as miserly beggars. He galled me, and I therefore consented to stake him —'

'When you can barely play?'

'O, he was too far gone to be dangerous. I had only to keep my head.'

'That was prudent of you, I suppose, but was it honourable? To play with someone so young and foolish?'

Edmund looks impatient. 'Good God, would you rather I had lost? A gaming table isn't a nursery! A man who goes there is responsible for himself.'

'But he'd been drinking.'

'So had most of the company. I don't know how *you* picture the tables – surrounded by maiden aunts, perhaps, and Methodist preachers – but I assure you it's quite usual.'

'If this be all,' says Sophia slowly, 'I cannot conceive why we should have fled Bath.'

'Directly I had revenged myself, his friends informed me he was not yet of age. I said it was a riddle to task the Sphinx how a man could be old enough to play, but not old enough to pay. This *bon mot* they failed to take in the right spirit.'

'You were playing deep, then, and won a great deal of money?'

He flashes her a smile. 'Yes – had I insisted on my rights. But I settled with them for less and trust that will be the end of it.'

'Why wasn't I told?'

'My dear girl, it was scarcely business for a young lady, much less one on honeymoon.' He rises. 'I succeeded in shielding you and we may now look on it as something past and forgotten.'

'May I at least know how much you received?'

'Twenty pounds. A pittance, considering,' and with a determined motion he flings open the door and is gone.

Considering what? It seems to Sophia that there is much to consider. Of one thing she is certain: Edmund is lying: lying as regards the departure from Bath and also concerning Papa's letter.

That woman in the street: does *she* know the truth of it? The thought brings on a familiar ache in her throat. She was raised to consider a wife as her husband's truest and most trusted friend, his beloved support, the intimate partner of his heart. Edmund has not merely declined her offerings, he has trampled them underfoot.

Her position as his wife, in some respects so baffling, is in this respect only too plain; yet what use is it to sit here and weep? She has made her bed, as they say, and must lie on it – but she need not hang herself in the bedlinen. I will *not* cry, she thinks, and gives a vicious tug at the bellrope. By the time Fan answers, Sophia's eyes are dry and her voice level.

'Send Titus to me directly.'

Titus arrives with a shifty expression, as if conscious of wrongdoing, but then he has always something of that air. Mama maintains that any servant with a hangdog look is sure to prove troublesome. This boy was a folly from the beginning, but Edmund would have his way. He said he wished her to have all that was fashionable. And here she is, in a wretched house, in an unsavoury district, with a servant whose speech provokes ridicule in everyone who hears it.

For an instant she is back in the boat with her intended, gliding over the Statue Lake, and with the recollection come sensations almost intolerable: a delicious tenderness, an exquisite longing to be dissolved into him, to exist henceforth only as that privileged slave, Mrs Zedland. A paradoxical longing. Such blissful solution was only possible, she now sees, in the dreams of Miss Buller, Mr Zedland's soul being marked off from his wife's as by a thick black line.

The boy's enquiring eyes recall her to the present.

'Wait in the lobby and should anyone knock, come and ask me before answering,' says Sophia.

'Yes, Madam,' he says. Plainly he finds it a curious commission, but it is not his place to hold opinions.

'Well, go then! You may not stir unless to relieve yourself.'

With Titus safely disposed of, she leaves her chamber and crosses the landing to Edmund's study.

22

Betsy-Ann squeezes the cards together. The edges must be precise, just . . . She prepares, takes a deep breath, tenses. Springs them. They drop to the table, turning over as they go.

Try again.

No.

Pushing them aside, she fetches a pot of ointment and massages her fingers, bending each one forward and back, stretching and loosening. That's more like it. She pours warm water into a dish and scrubs at her skin until not a spot of grease remains, then again takes up the cards.

Feel the edges . . . press, pinch and . . . spring.

Nearly.

Again.

Nearly.

She can't have lost the trick of it, she can't. She rubs her fingers, wiggles them, flexes.

Again.

The cards shoot from one hand to the other in an arc, a stream of paper in endless motion, court cards blurring into commoners. Her right hand glides along the pack, keeping up the pressure, until her left thumb closes over the last card, latching the pack snugly into her palm.

Betsy-Ann sits motionless, letting out her breath. Not until this instant has she dared to picture failure. Mam's voice, warning her: *When* I do it, child. *When.* Never say *if.*

She can still do it. *Will* do it, will turn her hands, her clever hands, to work. Balancing the books! She smiles at her own joke and blinks her sight clear before preparing, once more, to make the spring.

Again the bridge from hand to hand. She has the trick of the thing now, her fingers cunning, knowing the angle, sensing *when*.

She was playing at Loo when he entered in search of Jeanne. That lady was already engaged. Betsy-Ann saw him survey the room as if seeking out a substitute; he seemed in haste, and not inclined to wait. Some culls made this part of the business insulting, had the girls been at liberty to feel resentment, by looking them over in a peevish fashion as if finding fault. Ned was a man of a different kidney, whose glance rather seemed to imply that he found each so enticing that he would dearly love to take them all upstairs directly, had nature but made man's flesh equal to it.

It was Betsy-Ann's immense good fortune that she sat facing him and about to deal. She saw him consider the women at her table, held up her hands in a sudden motion to fix his attention and – *frrrrip!* – the cards, curving like the path of an arrow, shot from right to left.

Ned's gaze intensified like sunshine through a spyglass. Under the table, Betsy-Ann felt a girl kick her ankle. Her palms now sweating (for she had sprung the arc without time for thought and with a sense of staking her all) she laid down the cards as the others, exchanging the merest flicker of a glance, moved their chairs aside to make way for Kitty's son.

'A very pleasing trick, my dear,' said Ned as he seated himself. 'Pray show it again.'

'Willingly, Sir, as soon as I can.'

'Why not now?'

'My hands shake afterwards.'

'Then take your time,' he said kindly. 'What's your name?'

'Betsy-Ann.'

'You talk like a country wench, how extraordinary! I never

thought to see such a trick from a woman, still less from a bitch booby.'

She flushed at that word. 'My parents worked the books, Sir.'

'Sharps?'

'Fair people.'

He laughed. 'Lord, what care my mother takes! Could she but procure herself a Hottentot! And have you other gypsy tricks?'

She swallowed down the *gypsy*. 'Indeed I have, but,' (did he read *Harris's?*) 'not all fit to be shown.'

'*You* are certainly fit to show anything.' She was unable to see anything of his breeches but his tense, slightly parted lips were almost as sure a sign: she had him. 'Come, bring your cards away. We shall investigate these tricks of yours.'

He rose and Betsy-Ann with him, her ears buzzing. He took her hand as she had seen him take Jeanne's.

'Your fingers are cold,' remarked Ned.

'I warrant they'll soon warm up,' murmured one of the whores behind her back.

Oh Mrs Betsy, Mrs Betsy! In the morning, when trade is lax and they lie in bed, playing cards – in the evenings, when the bedsteads in the adjoining chambers slam against the walls, when the silence that follows is suddenly broken by the *whop* overhead of Selina's birch twigs and the joyous whimper of an admiral – through the long dull afternoons while Jeanne DuPont sits in the parlour, scarcely bothering to sulk since she cares for no man – in the night, when Betsy-Ann wakes in the aching darkness, urgent to possess him again, taste him, draw him into her, lover with hair of night, pleasure overwhelming as night itself – when she weeps in the moment of dissolution – when she fears all other women.

Of all times, this is *when*.

23

The study, as her husband insists upon calling it, would scarcely pass as such with Mama and Papa: a cramped chamber, smelling of damp plaster and mildew. Edmund has furnished it with a heavy desk, a bookshelf so understocked that its paltry volumes huddle together for company, and a curious marble table which he tells her was brought from Italy by his grandfather. She is prepared to admit that the table might possibly have belonged to a gentleman but the room, as an *ensemble*, has not a genteel air.

Sophia is aware that, let ladies protest against bachelor seclusion as they may, they do not, as a rule, meddle in these masculine dens. The study is sacred, be it a shrine of wisdom, its shelves groaning beneath the outpourings of genius, or one of those less inspiring but more numerous hideaways where the walls bristle with antlers, the books gather dust and a welter of papers, disagreeably impregnated with tobacco, threatens to overflow and bury everything else.

Edmund's study conforms to neither of these types. Long accustomed to Papa's clutter, Sophia marvels at the barren expanses of desk and table. To be sure, there are the accoutrements of writing, the pens, paper-knives, pen-wipers and sand, but apart from these one might fancy her husband had never any business to contend with. That this is not the case she is only too often reminded by Edmund himself. Where, then, does he keep his documents?

Inside the desk? The drawers are locked but the top one, out of true with its frame, yields half an inch. Grasping the sides, she rattles it back and forth, hoping to spring the lock, but without success.

As the frail hope of 'accidentally' opening the drawer evaporates, Sophia feels herself at the border of an unknown and inhospitable region. So far she has been supported, even at her most wretched, by the consciousness of correct conduct, of an integrity that could call upon the entire world to witness her every act. From these bracing heights she is about to descend into the vulgar mire of jealousy and suspicion where *spouse* is synonymous with *spy*.

Can she possibly be justified in stooping to such means? Good wives have reclaimed bad husbands, but she has yet to hear of any instances where this was achieved by sinking to their level.

There is, however, the question of natural justice. For what was Woman created, but to be Man's helpmeet? God himself assigned this role to the Sex, yet Edmund has deprived her of it. In breaking into the desk, she asserts merely her right to serve. She realises that her hands are trembling, and as she does so recalls how his arm shook in the street. Grasping a paper-knife with a tortoise-shell handle, she inserts the point where she judges the tongue of the lock to be, nudging this way and that, trying to coax apart wood and metal.

She makes a poor crackswoman. The knife blade snaps off and drops into the drawer. Sophia stares at the broken scrap of tortoiseshell in her hand. Then, rallying, she takes up a paper-knife fashioned entirely of metal and repeats the experiment. After some awkward efforts which bring on a cramp in her fingers, she is rewarded by a loud click.

The lock is sprung.

The drawer is full to the top with papers, packed tight without more division than an occasional ribbon. Plunging her fingers into the mass as if into a heap of lace, she snatches it up and carries it to the marble table, where, scarcely able to see for the excited throbbing in her neck and head, she begins to riffle through it without bothering to sit down. The first thing she finds of any interest is a letter in Papa's handwriting, addressed to herself.

She must remain calm. Forcing herself to breathe as deeply as her stays permit, Sophia reads:

My dear Daughter,

Had we not received the account of your excursion to Ranelagh, I might well fear for your health. My child, you do not write often enough, and when you do take up your pen you do not reply to my questions, or reply to no purpose. Excuse my writing to you in such a tone now that you are mistress of your own household, but these are matters of some importance.

Let me ask you again. Has Edmund collected from my representative the sum of 1000L, as agreed? Pray demand of him whether he has done so. Bracknell tells me it has been signed for, though from Edmund himself I have received no acknowledgement. London being home to such rogues as we daily hear it is, I cannot be easy until I receive confirmation in Edmund's own hand and am certain that he, and no other, took possession.

I am afraid, my dear, that your husband is sadly careless as regards business. You cannot but be aware of it since my last letter. If you are content that he should handle your monies in this come-day-go-day fashion then I must tell you plainly that you are not so awake to your own interests as I could wish.

Since your departure from home, I find that I have written to you four times on matters of some importance. My first two remain unanswered; your answers to the rest are barely satisfactory. Your repeated urging that I should not trouble Edmund does me an injustice on which I will not dwell except to say you are now out of the honeymoon and should not conduct yourself like a lovesick miss

Surely Papa is mistaken, and is recalling some letter from Cousin Hetty? Sophia has never written of a visit to Ranelagh, for the simple reason that she has never been there; nor has she urged her father not to trouble Edmund. But then Papa is liable to grow muddled in recalling conversations, misattributing words and sentiments; Mama often rallies him on it.

There is an omission more unsettling than any of this. In her last letter home, Sophia confided to her mother some of her perplexity concerning the departure from Bath; she even hinted that Papa might make enquiries as to any young heir that had lost heavily around that time. Of all that, Papa makes no mention. Out of discretion? If so, he does well to be discreet since Edmund plainly read – and confiscated – the letter she now holds in her hand.

What else has he confiscated?

She puts Papa's letter into her bosom to finish reading later, and continues to look through the pile. She is not the only person whose correspondence Edmund holds in his possession. There are a great many documents addressed to, or signed by, one Hartry: IOUs, bonds, bets signed and dated, some of them years before, some in the last few weeks. Of Mr Zedland himself there is no mention. Is this Hartry a relative of his, or has Edmund perhaps inherited the debts of a stranger? Is this the fruit of his mysterious win at Bath?

There is one note a single line long:

Ready in four days & sent directly. Shiner.

Evidently this Shiner person has a bent for the laconic, though the script – unlike the style – is exquisitely formed. Since the writer appears to be some kind of tradesman, she wonders at the familiar tone Edmund suffers the fellow to adopt.

She reads on, turning up each sheet as she goes but finding nothing of especial interest until her eye again falls on the word Shiner, this time coupled with her own surname:

Mr Hartry bets Mr Shiner five guineas that the Buller is broken into before New Year's Day, with or without benefit of clergy.

E. Hartry
S. Shiner

The word *paid* is dashed across this in a bold, flowing hand that Sophia knows well from her own correspondence. She stares at the words *broken into.* They dance about the page, flinging themselves in her face and dropping back again: *broken* into. broken *into.* What this Shiner and Hartry have to do with her she has not the faintest notion. She wishes she were equally ignorant of the nature of their wager, but the sense forces itself upon her.

In a stinking necessary house she lifts her petticoats as men's faces leer at her between the bricks. She whirls about, shamed and defenceless, as on every side they whisper and point and laugh.

The wager was made in August, the month when Edmund rowed her on the lake. How respectfully he handed her into the boat, first mopping its floor with his lawn handkerchief lest her shoes should be wetted, while all the time in his club he was making her the common talk of such creatures as this Hartry and Shiner: O, the duplicity, the heartlessness of the male sex!

Shaken, she reads on. The next few documents are deeds to Wixham in the county of Essex and these, at least, bear the name *Zedland.* Then come bills for shoes, gloves and a laced coat, followed by a sheet of calculations hastily scribbled down, various sums crossed out and others altered. On turning this last over, she finds a further letter, undated and written at speed, to judge by the frequent blots:

Child (for so you are to me, and ever will be, no matter how grown you think yrself),
*   I must ensist on telling you that you are headed the rihgt way*

to make yrself a most confirmed laughing-stock. To let a woman so tye you up! In a green youth there would be excuse for it, but in you it is not to be born. My indulgence has made of you a more finished man of plesure than fellos twice your age. My reward is that you help her away from me and set yrself up as her keeper, you dote on the creature like a raw schoolboy, ready to kiss the feet of any dirty trull that will obblige him.

Now I hear that you are promesing her marriage. Am I to believe you in earnest? Do you fancy I sent you to the varsity and to Paris, only so that you could wed a tinker?

Rest asurred (for now I come to it) that if you are so mulish I must needs stop yr allowence. Aye, let Madam earn it, and we shall see if she continues so lovesick.

Believe me when I say that I would not willingly see you reduced. I am ready to shower gold on you, only I would have you be wise and do as yr betters do. When you tire of the piece you will be ready to bite off yr tong, to think what you through away and will not have again. Picture yrself 10 years from now, chaned to a stinking gypsy and her brood; then fancy yrself with a rich wife, a purse full of gold and all those advantages my influence can secure. Though they are in no hurry to claim ackwaintance, I have some of the most celebrated persons of the Age in my pocket. Only consider what they have in their power to bestow, both now and in the future, and wether you can afford to turn up your nose at it. Should you not laugh to see another so infatuated and behaving so extravagant?

My son, this wench has sadled you and rides on your back. Only throw her and you will again walk easy. You make yrself ridiculous in the eyes of the world, enslaved to such a commen creature: I have now in my employ a pair of sisters something in the style of your Mrs Betsy, only far superiour. They come as a set, one most acrobatic and lassivious, the other the cunningest flute-player that ever made a man's eyes roll in his head. A

vicount pays 200L for an hour of their company but you, that
are Freeman of the House, may flitt from flower to flower sip-
ping necter where you will. Come, try if these girls do not make
you happy. Did ever parent make a kinder offer to a son? Sure
most young men would give their eyes for it! Did you but know
yr good, you were better apprentised to my trade than to cuck-
oldry, penury and a housefull of brats.

   Yr affect. parent,
   K. Hartry

Never could Sophia have imagined such wickedness. It is beyond anything: a father enticing his own son into debauchery! There are other letters in the same hand and these she pushes aside unread, not without a sense of contamination from their very paper and ink. So this is the company her husband keeps, un-known to her – this monstrous Hartry and his son. Supposing *Mrs* Hartry alive, and possessed of any womanly feeling, how the poor creature must have suffered to see her husband's profligacy begin to show, like spots of decay, in her child. Even the love affair of which the father wrote was evidently of a coarse and car-nal nature. Only suppose if she, Sophia, had a son, and Edmund should —

   Edmund. He said he would be out tonight, but he has been known to change his mind, particularly if the weather turned cold. Suppose he were to return? She has now worked her way through about half the mass of papers. Should she take some of them away with her? Caution urges staying where she is: from this room she can hear the front door, which allows her time to press them back into their hiding place. Once remove a doc-ument, and who knows when she will have the opportunity to make the return?

   How, though, will she explain the unlocked drawer? Directly Edmund finds it, she stands detected. She feels at the back of the drawer, finds the snapped-off tip of the letter-opener and slips it into her pocket. The lock itself appears uninjured. If so, and if she can find a key, all may yet be well. The maid (Sophia blushes) can be blamed for the damaged paper knife. Some tale about dusting – clumsiness – she will make it up to the girl.

Though the middle drawer is also locked, its contents can be exposed by lifting the top drawer clean out of the desk, thus revealing two rings and a stub of wax. There is, alas, no spare key. Sophia picks up the first ring, expecting to see the turtle-dove device that always appeared on Edmund's letters during their courtship. Instead she beholds a carved sunflower precisely like that on her own seal ring, the one she inherited from Grandmother Cotterstone. Sophia's ring is of bluejohn. This one has a dull reddish stone, perhaps carnelian, but as far as her eye can judge, it is the very same design.

There is a piece of paper shoved to the back of the drawer. She pulls it out and is faced with the words

Sophia Zedland
Sophia Zedland
Sophia Zedland

– followed by a few sentences of no great import but painstakingly inscribed in a character identical to her own. The proof is damning: here lies the explanation, dreadful though it is, for Papa's confusion. Sophia's breath seems to come through layers of muslin, as if she were straining the air, and she can hear her own gasps as if made by another person. Is this hysteria? Not at all. *Sophy is rational.*

Papa has been reading not Sophia's letters but Edmund's.

It is some minutes before she can command herself sufficiently to continue. The third and last drawer is unlocked and empty. Sophia turns back to Papa's letter and reads through to the end. He does not continue to scold her but offers the 'small beer', as Mama called it, of a country household: Mary-Ann's back is

159

improved, Rixam's grandmother has left him 20L. Sophia is not greatly cheered by Rixam's good fortune. She returns the letter to its place in the pile and closes the drawer, then hurries to her boudoir where she snatches up a handful of hairpins.

Eleven o'clock finds Sophia kneeling by the desk, hairpin in hand.

Midnight finds her, a prey to violent headache, in bed and endeavouring to sleep. The drawer is locked. Outside in the yard, bent pins and a broken paper-knife sink down in the privy-pit.

Edmund is still not home.

24

Punt's Coffee House makes itself known a hundred yards away, sudden heaves of heat and laughter pushing aside the cooling air each time the door opens. Betsy-Ann knows it of old: a nest for night birds, both cocks and hens.

Ned's there already, sitting some way off and watching the company. As he sees her approach, he turns the familiar smile full on her and despite herself, Betsy-Ann feels her heart kick.

He takes her hand and kisses it. 'Here have I been in a cursed funk.'

'What, you?' says Betsy-Ann, sitting down.

'I thought you might be afraid to come.'

Who does he think he is, Old Harry? She has sufficient courage to share a pot of capuchin, at any rate, and drinks from his used cup, the sweet milky coffee coating her tongue. This is a time to listen, not talk – what's his lay? – but now he has her here, Ned seems ill at ease.

At last he ventures, 'Queer times, eh?'

'I've seen worse.'

'And better. Speaking for myself, that is. Who'd have thought it, you with Sam, and me —'

'Spliced?'

'Damnably spliced.'

So she was right. She wonders if his autem mort is One of Us, as *Harris's* calls it. She didn't look the type, but on consideration Betsy-Ann's not so sure. It's possible to drown the whore in the wife. It's been done.

He says, 'I see you're curious, Mrs Betsy.'

'How?'

'Your eyes are all slitty.'

Too sure of himself by half! Betsy-Ann at once yawns in his face. He sees his mistake and says coaxingly: 'I flatter myself the tale isn't without interest. She's from Zedland, where the fine big wenches grow.'

'Is that why you went, then? To get married?'

'Nothing further from my mind, I assure you. When I binged avast, I hadn't the price of a hat.'

'You, Ned? You've never gone short in your life.'

'Ah, Betsy!' He makes sheep's eyes at her. 'You know I have.'

'You'll be telling me she's a fortune, next.'

'You are at liberty to laugh, Madam,' he says, but good-humouredly.

'That's a mercy. Might burst myself otherwise. So, let me see: you went there penniless and married an heiress.'

He grins. 'I grant you not every man could've done it.'

'O, it's been done before,' says Betsy-Ann. 'Mostly by tumbling her first.'

'That is, indeed, the beaten track. I pride myself on a little more *finesse*.'

'Christ, Ned!'

'Patience, you shall hear.' He's smiling; he's gained the upper hand. 'Now Betsy, in your gypsy days, when you went rolling about the country, did you ever fetch up at Bath?'

She shrugs. 'Don't recall.'

'Then my life on it, you never did. Bath's not a place you'd forget. Half of England's in lodgings there – the gaming half.'

'I know that much, Ned.'

'Well. It was in Bath that I set myself up.'

'Living off the loobies, I suppose.'

'Aye, such fat foolish trout as you see there! Ned tickled 'em into the pan.'

'But why?' Betsy-Ann is finally overcome by curiosity. 'Why *Zedland*?'

'The thing is, child, I didn't go there so much as leave here. Un-invited company, you know.'

'Uninvited — ?' For a moment she thinks he's complaining of fleas. 'Duns, you mean?'

'Aye. I was never so plagued in my life.'

'But Kitty – wouldn't she —'

'Put her hand in her pocket? It was she cut off the funds. I daresay you remember how *that* came about,' he adds with a touch of bitterness.

Betsy-Ann sits up straight. 'Don't you put it on *me*, Ned. I won't have it.'

'If we'd been spliced, nothing to be done, then perhaps she'd have come round in time. As it was, I saw she'd never leave off.'

She sniffs. 'I'm with Sam, for Christ's sake. What more does she want?'

'Curse me if she doesn't think Sam's a decoy. My dear mother is of a suspicious nature.'

Suspicious? Pitiless, more like. When Keshlie wouldn't go with a cull, but cried and clung to her, Kitty bent and whispered in her ear that if the man was not obliged directly, she'd have Kesh-lie's throat cut in the night and her body thrown into the Thames. She'd never have done it – easier just to shove a girl out on the street – but Keshlie was too green to know that. As for her elder sister, who did know, Kitty made sure she was occupied and out of the way. When Betsy-Ann was finished with her cully she went to the kitchen to look for Keshlie, who did such tasks as chopping and peeling, and was told her sister had gone for oranges.

'What's a fellow to do?' Ned shrugs. 'She wants me to give you up. I give you up, and she ruins me!'

Keshlie trailed downstairs and halted at the bottom step, grimacing, a slash of crimson across the front of her gown. Betsy-Ann hurried to her, took her by the arms and turned her round: another patch, and a faint hogo of salt and rust. Why, the child had started with her flowers! Bleeding like murder, right through her clothes. Behind Keshlie one or two whores were frowning and signalling across the parlour, indicating Betsy-Ann should take her sister away to their private quarters.

'Come with me and we'll get you some rags,' she said, putting an arm round Keshlie's shoulders. 'You're a forward wench, to be sure!'

Keshlie blubbed. Betsy-Ann could have done the same, seeing her start so young, but she squeezed Keshlie to her, murmuring, 'There, there, you won't die —'

She broke off, held her sister at arm's length, and stared. Earlier that morning, Keshlie had worn her green robe, with a little apron over it. Since then, someone had undressed her and put her into a long white garment like a nightgown, trimmed with lace and satin ribbon. At first Betsy-Ann had failed to notice the gown, so distracted was she by the patches of red. She ran her hands along her sister's body: neither stockings nor stays. Now she understood how the gown had become so bloody: there was nothing between it and Keshlie.

She understood everything.

When she first told this story to Ned, he insisted it must have been a bungle: a cully who'd paid to fondle and pet the girl, nothing more, but then things went too far. Betsy-Ann demanded what kind of fool he thought she was. They'd waited until she was busy, she shouted. They'd tricked out her sister like a bride. Yet still Ned resisted. His mother was no pious prude, but a child of Keshlie's age? Her house didn't deal in children. Kitty was a woman of principle, in her way, and much maligned.

It was a natural enough blindness in a son. Even so, there is a certain satisfaction in Betsy-Ann's remarking now, with an air of innocence, 'She ruined you! And she so soft-hearted!'

'It wasn't for lack of pleading, I assure you. I got down on my marrowbones – you'd have laughed to see me.'

'I reckon anyone would.'

'I said, Sam Shiner's her protector now, and she said, That'll change if you once get sixpence in your pocket.'

Betsy-Ann sighs. 'Didn't know you, did she?'

'I said, Be reasonable, Ma, you might as well cut off my baubles, and she said, At your choice. I never knew her so hard – to me,' he adds, noticing Betsy-Ann's expression. 'She said, I shall try if I can starve some sense into you. Nothing for it but to toddle. Fellows told me Bath was the place, so there I went.'

Betsy-Ann tries to picture Dimber Ned let loose in Zedland. All the time she lived there, she only once saw a man with good lace to his coat. In fact, *Zedland* was one of the first words Catharine taught her when she came to Town: the place was so called, she explained, because the inhabitants are too stupid to say 's' but must say 'z' instead, with their *zyder* and *Zummerzetzhire*. Zed was the last letter of the alphabet, said Catharine (Betsy-Ann not having learned her letters then, this was news to her) and it followed that Zedland was the last place on earth: Zed Land.

Yet here is Ned claiming to have married into it.

'So there you went,' she echoes. 'Is it so very grand?'

'The buildings please, and there's a deal of elegance in all their customs and contrivances, but lord, how it cramps a man! I lacked room to turn around in.'

'You mean they began to know you,' says Betsy-Ann, smiling despite herself.

'Aye, they made that pretty plain, so I took myself off to an inn outside Bath until there should be fresh trout to tickle, and there fell in with her father. A man of property, travelling on business and with a daughter at home still unwed, would I do them the honour of visiting? In short, Papa was quite charmed.'

'He took you for a gentry cove.'

'One would say so. He is, himself, a gentry cove. I arrived to find the premises snug, his wife as hopeful as himself and the wench —'

'I've seen her, remember —'

'I was *about* to say, a cursed mope.'

'So you worked a cure?'

'Had her blushing like port wine,' he agrees. 'A charming sight! How she did struggle against it! Were I not the most modest fellow living, such adoration might have swelled my head.'

'I daresay it did, a little, though you are so very modest. Had the lady no other suitors?'

'She's . . .' – his eyes go inward for a second or two – '. . . not calculated to please a man. I found her standing empty and put in for the lease, as it were.'

'But you —'

'I was a gentry cove, remember. Property in Essex. By which you perceive that I fought under false colours.'

'And was the lady in the deceit?'

'Not then and not now. What would you have me do? She would scarcely appreciate my mother's establishment.'

Betsy-Ann whistles. 'But if they find out?'

He shrugs. 'I've the dowry safe. Well, Betsy? Was it not a rum bite?'

She never fancied him capable of such things, certainly.

'They *will* find out, Ned.'

He shrugs. 'I'd put money on it.'

'But they'll come after you!'

'After who, Betsy? Edmund Zedland?'

Betsy-Ann blinks.

'There's a Mr Cant at Bath,' he says, laughing, 'and a Mr Blunt, and a promising pair by the name of Chase, with whom I had some excellent sport – the flats must think what very curious names some gentlemen have – but, Betsy! I must tell you, I ran into a friend of Ma's in the Assembly Rooms. I might almost say, a friend of *yours*.'

She shakes her head. 'I've no friends there.'

'Man of business, then.'

'A cully of mine, at Bath?'

'A hundred of 'em, for all I know, but the man I mean is Derrick.'

'*Sam* Derrick?'

'The same, and living most respectably. He's Little King of Bath now and a great favourite with the ladies.'

'And they don't object to his writing *Harris's*?'

'Your respectable lady's never heard of *Harris's*. As for the gents, some are just such innocents, but the rest! If you could see their faces!'

'I'm surprised they don't peach on him.'

'They'd peach on themselves into the bargain. And the thing amuses, no question, so providing he doesn't rub anyone the wrong way, Sam's safe enough. You should see him fawning on respectable females, petting their lapdogs and directing them to reading rooms and *chapels*!' Ned bursts into incredulous laughter. 'One expects him at any minute to lapse and introduce someone as *Lady Lushington, fine black pelt around the Grove of Venus*. He's been there two years now, and still not found out.'

'Who writes *Harris's* then, while he's in Bath?'

'Himself, I fancy. The style of the thing is his. King of Bath *and* King Pimp, what a blessed existence – eh, Betsy?'

Still laughing, he rises to go outside and piss. Betsy-Ann is left to ponder what she has been told, not about Sam Derrick but about

167

Ned's wife. The lady has been cruelly taken in, almost as cruelly as the Blore sisters when they fell into the hands of Kitty Hartry.

He's made a sweet business of it.

She's always known he had a wicked streak (how could he not, with Kitty as his ma?) but she never thought him so bad as this. And he isn't, she tells herself, he isn't! It's all down to Kitty – Kitty drove him to desperation – and things are never so hard for the rich, they've always something. Mrs Zedland (Mrs Hartry?) has family, and heaps of gold.

Or *had* gold, before she married Ned.

It was the common cry, among Kitty's girls, that Ned had twice the heart of his ma. They all said so, Betsy-Ann louder than any. Now it comes to her – with a sensation like something scraping at her breastbone – that twice nothing is nothing.

He's coming in from the yard. Betsy-Ann arranges her face in a smile.

'That's it,' he says, pinching her cheek. 'Good cheer and good company, the best things in life.'

'Not love?'

He grins. 'What, in the name of all that's ridiculous, has a married man to do with love?'

'If you don't know, you must ask your wife.'

'Pooh! Any whore knows ten times as much about it.'

'About lechery, you mean.'

'It's all one. That's why whores make the best wives.'

Betsy-Ann looks down, recalling the culls at Kitty's. Love!

'Yes indeed,' Ned insists. 'By love, you know, I don't mean your sentimental spew, your milk-and-water for young misses. There's but one kind, and if a man doesn't want that from a woman, what *will* he want?'

'Money,' Betsy-Ann retorts.

'*Touché*. You think I haven't lived by my own lights, eh?'

'Well, have you?'

'I have, indeed, married money – just a little. And what's the use of money? To buy pleasure.'

'I suppose,' says Betsy-Ann.

'We know too much to be prudish, you and I.'

His voice is softening, growing huskier. She looks up to see his eyes full on her, and recalls a fancy she had once, that those eyes of his give off black light. As a lantern shining in your face at night shuts out everything else, so to be caught in the beams of Ned's eyes is to find yourself alone with him; as a lantern turns flying things to crackling, so Ned sears his wife's skin, burns her cheeks to embers. The wife is a poor scorched fool, and Betsy-Ann is another: she sees him practising on her, plain as anything, but she'll dance up the stairs with him any-way. It's going to end the way it always did. She can no longer meet his gaze, and as she looks down at the table, Ned shifts in his chair. She knows that movement: it signals excitement. Yet he seems determined to take things coolly. He orders more capuchin and sits back as if to study her. She wonders if he's about to ask her about Sam but when he speaks it is to con-tinue his own story.

'I can go about now. Most of the duns are paid.'

'With her dowry.'

'And my genius. We began our married life with a visit to Bath – I wanted a last crack at it, so I persuaded *ma femme* to take a wedding trip there. And by God I was lucky!'

'You won a great deal?'

'A more pitiable flat you never saw. The merest pup.'

'Had he no friends?'

'Aye – damnably wide-awake ones. They'd have queered my pitch, only he was too drunk to heed them. They were not to be shaken off, however, so I thought it best to leave Bath and negoti-ate from a distance. Madam's been sulking ever since.'

'I thought ladies liked to come to Town.'

He grimaces. 'My wife, poor bitch, wishes to mingle with the Quality.'

'And will you?'

'How can we?' He runs his fingers through his hair. 'Where can I take her?'

'How about the bagnio? She'd see fine gents there,' says Betsy-Ann, only half joking since a bagnio is to her a place of luxury and splendour. To be invited to the bagnio, there to dine off plate and crystal and perhaps even bathe in the mineral waters! But Ned says sharply, 'She knows nothing of bagnios. Nor shall she, if I have my way.'

The capuchin is brought. Betsy-Ann, who rarely takes it, drinks half a cupful at once: the nearest she's likely to come to the joys of the bagnio.

'So,' she says, 'what will you do?'

Ned shrugs. 'She must wait, is all.'

'For what?'

'Until my turn is served. After that, she may go where she pleases. Christ, but I'm sick of her jaw!' He whines in mockery of a gentry-mort: '*I meet nobody! I meet nobody!*'

'Can't you introduce —'

'Who'd want to meet *her*, by God? If all a wife had to do was write letters and prink herself in a glass, she'd be the best wife in England.'

There is silence between them.

'You perceive how happily married I am,' says Ned at last. 'I fancy you and Shiner are better suited.'

Behind him, at a nearby table, a pinched, hungry-looking woman, her eyes closed in exhaustion, seems about to slide from her seat. Her gown is pulled aside to expose one breast and on her lap lies a swaddled infant. Betsy-Ann supposes the mother un-fastened herself but fell asleep before she could put the babe to suck. Unable to reach for the teat, it grizzles, a thin hopeless sound.

Ned takes Betsy-Ann's hand. 'There's money in resurrection – I take it he supports you?'

'*His* dowry's not up to much.' She pulls away. 'But you needn't put your finger in your eye for me, Ned, I'm not about to starve.'

'No, by God! I see that.' He's studying her bubbies. 'But you can still eat, I hope?' Though nobody nearby is listening, he leans forward and whispers into her ear. 'Suppose I ordered a private supper? I've a chamber upstairs and a fancy for resurrection. You can show me how to raise the flesh.'

Despite the capuchin she's drunk, Betsy-Ann's mouth goes dry. Not that she's surprised: what else are they here for? What astonishes her is the way her body, his loyal creature, sets to work. Like dried flowers dropped into water, it moistens and swells and blooms for him. Until this moment she fancied, fool that she was, that she had a choice.

'Wait, I've something to do,' she says, rising to go outside. In the street, she shades her eyes to shut out the coffee-house lights, and squints over the rooftops opposite. It's your true Romeville sky, a tight lid of cloud and smoke. Over to the east there's a flickering rose colour that means trouble for somebody; the rest is dark as the devil's arsehole – as dark as the inside of her own head, it seems to Betsy-Ann. She can't think straight: she's game, but is she flash or flat, here? If only she knew whether the cards would fall right for her: Ned kind and true and open-handed, and an end to Sam Shiner.

'You could've used the jerry upstairs,' Ned observes on her return.

'I was looking for the moon.'

He laughs. 'And what, pray, does that signify? Are you afraid of lunatics? Or is it the fashion now to relieve nature by moonlight?'

She shakes her head. 'If the sky clears, Sammy can't work.'

'Does he come home?'

'He might.'

'So you won't share my supper,' he says plaintively. Smiling, Betsy-Ann lays a finger to her nose.

'It's pitch,' she says. 'No moon to be seen.'

On their way to the stairs she stops and puts the swaddled child to its mother's nipple, folding the mother's arm over it for protection. The breast, when she touches it, is cold. She has a queer, bad feeling as if she's done this before, but perhaps that's just because so many things tonight are strange and yet familiar. She bends over and listens. The woman's still breathing and as Betsy-Ann moves away she groans in her sleep. Betsy-Ann silently wishes her luck before straightening and taking Ned's arm.

25

Clad only in her nightgown, Sophia is making her way across the rooftops. It is an effortless business: without any volition on her part, her steps soften, loosen, become long, low leaps, until she is merely skimming the slates, needing only to touch her foot to one before springing off again. There is considerable satisfaction to be derived from this floating motion, which is all quite natural. Somehow she has always known how it would feel to fly; she is ready to take off when the last, the longest, the endless step comes, after which she will have no further contact with anything resting upon the earth. In the meantime she churns the air with her hands, pulling herself along.

Thus she swims through the night sky, her destination a distant belfry where the bell shines out bright as a guinea. Sophia keeps her eyes fixed on the belltower, assuring herself of its solidity, for she has begun to notice, passing from one roof to the next, the great height of the buildings beneath her. Between them lie chasms, dropping sheer to the depths where London, all mouths and teeth, lies buckling and heaving. How easy, to fall into it and be devoured. And now she realises with horror that the belfry is swaying, undermined from below. She cannot reach it in time and as she passes over a great black gulf she feels herself sucked down, down, the walls hurtling up on all sides as she falls. The bell calls tenderly to her, its faint metallic lowing snatched away by the wind.

She is startled awake, the bell still pleading in her ears even as the threaded roughness of the winter coverlet tells her she is in bed and her husband, having kicked open the chamber door, is cursing his boots.

Perhaps she really did hear chimes. There is a clock over the hearth; were she alone, she would rise and ascertain the hour but Edmund is moving restlessly about, muttering something Sophia is glad she cannot understand. She is lying with her face towards his side of the bed. With infinite care, so as to make no sound, she rolls over until she is facing the other way.

At last he finds the edge of the coverlet and pushes his way between the sheets, bringing with him an eloquent if unspoken account of his night's adventures: the mingled stinks of punch, tobacco and burnt meat; the sourness of unwashed flesh and, most hateful of all, a sickly, clinging pomade.

His wife lies shamming sleep though she has never been more awake, almost afraid to breathe for fear of what she might suck into her lungs. Her thoughts come in a terrifying rush. Tobacco is nothing, though foul: even a man who does not indulge can pick it up on his clothing, merely from standing near. But the pomade, the pomade . . . if Edmund has been close enough for *that*, there can be little doubt of the rest. And now she remembers that vile, corrupting letter, the enticement to debauchery signed *K. Hartry*, testimony to the company Edmund has kept.

That the footsteps of vice are dogged by disease, and a wife's health at the mercy of a foolish or selfish husband, Sophia first learnt as a child, from hearing talk amongst the servants. At that time, with a child's innocence, she understood it to mean that a wife might become debilitated from constant quarrelling. Since then she has learnt more. Vice's punishment is visited upon the innocent as well as the guilty: not even children are spared. Very possibly, her husband carries such castigation within him; or, if not infected today, he may be so tomorrow.

Edmund makes an incoherent sound, followed by a full-bodied snore. The self-discipline required for perfect stillness means that Sophia dare not sleep likewise; coming to after a momentary lapse, she is cold with fear but Edmund snores on.

Her hips ache. The night would seem interminable but for the church bells: half past five, quarter to six. It is Sophia's habit to rise and be dressed by seven. She ought to get up, get away from him, but suppose he should catch hold of her? She cannot think how to proceed. Shortly after six, exhausted but still wakeful, she perceives a difference in Edmund's breathing. Immediately afterwards, her husband stretches his legs. Sophia's posture has never altered since he got into the bed, and now she feels his hand creep under her nightgown, pause on the curve of her hip, then walk crabwise, finger by finger, round the front of her body. Edmund pushes himself against her, nuzzling the nape of her neck. A sly, insinuating finger parts the flesh between her legs.

'Not now, my dear.' She attempts to pull his hand away, but his arm is stronger than hers. The finger stays where it is, and at the same time he slides his other hand around and beneath her in order to pinch at her breast.

She says more loudly, 'Not now,' but Edmund only murmurs into her hair, 'Ah, don't be coy, my dimbadell.'

At least, that is what it sounds like. Whatever it is, she has never heard the expression before and she thinks: Why, he has mistaken his bedfellow! Now he is putting a leg across hers, as if to turn her over. Sophia lies rigid with fear and disgust. In all the mortifications and cruelties of her married life, nothing has come close to this. Here in their bed, as if it were the most natural thing in the world, her criminally careless husband is proposing to ruin her health.

Edmund grips her tightly, giving a sudden heave and roll so that she is on top of him.

'Ride a cock-horse,' he mutters. 'Come on, ride St George.'

He paws at her nightgown in order to get at her breasts. She moves awkwardly so as to block him but there is the *thing*, straining, eager to plant death in her womb.

'No!' Sophia cries, flinching away. Edmund says nothing, but catches hold of her wrists. There is a moment when she thinks she might escape, but when he begins to grasp her in earnest she realises that, even sitting astride him, she is not strong enough to resist.

She screws up her eyes, deafened by the hubbub inside her, Mama's voice and the doctor's, and the physical effort, a squeezing, a forcing through. Surely it is impossible – for some seconds she feels nothing – her body has refused to obey, or has it? She cannot tell – and then there is the shameful, wonderful rush of warmth. Edmund gasps as the urine spreads across his belly and onto the mattress on either side.

There is a silence. She is shaking so violently as to be almost glad of his restraining grasp. The *thing* has shrunk away.

Edmund releases her left wrist. He lays her hand down by his side, stroking it as if to pacify her.

'Poor little Sophy.'

Sophia slumps with relief. 'Forgive me,' she babbles, 'I couldn't help —'

The slap wrenches her head to one side. She hopes she did not cry out. She might perhaps have rolled off him, but he still holds her by the wrist. Her cheek stings as, wincing, she opens her eyes.

'You couldn't help it, eh?'

'No —'

'I knew a girl took money for that.'

The room is too dark to see his face but it seems to Sophia that he derives pleasure from saying it here, to her. His voice is silky, as if he is smiling.

'She never pissed on *me*. If she had, by God, I'd have taught her manners.'

Again a silence. Sophia's left eye has begun to water. She wonders who this 'girl' might be: perhaps the person she noticed in the street.

'You'll be a pretty sight tonight and no mistake,' says Edmund, brisk and unconcerned. 'Now do as I told you.'

She makes as if to comply but flings herself to one side, so that she is no longer straddling him, and half slides, half falls down the edge of the bed. By the time Edmund has recovered from his surprise she is on her feet and about to escape onto the landing, but before she can haul open the door he is upon her and dragging her back. She refuses to let go of the doorknob: it comes away in her hand and both she and Edmund stagger backwards, through the door of her closet.

Sophia looks round desperately for something to cling to, and can find nothing better than the leg of the toilet table. Edmund gropes along the table-top, snatches up a pretty little tortoiseshell mirror that Mama gave her and throws it against the wall.

Sophia screams. 'That was wicked, Edmund!'

'Not at all, Madam. A man may do as he wishes with his own property. Even,' he shakes her, 'a stinking pisspot of a wife.'

Rage lends her courage. 'Stinking? *You* stink of smoke and —'

'Hold your tongue —'

'— worse, out till five, *I* heard you —'

He twists her fingers away from the table and wrenches her out of the closet. 'I know what'll settle you,' he mutters, pushing her against the mattress. 'I know you, of old.'

Once it has begun, her body remains inert throughout. She knew there would be no pleasure but nor is there any pain, nothing but a deathly numbness. This is how it must feel to drink off a bottle of poison: the flesh doomed, resigned, while the mind races. Is *this* the lethal moment after which there is no cure? Or *this*? Is infection already at work? *Feel the extent of my powers.* More than once Edmund mutters, 'Pisspot, bloody pisspot,' as if to render the connection as humiliating as possible. He himself, for all his huffing and pushing, appears to find little delight in it – precious few of Mama's *voluptuous sensations* – but at last he reaches the limits set by Nature.

'Cold,' he says, withdrawing his body from hers without any pretence of a caress. 'A cold, dirty little bitch.'

Hearing what she supposes to be her cue to beg and plead, Sophia remains silent.

'No man can be expected to sleep in a bog-house,' says her husband. Sophia would like to shrug, but does not dare; instead, she pictures her face as a wax mask, expressionless and colourless, except, of course, where he has hit her.

'I shall give orders for a new bed,' Edmund goes on. 'You may keep the old. Should I require your services, Madam, I advise you not to repeat that trick.'

He rises and begins to dress.

26

Fortunate starts awake. Was somebody shouting? Shouting and standing by his bed . . . He opens his eyes as little as possible, peeping between his eyelashes: before him is the familiar attic wall and the faint square of the window. After a while he raises himself on one elbow. He can just make out his soiled shirt and stockings lying over the chair and beneath them, keeping them company, his shoes.

Perhaps he himself called out in his sleep.

A bird frets on a nearby roof. In his village, at this time of morning, thousands of birds cry out together as the world is flooded with pink and green and gold. Creatures on every side, for many miles, pour their voices into a sea of song on which the village floats. If he was a grown man, he thinks, and had a woman, he would take her then, while that sea was rising.

Meanwhile there is Dog Eye and his pinched wife. Fortunate slides down into the bed again. Last night, fearful of her anger, he waited at the door until very late. He hoped that Dog Eye, who was out of the house, would return and dismiss him, but nobody came and Fortunate was shaking with fatigue by the time Eliza found him there. Eliza said the Mistress was in bed. She had made a mistake, and would not wish him to stay any longer. But Fortunate, though he went to his attic and lay down, was not so sure and half expected Mrs Dog Eye to rise from her bed and creep downstairs in order to catch him out.

There it is again: a cry, seemingly from under his bed. He rolls from under the sheet and kneels, ear to the ground. He already knows whom he expects to hear: below him lies the best bedroom, occupied by the master and mistress of the house.

It is the Wife who is crying, or rather uttering an indistinct string of sound varied by shouts and sobs. Now Dog Eye speaks, and Fortunate strains to catch the words. Something hard smashes against a wall. The Wife screams. Fortunate sits back on his heels.

A tapping: someone is outside his chamber. 'Titus!' a woman hisses. 'Titus, are you awake?'

A streak of light can be seen along the bottom of the door. Straightening his nightgown, Fortunate goes to unfasten the latch. Outside stands Mrs Launey, frizzled grey hair escaping from her cap, and behind her Fan, holding a lamp. Only after greeting these two does he see Eliza, hovering at the back. The women file into the room. Fan sets down her lamp on the sill where it lights up Fortunate's jerry, standing unconcealed next to the bed. Eliza nudges the jerry out of sight with her foot.

'Listen out, then,' urges Mrs Launey. The young women drop down as Fortunate himself did just a few minutes earlier, each pressing an ear to the floorboards, while the cook, who is plumper and appears, from her strange shape, not to have laced her stays, sits on Fortunate's bed and lays a finger across her lips.

'Ah!' The women on the floor breathe in sharply, both together.

'The brute!' Eliza murmurs.

'I reckon he's milling her,' says Fan.

'Cursed if I'd let a man take his fists to me.'

'When you marry,' says the cook, 'you'll find you've precious little say in the matter.'

'I wouldn't provoke him, at any rate,' retorts Eliza, straightening up. 'She *provokes*. Went to bed last night and left Titus asleep in his shoes, ask Fan if you don't believe me. If not for me he'd be standing yet.'

'Why'd she do that?'

'Forgot him.'

'Not provocation, then,' he hears Fan murmur. Eliza bends down again to the floor. Fortunate wonders if he will be able to get back into his warm bed but the cook shows no inclination to move so he puts on his coat over his nightgown. He has a pressing need to fart.

'Well?' asks the cook after a while.

The younger women exchange curious looks.

'*Well?*'

Fan shakes her head. Again the maids settle down into listening. Fortunate clenches his buttocks.

'I think they're making up,' Eliza says with a snigger.

'Then you've no business to listen,' says the cook, rising from the bed and pulling her by the arm.

'I'm only making sure.'

Fan straightens herself. 'It's sure enough. You won't tell, will you, Titus? You'd get us into terrible trouble.'

'Yourself too,' says the cook, puffing herself up and looking stern. 'Yourself worst of all.'

'Nothing, nothing,' says Fortunate, wishing he had pretended to be asleep instead of opening the door.

'I suppose I can take up the chocolate in a bit,' Fan says to the cook.

'When it's made.' Mrs Launey steers the younger women out of the room, one on each arm. 'You, Titus, time you were up.'

When they are gone Fortunate looks sadly at his bed. The warmth will be gone from it now. He farts, washes his face and begins pulling on his uncomfortable clothes.

'Your chocolate, Madam.'

Only a servant can smirk in quite that way. Only a servant would wish to, or would give off that precise air of mingled curiosity, pity and spite: it is Bath all over again. When Fan has gone, Sophia goes to the closet and pushes open the door. There lies the tortoiseshell mirror, its glass cracked and its handle broken off short. Even if repaired, it will never be the same: she will never be able to see it, now, without remembering this hateful scene. Nevertheless she takes up the mirror, cradling it in her hand, then raises it to the level of her face.

Having examined herself since rising, she already knows what awaits her. The left side of her face is swollen, her eyes crumpled and pink. The conviction rushes upon her that she has the face of a potato. In the whole of England, could there be found a plainer countenance? Useless, at moments such as these, to remind herself that Miss Beeston (now Mrs de Tronc) has a wasted arm, or Mrs Tench (*née* Balmayne) no ankles. These flaws are without importance, since both ladies are said to be loved and respected by their spouses. It is all the difference in the world.

Edmund is no such loving husband. He is dissolute and dishonest, piling up secrets of which the very imagination sickens her. Absurd to appeal for frankness, for integrity, between husband and wife: there will be more, always more, to uncover. Oh, to be back on the lake with him! How differently she would perceive his compliments and smiles!

Was there never a chance that things might have been otherwise? This thought is a torment to Sophia. Despite recent revelations, she remains, even now, unable to rid herself of a torturing doubt: had she been a more attaching female, sprightlier, given to piquant observations, endowed with beauty, blessed with perfect health, might she have charmed him into casting off his bad habits, and thus proved his redemptrix as well as her own? Many a bad man has been reclaimed by a good wife. Everybody says so. But Sophia has failed utterly and is more deficient, therefore, than either Mrs Tench or Mrs de Tronc. She is a mere vegetable, scarcely qualified to be one of the Sex.

If Mama were here . . . When Sophia was a girl, anxious beneath the scrutiny of gentlemen who might or might not declare themselves suitors, Mama would come to her before each social ordeal and stroke her brow. 'There,' she would say, 'perfect!' and present the maid with sixpence 'for arranging Miss Sophy's hair so very becomingly'. If Mama were here now, she would perhaps take Sophia in her arms. 'You have not your equal for miles around,' she would say, 'and Edmund knows it. Naturally your eyes are a little pink after a disagreement, with that sensitive skin! Who else has a complexion as delicate as yours?'

In the past, such maternal faith in her would have provided all the moral stiffening necessary, but Sophia, grateful as she will ever be for Mama's tenderness, has begun to doubt her wisdom. Having been put upon her wits lately, she has taken to making independent observations and has discovered, among other things, that although ladies set great store by the refinement of the complexion, gentlemen are not much swayed by it. Mama it was, also, who always insisted the *weakness* would heal with time. In this, and in other matters – such as leaving Edmund in ignorance of his bride's condition, while allowing the bride to believe otherwise – Sophia is forced to admit that Mama's judgement has proved sadly at fault. As for how to proceed after purposely soiling the marital bed with one's husband in it, such a question might perplex Mrs Delany herself.

The bedcurtains are drawn as if to conceal her sleeping spouse. Though Fan brought up two cups, as usual, Sophia observed that the maid avoided looking at the bed.

The girl *knows*.

Her chocolate is growing cold. She carries it with her to the window and stands looking down upon a street already full of hurrying people. I would change my lot with any one of you, thinks Sophia, and then reproaches herself: is she not fortunate, even now, compared with the twisted crone limping along on the far pavement? God places us in our stations and devises our trials, tempering the wind to the shorn lamb.

Edmund will have a new bed, well and good. Where does he intend to sleep until it is finished? With luck, pride will compel him to purchase one ready-made, and have it delivered directly. In the meantime, how is she to evade him? There is something perverse in his nature, something that recoils from her yet will not let her alone.

Is he trying to get her with child? A beloved infant would give him a powerful hold over both her and her parents: at the least displeasure, he could threaten to take the little one away. Her continuing resistance, then, is a question of great importance, to which she must give serious thought.

Yet even in the act of grappling with it she is distracted, forced to concern herself with all that other business. Her scrutiny of the contents of Edmund's desk was enough to show that he has made away with money or, at least, neglected to acknowledge its receipt. He has meddled with her letters to Mama and Papa, and gone so far as to substitute compositions of his own. It is an extraordinary thing to contemplate. Are the servants his confederates in that also? Lord! To think of herself snared like poor Clarissa Harlowe, surrounded by false friends – though if that be the case, the servants have performed their parts wretchedly, for she trusts none of them.

No: no domestic has duped her into misplaced confidences, and that is some comfort. She has kept her own counsel throughout, and – setting aside this morning's desperate shift – her dignity. As she contemplates her condition, it is borne in upon her that for an innocent and friendless lady, she has not, after all, done so badly. What folly, to fancy that a wife could reform such a creature as Edmund! The woman who could attempt it must possess dauntless courage, peerless virtue, the most entrancing beauty, the patience of Griselda, all the intellectual acuity of the one sex and the tenderest loyalty and devotion of the other. Which is to say, such a woman does not exist.

Since Edmund is not here she may as well drink his chocolate along with her own. As she sips at it, with a sense of having merited this small indulgence, a course of action presents itself. Papa may be about to send more money; if so, he must be prevented.

Fan, when rung for, reappears with unusual briskness – for all the world as if she has been lurking about the corridors – and an inquisitive, impertinent look. Sophia cannot judge whether the impertinence is deliberate insult or unwitting honesty: perhaps Fan is merely a bad actress.

'Help me dress,' Sophia says.

She cannot fault Fan in this duty: the maid is deft and painstaking. Even so, Sophia has to master a sharp revulsion at the touch of her fingers. She studies Fan's reflection in the closet mirror. The girl's pale skin is not unlike her own – one would wager that even as a nursling, Fan never had pink cheeks – but then her hair forms a pleasing contrast. Lack of contrast is a sad fault in Sophia's countenance. Fan has dark blue eyes, the brows curved as if in mockery; her nose is tip-tilted and it is these features, Sophia realises with surprise, that give her an expression of impudent amusement: do as she will, Fan cannot look otherwise. There is nothing impudent, however, about her mouth. It is a rose petal, a mouth made for kissing. Where once Sophia had utter faith in her husband, she now finds it impossible not to speculate on his dealings with the maidservants. So it is: one takes on the moral hue of one's companions.

Dressed and with her hair tolerably arranged, Sophia goes with some trepidation to Edmund's study, the door of which stands open. His desk appears just as she left it. She is tempted to enquire of the servants as to his whereabouts, but that would be at best a lowering of herself, at worst disastrous. Instead, she returns to her chamber and sits motionless awhile, thinking, before rising to fetch her pen.

My dearest Father and Mother,

Before you read further, I must beg that you will do nothing in haste as a result of reading this letter. I urge this lest natural indignation should overwhelm your judgement. Pray take time to consider. Consult with one another and with Mr Scrope. Above all, do not reply to me as affection might dictate since I am not mistress of my own correspondence.

I have not time to explain all, but trust to your faith in me and your knowledge of my character. You know that even as a young girl I was never given to vapouring and exaggeration, but ever sober, discreet and rational.

It is with regret that I inform you that Edmund is a dishonest, dissolute man. I believe him to be reading my correspondence, concealing letters from my family and even forging replies in my name; he has in his possession a sunflower seal exactly like my own. Did you, Papa, receive a letter in which I wrote of a visit to Ranelagh? If so, it was a brazen invention. I have never been at Ranelagh, nor have I ever urged you to repose more trust in Edmund, as one of your letters to me seems to indicate.

I also understand that Edmund has failed to acknowledge receipt of monies. Were I you, my dear parents, I should send nothing more and repose no faith in any document produced by my husband unless backed by a man personally known to you and of proven shrewdness and integrity. Be sure he possesses both qualities: integrity alone will not suffice.

As if this were not enough, I suspect Edmund of keeping a mistress. He certainly conducts correspondences calculated to disgust any well-formed mind.

I shall put this into the Receiving House at the Three

Castles, Marybone. Reply to me there. Though for the sake of appearance you must, if you please, continue to write to me at home, be sure to make no mention of any of this.

    Your unhappy

    Sophy

27

Betsy-Ann shakes out her bag of wipers onto the floor, taking stock and tutting: some of these patterns are going out of fashion, even among the poor. She begins to pick out the worst, then tumbles them all back into the bag and tosses it aside. Look here! She unwraps a watch, winds it and listens to its calm, measured tick, regular as music, as rich people's lives. Somebody risked a ride on the three-legged mare to lift this and she herself paid a good price. So why leave it here, going to waste?

'I don't know, I'm sure,' Betsy-Ann says aloud. She lays the watch back with the rest and stands, arms hanging at her sides, staring at the dingy walls of her hidey-hole. Someone else used it before her: there's a tally marked on the plaster, first fourpence a week, then fourpence-halfpenny. For what?

She used to turn a tidy profit. Still could, if she wished. She's never precisely let it go, never come to what you might call a decision; she's merely grown sick of it. Too much haggling, what with the buyers and the sellers, and then the trudge through the city with her bottles, the other articles tucked underneath. The lightning always sells, at least. Some things never go out of fashion.

There was a time she couldn't call her arse her own, when she'd have got down on her marrowbones and prayed for a snug little ken like this and a cart to flog goods from, yet Sam Shiner's managed to sour it all. She'd a bellyful of *him* even before she met up with Ned again, and now what's Sam playing at, to stay away so long? She'd wager a guinea he's not coming home, not ever – that he's Harry's man now, body and soul – except that he's got a knack of turning up when least expected. It's an instinct, the sharp's instinct for catching you off guard. Unless Ned opens his arms and his purse, she's not about to pack her box and walk out of the door, for fear of meeting Shiner, coming in. And a fine rumpus there'd be then!

She sees now how foolish it was, telling him she could always find the rent: he's taken her at her word. If she'd trusted him entirely she'd be in Queer Street, but Betsy-Ann Blore, thank Christ, is not such a daisy. At the side of the hearth there's a loose board she can pry up and underneath (not in the Eye, that's the first place he'd look) she's stashed about thirty guineas, all taken from Sam, a bit here, a bit there. Thirty, and he's not even noticed: the resurrectionists must be coining it. And you have to ask yourself, after that: Where's the rest going?

He's boozing away every penny or he's set up a new woman. Or both.

She comes out of the Eye, closing it with care so that the edge doesn't show. On the table stands a bottle of ratafia, brought this morning by a boy she'd never seen and isn't likely to see again. There's a card tied round the neck, with writing. It's a ticklish business, not knowing what might be on there, to ask someone else to read it for her.

The name always comes last, she knows that much. With scissors she snips away the final word of the message, trimming the card evenly to disguise the cut, then goes to the door.

'Liz? Liz!'

The stairs yawn beneath her, swallowing up the light. She's about to go in again when she hears a shuffle of feet and the crone's laboured, whistling breath. Liz hasn't enough puff to climb and talk at the same time.

'Up here, if you please,' says Betsy-Ann, who can now pick out a patch of shadow approaching from below. Though familiar, the woman's wheeze disturbs her; it's as though she herself can't breathe freely as long as she's aware of it.

'Mrs Shiner,' gasps Liz, emerging from the darkness. 'You want some lightning. Perhaps.'

'Not today,' says Betsy-Ann. 'Here, Liz, you can read, can't you?' Too late, it comes to her that she could have asked this before the woman dragged herself upstairs.

'My man. Taught me.' Liz flashes a hideous smile from between grey lips.

'Come in, Liz. You was spliced, eh?'

'Oh, yes. Sixteen years and more.'

'Kinchins?'

Liz shakes her head. 'All the boys was took, and then my husband was took.'

'God bless their souls,' Betsy-Ann rattles off. 'What about girls, Liz? Got any daughters?'

But Liz doesn't seem interested in daughters. She's looking round the room as if to spy something out. Betsy-Ann can guess what's next, and sure enough, it comes: 'How's Mister Shiner keeping? He well?'

'Thriving, thriving. Sit down a minute, get your breath,' Betsy-Ann coaxes. 'I want you to read something for me.'

'And you, Mrs Shiner, did you never "sprain your ankle", eh?'

'No, never.'

Only once did she get a bellyful and that was lost; it came before its time, a stunted rat of a thing, one day when Sam was out. Betsy-Ann hadn't even told him she was in the family way: she couldn't have endured his preening and pawing. She kept the wizened creature, bound up in a shawl, inside the Eye until she could find opportunity to drop it in an alleyway. She'd no wish to be tied to a bantling, not in her line of work, it would only be a clog hung on her. Yet afterwards, there was a sadness she hadn't looked for.

Liz coughs again, spraying the table with saliva. Betsy-Ann wipes away the flecks with her apron.

'Can you read this, Liz?'

The old woman holds the card at arm's length and squints at it. 'Maddox. Six o'clock. In a chair.'

'Maddox? I don't know any Maddox.' Unless Ned is teasing her, writing to her under a different name? But what's this about a chair? Sitting in a chair?

'I will settle all,' Liz says.

Betsy-Ann stares blankly at her.

'On the back.' Liz taps the card. '*I will settle all*, it says.'

'Maddox.' Betsy-Ann frowns, then fetches two glasses from the mantelpiece. 'Take a drop with me?'

A rich scent like that of Bakewell tart fills the room, sending Betsy-Ann straight back to Kitty's parlour.

The old woman's eyes glisten. 'O, my! Does you good to smell that!'

'Did you never taste it?'

Liz shakes her head.

'Ratafia,' says Betsy-Ann, pushing the glass towards her. She watches the scrawny throat rise and fall.

'It's very good, Missus.' Liz looks again at the card. 'He makes his M like an H.'

He? Betsy-Ann's stomach tightens. A very small word – *Ned*, say – spilt from Liz's grey lips at the wrong moment, and Sam Shiner might come awake in a way altogether to be reckoned with.

'A cove, is it? How'd you know?'

'A woman writes more finicky.'

'Ah . . . He makes the what?'

'M like an H. Maddox looks like Haddox.'

'Haddox. Six o'clock.'

'Is he sending you fish?'

'In a chair? A sedan chair, could be?' She pictures the chair-men's disgusted faces and in laughing it comes to her: Haddock's Bagnio.

'It's a puzzle,' she tells Liz, refilling the glasses. 'Never mind, here's to good cheer and good neighbours.'

'May we ever have both,' says Liz, who looks as if she's never had either. When she has finished her drink she shuffles her way downstairs, hugging the banister as she might hang on to a boon companion. Shutting her out, Betsy-Ann takes another swig of ratafia and leans back against the door, lost in remembrance.

'In your bagnios the cry is all for ratafia. Nothing is so eagerly sought after, or brings to such a perfection of enjoyment.'

The Mother's voice had been compared, by some sentimental sot, to the sweetness of the harpsichord. Her girls, better acquainted with the screeching end of her tongue, seized every opportunity to jeer this notion, yet there was something in it: Kitty's speech could charm the surliest culls, including the one seated opposite. Betsy-Ann herself could do nothing with him, but his frown had softened the instant Kitty began to speak. Possibly he was a fellow of a musical turn in whose mind Kitty figured as a kind of speaking harp, as in the story of Jack the Giant Killer, fitted out with a woman's head and bubbies.

'Its benefits are so well understood in those elegant establishments that nobody now questions them,' Kitty continued. To Betsy-Ann, perpetually hungry, her purring suggested not music but cream and sugar and eggs and wine, beaten up with spices into a thick, intoxicating draught. 'I confess myself surprised you should find ratafia at all out of the ordinary, but perhaps,' the voice was now shading into a rich, deep caramel, 'it is a thing out of your experience. In which case, you are to be envied, as having the most delicious discoveries to make.'

The cull, who a few minutes earlier had been about as gentle as a prison door, was already dissolving in the flood of sweetness unleashed upon him. Despite Kitty's show of surprise, he was to her that stalest of things, the timid fool wishing to be a dog upon the town, yet shocked – as well he might be – by the price of ratafia. The women, understanding all this as if he had shouted it from the rooftop, waited while he went through the usual calculations.

He said, 'The girl may have it and welcome' (Betsy-Ann lecherously licked her lips to show the wisdom of his decision) 'but for myself, I find the taste perfectly nauseous.'

He thought he'd got himself out of it. Poor fellow! So far Kitty had only been sparring; now she closed with him in earnest.

'Most gentlemen are of your opinion, at first, but with a little experiment, a little experience, they come to appreciate its benefits.' She turned on her prey the smile which, along with the voice (and other less mentionable talents) had made *Hartry* one of the most celebrated names of her day. 'Ratafia, Sir, is an inestimable boon to the male sex. Let a lady partake of a glass or two and she is pleasantly warmed and *tickled*, you might say.' She bent towards the man and murmured confidingly into his ear. 'That, in itself, is such an incalculable advantage to her lover that sometimes' (a plaintive sigh) 'I quite accuse myself of treachery towards the Sex, for so rigging the odds in the gentleman's favour.' Not even the stupidest cull could be expected to swallow this and Kitty did not intend it; her face, dimpling with wicked wit, invited anyone who heard her to share her in the joke. 'But Sir, a lover wise enough to join with his lady, and partake of a glass or two, profits ten times more. The refreshment cheers – strengthens – fills him with courage for the amorous combat. The mature devotee of pleasure finds himself flush and sturdy with regenerated youth. As a certain lord said to me the other day, 'O Mrs Kitty! I haven't ridden so long and hard since I was sixteen!' – and his lordship is seventy-two.'

'I'm sure it's of the greatest service to him. But if I may speak, Madam —'

Kitty cut him off. 'None of the *cognoscenti* would omit to take a glass or two. Why, Sir, they consider it as indispensable as rum before a naval battle – and you know, Sir, our navy is the terror of the world.'

Surely this must settle the business; but no, the man stared down at the carpet and would not be budged. Betsy-Ann perceived, by a hardening line at the edge of Kitty's mouth, that her employer was almost out of patience (a commodity in which she was never overstocked), and indeed, at this instant Kitty made a furtive sign to someone nearby. At the same time she began urging loudly, so that others could hear: 'My dear Sir, consider what you are about! You make yourself too ridiculous. You may *shop-keep* all the rest of the year, if you must, but a debauch is not a time to pinch and scrape.'

As many a plucked heir knows to his sorrow, it is easier to shame a man into extravagance than into virtue. Though he continued to study the floor, the quarry's cheeks grew hot. 'Ratafia may be of benefit for *elderly* gentlemen but in my case – at least, I am not aware —'

A big-built young buck, already stripped to the waist by a girl who was clinging to him and fiercely kissing his chest, appeared to have been listening to the lecture, for at this moment he interrupted.

'If I don't mistake, Sir, you were speaking of ratafia.'

The cull did not reply, so Betsy-Ann put in innocently, 'Why, yes, Sir. Do you care for the drink?'

'Worth a hundred pounds a glass. Puts a prick on a man like the town bull.'

The cull looked up.

'Don't *you* take no more though, John,' pouted the nymph, 'or you'll be needing two of us,' and she tugged jealously at his arm, as if unable to spare him even long enough for such brief talk. The young man shrugged amiably, as if to say *Such is the penalty for possessing such attractions as mine*, as she pulled him away and up the gilded staircase to Kitty's private rooms.

'You seem thoughtful, Sir,' remarked Kitty. 'You have perhaps seen that gentleman before?'

'Yes, indeed,' said the cull wonderingly. 'Going upstairs with that girl, there —' He pointed to another whore and broke off, harpooned by envy.

Betsy-Ann found it hard not to laugh. Men were so green! Only see this booby, who couldn't spy out something as plain as the nose on his face: the whores were under instructions to dote on John, an out-of-work footman hired by the day; tomorrow there would be George, another rented Adonis with a supposed passion for ratafia. These men went upstairs with one girl after another, hour after hour; once upstairs, they stretched out and smoked while the whore in question rested and perhaps had a wash. Not even John's good timing (for he had, of course, been on the watch for Kitty's signal) had awoken the suspicions of the wretched flat. He could only think that the handsome young fellow was mighty as a stallion, while he, twenty years older, was not availing himself of all possible advantages.

This last shift of Kitty's proved decisive: two bottles were purchased. Should the fool come to his senses while upstairs and grow as limp as his empty purse, Betsy-Ann would find ways. Later she would exclaim in amazement, finding him 'monstrous strong' for a man of his age, indeed, almost more than she could cope with.

Kitty smiled benignly and drifted away, surveying her realm. Even Betsy-Ann, whose skin stiffened every time she looked at the woman, had to respect her abilities. Appearing to carry off everything by sheer charm, Kitty was as practised a strategist as any Admiral of the Fleet. Every establishment of this type employed bullybacks to keep order, but Kitty went one further. She kept men whose constant task it was to spark jealousy and emulation: not only the athletic John and George, but fellows who appeared to bespeak suppers (at exorbitant rates) for the most beautiful whores and in return were publicly distinguished by doting caresses. There were also 'hollow legs' able to put away stupendous amounts of drink, and sharps who laid odds not only on cards, but on certain acrobatic games played in the parlour. All of these instructors combined to bankrupt, by their example, a great many fools. The experienced Corinthians knew who they were and what they were about; the naïve, particularly the young fry eager to compete in debauchery, were swept into the net.

The profit on ratafia being scandalous, Kitty's whores naturally took nothing else. Betsy-Ann, who had an unforced partiality to the drink, did everything she could to get a glass or two down her cullies: it did nothing for their pricks, but was a useful sweetener of the breath.

A gift of ratafia, an invitation to Haddock's: each a brazen call to pleasure, to the inventive and delicious vices of the Age. Betsy-Ann flatters herself she is woman enough to answer the call. Mr Shiner has departed. Long live Mr Hartry.

28

There are disadvantages to being waited on by domestics. One is that (as Sophia discovered during her honeymoon) they are liable to overhear what they should not. Another is the impossibility, even with no servant in attendance, of going out unobserved.

She has tried walking alone and has found the experience beyond anything she endured in Bath, so disagreeable indeed as to be almost impossible. On first arrival, she persuaded herself that such was the nature of town life. London is not like the countryside, where a lady travelling within her own district can expect to be recognised and looked up to. Life here is teeming and anonymous. The most infamous women go lavishly caparisoned and keep carriages, so that even the practised eye can scarcely distinguish virtue from vice. It follows that all females, even the most respectable, are subjected to advances from guttersnipes and even from men – she will not call them gentlemen – of family who have sunk and degraded themselves.

Such was her understanding a few weeks ago. Now she has come to a conclusion yet more distressing: while females anywhere in London may be exposed to casual insult, it would appear that the Zedlands inhabit a peculiarly unpleasant district. Impossible to imagine a gentleman of any delicacy wishing to live here, let alone bring home a bride. She wonders, not for the first time, if the house really belongs to Edmund. He has lied about so much, why not about that?

Not wishing to go alone to the Receiving House, she has ordered Titus to accompany her on her walk. It is high time he was let go and an English boy obtained in his place, but there is a use for everything and on this occasion Fan, with her sharp eyes and quick understanding, would never do. If only she had a footman! It was understood that a brace of them would be engaged but then Edmund said it was not worthwhile for such a short stay. Nothing, it seems, is worthwhile: engaging proper staff, decorating the house, inviting her parents have all been repeatedly put off.

So they progress along the pavements, first the mistress, then Titus. Sophia keeps her eyes downturned and clasps her bag in both hands, crossed over her stomach. Despite the awkward gait thus produced, she prefers to keep her arms in front, never allowing them to approach her sides, lest some brute should imagine she is twitching up the edge of her gown.

Gazing downwards is both tedious and uncomfortable, especially when one has been bred to hold up one's head. From time to time she is absolutely obliged to ask directions, lowering her voice in the hope that Titus will not understand. Even that proves mortifying: one young man shies away from her as if fearing to be accosted.

The humiliation of this last incident is still rankling in her when she at last spies her destination. Across the road is a large, comfortable-looking inn, its façade gilded by fragile sunshine. The picture thus presented has a certain old-fashioned charm.

It is the first time she has consciously approved anything in London and at the realisation Sophia suffers a pang. Everybody who can afford to spends time in this city: with a loving husband, she too would surely have come to relish it. She could defy the smoke, the relentless noise, the foul odours, even the improprieties enacted upon the streets, had Edmund only been what he ought, and her home a place of safety.

'Stay here,' she tells Titus before dodging the traffic and entering the inn where her business is swiftly transacted. The letter to Papa and Mama changes hands, vanishes, has already begun the first stage of its journey. When she comes out, Titus is lolling against a wall opposite, looking as stupid as ever.

'Where'd she go, then?' demands Mrs Launey.

'From here,' says Fortunate. 'Then along, and along.'

'Lord,' she mutters in exasperation.

'There was a corner.' He tries to remember something nearby. 'An inn. She said wait outside.'

The cook rolls her eyes. 'And did this inn have a name, Snowball?'

'A Receiving House,' says Eliza. 'She went to a Receiving House! Am I right, Titus?'

He shrugs.

Fan says, 'How d'you make that out, Liza?'

'She had a letter she didn't want him to see.'

'It could be, indeed,' Fan says to the cook. 'Why else would she leave him outside?'

'A rendezvous?'

Fan shakes her head. 'She was only there a minute. My money's on a correspondence.'

Eliza hops up and down, as if delighted with her own cleverness.

'I don't pretend to understand half of what goes on,' the cook complains. 'He's out so much it's not worth cooking him a supper.'

Fortunate suggests, 'Ask Mrs when her husband shall be home.'

All three women laugh together. Mrs Launey says, 'I tell you what, why don't *you* ask her?' and they laugh again.

He thinks, I will never understand these people. He feels something brush against his coat, then a gentle pinch at his right buttock: Eliza. He stares in disbelief but she only smiles and winks.

'Not the *very* best room in the house,' says Ned, lying outstretched on the bed, 'but I trust you'll be comfortable.' He waves his arm towards the mirror over the fireplace, a forest of silver candlesticks framed within its glittering borders. The waft of beeswax mingles with the scent of apple logs.

'I thought it was always coal in town,' she says wonderingly.

'These smell sweeter. Or shall I ring for coal?'

'O, no! Leave them.'

Burning apple wood: a memory of a place long gone, a lost field, grass sloping down to the hedge and a calf lowing in the night.

In the far corner, away from the fire, stands a marble table holding refreshments. Until now, the seraglio formed Betsy-Ann's idea of stylish debauchery, but this is several cuts above Kitty's.

'Who's got the best chambers, then?' she says, flinging herself down next to him.

'His Majesty and his dear friend John Wilkes, how should I know?' He laughs. 'Now *that'd* be worth seeing. You've heard of Wilkes, Betsy?'

'O, yes! Everybody says he's for the people.'

'For Woman, undoubtedly, though he's ugly as Satan – why *is* that, my sweet?'

'What?'

'Why is your sex so forgiving of ugliness? It pains me to see Beauty kissing a toad, even a toad as witty as Wilkes.'

'That's your vanity, Ned,' Betsy-Ann says, teasing. 'Any woman would wish to meet the celebrated Mr Wilkes.'

'Humph! Not Mrs Zedland, I assure you.'

'Is it true he's in France?'

'He didn't take me into his confidence. One thing I do know – he's safer away from here.'

The bolster has been polished with an iron. 'Starched,' Betsy-Ann says, nuzzling into it. 'Is there really a bath?'

'I believe there's a tub somewhere. So, we like the treat?' murmurs Ned, rolling over towards her.

She always forgets how big his mouth is. You wouldn't think so to look at him, but he has the jaws of a wolf, ready to swallow her entire. She doesn't dislike that thought.

'Naked,' she suggests. 'In the linen. Lie back, my lord. Allow me.'

'My lord, is it?'

She pulls back the bedcovers and helps him off with his waistcoat, untucking his shirt and sliding it over his head. He unfastens the breeches, wriggling out of them. Betsy-Ann pushes him back onto the bed. His skin: his fine skin. She runs her hands over him until he's tight and trembling as a stringed bow.

She takes her time in undressing. When she is naked she lies down beside him again, pulls the sheet across and feels it close over her, cool and inviting.

'Don't do that, Betsy. Let me see you.'

She reaches across to frig him and he pushes away the linen.

'Up – all fours.'

He throws himself onto her so hard that the bed shakes. They are dog and bitch, furious. It takes all her strength not to be pressed into the mattress.

'When did you last see him?' he enquires later, sitting up in bed over a dish of chicken in white sauce.

'A good while since. You wouldn't know him, Ned.'

'Is he so changed?'

'Not to look at. But he's not the man you remember.'

'I should damn well think not. A resurrectionist!' He makes a disgusted face. 'Tell me, Betsy, does he ever ask about me?'

She laughs. 'Why should he?

'O, I don't know – old companions.'

'He hardly talks about anything, hardly comes home even —'

'All the better for us —'

'And when he does, he's reeking.'

Ned feels for a chicken bone between his teeth. 'How does he stand it, Betsy?' he says in a voice of unfeigned wonder. 'How *does* he stand it?'

Betsy-Ann holds out a spoonful to him. 'You should ask how I stand it.'

'That I already know.' Ignoring the proffered spoon, he kisses down her neck to her left breast, little feathery kisses. 'Under here beats the heart of a lion. And here,' he tickles between her legs, 'the cunt of a lioness. A biter.'

She wriggles at the feel of his hand. 'For Sammy, I can tell you in a word – nantz.'

'Was it nantz that lost him his finger?'

'O, no! He hired a bully to squeeze the flats —'

'And did he?'

'Like oranges.'

'There you are, ' says Ned. 'Exemplary. O my dear brethren in Christ, only see what a man may become by diligent labour. Would that we were all like this admirable fellow, able to wring gold from a bankrupt. But what of the finger, the moral of our sermon? Pray point out the finger.'

'Morson – that was the bully – got fuddled and let a man go.'

'Tsk, tsk! And what said the Honourable Samuel to this?'

'Threw drink in his eyes.'

'And got himself docked.' Ned looks thoughtful. 'Well. Could've been worse.'

'For a gamester? For Christ's sake, Ned!'

'True, my dove. What became of Mister Morson?'

'Took the King's Shilling.'

'But naturally. A butcher born.'

'And dead and buried, I hope! Though it's no good to Sam. Sometimes I think – I think I brought him bad luck.' She flushes. Up to now she has never put such thoughts into words, even to herself; if ever her mind began wandering that way, she hauled on the reins and turned it aside.

Ned gives an incredulous laugh. 'Nonsense, Mrs Betsy! You're his *good* fortune.'

'I once thought so.'

'But not now? Isn't he kind to you?'

'Not like at first.'

'Kind enough, though, hey?' When she doesn't answer, he takes her by the chin and tilts her face until she's looking into his eyes. 'He doesn't beat you?'

'He couldn't if he tried. He's sodden.'

'With such an intolerable trade, he'd need to be. If a man may be so impertinent as to ask, why did he take it up? Even without a finger, I'd have thought Sammy could do better for himself.'

She sighs. 'Harry lost one of the crew. He thought Sam'd be more trusty, see, on account of being with me.'

'Any man of sense would.'

Ned strokes her cheek. She loves it when he talks like this: as if it matters what happens to Betsy-Ann Blore when Ned Hartry isn't with her. Such sweetness never lasts. Soon he'll be singing the old tune and Betsy-Ann left to get by, as usual.

'Better Harry than a stranger,' he's saying now. 'He'll look out for Sam.'

'Same way he looked out for me and Keshlie?' Betsy-Ann flashes back. 'I believe you know where we ended up.'

Ned frowns and stops stroking: a warning sign. Like others she's known, he prefers to think of whores as 'given up to love', as *Harris's* puts it, slaves to their passions, rather than to despair and Kitty Hartry.

In her early months in the seraglio she marvelled at this

blindness: how could a fellow who paid for every caress fancy himself desirable and desired? Later, she came to understand that fancy was in the very air of the place, was its bricks and mortar. More happens inside the skull than between the legs: a man would favour an ugly whore over Venus herself if she had but the face or voice to fit her for some private play inside his head. If you only had that, imagination did the rest.

There were others, stony-hearted culls who knew themselves unwanted and took delight in it. Kitty kept a list of such, supplied them with innocents – real or fake – and charged extra. She had rules to protect her property: these men were only to be catered for in certain rooms, with concealed doors that could be pushed aside and a member of the household on spyhole duty. The spies – said Lina Burch, an old hand at virginity – were sometimes slow in opening the door. It was even whispered a man could pay to have them dismissed entirely.

Yet here is Ned, knowing all this and utterly out of tune with his mother, still so much her son as to talk, on occasion, of 'love' between a sixteen-year-old rose and a pox-ridden gargoyle of sixty.

She'd better watch out. Mustn't cross him just now. She smiles and says, 'Well, I met you there, so I can't ever regret it, can I? For myself, I mean.' She has to add those last words because of Keshlie: a regret if ever there was one.

'A blessed chance for both of us,' Ned says, lowering the tray of food to the carpet and lying back in bed. 'Ride St George, there's a dear girl.'

She does so, squeezing him inside her, holding him tight and snug. He loves the woman on top, says he can get in deeper that way.

He gives a curious sigh, half pleasure, half regret. 'I wish I could do you good.'

'But you do, Ned.'

'Should you be in need – real need, but you understand that Betsy, you're a woman of sense – send word by the blackbird. He's mine entirely, can't stomach *her*.'

'And if I asked you to visit Sam?'

Ned cocks an eyebrow. It seems he's not willing to descend quite so low as a resurrectionist's ken.

Very well, let us enjoy what we have. She pulls away, slides against him, belly to belly, tongue in his mouth, in his ear, kissing his neck, stroking his chest, running her nails across his back. He's smooth and slippery as satin and oh, the smell of him. Knave of Hearts. She moves more slowly, more deeply, then faster. *Chink, chink*, from a dish tangled in the bedclothes. Ned stares at her body, arched and thrust towards him. He reaches forward and takes her titties between finger and thumb, pinching, teasing. She rides harder, nearly there, there. Pleasure breaks over her and she clenches and bucks under the force of it. Ned's hands tighten, expertly cruel.

During the hours of darkness they continue to talk, weaving in and out of sleep, touching, lying tumbled together and apart. Betsy-Ann is exhausted, hollowed out. She'd like to drop off entirely, the way she used to when in her own rooms – curl up, Ned curled round her, and wake with the two of them still folded together – but she's reluctant to waste these last few precious hours.

'You're thrown away on that sot,' says Ned towards morning. 'You should get yourself another keeper.'

Is it an opening? She hesitates before she ventures, 'Do you know a man who'd suit me?'

'I know one who'd love the position but he's no good to you, Betsy. There's still a creditor or two. Until all that's settled —' He presses a finger against her lips. After a moment he adds, as if to himself, 'And what a figure he cut, tied to his ma's purse-strings!'

She brushes his finger aside. 'Is he better off tied to a wife?'

'Of all ties that's the most damnably . . . damnable. It's a species of . . . of . . .'

He trails off. Betsy-Ann waits and waits but he seems to have fallen asleep. At last he mumbles, 'It can be done.'

At least, that's what she thinks he said, since her ears at once start up a stupid buzzing that means she can't trust them. Or was it, *can't be done?*

Perhaps she's dreaming.

Daylight. She's revelling in the luxuries of the toilet table – cold cream, toothpowder, rose cologne, comfits to freshen the breath, an ivory brush and comb – when he slaps down a sealed pack on its marble surface.

'What's this?' she says, turning. 'You're going out?'

'It's eleven, my sweet. At the private tables your industrious sharp is already up and tearing at the prey while Ned, like an idle 'prentice, puts pleasure before duty.' He laughs. 'As would any rational man. No, I'm not going out.'

'Are *we* playing, then?'

He bends to kiss the nape of her neck. 'For love, for love.'

Just as well: her stash, even had she brought it, would hardly suffice.

'Very well, but first help me lace my stays.'

'We'd only have to unlace them again. You can play in *déshabille*, surely? All the better to distract me with – you know the rig.'

Betsy-Ann brushes her hair and sprinkles it with cologne while Ned fetches the little card table from the far side of the room, setting it at a comfortable distance from the fire.

'Now,' he says, unsealing the cards. 'What shall it be?'

'A queer thing,' she observes, 'a sharp playing a sharp.'

'Novelty pleases. Come, your game.'

'If we was in company, I'd say Loo.'

'Loo? Where *have* you been, my dove?'

She blushes to think how near she was to wearing the little fawney with its inscription. 'Don't you remember we used to play sometimes? Catharine was fond of it, and Lina.'

'And I rode a hobby-horse – during the last Age. I beg to inform you that no person of fashion sits down to Loo, these days. It is most extremely decayed.'

'What, nobody at all?'

'Perhaps an old squaretoes, here and there – your booby squire, dining off a boiled ox, bones and all, with a dried pippin.' He begins to shuffle. 'And as you observed, we are not enough for Loo. Here, ask any card.'

'Pam.'

'Always your darling.'

So he hasn't quite forgotten. He is, indeed, always her darling.

No doubt about it, Ned does her credit. She watches him drop the cards like any cack-handed fool, then sweep them up, seemingly flustered.

'Bravo,' says Betsy-Ann, knowing not a picture will be out of place.

When she examines her hand, she laughs out loud: there is Pam's melancholy face gazing off into the distance, surrounded by a gallery of kings and queens. When Ned sets himself to please, he excels. It is like their best times together: the joys gathered beneath Kitty's nose, the more defiant days of Covent Garden.

He winks. 'I wager a pretty fellow has come to see you.'

'Pretty, aye, but he looks sulky.'

'That's because I've trained him to *my* hand,' he says, with a lewd grin. 'He's accustomed to find his pleasure there and nowhere else.'

He holds up his own cards. For each of her queens he holds in reserve a king, and for each king, an ace. It is, she sees, calculated to a hair's breadth. They abandon the game while Ned demonstrates the rig.

'Naturally a man can't beat Pam,' he observes with a wink, 'but once he's gone —'

'Here, give them to me.'

She lays aside the important cards, inserts them and tries the shuffle, Ned instructing her: take a grip with your thumb, it's this way not that way, hold the cards *so* and count off, one, two. She deals, asking Ned to hold up his cards. There he is: Pam, flanked by nobility and royalty. She checks her own, laying them on the table beside his. How could a flat, dealt these, understand that he held a losing hand? Not only would he be done to a turn, but he would surely blame himself.

'My own work, you know,' Ned says. 'An entirely new thing.'

'I never made up a rig in my life,' says Betsy-Ann, delighted.

'Am I good to you, my doe?'

She replies with a kiss.

'You know, I suppose, that a man can bring anyone he wishes to this place?'

She shrugs.

'But I don't wish,' Ned says. 'I don't frequent it. I came only for you.'

Betsy-Ann holds back the words, 'That's my eye,' but it seems he reads them in her expression, for he adds, 'Not a word of a lie, Mrs Betsy. I miss our old times.'

'Then it's a pity you —'

Ned holds up a hand. 'No need to remind me, I assure you.' He looks melancholy, and all the handsomer for it: a little goose would kneel before him, embrace his thighs and plead, *take me back, take me back.* He would recognise his cue, would raise her, take her in an embrace and promise never to part – what bliss! And what a blunder, since he's already warned her off, and since Ned pays court just as long as some part of the woman remains unconquered.

'I'm kept on short measure, these days,' he says. 'She thinks to raise her value by rationing.'

So she knows him that well already. Betsy-Ann supposes he wants to go back to bed and wonders if she has time to chew one of the sweet comfits when she realises that's not his game. 'Do you know, Betsy, I'm still in hock to Ma?'

Is he asking her to settle the score with Haddock's? She feels a twist of panic: she hasn't the readies for that sort of kindness and besides, it'd make her a fool.

'I thought your autem mort was a fortune?'

'Up to a point.'

'So you're not —'

'The truth, Betsy, is that from being saddled with one female, I've gone to being saddled with two. At least Ma is a beauty, or was before she sported so much blubber. That's more than you can say for Mrs Zed.' He's working up to something. Moving closer, he takes her hand between his. 'I can get free of the pair of them, if you . . .' He gives her the benefit of his most imploring expression. She guesses now what's coming and pulls her hand free, clenches her fists to keep him off —

'I can get away, my darling, if only you'll teach me the Spanish trick.'

Betsy-Ann looks down. He's too fly to snatch at her again, but his hands are clenched.

'With that rig, I can make a clean sweep. Tell Ma to kiss my arse.' His voice loses its edge, softens, grows more intimate. 'I can set you up again, my dove. Picture it. The two of us, just as we were.'

Paying the bagnio is nothing to this. The Spanish trick came from Mam; it's the one thing she's never shared. Giving him *that* would be like tearing the heart out of her breast. She stares at him, tears rising in her eyes, the elegant glitter all around dissolving into sodden misery like rain in clay country.

She says, 'I'll show you the bridge of cards —'

'A very pretty trick, indeed, but what I need is the Spanish.'

'I can't, Ned, you know I can't. My mother told me to —'

'Your feelings do you credit, love, but what difference can it make? Pardon my bluntness but your people are dead —'

'Harry's not.'

'Dear child, I'm not such a fool as to trumpet where it came from! What do you take me for?'

She isn't sure what she takes him for. It occurs to her that perhaps his 'treat' has been only for this, and Betsy-Ann Blore merely another Mrs Zedland. Not for the first time with Ned, she feels as if someone has stuck a shiv between her ribs; yet there sits her lover, those black diamonds of his shining with hope. No man ever looked less cunning than Ned at this moment. He could pass for a bridegroom, thinks Betsy-Ann, taking breakfast, with his new wife blushing with mingled shyness and delight at last night's discoveries. Even in debauchery there's always been something boyish about him.

She says, 'Harry would know, if he ever saw it used,' though Harry knows nothing of the trick, which passed from mother to daughter. Women have their secrets, as well as men.

'But how could he see it?' asks Ned, practised in the art of pushing others round the chessboard. 'He's not admitted to the establishments where I spread my net. Just think, my honey. Think how snug we'd be.'

'Aren't you forgetting Sam?'

'O, Sam!' He waves dismissively. 'The merest sot!'

'So you said before.' She fixes him with an accusing eye. 'Who was it begged me to stay with him? Your great understanding! Christ knows, I heard enough of it! In *honour*, you said, *in honour*.'

'How many times, child? I never thought he could win. It damn near broke my heart.'

Damn *near*, thinks Betsy-Ann. No more than that?

29

Before Sam Shiner was himself shorn by Morson, he and Ned often joined forces to shear those lambs who came wandering among the tables. Sam was celebrated among sharps for the extreme delicacy of his fingers, which impressed even Ned: 'Put a picture a hair's breadth out, he'll feel it.'

'Takes more than good fams,' said Betsy-Ann.

'True, and nothing is neglected. Shall I paint you the picture? There's Sam, in his wool, and me in lace. Not a glance between us, we haven't the pleasure of each other's acquaintance. The flats don't take to me.'

'Why?' asked Betsy-Ann, surprised. 'Surely you want —'

'I'm the bonnet, my dear. And I flatter myself I cover Sam tolerably well.'

'With what?'

'Prattle, mainly. A pound of prattle to an ounce of wit. They distrust me from the start, and never stop watching my hands.'

'While all the time Sam does the business.'

'He's his part to play, too – he's the Plain Man, pursing up his face at my sallies, as if to say, Who's this fopling? They consider him no end of an honest fellow.'

'And so between them both, you see, they licked the platter clean?'

'Dear Prodigy. How well you understand the world.'

Betsy-Ann liked the sound of this Shiner, but when Ned brought him to the rooms off Covent Garden, she drew back. Though Shiner would take nothing but small beer, his blue eyes clung so moistly that she felt them sticking on her skin.

'Your friend has a letch for me,' she informed Ned afterwards.

'He shows admirable discrimination.'

'*Admirable discrimination*! I'd call it slobbering, myself.'

He said lightly, 'How refined you've grown, my dear,' and Betsy-Ann's cheeks burned.

'You needn't fling it in my face, Ned.'

'Damme, my tongue's so sharp I cut myself sometimes.' He kissed her hand, bowing his head in a gesture of contrition. 'Shiner's susceptible to the Sex, that's all.'

'I don't like him.'

Ned shrugged. 'You needn't see him, except when he's with me.'

About the same time, letters started to arrive from Kitty. Ned would read them aloud. He had a sly knack of imitating his mother's voice, particularly its sudden shifts from dove-like cooing to the screech of an angry crow. Betsy-Ann laughed. She kept the laugh in her mouth even when Kitty offered Ned two beautiful sisters, though she saw it now: how clearly she saw it! Every whore in the parlour, a weapon in Kitty's hand.

Ned snorted – 'She forgets I've already seen the livestock' – and continued to read.

'Are they so dimber?' For the life of her Betsy-Ann couldn't help asking.

'Fishwives. Ma should keep her trash for *Harris's*.'

As the weeks passed and Kitty drew her purse-strings tighter, it became hard to obtain credit. Though the butcher and the vintner were the most insistent, all the tradesmen seemed to raise their snouts to the wind at once, sniffing out weakness and 'howling like a pack of wolves', as Ned put it. Betsy-Ann's bracelets were returned to the jeweller but the howls continued. People of means were beginning to decamp for the country, so that Sam and Ned, for all their talent and industry, sometimes found themselves without an opening. There came a month when, the meat bill being at last settled, Ned's winnings barely stretched to the rent on the rooms.

'I could entertain here, if you wished,' said Betsy-Ann. She needed all her courage to propose it, having forgotten neither Ned's jibe at her 'refinement' nor his mother's suggestion, in one letter, that she should earn their expenses on her back.

'If I wished!' Ned exclaimed. 'Pray, why did I take you out of Ma's place?'

'To have me to yourself.'

She would never say, 'To spare me.' Ned preferred not to reckon with the sufferings of the 'sweet criminals'. Nevertheless, his refusal did much to comfort her.

Sam Shiner, unlike the Corinthian, was a saving man, notable even among sharps for his watchfulness. He drank mostly beer and stayed away from disorderly houses, preferring to visit a lady in Long Acre on Sunday evenings. He paid two guineas for the entire night and (Ned told Betsy-Ann) never occupied her without first donning a sheep's-gut cundum. Shiner claimed that this arrangement, a decorous and long-standing one, suited them both.

He maintained two good plain suits of clothes, which apart from the Long Acre lady constituted his principal expense and were essential for the role he played opposite Ned at the tables. All this Ned reported to Betsy-Ann with a certain amusement at what he called Sam's 'puritanism in debauchery'. Sometimes she thought she detected something like envy, for it seemed that Sam planted his money where it would grow, while Ned's dribbled away in momentary pleasures and lasting debts.

He called a few times at the rooms, always with Ned, and

she was forced to recognise his quiet usefulness. To this man, in part, she owed her silk and linen, her soft mattress and pretty china. She was fly enough to be civil: never let it be said that Betsy-Ann Blore quarrelled with her bread and butter. Her distaste to his person, however, did not diminish, any more than his evident appreciation of hers. He would hang over her bosom as though about to snout and truffle there, while Ned affected not to notice. Later, when Shiner had gone and Betsy-Ann complained of him, Ned would say no more than, 'If a man chooses to make an ass of himself, that's his affair.' Like Betsy-Ann, he would not quarrel with his bread and butter and besides, he disdained to be jealous.

'I should like a greyhound,' said Betsy-Ann one afternoon.

Ned stared at her. 'A greyhound? Can't you amuse yourself without?'

'Surely you don't grudge me, Ned? Only a little Italian one. All your ladies have them.'

'O, ladies! Ladies want everything they see. I've no desire to be forever tripping over a cur.'

'It's something to love.'

'You've got me to love.'

'I mean company. When you're at the tables.' Recalling the previous week – during which he'd stayed out every night except one, and *that* only because he'd overdrunk himself the previous day – she started to pout.

He said, 'Sam and I are hard put to it, don't you understand that? I can't have another useless mouth.'

Betsy-Ann abandoned the pout, a habit picked up at Kitty's which had never come naturally to her, and drew herself up. '*Another* useless mouth? Pray, who taught you to handle the books?'

He dismissed that with a noise of impatience. 'Your cur will piss everywhere, the place'll stink. Besides, I'm not paying for lap-dogs or dog's meat or cushions or any of it.'

'I offered to entertain,' said Betsy-Ann.

'You are too good, Madam. But I don't propose to make myself a keeping cully, maintaining a mistress for the benefit of every strolling beggar.'

'Beggar!'

'Bishop, then, if you prefer. I still won't have it.'

'Very well, I shall just sit here and love you.' She gave a frigid curtsey. 'Lovable as you are.'

After that Ned slept awhile, so as to be fresh later on, and went out without any supper, telling Betsy-Ann, 'They'll feed me where I'm going.'

She took the hint and didn't wait up, but could find no rest in bed, where she lay sleepless, anger heating her like wine. Hadn't she already given up her jewels, the best pieces she possessed? He'd no call to beg and plead: she'd parcelled them up directly and presented them with a kiss, keeping back only his first gifts: the earrings and the little fawney with the red heart.

What a daisy! She thought of his mother's pearls, great ropes of them. Kitty's sort never stopped angling: for rings, for gowns, for carriages, houses and land.

Could any lover worthy of the name begrudge such a trifle as a dog? She'd known many a man who'd abandoned wife and chil-dren to smile indulgently on a whore who petted pups and kit-tens. It was natural that the Sex should find these little creatures appealing, and some culls found irresistible the toying and whis-pering that they inspired in ladies of pleasure: for such men as these, a kitten nestling in a white bosom was as good as a dose of Spanish fly.

As for Ned, what would it cost him, after all? Scrimping was what men did with their wives. A keeper had to be open-handed, or his doe would wander into someone else's field.

With that thought came fear: did Ned *wish* her to wander? She'd never seen him so ill-humoured, or so beset by debt. In the seraglio he'd gamed with the best of them, throwing gold about like a nabob: Betsy-Ann now understood what she had failed to grasp at the time, how little he controlled the supply. Kitty had wasted no time in cutting it off. Ever the strategist, she'd known just how to have him.

Some said you should husband your resources. That, too, was easier said than done. How many fellows of the middling sort had she heard in Kitty's parlour, boring the company with their debts? So common were they that Kitty complained that they lowered the tone. The wretches would sit spouting resolutions – to repent, give up their evil ways, no more gaming, whoring, lushing – then call for a fresh jug and continue to drink till they fell from the chair. She didn't think they were shamming, just overcome with hopelessness. Betsy-Ann knew nobody who'd got out of debt. She herself had never tried it; never, until now, even considered it.

She thought back to the time when all this would have seemed riches beyond imagining. Her life revolved in those days around potatoes, cabbage, oats and salt fish, with the same rags on her back from April to October. The question was always: of what use is it? Nothing mattered but your back and your belly.

Genteel economy was different. So many pieces of plate and china, so many vases, hangings, glasses, finishes, so many *surfaces* making up the fabric of her existence. There wasn't a rug or a knick-knack of which she could have said, 'Now *this* is of the first quality,' or, 'This looks well, but is a sham,' or, 'What need of this?' When had Betsy-Ann Blore enjoyed the opportunity of learning such things? She'd passed from a hand-to-mouth life, in which a dish of fried beef made a holiday, to Kitty's house where she'd been fed and 'found in' robes, a slave in Spitalfields silk, paying off the cost of her finery at a rate of interest fit to beggar a duchess. When Ned set her up, she'd played no part in managing that affair, either: he'd chosen the rooms, arranged for their decoration and opened tradesmen's accounts for her. Even the little girl who served as maid-of-all-work, and who brought warm rolls each morning, had been engaged by Ned – and he had not seen fit to engage other servants. For such a small establishment, he said, there was no need. She entertained no visitors, kept no horses. For a whore in keeping, she lived in a damnably small way: *high* keeping it was not. Where, then, should she cut back?

There were women, she knew, who understood the mysteries of cheap fish and small coal. They bought plain stuffs to make up at home; they could detect chalk or bones in the bread, crushed snails in the milk (a knack she'd once had herself, before her nose and mouth grew numb to London food). Kitty's female servants were all of this kidney: shrewd, active, contriving women. They prepared ragoos for those in whom lust, once satisfied, brought forth greed; they stitched torn gowns, emptied and sweetened chamber pots and dabbed bread over spilt wine. Betsy-Ann had wondered at these grey tabbies, thinking them tame creatures who bedded with tame men, never once throwing back their heads and drinking pleasure down to the dregs. What could they know of such things, when they had no Knave of Hearts? Now, lying alone in her apartment, she saw them differently. Grey tabbies they might be, but they had thoroughly mastered the business of getting and selling, which in London was to say, of living.

She must learn. One thing she did know: some people did without wine, drinking ale or cider instead. Would Ned consent to that? He might not, but surely could not resent her asking. Putting the question was itself a pledge of loyalty.

She pictured Ned's adoring gratitude. 'My dove, my doe,' he murmured, kissing her eyelids. 'What would I do without my

Betsy?' She pulled open her gown to display her breasts. Ned knelt in worship. She was tall and beautiful as a statue: there was nothing left to wish for, now, her every wish was answered . . .

She started out of half-sleep, her statue-body crumbling around her, the air cold on her shrinking shoulders. As she pulled up the bedclothes, she fell prey to a thought so terrible she couldn't properly frame it at first, not even to herself. The thought was this: Ned mightn't be short of blunt after all.

A good sharp with a trusty second could take enough in one night to keep himself and a mistress for months. Not in your paltry, threadbare style, scraping along like a tailor's widow. No, your winning gamester lives like Irish gentry, a good, strong, rollicking life: hot punch and silk gowns, diamond rings and beef-and-oyster pie. Ned had been out every night for weeks. If his luck had deserted him, he must be over his ears in debt; if not, was he crying poverty?

Certain past talks came to mind. He'd spoken more than once of Sam Shiner's having scraped together a handsome nest-egg. It was done, said Ned, by lodging very cheaply and dining once a day on bread, meat and beer.

Another time, he'd said to Betsy-Ann while dining, 'They say a fellow can be bred to anything.' When Betsy-Ann asked what he wished to be bred to, he said, 'Nothing in particular,' then went on to remark that Shiner had advanced him a loan, 'as he has plenty laid by'. There was no mention of Sam's contenting himself with the weekly use of a woman, but Betsy-Ann remembered it: how could she not?

She was on the watch for his next mention of Shiner's prudence. Directly it came, Betsy-Ann said, 'But my love, such a cramped way of living! Everything so pinched and mean!'

'My sentiments exactly,' said Ned. 'What intrigues, however, is that he finds it quite enough. One wonders at him.'

'When I lived in a wagon, Ned, I found *that* quite enough.'

'Aye.' He looked thoughtful. 'It's a deal more comfortable to rise than to sink.'

'We could try for cheaper lodgings, I suppose,' she said, studying him. 'Should we give notice here?'

'No, no,' said Ned, shuddering.

The bad day came. She'd been in ill temper and ill looks from the beginning: the little maid who helped her had been called home to her mother's deathbed, and without help Betsy-Ann could not dress her hair becomingly nor lace herself tightly enough. Her sacque, a blue-and-green silk, did not show to advantage. She sat at the window, frowsy and irritable, wishing for a pretty greyhound to stroke and pet.

It was three in the afternoon, long after his usual time, when she heard two men on the stairs. Ned came up slowly, followed by Sam Shiner. Both men had a greasy, wilted appearance suggesting that play had been followed by a visit to a boozing-ken and that Shiner had indulged, for once, in more than beer.

'Curse me for a bear,' said Ned, crossing to Betsy-Ann, his arms open for an embrace. 'A damnable, cross-grained bear. Betsy, I don't deserve you – by Christ I don't —'

He staggered as he approached and instead of embracing, half leaned on her. He had a sharp hogo on him, like gin drunk from a metal cup: liquor taken many hours previously, coming out in his sweat. It was an unlucky smell for a gamester.

She wondered if his apology meant she would have her greyhound after all. At Ned's request she fetched drink for all three of them – beer for Shiner, lightning for herself and Ned. There was some gingerbread left over from the previous day, so she arranged it on a dish and brought that, too. Shiner grinned at the sight of the gingerbread. She wondered if he ever permitted himself such luxuries.

'Your hair's ruffled, Betsy,' said Ned. 'You're not in looks today.'

She started, stung. 'I slept badly.'

He began rearranging her curls. 'You were unhappy, child, I'll be bound. When she's happy, there's not a woman to touch her. I'm a brute to her, a cursed brute,' he said in a strained, maudlin voice, like a man speaking of a dead wife. Betsy-Ann noticed that he turned away from her as he spoke, addressing himself to Shiner. 'She wanted a little dog and I wouldn't let her have one.'

She had never before heard him whine in his cups. Some queer game was certainly afoot.

'Mrs Betsy is an example to the Sex,' said Shiner, 'and deserves any number of dogs.'

Though he spoke as if to Ned, he was watching Betsy-Ann. She wondered what he meant by talking such gammon to a whore in keeping. Example to the Sex, indeed.

Ned said, still in that strained voice, 'Damn you, Sir, I know it. Some napkins, if you please, my love.'

She brought napkins and the men wiped their fingers. Sam produced a pack of cards.

'And now, my sweet, be so kind as to leave us.'

She froze. 'You don't wish me to play?'

'Not now. If you would be so good, Betsy.'

He still wouldn't look at her. Sam Shiner, on the other hand, was peering up from the table with hot little blue eyes. She turned her back on the pair of them and went into her chamber. At Kitty's, they were encouraged to refer to the chambers as *boudoirs*; Jeanne DuPont said it meant a place for sulking in. Betsy-Ann lay down on the bed, unsure whether to sulk or rage or weep. After a while, feeling the cold, she covered herself over with the quilt.

'Betsy.'

She and Ned were travelling across country in Mam's wagon, now hung about with velvet curtains.

'Betsy.' The wagon stopped jolting as its familiar shape settled down into that of her bed in Covent Garden. It was daylight, and Ned was bending over her. Her legs were difficult to move and she realised that under the quilt she was still wearing her sacque. Ned was holding out a cup. Chocolate.

Betsy-Ann frowned. 'Couldn't the girl bring it? Where is she?' Ned shrugged and she remembered the maid was at home, waiting for her mother to die.

She realised it was not tomorrow morning, as she had at first thought, but evening of the same day: all she had slept away was part of the afternoon. The room seemed to change as she understood this. It shrank and grew stale before her eyes.

'Did *you* prepare it?' she asked, still not taking the cup. She'd never known him so much as boil a pot of water; he scorned any man who meddled in women's business.

'Sam.'

'He makes free with the place.' She again caught that metallic stink on Ned's breath. There was something menacing in the thought of Sam searching along her shelves, spying out her chocolate and sugar.

Ned said, 'I want you to come and talk with him.'

'You sure about that? You wouldn't rather I stood outside on the stairs?'

He laid down the cup without further speech and went out of the room.

Betsy-Ann sat up in bed, her heart stammering. Evening sunlight threw apricot-coloured squares onto the wall opposite the window: he would soon be setting off for the tables again. What a wretched day was this! She perceived a wisp of steam trailing upwards from the rim of the cup: despite the sunlight, the room remained cold.

She rose, tidied her hair and smoothed down, as well as she could, the rumpled sacque. The men, when she returned to them, were still seated at the table. Ned stared down at the cards lying there; Shiner glanced up and smiled.

'Well, mort, I trust the chocolate was to your liking.'

'I didn't care for it.'

Ned said, 'Betsy, don't,' and something in his voice told Betsy-Ann that, since she was last in the room, Shiner was become king of his company.

She thought, Ned owes him.

Shiner was watching her. He said, 'No? I've been told I've a knack with chocolate.'

'Much obliged, I'm sure,' said Betsy-Ann, her hands now icy. Too late, she wished she still had the cup with her, if only to warm her fingers. 'Have you something to say to me, Mr Shiner?'

'Hartry speaks for both of us.'

'Sit down, Betsy.' Her lover looked like a dying man, his face waxen and his brow all of a sheen. Betsy-Ann thought he would be cold to the touch. She pulled the sacque straight, as well as she could, and sat.

'We've been talking, Sam and I,' Ned tilted his head towards Shiner in a ghastly attempt at lightness, 'about this and that —'

'In a gentlemanly way, you know,' Shiner put in.

'About the troubles that might – on you, I mean. Descend on you. As a result of my affairs being so – irregular.'

There was a pause. Ned's breathing came ragged, as if he had run a race.

'I'm not liable for your debts,' said Betsy-Ann, a tremor starting up in her hands so that she had to squeeze them between her knees to conceal it.

'The rent's in my name,' Ned replied. 'The coal, the butcher, the wine.'

Betsy-Ann thought, He's forgotten the plate.

'There's no more credit to be had, Betsy. Ma and me – word's got round.'

She said, 'I was thinking about that, Ned. What if I —'

He burst out, 'No, child!' and then, more softly, 'Don't you see? There isn't time for anything of the sort. And here's my good friend Sam Shiner – my right hand, Betsy. He's agreed to help us out.'

Agreed. They'd settled it, whatever it was, without so much as a word to her and by God it must've been a filthy bargain. No point sending her out of the room, else.

He'd have to say it to her face, then. Say it himself, all of it; she wouldn't carry him an inch. She smiled like a daisy and said, 'A friend in need, eh? So how is Mr Shiner to help?'

If they hadn't been sharps they would have looked at one another. The cold had spread from Betsy-Ann's hands all over her body, except for her face which was burning. She pictured it a mottled red, peering over the crumpled sacque. What an enticing prospect for *Harris's*.

'Sam and I had a wager,' Ned said. 'Best of five games.'

She waited.

'Sam's stake was that if I won, he'd settle everything in my name.'

'Not in mine?' Betsy-Ann asked.

'Yours too. You see the use of it, Betsy? For both of us.'

He'd lost, then. It was hard to speak or even nod, so painfully did she strain towards him. Both men were now staring at her, Ned as if imploring, Shiner with a mask-like absence of expression.

At last Betsy-Ann said, 'So that was his stake. And yours . . . ?'

Ned said, 'The best thing I had in the world, Betsy. The one I loved most.'

Betsy-Ann's mouth opened and let out a wail. She could not, for the world, have held that sound in; she felt as if it were crying her, and not the other way round.

'There, there – there, *there*.' Shiner murmured as he might to a kinchin but Betsy-Ann barely heard him. She held out her hands to Ned, as if by taking them he could haul her up from the pit of a nightmare. Ned observed the outstretched hands but made no move to touch them, and Betsy-Ann's arms fell back to her sides.

'He'd nothing else so precious, you see,' said Shiner mournfully, as if he, and not Ned, had lost.

Her tongue was dry. She scraped it round her mouth until the spit came. 'I'm not some damn fawney you can pass from one finger to another.'

'Of course not,' Shiner said.

'Dear girl, nobody said you were,' Ned protested. 'Nobody would ever think it —' She waited, watching him fidget. He cleared his throat. 'Will you hear the conditions?'

At that she rose, walked to him and caught him a good slap across the cheek. Ned stiffened but remained motionless, the mark of her fingers darkening on his skin.

Betsy-Ann said, 'No conditions, no nothing.'

'You shall have your dog,' put in Shiner.

She gave an incredulous shriek of laughter. 'I'm not wapping you for the price of a greyhound!'

Ned looked from one to the other. 'Go out, Sam.' Shiner hesitated, frowning. 'Give us some time alone.'

Betsy-Ann ran to the door to make sure Shiner had descended the stairs. She stayed there, peering over the banister, until Ned pulled her back into the room. Now that Shiner was gone, he attempted to embrace her. Pushing him away, Betsy-Ann saw him open his eyes wider, as if to snare her in his crackling black gaze. She observed with pleasure the handprint on his cheek, and was conscious of something hard pressing against her stays, a steely point about to burst out of her skin. It travelled up her chest and throat into her face, into her own eyes, which she fancied must be glittering as much as his. In a voice like the sharpening of a blade she said, 'I wonder what you can find to say for yourself.'

'I thought I'd win.'

Betsy-Ann gathered the last drops of moisture left in her mouth and spat in his face.

Ned wiped away the spittle with his sleeve. 'He'll take you under his protection. You're made.'

'And you, I bet.'

'Me? There's nothing for me, child. Your debts only.'

'Sam Shiner's —'

'A coming man, Betsy, a coming man! And he worships you, you couldn't wish for more – and in honour, in *honour* —'

'You – slaver!' She lunged at him but Ned caught hold of her arms. 'I've heard it all, now,' she moaned. 'You might as well sell me in the street. How can you, Ned?'

'Don't you see? I staked so that if I won, we'd both be free, and if not, you'd be safe. No matter how it fell out, *you'd* be safe.'

Safe, away from him? She bowed her head in despair, seeing now how it had been: their vows of love, never set down on paper but made a hundred times over in words, in smiles, in caresses, in cries and moans – they were all on one side.

'He's no duddering rake, Betsy, he'll do you no harm. You'll see, my sweet,' he raised her chin with his finger, 'it's not so very bad. And when you've shaken down together, I shall call on you.'

He did not shrink from her gaze. There was even a faint glimmer in his eye, a hint that Sam Shiner couldn't keep watch on her seven days a week. There might be times, said that glimmer, when she would be glad of company.

Betsy-Ann said, 'If you come near me again, I'll cut off your prick.'

This seemed to amuse Ned. 'You, my doe, maim a pretty fellow? It's not in you to hurt a man.'

'Is that what you are?'

After some whispering on the stairs between him and Ned, Shiner sidled back into the room. He promised to call for Betsy-

Ann the following day but she refused to look at him, preferring to stare out over the piazza. Shiner addressed himself to the back of her head: he was vastly sorry she chose to take it in that way, he could assure her there was nothing to fear, he was confident that a connection begun in such an unusual fashion could prove a happy one. Betsy-Ann only continued to stare, twisting her hands together.

'So. I'll call here tomorrow, at two,' Shiner said. 'And you, Ned, shall I meet you at —'

'Not *now*,' Ned snapped.

Shiner hemmed, crossed to the door and went out. Hearing his footsteps, light and rapid, die away on the stairs, Betsy-Ann at last turned away from the window. 'I'm surprised you don't go with him,' she said, 'you being such very good friends. Watching over the goods, are you, so you can deliver them in person?'

'No.' Ned hesitated. 'Indeed, I shan't stay here. I've – taken rooms.'

'Rooms? Where?'

'In the New Buildings.'

She thought: Never! Kitty's, more like. But what did it matter, now? 'Your Mister Shiner,' she said, 'he'll clear everything that's owed?'

He bowed. She didn't care whether the tradesmen were paid – she needed all her pity for herself – but she itched to give her new keeper any little trouble she could.

'What if I pike off?' she demanded, glancing back towards the piazza. 'Suppose your coming man gets here and finds I'm a going woman?'

'I hope you're not such a fool.'

She stiffened. 'Are you threatening me?'

'Not at all,' Ned returned. 'But you know how it is with a woman on the town. One false step and —' He drew a finger across his throat. 'Sam's trusty. You'd do well to bear that in mind.'

That night she again lay sleepless. Wakefulness was no stranger to her; she knew every lump in the mattress. Now some other mort would lie here. A few words, a wager, and her time had ended. She lay on her back gazing up into blackness. Was death like this? An emptiness, a light, numb sensation. She closed her eyes, trying to escape into sleep, but the shrieks of a night reveller down in the square returned her to herself.

Keshlie had died in bed, a year or so after her breaking-in. When the symptoms first showed themselves Kitty called in a physician – the girl was in demand, so it was as well to be sure – but his diagnosis was the inevitable one.

'He said I was a very bad case,' Keshlie whispered to her sister. 'And he asked if any of them had no hair, you know, down there.'

'And did they?'

'Yes, some.'

'Christ, Keshlie, you never told me!'

'I didn't know it was anything,' Keshlie said. She seemed afraid she might be blamed.

A 'rose never blown upon' was a commodity for which a bawd could charge the highest rates. Betsy-Ann was, of course, aware of this: both she and Keshlie, after their initiations, had been douched with 'pucker water' to disguise the damage and sold several more times as innocents. Even so, Betsy-Ann experienced extreme good fortune: it so happened that her early clients were men excited by seduction and rape. What she underwent at their hands was unforgettable, but by the standards of the brothel, far from being the worst.

That worst was reserved for Keshlie, who was sold as a cure for the pox. Her fragility was an additional attraction – such a childish creature must surely be clean – and Kitty made the most of it. Then, when the infection began to show, she swept Keshlie from the premises before she could publicly sink from being a 'sweet feast of love' to a spectacle more likely to bring on a vomit. The seraglio could not be expected to support such cases, which were a drag upon trade. For them, there was the Lock Hospital.

So to the Lock Keshlie went, but the disease had been working unseen within her for too long, and the cure did not take. She came out of the hospital poisoned with quicksilver, barely able to walk.

By means of tears and pleading Betsy-Ann managed to extract a loan from Kitty. With it she rented a room, cramped and filthy but not too far from the seraglio, and there she installed her sister along with a nurse, a broken-down old woman who was paid to tend the fire and give Keshlie tea and slops whenever she could take them.

On the day of Keshlie's death, Betsy-Ann obtained permission to visit her as soon as she had finished with her last cull of the afternoon. She bade the man goodbye with languishing smiles and sighs, all the time wishing him in hell, before throwing on her pelisse and hurrying to the house where Keshlie lay. Panting, Betsy-Ann pounded up the stairs and struggled with the lock. Even before she had the door properly open, her heart misgave her: a waft of stale, cold air from within told her that no fire had been lit that day. Keshlie lay on the bed without so much as a sheet, her cheeks fallen in and the inside of her mouth showing black. The nurse was nowhere to be seen, but the landlady was already peering round her door, wanting to know what Betsy-Ann proposed to do.

'I've no money to bury her with,' Betsy-Ann said.

The woman looked sour and said that was strange, in a wench so well turned-out.

'None of it's mine.' Those were the last words she spoke for some time, being almost strangled with sobs. The landlady's face softened. She said that in return for Betsy-Ann's pelisse, she would arrange for Keshlie to go to the poor's pit.

'When?'

'Tomorrow morning, if I can. I've no call to keep her here.'

Betsy-Ann unfastened the pelisse.

'Dear God, the poor's hole!' Kitty had exclaimed, pouting in disgust. 'Surely you can't wish to see her coffin shoved in there with the rest of them, all . . .' She shook her head.

'I've no wish to see it, but —'

'Then don't speak of such things.'

'— it's her grave. My sister's grave.'

Kitty stared. 'You did all you could. Your duty now is to work off some of what you owe.' Perhaps Betsy-Ann's expression was rebellious, for Kitty caught hold of the young woman's hand and marched her to the room near the front door where the bully-backs sat at their card games.

Kitty clapped her hands for attention. 'This one,' she announced, pointing to Betsy-Ann. 'Never mind what she tells you, she's not to go out.'

The Mother charged interest and kept tally of every farthing, so that Keshlie's sickness and the loss of the pelisse sank Betsy-Ann further into debt. She spent the morning of her sister's burial chafing the withered parts of an elderly gentleman, a service known in the trade as 'raising the dead'.

And now she was through with the Hartrys. Bad luck to the pair of them, mother and son: it was an evil hour when she flew under their net.

Indeed, she was better off without Ned Hartry. Much better. Much . . . Betsy-Ann gave up the struggle. She cried in the darkness until her face turned to raw meat.

At half past one the following day, her features pale and swollen, she was standing at the window of the apartment, surveying the piazza. The strollers below, knowing themselves observed by their fellows if not by Betsy-Ann, carried themselves with the usual swagger and sparkle of a Romeville crowd, even the beggars plying passers-by with an insolence that was their version of wit.

To Betsy-Ann's experienced eyes nearly all those in the piazza fell into two groups, the one's pleasure being the other's profit, and her sympathy lay entirely with the profit-seekers. From time to time she would recognise a face: a street girl noticed on another day or a wench who once worked at Kitty's. These she would watch with interest to see what fortune had in store for them: a pretty young fellow, kind-hearted and open-handed, or one of those miserly debauchees whose ruined constitutions demanded refinements for which they were loath to pay. Some of the shabbier women continued wretchedly pacing the piazza for hours on end. She watched them come round and round, dragging their feet for weariness: no supper and perhaps no lodging either.

Since taking possession of these rooms, Betsy-Ann had watched the heaving shoals outside with the blessed sense of having been lifted out and placed in a calmer sea. Now she felt herself tossed back again, one fish among hundreds.

Her feelings towards Ned had softened with daylight. Though she could never, never hold with what he'd done, it might be considered an act of kindness, a damn fool way of doing her good. Suppose she piked off now, leaving Shiner empty-handed? He'd think she and Ned were in it together: it was how he and Ned pulled in the flats, a lay he thoroughly understood. Who knew what Shiner might find it in himself to do, what revenge he might take on Ned, after that?

This morning she had risen and moved about the place with an intense awareness of doors slamming shut behind her: her last cup of chocolate, her last putting-on of her stockings in this bedchamber, her last spying out of the window. She was going to play her part. What else did a whore ever do?

She wondered what Shiner had in store for her. She hoped there would at least be a window.

He was punctual to his time. She saw him approach just before two and at once turned away: he should not think she was looking out for him.

His footstep was light on the stairway. Cock-a-hoop. Before Betsy-Ann could answer to his knock, he'd opened the door for himself. Ned must have handed over the key. She was caught unprepared, betrayed as Shiner stood masterful in the doorway, his blue eyes gleaming.

'I trust you are ready,' he said.

Perhaps this was how it felt to be mad: like two women in a single body, one holding up her head as she went down the front steps, the other thinking, *This is Sam Shiner, Sam Shiner*, yet continuing to walk beside him, right into the carriage. Shiner patted her hand, a satisfied smile on his lips, as the driver loaded up her boxes.

Though Shiner still occupied the plain old lodging once described by Ned, his landlady had agreed to let him an extra chamber at the house back. The few rooms were spare and precise: everywhere the mark of the meticulous man. Betsy-Ann walked about stupidly touching the walls, except in the new room where Shiner explained that she would be able to enter in a day or two; he had engaged a man to paint and paper but the job was not yet complete.

'For you,' he said, holding open the door to show her. The room was almost empty, the window big and light. A tree outside cast green shadows onto the floorboards and she realised that the window gave onto someone's garden: a city man's notion of a rustic retreat, in which she was to provide the birdsong.

So many knick-knacks as she'd had in her Covent Garden rooms! She wondered what Shiner had made of the place: was he impressed by the comfort in which Ned had set her up, or disgusted by her extravagance?

'I hope you find it satisfactory,' Shiner said. As if she had a choice in the matter. She looked round at it all, plain as a nunnery, and nodded.

'You'll be known as Mrs Shiner.'

'What of the other Mrs Shiner?'

'I'm not spliced.'

'You've a friend, though, haven't you? Ned told me.'

Shiner turned to her in surprise – 'He did?' – then fell silent a moment, picking with a thumbnail at something between his front teeth.

'Shall you give her up?' Betsy-Ann persisted.

'Yes. Poor Nancy.'

So that was settled, *if* he intended to keep his word. You never knew with men. Shiner himself carried her box into the room she was to share with him – he kept no servants, she was to discover later – and stayed with her as she unpacked her things. She dearly wished he would go, but could scarcely order him from his own chamber. Worst of all was when she took out her blue silk. The light shook off it, as if some exotic bird were flying about the room: O, the times she'd had, the memories! She resolved there and then to sell it and never look on it again. But Shiner said, 'I always thought you perfection in that gown, Mrs Shiner,' and she knew it for her livery.

The following week a man arrived with a box, pulling back some straw at the bottom to reveal a pup the colour of cinnamon. She recalled her words to Shiner – *I'm not wapping you for the price of a greyhound* – and bit her lip. But she'd wapped him anyway, and it wasn't so bad: the simple act satisfied him, no filthy letches. And here was the dog. She might still have stood on her pride and sent it back, had the little thing not chosen that moment to raise its head from the box and look around, some straw behind one ear. Seeing its delicate whiskers, the honey of its eyes, she was lost. She reached into the box for it, taking it in her arms, and it at once pissed over her. Betsy-Ann burst out laughing. The man said it was nothing but fear: the dog would soon know its home. She kissed the top of its head, inhaling its biscuit smell.

Some men can tolerate any amount of dirt provided it arises from horses or hounds. Not so Sam Shiner. On coming home he cast an anxious eye around the rooms, noting wet patches and torn paper. Betsy-Ann waited, enjoying his discomfiture. In the end he said nothing except, 'Did I choose right?'

She couldn't deny it warmed her to him.

From that time they began, though slowly, to shake down together. Even after the little dog vanished, stolen by someone who scaled the wall of the yard, the gift bred a certain kindness in Betsy-Ann. She could never love Shiner as she had the Corinthian, but she thought of him now as Sam: there was a steadiness between them, a trust you might say, that went on growing until Roderick Morson struck at it with his knife.

She remembers the morning he came home, his fam bound up in a wiper. At first he wouldn't unwrap it or talk about it. He sat awhile staring at the wall, then started up and hurried downstairs. Betsy-Ann hung over the banister.

'Sam? Are you going out?'

When he returned, he told her he'd talked with the landlady. They could no longer afford to rent the room with the green shadows in it. From now on, she'd be in with him entirely.

30

'Titus?' Eliza says. 'What's it like, being a slave?'

Surprised, he looks up from polishing the spoons. When he first came to England, people talked to him more kindly than in Annapolis. Since they seemed sympathetic, he thought they might ask about his family: whether they were people of importance, what language they spoke together, if he felt loneliness at being taken from them. He soon realised that they had little interest in that. What they most liked hearing was how he had been enslaved by his fellow blacks: they wanted tales of savagery, full of cannibalism and sacrifice, and to know how England seemed to him – didn't London fairly knock him sideways, at first? Wasn't it the finest place in the world? Then they would look pleased with themselves, and say, 'Well, we won't eat you *here*.' As his speech improved, matters only became worse: if he spoke of what he had witnessed in Annapolis, they would fidget and say things like, 'My brother was there on business, and found them extremely civil,' and one man even told Dog Eye that no Maryland gentleman would behave so, and that the boy was a liar and deserved a whipping. They asked, but they did not want to know. So now he has stopped talking about Annapolis.

'Launey said you get wages, like a servant,' Eliza goes on. 'Why's that?'

He shrugs. Dog Eye always paid him something, even before the marriage. The Wife thinks that he eats too much and does too little, but he did not ask to come here.

'Were you a slave in Africa?'

Now it starts. 'No. My father was an important man.'

Her face lights up. 'From Ethiopia?'

This, too, he has been asked before. Dog Eye explained to him that a famous Englishman wrote a story of an Ethiopian prince; even some ignorant people – like Eliza, who cannot read – have heard of it, and take it for truth.

'That's another country.'

'Not Africa?'

'Another part of Africa.'

Her face falls. He is secretly glad to displease her; it is an effort to remain patient with a woman who pretends to be interested in you, but is really only puffed up at the idea of mixing with princes. He says, 'Some men took me and sold me for a slave.'

'Which is a better master – an Englishman or an African?'

For an instant he considers taking the question seriously, before replying, 'Englishman, of course.'

She smiles. 'I thought so. But the Abolitionists say it's all the same! You've heard of the Abolitionists?'

He has heard of the Abolitionists. Every time he meets with the word, so long and slithering and alien, it catches him out for a second, but he knows what it means. He waits for Eliza to tell him that they are a race of meddling busybodies, as he has heard else-where, but it seems he has exhausted her meagre stock of interest: she is content to smile and go on grinding sugar.

What does it mean, *master*? Not the kidnappers. He would not dignify them with such a name: they were devourers of hu-man flesh. He remembers being found, struggling in their sack: someone slit the top of it, pulling the fibres away from him where they had stuck to his skin. The rescuer was a man he had never seen before, who at once pushed him to the ground. Fortunate held his arms up over his head for protection, looking down at the sunburnt grass and the man's scarred and dusty feet.

He heard another person shaking out the girl child from her sack. Between splayed fingers Fortunate saw her fall to the earth, folding upon herself like cloth. The man who had taken the sack from her turned up her face, then with a disgusted noise let her drop back. It was the first time that Fortunate had seen the girl. He did not think she was from his village.

Both men now stood staring at him. One of them bent to untie his feet, leaving his hands tied, then dragged him upright. Fortunate made a little coughing sound and the man understood: he felt in Fortunate's mouth for the cloth and threw it away but did not speak to him.

Leaving the dead child, they began walking towards the sun. Very soon they passed one of the kidnappers. It was the man, lying with his face to the ground and an arrow sticking up from his back. Where the blood was, the body glittered with flies. The man who had taken the girl from her sack went to pull out the arrow and the flies rose in a cloud. He listened for a while, then called out something. The other man went to him, Fortunate following behind.

The woman kidnapper was lying on her back. The arrow had pierced between her breasts. Her breathing bubbled and rasped: she looked at the men with half-closed eyes. The men talked to one another, seemingly unsure. In the end they left the woman where she was and set off at a slow pace that told Fortunate they would be home before sunset.

It was not so very far, but by the time they arrived he was staggering from hunger, thirst and fear. The men indicated that he should sit down while a woman sent a small boy up a tree for mangos. Fortunate's hands were still tied, so the boy came to feed him. The sweet pulp of the fruit cleaned the dust from his lips and ran from the corners of his mouth. He looked around and saw a green country, greener than his father's and seemingly close to a river.

His family would know by now. Everyone would search for him, the women wailing. A slave would be sent to the next village to ask if strange men had passed that way, and if anyone had been taken from there. The younger ones would cry, and Father would say to them: 'You see what happens when children stray too far from home!' Most likely nobody had seen the man and woman enter the compound. It grieved him that his father would never know of it, and would die thinking him a foolish, disobedient boy.

After eating three of the fruits, he bent forward and lost consciousness, his weariness mastering him even in this dangerous situation. He dreamed of the evil woman lying in the grass. Vultures and pigs broke her open, ants hissed in her bones.

He woke to the smell of cooking fires. Some distance away a young girl was seated on a log, stirring a pot. He was given rice and something strange and hot-tasting, which he ate in the company of two older men. From their poor clothing and humble manners, he understood that they were slaves, even before one of them, who could speak his language, told him he should always eat with them, never with anyone else in the compound.

That was when he understood. The rule was the same in his father's house: slaves do not eat with the freeborn. He had been rescued from the kidnappers in order to become a gift elsewhere.

Even Dog Eye, sitting late over his wine, once called to Fortunate to come and sit by him, demanding to hear the story of his life. Fortunate could see that Dog Eye thought of this as a kindness, though he himself spent much time pushing the memories into darkness and did not want to bring them out into daylight for the pleasure of Dog Eye or any other white person. With a man of his own race, who knew what such sufferings were, he might speak more freely.

Dog Eye, however, knew nothing of these feelings and was not accustomed to be checked in his desires, so Fortunate told him quickly, squeezing weeks and months into a very short time: that he was seized by kidnappers, then taken from them and made a slave in a village near the west coast.

'Were they cruel to you?' Dog Eye at once asked. 'I've heard the natives trepan each other as easily as they take a bird.'

Fortunate did not know the meaning of *trepan*. He said, 'African master is not cruel.'

'Not so cruel as a white, you mean.'

'My father having slaves. It was —'

He lacked the words to explain that inferiors were given good food and not overworked. 'Not cruel,' he repeated.

'And *your* master wasn't so bad?'

Fortunate shook his head. The women were especially kind: one of them had dealt with him in a motherly way, patting him when he cried. Yet Fortunate never felt safe in their compound, especially when one of the older slaves told him that further downriver lived evil, red-faced people who had no pity and who bought slaves from the local chiefs.

'Will they sell us?' Fortunate had asked.

'Perhaps,' the slave said. 'Men are taken downriver from here and put into boats.'

'To row them home?'

'The red-faced people have no houses. They have no crops. They live on the water.'

'What do they eat?'

'Human flesh. They take hundreds of men and come back for more.'

After about a month, the same slave told him that he was indeed to be sold on. Fortunate went to the master, the slave translating, and begged with tears in his eyes not to be given to the red-faced cannibals. The master said he should not be sold to them but to a kinsman, who would treat him well.

This was the sort of lie told to children, to make them go meekly. When the time came, Fortunate was taken downriver to an island the cannibals called *James*. It was here that he at last saw one of the ships he had been told about, as big as an entire village, and its red-faced monsters. It was riding in the river below the island, but they were not to enter it, so, along with hundreds of others, Fortunate was chained in a suffocating room until the ship should be ready. A man who spoke his language told him he was lucky. He had arrived shortly before sailing, whereas some of those waiting in chains had been rotting in that room for weeks or even months.

He wondered if he would ever tell Dog Eye the story of the cannibal monsters. He knew now that the people were not cannibals, and was almost used to their ugliness. They seemed not to see their own red faces, but called themselves white. They thought pallor was beauty, even when it came with twisted bodies and bad teeth. None of this could be said to an Englishman.

'You made the middle crossing, did you not?'

'Middle — ?'

'You went by boat to Annapolis.'

'Yes.'

'I've heard philanthropists say it's an earthly hell. What'd be your word for it?'

Fortunate ignored the puzzling word *philanthropists*. He was astonished at Dog Eye: a word to call the voyage! How could he imagine one word could convey it?

After two days they were herded on board. The ship gave off a loathsome smell, as did the men whose faces resembled those of evil spirits. Fortunate was amazed to see that they behaved almost as viciously to one another as they did to the Africans, punishing accidents with blows and whippings. There was one good thing, however: they kept blacks with them who could speak various languages and who were sent among the people for reassurance. For the first time, Fortunate understood that the monsters had fields and crops. He would not be eaten but put to work, growing tobacco.

Then came a time he would gladly have been killed, a time

he cannot keep out of his dreams but never willingly remembers when awake. At Annapolis he came off the boat like a mad animal, cringing and half blind.

'Well?' said Dog Eye.

He looked into his master's face and said, 'Death.'

'Indeed! If it's so bad, why don't they all kill themselves?'

'The masters,' was all Fortunate could say. Again he saw the nets spread to stop people from flinging themselves over the side, but though his eyes filled, he lacked the words to make Dog Eye understand. 'Maryland. Cruel there.'

'To you?'

In the elegant house near Annapolis he saw whites sitting back to be fanned in the summer heat, while black men and women went about their labour hampered and tortured by metal contrivances: chains, muzzles. This was done for the least fault, perhaps the oversetting of a pot.

'Chains in mouth,' he said. The words are inadequate for the hideous thing he saw screwed into the cook's face, but Dog Eye stares.

'Whose mouth, in the name of Christ? Yours?'

'For a woman not to eat.'

Yet when Mr Watson sailed for England, bringing Fortunate with him, Fortunate's terror was greater than before: each time he had changed masters, it had been for the worse. When he first understood his position – that because of a game, he now belonged to Dog Eye – Fortunate could have gone on his knees to Mr Watson and begged not to be left behind. He had seen so many tricks played on Africans that he sweated with fear of this laughing man who put wine and gold in his hands while those around watched and also laughed.

'You were glad, then, to come into my service?' Dog Eye said.

He nodded.

'You didn't look it.'

'Afraid. Afraid hurt.'

'O no,' Dog Eye assured him. 'It was Mr Watson I hurt.'

Fortunate could make nothing of this, but then many of Dog Eye's sayings and doings were hard to understand. The master sometimes treated him with such indulgence that they dined together at the same table. At other times he was taken among hard-faced men who frightened him, or women who fed him sweetmeats and patted him as one might pat a child. He was taught to make punch and was sick after drinking it. He learned the loading and firing of pistols, something of the games of cards, and a couple of dances. It did not escape him that Dog Eye often went among people who were drunk, or that the women who came to the house were of the lowest kind. Fortunate puzzled over that mysterious thing, the honour of an Englishman. His father would not have liked to see him the master, let alone the servant, of such a man as Dog Eye.

Yet in all this disorder and unseemliness were moments of joy, as when one of the women taught him an English dance. All three of them laughed so heartily that he saw tears run down Dog Eye's cheeks. A man grows accustomed to strange, even shocking things, if they ease his loneliness. After a few months Fortunate thought of Dog Eye as a kind master and protector, almost a friend.

Since the marriage there has been more bickering than dancing. Still, what has changed once can change again, and in ways impossible to imagine: how could Fortunate have understood, before leaving his father's house, what lay in wait for him? Why should Dog Eye not go back to the old ways one day, taking Fortunate with him, and their life together begin anew?

31

Betsy-Ann steps away from Haddock's and hails a pair of chair-men who promptly size her up.

'One-and-sixpence,' says the front man. 'In advance.' An old hand, he can tell your rising courtesan from the commoner who might find it worth her while to bilk him and he's put her down as the second kind. All this Betsy-Ann, as shrewd as he, reads in his rapid, calculating glance. Ned has provided, however, so she produces the fee with a flourish and settles herself inside the chair. She has no desire to trudge through the city, keeping a wary eye out; she wants to mull things over.

She set off yesterday to Haddock's for pleasure and pastime. Pleasure and pastime there was, and still is, if she includes the parting indulgence of this chair-ride. Why, there is scarcely a jolt: trained to hold steady, the men take each cobble in their stride, imparting a wonderful smoothness to the motion of the whole. It comes to her that the chair-men are her brothers, sweating for the gratification of others. From the look they bestowed on her, however, she doubts they would acknowledge the relationship.

But enough of the chair-men; this is a time to think of Ned, with whom nothing is ever simple. Does he truly wish to set her up again? Or is his smiling free-handedness nothing but a rig to get the Spanish trick and make it his own? Suppose he had it, and could thumb his nose at Kitty, would he then cast off Betsy-Ann? 'Once bitten, twice shy' – there's wisdom in that. And Ned's a known biter – only look at his autem mort! The poor thing's bitten to pieces!

She told the men to set her down some way from home. For a second she's tempted to call out to them and ask, instead, to be taken to where Ned lives – it's about the same distance – but that's the sort of thing a lovesick child would do, a sure sign, should he catch her at it, that he could count the trick his own.

Was there ever a time when, for such a sweet rendezvous as last night's, she would have surrendered it? Perhaps, at the very beginning. Since then, the game's moved on. She knows now what it is to be put aside, left to shake down with another man: damned if she'll be caught that way again. Dimber Ned must show a bit more spirit: he must join hands with her, pull her free, take her once more into his keeping.

After the spotless elegance of Haddock's, the casual filth of her street leaps to her eyes like spilt blood. She sees it all afresh, even the scar on the front door where there was once a brass knocker, long since twisted off. In the passage Liz-the-Moan has found herself a chair from somewhere and sits with it pushed up against the wall since the chair is missing a back leg. For a miracle she contrives to get up without oversetting the thing, but despite her eagerness to pour out the usual medley of tittle-tattle and complaint, Betsy-Ann won't be held back and gives her a bare good-day before hurrying upstairs, eager to get a fire going.

Unlocking her door, she finds the main room unoccupied but disarranged: a gown that she laid over a chair now lies crumpled upon the floor. With a tut of irritation she hurries to it and shakes it out. Here's a nuisance! The bodice is blotched with dirty finger-marks as if fumbled by a coal-heaver – that won't come off in a hurry. A faint sugary perfume hangs in the air. Turning to see what else has been soiled, she observes a heel of bread on the table next to a plate of cold beef, and on the other side of the plate, a jug. Ah, yes. She knows the smell now for spiced nantz and also perceives, lurking beneath it but growing stronger as she approaches, the sickening stink of *that coat*, which she at last spies thrown down between the table and the wall, seemingly flung off and left there. All this is the doing of Sam Shiner, once so particular that he would run his fingers along the shelves for dust.

But why leave the meal untouched? Has he dropped into bed drunk? No: from where she stands she can see the bed. The bedchamber itself is scarcely more than a cupboard, its contents a bedstead and a box of clothing. Nevertheless, she cannot rest until she's stepped inside and looked all round. He's been home, but when? He's been away so long, surely – her heart misgives her – he didn't pick last night?

The bedchamber, having gapped floorboards and no hearth of its own, is always cold. She closes the door to it. Still a draught from somewhere. Not the window frame; that was stuffed with rags long since. It's blowing from the far corner – and now, for the first time since entering, she notices a faint line of shadow around the cupboard door where the Eye lies concealed.

He's been in there.

She runs to it, fearing the worst, and with clumsy fingers searches through her baskets and boxes. She's forgotten how many she had of each – this is what comes of neglect – but it seems to her he hasn't taken anything. Or if he has, he's been fly about it.

At last she comes to the box containing the satin shoes. They lie snug within, white and innocent as butterbeans, her black pearl earrings pushed down into the toes. She's about to replace the box lid when she sees something is wrong. Her shoes are lying the same way round, one treading on the other. Betsy-Ann always packs them the same way, soles outwards, so as not to soil the satin.

So he took them out. For what? It comes to her that he might have started poking about the Eye long ago, or . . . more recently. Betsy-Ann shivers. Suppose he saw the coral fawney in this box, before she took to wearing it? Seeing a trinket in a box proves nothing, to be sure, but she recalls how curious he was. He seemed to have an inkling, even then. She pictures it: Sam comes in, finds her gone. He knows what's in the boxes, and he remembers the fawney, so he looks to see if she's taken the shoes with her. He turns them up in their usual place.

Well, that's all right. He could make nothing of that. And he's no notion what they are to her. Has he? But when was he in here? Last night?

Was he home last night?

She closes the Eye, then stands listening a few seconds before turning her attention to the floorboard by the hearth. Snatching the knife from the table, she levers up one corner until she can distinguish a faint gleam beneath, then pushes the board down flush with the floor surrounding it. She wipes the knife and returns it to its place.

What more? She'll have to wait until Sam reappears, hear what he's got to say for himself. In the meantime, she may as well make up the fire. Let's warm ourselves at least. A quick stir with the poker reveals rubies among the ashes. When was that lit? She hurriedly criss-crosses pieces of kindling and tips a glistening mound of coal over them. The usual greyish-yellow fog bubbles up and blows off into the chimney and Betsy-Ann realises how cold she is. She can hardly wait for the brisk flames of the mature fire in place of this sulky, smoky beast.

All at once her sleepless night comes over her. It's too much trouble to get up again and go about her business; she sits back on her heels for a blessed minute or two, closing her eyes, and allows herself to doze. It is thus that Sam Shiner finds her kneeling before the hearth, her chin dropping on her chest.

'Why, Betsy-Ann,' he says, and she is at once awake and on her guard: something different in his voice.

'I dozed off,' she says, struggling upright. 'Lucky I didn't fall in the fire.'

Sam's hands are scrubbed and he's steady on his feet. Is it possible that he's sober? 'I've been talking with Mrs Ward,' he says. 'She'll give us the rooms another year, same rent. But you, where'd you get to? You had me worried.'

He *is* sober.

'I can't be forever shut up in here, Sammy.'

'No more you can,' he says, studying her. 'By the look of you, you're fairly worn out.'

'I've been with Lina. The poor mort's nothing but one big ache.'

She's expecting more questions but instead Sam crosses the room and embraces her. A flash of terror goes through Betsy-Ann: she's breathing ratafia, she's been smoked with beeswax, basted in Ned's juice and sweat. And now she remembers the toilet table with its rose-scented cologne which she, stupid bitch, must go splashing in her hair. Her only hope is the dullness of Sam's nose: were it any sharper, he'd hardly have lasted a week in resurrection.

He says nothing, at any rate, but releases her and sits down opposite the meat and bread.

'You've come at the right time,' he says. 'Fancy a morsel of beef?'

Betsy-Ann seats herself beside him, catching an evil whiff from the nearby coat. Sam rises again to fetch the mustard pot from a shelf.

'I don't care for this bread. You have it.'

'How finicky we're getting,' Betsy-Ann says. She takes a bite from the bread, which tastes no different from any other, and puts it down.

'And a drop of nantz. You won't see it again. I'm packing it in.'

'Are you, Sammy? What'll you drink?'

'Beer.' He shoves the plate towards her. 'Here. There's enough for two.'

Does he suspect she's been feeding elsewhere? She takes a mouthful of bread and beef and makes a show of enjoying it.

'Your Englishman's natural food, is beef,' Sam observes between chews. 'Unless he's one with peculiar tastes.'

She giggles. 'You mean like buggerantoes?'

'That's peculiar, all right. But I was speaking of food.' He takes another bite, munches it. 'Females, they're worse. I've known females eat the strangest victuals.'

'In the family way.'

Sam shakes his head. '*I* knew one never had a kinchin in her life, and you'll never guess what she was *most particularly* fond of.'

'Raw onion? I heard of —'

'Haddocks.'

He opens those blue eyes as wide as they will go, mimicking astonishment, and it's as if she's glimpsed a dagger under the table. She shrugs and says, 'Nothing so strange there. Though I can't say I care for 'em.'

'No?' says Sam. 'I expect you're more for oysters, or sparrowgrass, are you? Spice you up?'

'Why would —'

'I heard all Mother Hartry's chickens were fed provocatives. Regular feeding, to keep 'em in a state of heat.'

She can't tell whether he's backing off or merely circling round to come at her another way. Her mouth dry, she offers: 'That's all play-acting, provocatives.'

He guffaws. 'Why have 'em, then?'

'The culls believe in it. And they like to see.' She takes a little nantz to help her parched tongue. 'We had one fellow paid a guinea just to watch a girl eat sparrowgrass.'

'Good eating, boiled and buttered.' He clicks his tongue in appreciation.

'Practically raw, it was, so it didn't fall apart. You had to suck and suck till you was fair put off your supper.'

Sam smiles slyly. Betsy-Ann could wish she had a plate of sparrowgrass in front of her now, not the beef which has turned to pap in her mouth. The more she chews on it, the stringier it becomes.

'Aren't you going to ask me?' Sam says.

She forces a swallow, the compressed wad of meat scraping her gullet all the way down.

'Ask you what?'

'Oh, nothing in particular. If you can't notice a thing, you can't.'

She tries to look pleased. 'Course I noticed. You didn't go boozing, then?'

'No.' He never takes his eyes off her face. 'We got word the traps were out, so Harry passed the night here for once. Left this morning.'

She says, 'Least you got a night's kip, eh? I didn't hardly get a wink, what with Lina coughing. Like a broken-winded nag, she is.'

'Harry was vexed not to see his sis. I wonder where she can be, he said. How is it she's roaming when you've got this snug little ken, he said. And I had to say to him, I don't know, my friend, I don't know indeed.'

'He wants to visit more often,' Betsy-Ann observes tartly, even though Harry's visits fill her with dread.

'We was both vexed,' persists Sam. 'And I thought to myself, where *would* she be?'

'Well, now you know,' says Betsy-Ann, wondering how much truth is in those words, and which of the two purposely spoiled her gown. Sam's got more cause, all said and done; but it's more in Harry's line.

32

Turning over the pages of her letter, Sophia paces the bedchamber. This morning she went so far as to risk the journey to the Receiving House unaccompanied, lest Titus take notice, and was rewarded by the sight of Mama's familiar hand. As she broke the seal, her pulse quickened, but as she peruses the contents, it seems her excitement was premature.

> *You must not let your fancy run away with you,* Mama scolds.
> *I confess I did not expect such a message, and am distressed not because I am inclined to regard Edmund as a monster, but because I find my daughter so lacking in judgement.*
> *Let me speak frankly, as one married lady to another. No husband is perfect and yours has his faults like the rest: he is careless in conducting his affairs. I am puzzled why, if Edmund does not like to take things into his own hands, he should not follow the usual course and employ some trusted person.*

Quite.

> *He has now, however, sent a receipt to Papa so you may cease to fret about that, at least.*

He sent the receipt only because he opened Papa's letter, thinks Sophia, and saw the thing would not do.

> *You may also set your mind at rest as regards Ranelagh. Papa got into a muddle, that is all. One of his correspondents mentioned a visit there and he thought he had heard it from you —*

quite the usual thing with him, so we need not suppose any villainy. My love, you will never be happily married if you are given to fanciful imaginings, and in particular to suspicion. Do you remember when you and Hetty read Othello together? There are lessons in that play which might benefit any young person recently wed.

As for your reading his letters, for it is clear that you have done so: my dear Sophy, what can I say? If Edmund is guilty of meddling in your private affairs, are not you equally to blame? I believe I impressed upon you before your nuptials that men and women are differently constituted. I take it your spying has turned up some keepsake or billet-doux of a warmer nature than you anticipated. You must remember that it was never Edmund's intention that you should be thus offended. You are to blame – you are, Sophy! – for officiously seeking it out.

A wife should consider her husband's past a sealed tomb, as indeed it is. I will not deny that it takes more than a month of honeymoon, or even six months, to bind two people into one flesh. I know whereof I speak; I positively hated your papa, at first! But one shakes down, child. One shakes down. These days, Papa and I jog along very well together.

And now I must make myself plainer still. You write, Sophy, as if you contemplated a separation. Let us assume Edmund has indeed some sort of hole-and-corner 'friend' – my dear girl, a separation on such grounds is unthinkable. You cannot imagine the sea of troubles in which you would be plunged. No, the surest policy for a deceived wife (which I sincerely believe is not your case) is to please. Remain resolutely obliging and cheerful – in other words, feign ignorance. To nag, whimper or reproach him is a shocking blunder and will only benefit your rival. She will endeavour at all times to be delightful company, on that you may depend, and a man who feels himself caged is liable to roar.

To cage Edmund was never Sophia's intention, nor can she think him lacking in liberty. Mama's meaning, with the sugar and vinegar taken out, would appear to be this: Woman's sway is pitifully brief, the marriage vows do not apply to Man and a wife goes most safely through the world bound and blindfolded.

> *I send this via the Receiving House,* her mother concludes, *not out of suspicion of my son-in-law but that you may be convinced of its authenticity.*
>
> *I hope, my dear, that you and Edmund may soon reach a more comfortable understanding, and pray it will not be too long before a certain desirable event occurs. My girl will then find herself too much occupied in tender duties for such fanciful notions.*
>
> *We could join you in London for the rest of the season, or – should Edmund be entirely set upon neglecting the Town for domestic pleasures – at Wixham. Pray write and let us know which it is to be.*

Intolerable! Sophia crumples the letter in her fist. To have so opened her heart, so appealed to her natural allies, only for this! Seeing that Mama ranges herself – along with the rest of society – on the side of Mr Zedland, of what use is a visit? And what of Papa? Has he nothing to say on the subject? He concurs, then, in the diagnosis of hysteria, and believes that the fittest person to minister to such feminine distress is a mother.

Concerning the sunflower seal and the forged signatures, Mama can hardly argue Edmund's innocence. She therefore declines to address those subjects at all. The message is clear: you have made your bed, and must lie on it. Though your bargain be dreadful, it is for life. A horrifying thought strikes Sophia: are mothers always so treacherous? Is it possible, for example, that in secret Hetty is equally miserable with her Mr Letcher, and that the whole thing has been thus smoothed over?

Evidently Mama thinks she should be grateful to be married at all. Was she not nicely palmed off with no mention of 'the weakness'? Now the mother's work is done, no matter how botched, it cannot be unpicked. Doubtless Mama had the same reply from her own mother, before she and Papa 'shook down'.

Never has Sophia felt such rage. She flings the crumpled letter into the fire and pokes at it until the thing is consumed. One thing, at least, she has learned from Edmund: the importance of destroying evidence.

33

A fiery smell, one Fortunate has learnt to recognise, lingers in the kitchen. Mrs Launey keeps a bottle corked up on the top shelf of the pantry: whenever that bottle is brought down and the smell let out, the cook becomes friendly and calls him her little hobgoblin. The first time he saw her in this condition, with her face all scorched, she reminded him of the red-faced devils at James Island. The second time, he thought she must have stood too close to the spit. Now he knows that the scorching comes from inside, from the contents of the bottle: she cannot drink without burning her face.

The usual thing is for Mrs Launey to pass from friendly to prickly, from prickly to tired, then fold over the table, head across her arms like a sleeping dog. Sometimes the table is floury from baking and when she at last snores and pulls herself up, it is as if someone has painted white breasts on her clothing. The other women can't see that without laughing, though they are careful to conceal their laughter from the cook.

This morning Mrs Launey's bottle was again in play. The maids kept nudging each other behind her back, but once she slept they took up the bottle, which Mrs Launey had forgotten to return to the shelf. Fan fetched cups from the dresser and poured a little into each, then took the bottle to the bird's-head tap and added water.

'She'll never know. It's strong as horse-liniment.'

'Medicine for horses,' Eliza explained, seeing his confusion. 'Come on, Titus, give us the toast.'

'Must be burnt toast, if he gives it,' said Fan. The two of them laughed. Eliza is kinder than Fan, yet she always joins in a joke against him.

In his best English he said, 'Thank you, I take tea and beer.'

'Do you a world of good, provided you're not like that.' Fan jerked a thumb towards the cook. Eliza held out a cup to Fortunate, who shook his head.

'Go on, Titus.'

'With us, for luck.'

'No, I thank you.'

At last the maids shared out the extra cupful between them and Eliza stood on a chair to put the bottle back in its place.

He does not like to drink. This was not the first time they have behaved so wickedly: once, when the master and the mistress *and* Mrs Launey were away, Fan and Eliza let a young man in by the kitchen door. The man had brought a bottle of the same fiery drink that burns up Mrs Launey, which he handed to Fortunate saying, 'Here, Blackbird.' Fortunate disliked *Blackbird*, and disliked even more drinking after a man with grey stumps for teeth, whose unclean spittle he could see on the bottle-neck, but the man was insistent. The drink stung like scorpions; he spat and the women rocked up and down, laughing. Afterwards they danced with the young man and then quarrelled. There was shouting and sobbing. The man lifted the latch and was gone. Fortunate was certain that beatings would come of it, but when the cook came back she only looked round her and sniffed. He realised later that she did not dare complain to the Wife.

Now they are busy with this other bottle, nobody to stop them but burnt and snoring Mrs Launey. He wonders if they will bring back the man with the rotten mouth.

For himself he has other plans. Noiselessly he mounts the stairs. Moving with such care is like tracking, and for a moment he sees again his yellow dog with its shining eyes. The dog will be dead now. He does not like to think of it creeping broken around the village, stoned away from the hut doors. Surely it is dead.

Though the master is out, Fortunate's heart pounds as he approaches the study and silently eases open the door.

The first thing he sees is the marble-topped table and after that the shelves. He moves on soft feet, in case someone should be in the room below, and with trembling fingers catches up a box from the middle shelf. The lid has been pushed down tight but not locked. With some little effort, he is able to ease it up.

They are stretched out like dead men laid head to toe. He knows what they are: once, in Maryland, he was taken by Mr Watson to hold coats while two white men shot at one another. It was a quarrel, and the younger man so sick and faint that Fortunate could see at once he was the fated one. It was a strange way to fight: this faint, sick man was also the taller and heavier of the two. Had they met with cudgels, or swords, or simply wrestled, he might have lived. As it was, his strength was no help to him.

Later, when he felt able to speak with Dog Eye, he struggled with the English words to convey his sense of injustice: 'The man does nothing.'

Dog Eye said it wasn't as simple as that. Firing a pistol was like riding a horse. You had to learn how. That was why the man was afraid: he had not enough knowledge, and his fear took away the little knowledge he had.

Fortunate understood. It was the same with any weapon: you had to have the understanding of it.

He takes a pistol from the box and goes over to the window. He likes this window; from it he can observe people who never think to look up so high and see him. Fortunate gazes down to the pavement below, searching the street for a Bad Spirit which sometimes stands opposite the house. That is its favourite place, but Fortunate has seen it right up against the windows, staring into the rooms. Most of the time, though, the shutters are closed so the Spirit cannot be seen. It fills Fortunate with dread, the more so in that it only appears when he is alone in the room. Nobody else ever speaks of it or seems to see it, which suggests it has come only for him, to do him harm. Even from across the road the boy

256

can see its power: it is in the shape of a man but taller, as tall as a warrior in his own country, its hands enormous and its face eager for cruelty. Once, when Fortunate went out behind the Wife, he became aware of a fearful smell that he knew from his time on the slave ship: the smell of dead flesh. He looked up and saw the Spirit beside him. It grinned down and drew a finger across its neck, as if to say Fortunate's throat would be cut. He thought it meant to kill him there and then, and closed his eyes.

'Titus!' The mistress was prodding him. He looked up, stupid with terror, to find the Spirit gone: it had been mocking him. Useless to tell the woman. She would say, 'Some fool,' as if the thing were gone like a passing bird, never to return.

Could a weapon like this frighten such a creature away? Dog Eye said pistols and rifles were like spears: unable to work by themselves, even to choose whom to fire at. So it was the man who fought, and not the gun as Fortunate had first imagined. He knows very well by now that guns are not magical, but he has nothing else.

Bringing up his hand, he trains the pistol on a chimney-pot opposite. He has learnt a great deal since his first conversation with Dog Eye. He knows how to aim and fire because, in the happy days before the Pinched Wife, Dog Eye taught him; he said he had a hankering to instruct a black and perhaps write up the experiment, like the accounts of children raised by beasts but brought with much trouble and expense to eat human food. Fortunate understood enough of this to feel such offence that for once he could not conceal it. 'You needn't sulk,' Dog Eye said, seemingly surprised. 'I find a deal of capacity in you.'

He took Fortunate over to the common, where they spent time shooting at a paper pinned upon a tree, and Dog Eye said he did it all 'quite natural'. Fortunate was at first ashamed because he knew that *natural* meant *fool*, but it seemed the very same word could also signify a man of great ability and he rejoiced, even as he despaired of the English language.

That was a happy time. Life was easy-going, for Dog Eye was strange but often kind and men understand one another. At times Dog Eye would say little, merely holding out his glass for more wine, or pointing to his coat. It was all that was needful, though women must always be chattering. Dog Eye often dined in company, but the days Fortunate liked best were those with none, when master and servant ate at the same table. On these days Dog Eye grew talkative; instead of pointing, he would question Fortunate about his childhood, which he pronounced most curious. Once he said, 'You were raised in Arcadia, I do believe,' and another time, 'We are outside the circle, you and I.' Fortunate could never understand what his master meant by this: was he not an Englishman in England?

He said, 'You are a rich man, Sir.'

Dog Eye laughed and offered to teach him a song, but Fortunate could not pronounce all the words. Such doings would greatly surprise the mistress, were she to hear of them.

It comes to him that he has perhaps been tricked, and was not truly a friend. He was brought here to take orders and nobody – not even Dog Eye – cares to hear him speak.

No, it is the Wife's fault. You have only to look at her cold face. He steps back from the window and beds down the pistol next to its mate. Suppose the mistress came into the room now, while he is putting the lid on the box. She would scream to think he had touched them, foam at the mouth if she knew her husband had taught him to shoot. He smiles, picturing it, and remembers something else Dog Eye told him.

'These aren't like a knife or a rope,' Dog Eye said. 'They're made for only one thing.'

The smell of that thing is on them: metallic and corrupt, a foretaste of darkness and pain. It sticks to his fingers. He snuffs it up, intoxicated for an instant with its bitter power.

34

Nothing more has been said about haddock or provocatives, but Sam Shiner is a changed man. Though Liz hovers on the stairs, peering up though dulled eyes, she gets little by it: all he sends out for is the occasional jug of small beer. Sam's given up nantz entirely. He's returned to his old particular habits, washing his hands and face in a bowl of warm water and donning his night-shirt, neat as a nun, before bed.

'You never thought I could, eh?' he says to Betsy-Ann as she turns back the sheets.

'Could what – turn Methodist?'

'In sure and certain hope of resurrection, at any rate.' He catches her smiling at that. 'I trust you're pleased?'

So pleased is Betsy-Ann that she's tried sending Liz for nantz and leaving the open bottle on the table. She's on the lookout for the blessed *just this once* that will end his career as tea-and-beer man, but it's a long time coming – a cursed unlucky time, too, with the moon waxing and a clear sky full of frost. Nothing do-ing for resurrectionists: a full moon and a quiet churchyard. She wheedles, 'Don't it make you poorly, though, Sammy, giving up so sudden?'

Sam considers. 'I see better these days.' He raises his eyebrows as he did when he said *Haddock's*. After that, she doesn't want to know what he can see.

Next day she's restless, cudgelling her brains. How can she get word to Ned? She could slip Liz sixpence to write a note and de-liver it. Then she realises: even if she directs the old woman to the right street, and Liz has the strength to creep there, she still can't describe the house. And suppose his autem mort got hold of it, what then?

Taking the cards from the shelf, she sets herself to practise. She can't ask Shiner to watch her while she's drilling: that would be to teach him the trick, and if she won't give it to Ned, she won't give it to Sam. Much good it'd do him, with his ruined hand, but still.

She lines up the books and plants them, idly flicking backwards and forwards through the pack as if to amuse herself. Sam sits by the window, drumming his fingers on the ledge.

'Look here, Betsy.'

She ignores him. He has a habit of pointing out little oddities – a pigeon with a broken wing, a beggarwoman wearing a man's wig to keep her head warm – and calling her to the window to witness them. His drunken time put a stop to that, but now he's started up again.

'Look here,' he repeats. 'Look.'

Suppressing a sigh, she goes to the window. Below in the street is a dwarf, a man in a full-sized coat turned up at the cuffs and cut short across his knees. The dwarf is dragging a kind of sled behind him, laden with tarpaulin tied up with rope.

'Now where's he going with that?' Sam murmurs as if to himself. 'It's near as big as he is.'

'How should I know?' There's something pitiful in the sight of so small a man tugging so awkward a load and she turns away from the window.

'Makes you think,' Sam says. 'Looks like he's pulling a dead kinchin.'

'That's your trade, preying on your mind.' Betsy-Ann sits again and takes up the cards. 'He's carrying goods.'

'A kinchin's goods, ain't it?'

He seems low in his spirits. Now might be the moment to propose a cheering glass.

'Betsy-Ann.'

'Sam.'

'I don't care for the resurrection lay.'

'Nobody cares for it,' says Betsy-Ann. 'Here, how about a warming drop of —'

Shiner bursts out, 'I hate it, Betsy. I can't hardly stand myself.' He stares at her, mouth compressed, eyes swimming. Caught off guard, Betsy-Ann stares back. She'd forgotten how he was once, a man capable of turning things over in his mind, of drawing a line, saying, *That's as far as I go.* Now he's capable again, and miserable as only a sober resurrectionist can be.

He says, 'Suppose I was to pike.'

Betsy-Ann's stomach turns over. 'He'd hunt you down,' she says, snapping shut her fan of cards for emphasis.

' I won't peach, Betsy. I'll swear any oath he likes.'

'An oath!' Betsy-Ann looks pityingly at him. Who'd swear a cockerel not to crow, when you can just wring its neck?

'You're his sister. He won't make you a widow-woman.'

She could agree. It's a way out for her – urge him on, get him to pike and leave the rest to Harry – but at the thought of it her insides go cold. Whoring's one thing, setting up a murder another. She snaps her fingers. 'He'd do it like *that.* Christ, Sam! I'm sick of telling you!' *Go back on the nantz*, she silently urges him. *It's suited you this long.*

But of course it doesn't suit him any more. He wants to be sober now and keep an eye on her. Betsy-Ann could weep.

'I need blunt,' he says, scratching his head.

'You've got blunt.'

'I need more.'

'What for?'

'Change of air. He can't look for me forever.'

I wouldn't bet on it, thinks Betsy-Ann, but she holds her tongue because it's hopeless, he might as well be deaf. Besides, fancy's painting her a pretty picture in which Sam doesn't figure:

herself at the window of a new lodging, watching Ned come down the street. She's tearing herself in two as she says, 'Don't cross him, Sam.'

'Damn your advice.'

Betsy-Ann's come to the end of her strength: she can't go on. 'Very well,' she says. 'Be a fool, if you've set your heart on it.'

'But will you help me?' Sam says. 'What have you got?'

'There's stock put by.'

He snatches up her hand and kisses it. She stands ill at ease, arm extended, making no move to embrace him. How he's lowering himself, she thinks. When he raises his face to hers, his voice is husky.

'You're a diamond. Take that nantz, will you? I don't want it round the place.'

She nods. He widens his eyes again in the way she has come to distrust. 'You're a good mort, though,' says Sam Shiner.

35

'Sophia, have you been in my study?'

Edmund's voice, though polite, has the effect of trapping Sophia's breath in her throat. She forces herself to look up slowly from her newspaper, as if reluctant to leave off reading.

'No, Edmund. Why do you ask?'

'Something's been moved.'

'Oh?' She hopes she looks sufficiently puzzled. 'If I went there, I'd be sure to leave everything in place. May I ask what you've lost?'

'I didn't say I'd lost anything.'

'I thought —'

'Someone's moved my pistols.'

Sophia starts. 'You have pistols?'

'Like most gentlemen,' he says, evidently enjoying her dismay. 'And have even been known to fire them. You may now worry to your heart's content.'

'Edmund, don't.'

'Don't what?'

Joke about something so terrible, she was about to say, but his amusement acts as an astringent upon her so that she says instead, 'Surely you would never be so stupid as to demand satisfaction?'

'Perhaps another man may call *me* out, and I be obliged to meet him. But if I did, I'd be sure not to tell you.' She can't tell if he's mimicking her. 'One doesn't frighten the ladies for nothing.'

No indeed, thinks Sophia: you have always some purpose. 'Quite right,' she says. 'Die first and tell me afterwards.'

Her husband almost smiles. 'I've no intention of duelling, you goose.'

'Then why did you want the pistols?'

'You persist in misunderstanding me. I didn't want them, I noticed they'd been moved. Not at all the same thing.'

'O! Not at all.'

'So you know nothing about it?'

'Nothing,' she repeats, nettled at the repeated question. 'The people to ask are the servants.'

'I am quite of your opinion. Suppose you ask them.'

He is gone. Sophia remains sitting with the paper open before her, her eyes focused on a grease-mark on the opposite wall. She finds herself simultaneously noting that she must have the mark rubbed with bread, even while she considers what Edmund has just told her.

It astounds her he can talk in this half-teasing, half-bullying fashion when by night she has to endure his repeated assaults. The first occasion was only the most violent one; he still comes to her chamber upon occasion and woe betide her if he finds the door bolted against him. She has tried that and it does not answer.

How weak are the Sex at all times, how ill-equipped for defence! How much more difficult to resist one who attacks in the marital bed, his ring upon her finger! Resigned to the futility of resistance, Sophia does her best to shorten the ordeal by yielding directly. He takes what he has come for, then retires to his own chamber with its unsoiled mattress. His wife lies in darkness, staring upwards, her mind as frenzied as her body is motionless. When she is at last able to sleep, she dreams of foulness proliferating within her, of worms thick as ropes coiling about her womb, lying packed beneath the skin of her breast.

Yet morning after morning she awakes to find her body apparently sound; if disease mines within, it mines unseen. Nor has Edmund struck her again. To her astonishment – considering what has passed between them – it appears he can still be pacified by animal satisfaction. At times it even appears to produce a mechanical affection: his *you goose*, as he dismissed her fears of the pistols, was not unkindly spoken. She was aware of something similar after that first hateful time: a few hours afterwards Edmund was already talking as if nothing untoward had occurred, as if the memory of it had fallen away from him even as he rose and dressed. Sometimes he smiles at her, rallies her, as if with a little give-and-take they might yet be happy together.

It is as if there were two Edmunds: the gentleman whose very person emanates refinement and the nocturnal brute who can mate without esteem. Even this she can comprehend: there is said to be a certain admixture of the animal in the make-up of every male, which a Christian, manly fellow makes it his business to subdue. What she cannot fathom is how the daylight Edmund, knowing what he knows, can talk to her as he does. But then she, taking her cue from him, responds in like fashion. She wonders what marital horrors are concealed beneath Mama's words: *I positively* hated *your papa, at first! But one shakes down, child. One shakes down.*

These days she weighs Edmund's every speech, trying to judge how much truth it contains, how many lies. *Does* he have pistols? She has never noticed them, but supposes they are kept in a case.

She sees him lying in a field, his waistcoat dark and sticky, herself kneeling beside him. *Forgive me*, he says.

Is he home? Betsy-Ann's been backwards and forwards, forwards and back to the street-end. Twice she thought she saw him approach: each time, her heart came so far up her throat that she could have coughed it out, and then as the man drew nearer, she saw that he wasn't Ned.

Business is middling. The nantz went first, raising her hopes, but after that only trinkets and wipers. Hard luck, Sammy.

What now? Shift her pitch and try elsewhere? After all the

time she's put in, surely it can't be much longer. Ned will walk out of that door or better still, come towards her, so she can collar him before he gets home.

She wasn't thinking straight when she brought the cart. She fancied they might go off somewhere together, but it can't be left unguarded; she's tied to it like a tinker's dog, trotting behind. She's pushed the cursed thing so long now that she's constantly re-crossing the tracks left by its wheels; perhaps it'll wear a groove in the road, big as a ditch, and by the time Ned arrives she'll be sunk down in it, never to be seen again.

His house has a discouraging, shut-up air. The downstairs shutters are pulled to, either to keep in the warmth or keep out the spying eyes of such riff-raff as herself. There's also the odd cheering detail such as the house number, forty-three – remember that, girl – and a scrap of string on the area railing, fifth rail from the end, just beneath the spiked arrow-head. To Betsy-Ann it shines out because she put it there: the merest twiddle while she leaned against the railing as if for weariness. Jack Ketch himself couldn't tie a sweeter knot.

The sky is dark even by Romeville standards. Ned, where are you? Once more she scans the street, her eye caught by a tall cove on the other side of the way, talking to a young woman. His back is turned to her. He's sporting a fine coat, something about him . . . ? No, not Ned. At first Betsy-Ann assumes he's a flesh-hound closing on the prey, but then the woman points as if to give directions. A lot of folk get lost round here, on account of the New Buildings.

Here comes the rain! Stinging her face, beading the sleeves of her pelisse, it acts on those around her like a whipping: respectable men hasten towards their business, idlers strike out for the taverns, servants hoist baskets over their heads to keep off the wet. A few of the prowling women flock together and move off towards some nearby panney, while others dart into an alleyway just to her left.

No point in staying now. All she'll get is mud up to her arse, a bonnet like a squashed bun and her death of cold into the bargain. With a sigh of disappointment she turns the cart around, causing a passing coachman to curse her for a witless bitch.

But wait. It's the walk she recognises, even before the phiz: hurrying like the rest but slipping between them, no shoving. A flick of the brows: he's seen her. At once her heart's up in her throat again, worse than before: too bad about the limp bonnet, but perhaps he won't notice.

He's only a few yards away now, and smiling.

She can't help calling, 'Ned!'

He takes another step and halts. She sees the joy drop from his face. His mouth works; he's like a man paralysed, twitching back and forth before recovering the use of his legs, turning and diving into the alleyway.

'Ned!'

Betsy-Ann stands confounded, rain dripping from her front hair. Impossible to follow with the cursed cart. Damn the man, what's got into him? She'd lay a hundred pounds he saw her: there was the black-and-white flash of the eyes full on, the smile, and then —

Someone taps her on the shoulder. Betsy-Ann gives a little cry as she flings around to find herself face to face with the man she noticed earlier.

'You're like a drowned whelp, Sis,' says Harry Blore. 'Reckon you'd be best in your own ken, don't you?'

It is a dreary traipse back to the rooms, Harry lumbering alongside but not offering to help with the cart, Betsy-Ann tormented by Ned's flight. Why should he be afraid? In any particular way, that is. Most people fear Harry on sight – the damp and dispirited stragglers coming in the opposite direction take care not to meet his eye – but that's only the common prudence of the streets.

Walking with her hulking companion is like being taken up by the traps: others move aside at their approach, some of them glancing at Betsy-Ann with curiosity and even pity. There are no manacles, to be sure, but there's that feeling of being *for it*, afraid to stay yet unable to move off.

Betsy-Ann has the advantage of the onlookers, having studied Harry's moods over the years as a cat studies a mousehole. One thing she can rely on: he loves to be praised, and even more to praise himself.

'That's a grand new coat you have on, Brother. New hat too, unless I'm mistaken.'

As good as a disguise, she could have said. In them he can pass – on a dark day, with his back turned, from the other side of the street – for an almost-respectable man.

Harry struts. 'The tailor was for pinching and scrimping but I told him, Be damned with that, Harry Blore wants something worth wearing.'

What gammon! Close up, she can see how the fabric strains across his shoulders. Harry was never at a tailor's in his life: the coat is some cast-off purchased from a footman.

'I'm told it sits well,' Blore adds, by way of a nudge.

'Vastly well. But then, you're a fine figure of a man.'

'So *she* says.'

'An affair of the heart, Brother?'

Harry remains modestly silent, but his answering leer makes as sinister a phiz as Betsy-Ann ever hopes to see. She gushes, 'A beauty, I'll be bound. Eh?'

Harry grins. 'Tall. Fair. Lush around the dairyworks.'

'Gay company?'

He doesn't answer. Betsy-Ann supposes her dairyworks are company enough. She's about to ask if he has these pouting bubbies – and the lady attached to them – safely in his keeping, when Harry says, 'How's Shiner?'

'A touch sickly, but tolerable.'

He walks on a few steps, frowning. 'Tolerable. You surprise me. *He* surprises me.'

'He's as hale as most, Brother.'

Harry shakes his head. 'My meaning is, he gets a good whack, yet here's my sister behind a cart.'

'O, don't fret yourself about that.'

'You like tramping about in the wet?'

'I've goods on my hands. No point keeping them for the priggers.'

'Shiner never said you had priggers.'

Fat lot he cares. 'Through the skylight.'

Harry nods, as if to say that he understands now. She breathes more freely, despite the effort of pushing the load.

'Why'd you go there, Betsy?'

'Sam was already settled when I took up with him.'

'Not the ken. Back *there*. Good run, is it?'

'Never tried it before.'

He purses up his lips as if in disbelief. Rain trickles off Betsy-Ann's forehead into her eyes.

'And what brings *you* here, Brother?'

'Something and nothing.'

When Sam opens the door she takes a good look at him, since that's what Harry will do. Sam is pale, greasy, eager to please: a kinchin could smell the fear coming off him. He's doomed, she thinks, as Harry strides towards the fire and Sam, having found a smile from somewhere, steps back out of his way.

Her brother announces that he's come to see his old trusty, his friend Sam Shiner, for mutual merriment: perhaps a bowl of something hot?

'We've beer and lightning,' says Betsy-Ann. 'Shall I send Liz?'

'She'll be an eternity,' says Sam. 'You go. Get nantz, lemons – will they have lemons?'

She shrugs.

'If not, try at —'

'I know the drill.' Betsy-Ann takes up the empty jugs. Looking sick at the prospect of being left with Harry, Sam produces a coin from his pocket and then, after some fumbling, two more.

Laxey's isn't too busy at this time of day. She's able to bring away a big bottle with the proper French label on: it'll set Harry up, and finish Sam, most likely, but then Sam's finished already. Wine, the cheapest sort. It won't matter when it's mixed.

After that it's a long walk for the lemons. The woman watches to see she doesn't lift anything and when Betsy-Ann hands her a coin she bites on it.

'Charming manners you have,' says Betsy-Ann. 'I daresay you was in one of those young ladies' academies.'

The woman glares but there's nothing wrong with Betsy-Ann's money.

Harry will be stamping with impatience. Her breath huffs as she runs back to the ken, taking two stairs at a time. The men are seated at the table, glasses out; the talk, it seems, is no longer of punch, but of straight drinking.

'Here,' she cries gaily, banging down the nantz between them. The lemons, escaping their paper, trundle along the table-top. Harry snatches the bottle, for all the world as if *he* was standing treat, and reads the label before pouring out for himself and Sam – both glasses brim-full, Betsy-Ann notices. Sam's gone all cringey, folding in on himself like a dog that fears a kick.

He's going to drink the nantz.

'Come on, Sis.' Harry waves his hand, inviting her to sit down. 'Drop of French?'

'Not for me, Brother. Lightning for me.'

'Then take a flash directly, because me and Shiner are talking business.'

'You want me out *again*?' She can't keep the anger out of her voice. 'In this weather?'

'Didn't bother you earlier,' comes Harry's voice, soft and nasty.

Betsy-Ann clenches her fists behind her back, where he can't see them. 'Give me five minutes.' She goes to the Eye and rummages in there for the lightning, slipping a couple of small bottles into her bosom and snatching up a thick woollen shawl.

'I'll be with Liz.'

Harry shrugs as if to say she may go to the Deuce, for him.

Liz is a long time answering her knock. When the door judders open, Betsy-Ann is shocked: the poor woman looks like Death's Wife, so shrivelled and bleary that her neighbour forgets, at first, what she came to say. Liz, meanwhile, hangs in the doorway, spent.

Once inside, Betsy-Ann begins to understand. Just to stand in the room is like being pressed between blocks of ice.

'When did you last have a fire?'

'Not for weeks.' Liz holds out purple hands. 'Can't hardly break a bit of bread, look.'

'Don't say that. I've a message for you to put down and take.'

'Who for?'

'The master of the house. Or there's a servant, a blackbird.'

'You can't trust them.'

'This one you can.' Bracing herself, Betsy-Ann pulls off the shawl and drapes it over Liz's bony shoulders. The rush of chill air to her own neck and shoulders makes her wince. 'Now,' she says, producing the lightning. 'Do as I ask and bring me luck, and you'll have this, and a cloak, and coal. Like roast beef you'll be, warm all the way through.'

Betsy-Ann smiles encouragement. She reaches out, takes the older woman's fingers and begins to chafe them.

36

'You may be sure he knows,' Ned mutters. 'Why else would he hit on Haddock's?'

'He knows something, not everything. But he's suspicious, all right, and he won't drink, and now I'm hearing fifty times a day how he can't stick his work. He talks of piking off.' She glances at Ned to see how he'll take this: with fear, because he might lose her? With joy, seeing as Sam might flee and leave her behind?

What she gets is temper.

'Well, let him pike if he wants to! If he can't stick resurrection he could at least stick to nantz.'

'It's very hard on *me*, Ned,' she says as piteously as she can. 'Being watched all the time, with him looking out for proof —'

'Proof? My dear Prodigy, in such cases a man generally convicts upon suspicion.'

Convicts and executes too; even with nine fingers, Sam's equal to that job. She wouldn't be afraid, however, if Ned would only show more spark. If he stood up and declared, I'll be your protector, Betsy! Come what may, I'll defend you! — what wouldn't she venture? Instead of which he sits there looking sulky and vexed.

To be defended as a darling pleasure, even that would be something. She lays her head upon his shoulder, hoping to be gathered to him, but his arm remains motionless against her side.

'We only went there the once,' he says, signalling for another pot of capuchin, after which he sits staring into space. Betsy-Ann shifts awkwardly. This morning she enlisted Liz to lace her extra tight and her stays are making themselves felt. All this to set off her new gown, yet he's hardly given it a glance.

'You said Haddock's could keep a secret.'

'And I maintain it. Consider what would become of the place, otherwise.' He pauses as the coffee is set down in front of him, continuing with growing conviction, 'Someone outside spied on us.'

'Us? We went in separate, came out separate.'

'Precisely.' He's waiting for her to twig. She stares at him, nonplussed; then realisation comes. 'Someone that knew us – knew us before.'

'Very good, Miss Blore. Pray proceed.'

'How do you mean, proceed? It wasn't Sammy. He was at home, I saw him.'

He pushes a cup towards her and this time he meets her eyes. 'Certainly not Sam Shiner. Our man is a Mr Blore.'

'Harry!'

'He, or someone very like him, was in the street when I came out.'

'And you kept mum?' Betsy-Ann stares in astonishment. 'You saw him spying and you never *told* —'

'What I saw was a man near a bagnio door. What should I think? You know the trade, child. Men hang about such places like flies, drawn by the scent of flesh.' He plainly expects her to smile at this witticism but instead the coffee house shifts and blurs. She turns away from him, wiping her eyes on her sleeve.

'I wasn't even sure of my man,' Ned says to the back of her head. 'He moved off directly I saw him. But now Shiner's acting queer – it has to be.'

She nods. 'Has to.'

'Still, who'd have thought Harry would peach on his own? And to Shiner, of all people!'

Betsy-Ann gives her eyes a final wipe and turns to study him. Is it possible he's forgotten? She told him long ago how Harry barred the door and sent his men to fetch away Mam. When Ned first heard the story, he called Harry a foul name and pressed Betsy-Ann to his heart as if he bled for her.

Yet he's forgotten. She feels it in the casual way he now drapes his arm about her shoulders. 'Ah, Betsy!' he says, as if disappointed in her, 'How was it *you* didn't notice? Your own brother.'

Betsy-Ann breathes fast and thinks of potatoes, a trick for staving off tears discovered in childhood and strengthened by long practice. Had Ned embraced her ten minutes ago, she might now give him some lover's prattle: I was too happy, something of that kind. As it is, she replies, 'Suppose I noticed, what could I say?'

He takes her hand, squeezes it and says, 'Afraid to speak to him, eh?' as if she were a kinchin with a fear of dark cellars.

'I've seen him frighten *you*,' she retorts.

'I think not.' He grins. 'Though I admit he's not to my taste. Too much of the driven ox about him.'

'Say what you like, I notice you keep away. When you cut me the other day —'

'Cut?'

How black and glassy his eyes can go, and how his fingers have tightened on hers. Betsy-Ann braces herself. 'Outside your house. You saw me and you went into the alley. Ned – you're hurting me —'

His grip relaxes. 'Darling girl, when? As if I would cut you!'

'That's my eye, Ned! You saw me and toddled. Harry was behind me, I know that now, but I never knew it then.'

He stares at her. 'Have I accused you? Would I give you the rendezvous, if I thought you were in league with – anybody?'

Of course not. She bows her head. 'No. I never said so. But there's something you've not told me. About you and Harry.'

He scowls and flings her hand away, striking her knuckles against the table. 'Sometimes, Prodigy, there's not a hair between you and my wife.'

'I only want to help.'

274

'Sophia's precise words, as I recall.'

Betsy-Ann nurses her fingers. Ned sighs, glances towards the door and asks, 'Is Shiner out of blunt?'

'He soon will be.'

'He should take up a new calling. A man of his talents . . .' He smiles to himself. 'I see him as a wigmaker. What do you think? Would it not suit him admirably?'

'He *can't* leave the crew. Harry came —'

Ned whistles. 'Did he, by God!'

'Don't you understand me, Ned? Sammy's not free to leave.'

'So your brother came to remind him of his obligations. Excellent Harry! The moral polestar of this erring Age! If any will not work, neither shall he eat.'

She looks at him, blank.

'St Paul,' Ned adds. 'And for once I'm of his opinion – cadavers won't steal themselves. *Ergo*, Mr Shiner must go back on the bottle. As I'm sure Mr Blore persuaded him.'

'He wasn't short of persuasion.' Indeed, what with the nantz, beer and wine they'd had a pretty batch of it. 'They sent me out of the way. That's how I got my note written, see.'

He's not interested in how she got her note written. 'A man can talk as he likes about leaving off drink, one cup generally settles him.'

'Not Sam. Guess what he did when Harry was gone.'

'Threw sweet herbs on the fire?'

'Put a feather down his throat and was sick as a monkey. Got himself sober.'

Ned makes a disgusted face.

'Yes, I grant you,' replies Betsy-Ann, 'but determined.'

'So where is he now?'

'Seeing a lodging in St Giles. O, Ned, I'm weary of it, so bloody weary.'

'Ah, my sweet, my honey,' says Ned, embracing her. She leans into his shoulder, smelling coffee on his breath and the bitter amber scent of his skin. But only his right arm squeezes her, pressing her against the buttons of his coat. The left is occupied with the coffee pot, lifting it and setting it down.

How small, the word that could change everything. Ned must know that word. She can almost see it on his lips, poised like a bird – a tiny, daring wren – about to fly the nest.

'I should be wretched in St Giles,' she whispers.

Ned studies the inmates of the coffee house as if to commit them to memory. A silence grows. Betsy-Ann sees herself and Ned as they must appear to others: a handsome man, looking about him as if bored, and a shabby, spoony female glued to his side. Her cheeks growing hot, she pulls away. Still he does not speak. Betsy-Ann takes up the coffee pot and empties it into her own cup.

'My affairs are so – so irregular,' he says at last. 'I should be a brute to make any poor bitch dependent upon them.'

'Like your autem mort?' It is out before Betsy-Ann can stop herself.

'A different case entirely.' Ned stares at her, unsmiling. 'It seems to me, Madam, that you spend a deal of time, lately, considering how best to worm your way round Ned, how to make Ned say this or that. Let us understand each other for once.'

'For *once*?' She gives him the stare right back, though doing so produces a near-unendurable sensation, like boiling water bubbling up inside her body.

'You don't consider my position. Being caught by your bull-calf of a brother – that's bad luck for you. Well, it's *deuced* bad luck for me. Suppose Shiner asks him, by way of a favour, to break my hands?'

She can find no reply.

'No,' he says, 'I prefer to keep in one piece. If that makes me a coward, so be it.'

'I can never think you a coward, Ned,' says Betsy-Ann.

His voice softens. 'I'm not too proud to return the compliment. If a woman may be judged by strength of character then you, Miss Blore, are the finest woman I've known. You meet a man, as it were, face to face – or did so until recently.'

At the last few words Betsy-Ann feels a stab. To be accused of deception, while all the time persuaded that he is hiding something from her, is too cruel.

'I understand your hints,' Ned says. 'You wish me to set you up again. There's nobody I'd sooner take into keeping, but —' He gives a regretful shrug. 'There's Ma, too. She won't endure you.'

'So our meeting's for nothing? I'm to continue with Sam?'

He lays his hand over hers, stroking her wrist with his thumb as if soothing a child. 'You can get out from under him. There's many a man would be glad enough – yes, indeed,' he insists, catching at her fingers as if she might pull them away.

'But us, Ned.'

'What of us, my sweet?'

'Shall we keep on with Haddock's?'

'We've been beaten from that bush.'

If he has a chamber here, now's the time to say so. With a final pat at her fingers he pulls away and begins buttoning up his coat.

'Easy as that,' she says as if to herself. 'Like some old shoe.'

He pauses in the act of fastening the buttons and regards her, head cocked, in silence. At last he says, 'I should never have followed you that day.'

'You'd no business to.'

'Inclination I certainly had.'

'I could help you,' Betsy-Ann says.

'Oh, child, let us be done! Spare me your —'

'Teach you the Spanish trick.'

'Ah.' His eyes flick over her, searching her face for deceit. Then, '*If* you did,' (biting off each word) 'I could tell Ma to go hang.'

277

'If I did.'

'If.'

She has his attention, all right; he's a dog shivering for the hare. What does it mean? A brief chase and thrown aside bloody, her mystery torn out?

'Understand me, Betsy.'

'I'm trying to,' says Betsy-Ann.

'With that rig I can pay off all the creditors in a few months. I can carve us enough to live on.'

'Together?'

'For as long as we want. She'll be glad to see the back of me. We'll set up genteel, away from Shiner and Harry.'

'And Kitty?'

'Kitty can't touch us. Can't touch us, my honey,' and Ned's face shines. It's the face she remembers from their first days together; she hadn't learnt, then, to be wary of him. Still, what a look to turn on a woman. Like a purseful of gold. He says, all sweet and tickle-mouse, 'No other woman ever gave me such a gift, Betsy, no other woman could, but you' – though the tilt of his head says, *To me, such incense is due.*

She raises her chin in turn, eyeing him: one gamester to another. 'I might possibly be persuaded.'

'And your condition is . . . ?'

She folds her arms. 'I can't talk of it here.'

Again they eye one another, until Ned laughs. '*Touché.* You shall have your chamber.'

'And my chamberer, to attend on me?'

'Him also.'

'Your word upon it?'

'Damn my word. My wife has my word. Whereas you —' He grins. 'You have something of far greater value.'

'What's that?'

'My inclination.'

37

On entering the room he sees a strange woman peering through the window. Today both grate and candles are cold and dead; anyone standing on the pavement would be looking into a dark pit, which is why she screws up her face like that. There is a moment's fear as the woman's eyes lock with his, but they lock blindly: she has not seen him and she moves away.

Fortunate takes what he came for – Mrs Launey's account book, left behind after this morning's consultation with the Wife – and is crossing the hallway when someone knocks at the door.

He dodges into the corridor, but too late. Before he can turn again and be out of sight, Eliza is upon him.

'I'll have that, if you please! Now go and answer, and don't ask me why!'

She swipes the book from his hand and hurries back to her work.

The knock comes again. Of course it is the spying woman. When he opens the door her face is composed and superior, her eyes commanding where before they squinted. There is even a little smirk on her lips. He would like to say to her, I saw you! And you looked very foolish!

Instead he asks her to wait and takes her card to the Pinched Wife.

'Send her in and fetch us tea,' the Wife says. '*You* are to fetch it, mind, not one of the maids.'

Today is strange, everybody seems to want him. He must go for the book, must answer the door and bring the tea.

The woman follows him along the corridor to the Blue Room. He can tell from the tiny sounds made by her clothing that she keeps turning and staring about her at the furniture and wall-paper. It is not pleasant to have such a person at your back. He is glad to deliver her to the mistress and hurry away.

In the kitchen, Mrs Launey wants to know the woman's name and if she appears respectable.

'Yes, I think,' says Fortunate, who understands that by *respectable* these people mean someone cold and overbearing. 'Her name is Mrs Howell.'

The cook picks at her front teeth. 'Can't say I know any Howells.'

'Me neither,' says Eliza, placing a loaf upon the table. 'She doesn't visit here. Did she seem a kind sort of lady?'

'Not kind.'

'What's she like, then?'

He shrugs. What can he say? The woman made a bad impression.

'I wish Fan was here,' says Eliza.

'He's taken against her, we don't need Fan to tell us that. Can't you cut the bread any thinner, Liza? You weren't taught to make doorsteps.'

'Begging your pardon, Mrs L, but it's crumbly. Listen, Titus. Do you know why this lady's come?'

Fortunate suggests, 'To look in the house?'

Mrs Launey raises a warning hand, which Eliza ignores. 'It's you she's come to see, Titus. Mrs Zed advertised you for a good servant.'

'The mistress is pleased with me?'

The girl looks at him with what he now sees is pity before turning again to the loaf and slicing it in half. 'No, you noddy. She wants you off her hands.'

He shivers. So he is to be passed on once more, like an animal – is this possible? Has Dog Eye permitted it?

'Here.' Eliza arranges the items on the tray. 'Your bread-and-butter, your teapot, china, water, cream, sugar, lemon, sugar-tongs. And spoons. I'll hold the door for you.'

'The master,' he stammers. 'Is he know?'

'Couldn't say, I'm sure,' the cook replies. 'Don't take on, love. Eliza, *you* carry the —'

'No, it's got to be him. Hey, Titus!'

He is about to pick up the tray. He looks up and Eliza fetches him a stinging slap across the face. He freezes, unsure whether to retaliate but determined not to cry at the hands of a woman.

'Go on,' Eliza urges. 'Blubber. Cry your eyes nice and red.'

The cook bends toward him, interested. 'Do what she says, child.'

'Titus, you must be a bad servant. Bad, bad! Do you understand? You must have nasty eyes and drop things, then Mrs Howell won't take you. Here —' She pokes her finger into the butter dish, smears it along his sleeve, then runs to the flour bin and fetches out a handful, sprinkling it over the butter.

'Rub it in,' she says. The result is terrifying: an impressive white stain blooms along his forearm. The mistress will surely kill him. In his soiled livery, with his eyes watery and his cheek burning, he creeps towards the room where the ladies wait.

'Poor creature, it was a blessed release,' patters Betsy-Ann, her head cocked in at the doorway. 'Such affliction, Sir, as you'd have wept to see.'

The Uncle says, 'Don't stand there letting in the cold.'

'I can't leave my cart, Sir. If I could bring it into the yard, now.'

He grunts, slides off the stool and disappears through the back of the shop. Betsy-Ann ducks back outside, to the gate flanking the shop front, and hears a bolt shoot. The boards quiver on their hinges.

'To pledge?' asks the Uncle, peeking through the gap. His head with its small round eyes reminds her of a parrot at Kitty's: it was forever poking its head between the bars of its cage, and one day the cat got it. She shoves at the gate, pushing in her handcart before he can change his mind. 'To sell, Sir. All to sell. I've wipers, dummees —'

'Don't give me your cant.'

'Kerchiefs, pocket-books and watches. And fawneys, Sir.'

He allows that word, or perhaps doesn't hear it since he is now bolting the gate behind her. Betsy-Ann safely inside and his defences back in place, he unlocks the side door to the premises.

To her surprise, what lies behind is almost the same as the shop front: another counter, another grille. 'Stop there,' says the Uncle. Yet another door opens, fast as a whore's legs, and he dodges through it. Again the sound of bolts. In a few seconds he reappears behind the grille.

'I don't go armed,' says Betsy-Ann. 'Is this all the same place?'

'Same only privater. Now, show me,' he says, unlatching the little door in the grille.

'There's more left behind.' Betsy-Ann wipes her eyes. 'Such a lovely shop as she had. To think of her ending up skin and bone.'

'Show me.'

He claws at the first thing she picks out for him, a mother-of-pearl toothpick case with silver trimmings.

'I've wipers, different colours —'

Through the gap in the grille she offers him a fine big one in scarlet silk. He pushes that aside and reaches for a gold-and-turquoise fawney.

'I shouldn't be standing here with my constitution,' he says. 'Show me the lot at once and I'll give you a price.'

'Piece by piece is my way.'

He's weighing her up. 'It'd be quicker.'

'We might forget something, Uncle. You wouldn't want that, would you?'

They settle to the business of haggling, though Betsy-Ann relents so far as to group the handkerchiefs together. As he examines each item he adds it to a list, Betsy-Ann watching to make sure nothing is left off. When a price has been agreed for everything, he reads the list aloud, pointing to the price and at the same time moving the goods from one pile to another so that she can see for herself. She insists on him going slowly; she can't read but she can add up. Even so, by the time she is satisfied that everything tallies, her hands are nearly as blue and corpse-like as his. The pawnbroker's cough smokes in the hard, dead air.

Before his eyes she bites each piece of gold he slides across the counter, then signs, with a cross, a receipt he's made out for her in the name of Mrs Flatt: their one shared joke.

On the way home she stops to buy bread and sausage from costers. Her feet are light; she trips along humming one of Mam's favourites, *Young Robin and His Love*.

> *Young Robin was of high degree,*
> *He loved a simple maid*

She's offloaded about a third of the Eye's contents. First she took the small precious things, leaving the bigger ones to make a show. At a glance, which is all he'll spare them, the boxes and buckets look as full as ever. Thrust down her stays, digging into her ribs, is the fruit of her labours: a tight little leather bag. What Sam'd give, to get his crippled paws on that! In a couple of days she'll hand him a guinea, tell him she's doing all she can to get him to St Giles.

> *And there he saw a wondrous sight*
> *The like was never seen*
> *A thousand horses, red and white*
> *A-riding on the green*

He'll be well and truly bitten. She tries not to think about how he'll look when he finds out: though he doesn't trust her any more, he did once, or wanted to.

Damned if she'll weep for him, though. When *he* had gold he got a piece tight in each fist and struck out like a man that meant business. A regular prize-fighter he was, coming slashing in with his old one-two, when she and Ned were at their weakest.

> *He is not here, the mother cried*
> *For Margaret is dead*
> *And 'neath a grove of willows green*
> *Are she and Robin laid*

Now Sam's star is on the wane and the Age of Ned dawns. She's game enough to take that chance, go where it leads: Pamphile and Prodigy seated at the table, playing to the end, Prodigy with aces roosting in her hand, aye, and Pamphile in there too.

For a while. No man is in the palm of a woman's hand forever. Her time in Kitty's would have been spent to little purpose indeed, had she failed to understand *that*.

Shiner is asleep in a chair, his cheek pressed to the window. He must have dozed off while watching for her. Even the rattle of her key in the lock fails to bring him round; he only grunts and shifts position.

Betsy-Ann puts down her basket and sits to study him. He's a ruin, his face crumpled all on one side. His fam lies palm upwards in his lap, the purple gristle of the scar exposed. When he wakes, he'll put that out of sight.

There was a time, a little breath of a time before he lost the finger, when she thought she and Sam might do something, after all.

Not at first. At first she couldn't talk for grief. She was a blind girl, Ned's pretty picture burnt in at the backs of her eyeballs, a girl sitting dumb and motionless while somewhere in the room Shiner bustled about, taking pains to please her: bringing coal upstairs to spare her the trouble, washing his face before bending it towards her for a kiss. She did not turn her lips away but let them hang slack. One morning she woke to find him bending over the pillow, his blue gaze no longer sly but bruised. *Poor bastard*, she thought. Her pity made him real.

Slowly they began to shake down. It was true what Ned had said: Shiner adored her, watched her like the little dog did, until it was stolen away. Never what you'd call well favoured but still, he talked with her. Gave her his name.

Now he's gelded, his power over the cards cut away. Terrible to see a man so reduced. It comes to her that this is perhaps how she looked, all those months ago: collapsed to one side. She sees his eyelids flutter, hears the faint *pop* as his dry lips part. He might be saying *Betsy*. Perhaps a figure in her shape floats about the inside of his head, dancing, laughing. The ghost of Betsy-Ann leads Sam into the bedchamber, bright in his dream with the best wax candles, and there pulls him down, gluey kisses in the damp, death-scented sheets —

Sam farts, opens his eyes and peels his face off the windowpane.

'Your neck'll be stiff and no mistake,' says Betsy-Ann, watching him rub it. He flinches and she realises that until she spoke, he hadn't known she was there.

'You just come in? Where you been?'

She shows him her basket with the sausage and loaf in it. He turns towards the sinking fire, as if calculating how long ago she left, and covers the move by saying, 'Warm enough for you?'

'I'll put some coal on.' She places the basket on the table, ready to unpack. Shiner lays his good hand on her arm.

'Harry's been here.'

'Has he, now.'

'I told him straight. Said I'm not going back.'

She leaps with the shock of it. 'Christ, Sam! He'll kill you – kill you.'

Sam's grip on her arm tightens. He pulls her down until their faces are almost touching. 'Not a tear, eh? You might shed a tear for me, Betsy.'

She looks away from him and in the end he lets her go. She reaches for a chair. By the time she's pulled one close and sat down by his side, he's slid the maimed hand into his pocket.

'I can blub all you like, it won't do any good,' she says, sugaring her voice. 'Go and take him something, Sammy. Bottle of nantz. Tell him you meant nothing by it.'

He stares straight ahead now. 'And is that the advice you'd give Hartry?'

'It's not Hartry we're —'

'If it was, you'd be giving fourpenny flyers in the street, paying his passage to India. Anything to keep him safe.'

'I'm trying to keep *you* safe.'

'So you say. I don't see any love in you. Damned if I've ever seen any.'

Very quiet and cold she says, 'He wasn't in a position to stake that.'

He turns his head and she is surprised: just for a second there's a flicker of something she hasn't seen before, something that in another man she might call pity. What's he sparing her? Ned's catalogue of sale, perhaps: *lush around the dairyworks. Deep purse.* If so, he could spare himself the trouble. Since Kitty's, she's beyond caring. She says, 'What'll you do for readies?'

He says nothing, but takes the sausage out of the basket and unwraps it.

'Wait, I'll cut you some bread.' But Shiner shakes his head. He

286

casts aside the sausage and smooths out the wrapping paper on the table.

'Get us a piece of coal, will you? With a bit of dust on it.'

He's a case for Bedlam. Betsy-Ann fetches a lump and he takes it not in his good hand, but in the maimed one. He turns the coal over, running his tongue between his lips, almost as if he wants to eat the thing. Then, smiling as if at some private joke, he puts it to paper, avoiding the grease spots, and begins to scratch. She watches, fascinated, as his fingers travel about the paper on tracks only he can see, a curve here, a mass of shading there. The coal cracks, spattering the surface with black flecks, so that he is obliged to turn it about frequently in his hand. He works fast, for all that. A knot of lines becomes brows, lashes, a circle of iris, another.

'Fine pair of ogles, eh?'

'Dimber.' She wonders how he'll do her ringlets, down on her shoulders or fastened up.

'It should be charcoal. If you saw me with charcoal, now. Or an engraver's pen.'

'So the plan's to be an engraver?' She stops looking at the picture and stares at him, at his intent profile. 'Do you know the trade?'

'I'm time-served. Never set up my own shop.'

'Why was that?'

'Fell in with bad company.'

When she looks back to the picture, she gasps. The hair is in place, but not as she pictured it, and Shiner's hand is just touching in the lips: a wide, greedy muzzle. Even drawn in coal on coarse paper, the face compels attention.

'Dimber. As you so kindly observed.'

'I thought it was me,' is all Betsy-Ann can say. And indeed, the picture does have a look of her about it. She's not sure whether the resemblance has always been there, and the sketch has merely shown her what everyone else has seen from the start, or whether it comes from Shiner's coupling them in his mind.

287

'Is it a good likeness?' he enquires, head on one side.

'I'm no judge of likenesses.'

'You see I can earn my way. Should you like to have this? As a memento of me.'

She turns over the possible answers in her mind. None of them is safe.

'It's fine work.'

'You show your ignorance, my dear. Before I was cut, *then* you could call me a draughtsman.' Shiner takes the portrait over to the fire and drops it onto the coals. Ned's eyes light up, defiant, as the grease on the paper catches. The face itself goes next, a red-rimmed hole appearing at his temple. Though he grins to the last, there is soon nothing left of him but a grey rag of ash.

Shiner whoops like a savage, startling Betsy-Ann. He claps his hands and crows. 'What a pretty fellow! What a pity!'

'Is that all you drew it for?'

He smirks. 'Don't you understand what I just showed you? No, nothing. Cunts and the use of 'em, that's all the Sex can compre-hend.' Bewildered, she lets him run on: 'A mort can't know the hundredth part of what a man knows. Not the hundredth part.'

It's on the tip of her tongue to say, *You talk more sense when you're drunk*, but she is wary of this bitter Shiner who has opened up, like a magical box, to show inner workings previously unguessed-at. She says:

'If something's *told* me I can understand it.'

'Ah, but you shan't be told.' He lays his finger alongside his nose. 'You'll have to wait and see.'

What she sees is that between Harry's spite and Sam's jealousy, she stands a fair chance of being crushed. She has to get out from under him. Ned or no Ned.

38

'Bless me,' cries Hetty, entering with a bustling haste which, though inelegant, speaks eloquently of her affection, 'Who have we here? Cousin Sophia, I vow! And mistress of all she surveys.'

Sophia composes her features into the smile demanded by politeness. There is nothing she can do, alas, about her flaring cheeks.

She is quite fit to be seen. Her toilette is respectable and the room where she sits clean and orderly; even at her most wretched, she has never descended into sluttishness. Her sense of being caught out arises from the consciousness that she cannot produce Edmund, who has not been home since yesterday evening. To add to her misery, there is nobody she less expected to see than these two and nobody to whom she would sooner offer the warmest hospitality, had she only known. Though there may be something in reserve: Mrs Launey seems a competent enough person and Sophia has yet to test her mettle.

'Darling Hetty —' She embraces her cousin and shakes hands with Mr Letcher, her mouth bringing out congratulations and civilities while her mind flaps moth-like round the burning questions: how has this happened? Are they expecting to stay?

'And such a cold day, too! Pray sit near the fire and warm yourselves.' She installs the smiling couple on the sofa; it is rather cramped for such a big man as Mr Letcher but the chairs are no better. 'Fan, bring tea and cake.'

The girl curtseys and is gone. Sophia seats herself opposite her guests.

'Well!' The word comes out breathily, as if she is over-laced. 'This is indeed a charming surprise.'

Hetty's dark eyebrows arrange themselves into graceful arches. 'Surprise? But I wrote we should come if —' Her hand flies to her mouth. 'You haven't received — O, Sophy! O, Lord!'

'It's of no consequence,' Sophia assures her. 'Were you intending to pass the night here?'

'You see how splendid she is, Letcher? No, my love, we shan't be billeting ourselves upon you. Our lodgings are quite satisfactory. Good God, what a shock you must have had!' Hetty is laughing now, her eyes not quite as blithe as the rest of her face. Sophia can guess at her thoughts: *Such a street for a gentleman's house, I do hope Sophy is not unhappy.*

'Dearest Hetty, you mustn't apologise. Though I never saw your letter, I couldn't be more delighted to see *you.*'

Now that Sophia has begun to recover herself, she is indeed filled with pleasure at the sight of her cousin, with the pink cheeks of one newly entered from the cold, installed by the hearth while her husband, the estimable Josiah Letcher, compliments his hostess on having a first-rate fire. Her initial impressions of this gentleman were principally of height and solidity. Now that she has looked at him a little longer, she can add to those attributes a good-tempered mouth and a pair of small but benevolent brown eyes. Mr Letcher is scrupulously but not foppishly groomed and his clothes well cut. He is a man upon whose arm one might lean in confidence and Hetty (blooming with precisely such confidence) a charming exemplar of wifely happiness.

Like most plain women, Sophia has endured her share of complacent looks from more fortunate members of the Sex. From Hetty, however (so sprightly and attaching, so admired by gentlemen) nothing of the sort has ever been forthcoming; Hetty is, was, and always will be all generosity and good nature. And since Mr Letcher, beaming goodwill from the sofa, appears to be Hetty's masculine counterpart, Sophia feels her awkwardness thaw to the point where she can boldly confess her predicament: though her guests will not starve, the kitchen may not rise to the occasion. It is, of course, possible to send out for something and when they have drunk their tea she will speak with the cook.

'O, that won't be necessary,' Hetty says. 'My plan was to call this morning, take the air with you – if you wished – and then have dinner somewhere.' Seeing Sophia hesitate, she adds at once, 'Mr Letcher's treat, you know. He insists he shall indulge us this once.'

'But you are too kind,' says Sophia, a girlish excitement rising within her at the thought of such an outing.

'Kind? I shall thoroughly enjoy myself,' replies Mr Letcher. 'What's the use of money, if not to spend?'

His wife chimes in, 'Or of matrimony, unless one may also enjoy a *partie de plaisir* with one's dearest friends?'

'O, I should like it above anything! I remember last year you went to Ranelagh.'

'Yes, with Mama and Mrs Jamieson – I don't think you know Mrs Jamieson. We thoroughly enjoyed ourselves. Everyone should visit Ranelagh, if only for the Rotunda.'

'And the music?'

'Charming, if you like the English style. The price of refreshments is a scandal, of course. Everybody is shocked, and everybody continues to go.' Hetty looks thoughtful. 'Do you know, Sophy, I believe I wrote to you proposing this visit – now, I mean – while you were in Bath. Didn't you receive my letter?'

'The post's very bad. I've only heard from Mama and Papa, and not always from them.'

'How odd! *We* haven't been inconvenienced, have we, Letcher? And you've missed more than one letter from Buller?' Hetty leans forward, lowering her voice. 'In your place I should look to the servants. I should never suggest such a thing in your mother's house, but *London* servants!' She shakes her head. 'Mr Letcher's mother once engaged a boy who wouldn't take the trouble of collecting the post during cold weather, can you imagine? He sat in the kitchen eating buttered toast – the best butter, at sixpence a pound! – and she only found him out by accident.'

'You may be right,' says Sophia. 'As for the letter to Bath, we left early and it was perhaps lost that way. Where shall we go, Hetty? It sounds as if you would recommend Ranelagh?'

'Marylebone Garden is more convenient than Ranelagh at this time of year,' says Hetty, 'though you've perhaps seen Marylebone already, since it lies so close at hand.'

'No, I haven't. But I read in the papers that Ranelagh is by far the most elegant, and patronised by the *ton*.'

'The thing is . . .' says Hetty, glancing across at her husband.

Mr Letcher spreads his hands appeasingly, 'Alas, Ranelagh is now closed except for very particular events. The weather, you know.'

'O, how disappointing!' As indeed it is. 'But surely the Rotunda is heated? I've read that its warmth is much appreciated.'

'On a chilly summer day, yes. Its fires are not equal to autumn and winter. But never mind,' says Mr Letcher with what Sophia already recognises as his usual kindness, 'we shall promenade quite as healthily in Marylebone Gardens. Unless, of course, there is somewhere you would like better.'

Hetty, seeing her cousin's difficulty, moves to shield the raw ignorance of a bumpkin who doesn't even know the months for Ranelagh. 'One is never sure what to believe. Yesterday's great project, Sophy, was to dine at an inn – a celebrated place, recommended by a man of taste. When we got there I couldn't touch a thing. The mutton they brought! So high it was practically green. Was it not, Letcher?'

'Quite green, my love.'

'Well, you shall eat no green mutton at my house,' promises Sophia, her mind reverting to her lost letter. That Edmund might have confiscated it she does not doubt, but would he not have put off the visitors by a counterfeit reply? Unable to solve this riddle, she pushes it from her mind as Fan reappears bearing a tray with tea things and – Mrs Launey having risen to the occasion – an entire unbroken seedcake.

'O, Sophy, I quite *forgot*!' Hetty exclaims as Fan sets down the refreshments, causing the maid to start. She begins to root in the knotting bag which she has evidently taken, like Sophia, to carrying outside the house. 'I do hope you haven't got one already. I thought, Why, that's the thing for Sophy – ah!' With this cry of triumph she fishes out a rectangular package wrapped in white paper. 'Yes, the very thing.'

Smiling, Sophia smooths back the folds – so fresh and immaculate as to be a pleasure in themselves – to reveal a gleaming new binding. Her gift is the plays of William Shakespeare, edited by Samuel Johnson.

'O, my dear — !'

'Aunt Buller seemed to think you didn't have it. There are more volumes, of course —'

'Seven,' puts in Mr Letcher dryly.

'— which my dear husband had to carry. We've left them with the maid. You *don't* have it, do you Sophy?'

'No, my dear.' Sophia hugs the book to her bosom. 'I can't think of a better present, Hetty, nor can I thank you enough,' and she rises to kiss Hetty on both cheeks, noticing in the process that Hetty's eyes are moist at the success of her gift.

'Now let us do justice to that seedcake,' says Mr Letcher, rubbing his hands together in high satisfaction.

Cutting up the cake, engaged in family gossip with Hetty and civilly addressed by Hetty's husband, Sophia can imagine herself engaged upon the married life of her innocent expectations, the life she believed herself to be choosing when she gave her hand to Mr Zedland. It is a poignant sensation, such as a beggar might experience on being handed a plate of turtle soup: surely he would swallow the precious treat in drops, lick the bowl and spoon and do everything in his power to lengthen out the pleasure. So does Sophia endeavour to extract every last scent and savour from her impromptu tea-party.

After a while, Hetty asks: 'Is Mr Zedland away from home?'

Having perceived her repeated leadings-up to this question and her very natural curiosity, Sophia is ready with a smile.

'He dines today in town.'

'And tonight?'

'It depends. He is often engaged with men of business until very late, so he prefers not to bring them here.'

'Do you hear that, Letcher? How agreeable, not to have one's men of business in one's home. Will you stay for him, Sophy?'

'No. I'll join you.'

'O, I hope he does come! Aunt has raised my curiosity to such a pitch, you can't imagine. She says he's the handsomest man in England.'

'I haven't yet seen all the men in England. He has certainly a prepossessing appearance.'

Hetty's eyes narrow a shade. Sophia is possibly the only person in the world who could interpret the precise degree of unease conveyed by those narrowed eyes. 'If he's detained by urgent business, I must resign myself to missing him, I suppose. But not the house, Sophy. You shan't get off that.'

'If not inconvenient,' puts in her husband.

'Of course it isn't inconvenient.' Hetty rolls her eyes. 'What can possibly be of more interest? Between ladies, that is. Gentlemen never understand.'

'Slander, my dear. Every gentleman of sense appreciates domestic comfort. But we mustn't impose on Mrs Zedland.'

'No imposition, I assure you. Hetty is right – were I in *your* new home, I should fairly boil with impatience for the Grand Tour.'

'There, you see, Letcher?'

'But Hetty, you mustn't expect to see anything of my choosing.

Edmund digs in his heels and refuses to decorate. When we first arrived, he was adamant that we should soon decamp for Wixham. And yet we linger.'

'Perhaps he'll change his mind.'

'Hum! Perhaps.'

Mr Letcher is sympathetic. 'Husbands are crusty, disagreeable things. My spouse often complains of it. But never mind, Mrs Zedland. If the new spring patterns are charming, and I am told by ladies that they always are, your patience will be amply rewarded.'

'Who's slanderous now?' exclaims Hetty. 'I never called you crusty and disagreeable in my life.'

'Did you not? Then it was perhaps some other spouse. I follow the Mussulman custom, you know, Mrs Zedland, and permit myself four.'

'Gracious!' Sophia helps him to more seedcake. 'The laundry bills must be shocking.'

'I knew you would appreciate Mr Letcher, Sophy. Mama, bless her, is frequently at a loss. But to your house. If Mr Zedland wishes to stay, all the better, surely? Time enough to rusticate after the Season.'

'You underestimate us, Hetty. *We* contrive to rusticate in Town.'

'Come, this isn't so far out! Lord, to think of Buller, with those dirty roads around, yet you contrived to visit. When you and Mr Zedland come to our seraglio,' she darts a mocking glance at her husband, 'you shall see the grapevines.'

'Really, a vineyard? How delightful that must be.'

'They are famous throughout the district, but my Mussulman husband refuses to drink the wine.'

Mr Letcher roars with laughter. 'Not one tolerable bottle in ten years! The gardener warned that it wouldn't do but Mama insisted upon making the experiment.'

'And now blames *him* for it. The gardener, I mean. But he's trained some of them up a loggia and they give the prettiest shade imaginable. Come in summer, Sophy, and we can dine beneath them.'

'I should love to. Do the grapes make good eating?'

'Sour, alas. But ornamental. We must not expect too much of beauty.'

Her eyes, meeting Sophia's, seem to hold them an instant. Not until Hetty has looked away, and is demurely nibbling at her slice of cake, is Sophia even aware of it.

The refreshments disposed of, Sophia and her cousin are ready for their tour of the house. Upon Mr Letcher's rising to accompany them, Hetty suggests he stay and rest. 'We've a campaign to plan, my love, right down to pelmets and fringes. Best stay out of the firing line.'

'If Mrs Zedland will not think me impolite,' he says, hovering.

Sophia assures him she will think nothing of the sort. Indeed, her thoughts are entirely engaged by one question: what Hetty will make of what she is about to see. So Mr Letcher remains, digesting seedcake, while the ladies mount the stairs.

The first room opened is Sophia's own chamber. The mattress, sponged and scrubbed but not replaced, retains a faint odour but at this time of year it is weighted down by coverlets and quilts; the bed is tightly made and the room pitilessly aired. If Hetty is aware of any taint in the atmosphere, she is far too well bred to reveal it.

'Don't fear to insult my taste,' Sophia prompts. 'I chose none of this.'

'Well. It's a *little* drab.' Hetty, linking arms, gives an affectionate squeeze. 'And those boards need varnish. But only think, my dear, once you get started – how glorious to sweep it all away at once! I've often thought that in decorating, the first time must be the best. After that, you know, one patches and pinches and has nobody else to blame.'

Sophia, persuaded that genteel economy will form no part of her cousin's married life, feels Hetty's kindness. She is about to consult her on the relative desirability of green and yellow bed-hangings when Hetty's arm stiffens in hers: it is the involuntary frisson that accompanies a hastily restrained impulse. Sophia has been anticipating this moment. She composes herself and waits.

For a short while Hetty also remains silent. When she does speak, it is with an assumed lightness.

'If only my husband were as tidy as Mr Zedland. Letcher's like a romping pup, things flung everywhere. It creates so much work for the servants.'

Sophia's eyes turn with Hetty's towards the bolster with its tell-tale single indentation and then back towards her cousin's face, which just now resembles that of the maid in Bath, the one who said, 'Oh, *Madam* . . . !' before spilling out the business of the bubbled heir. On this occasion, however, Sophia is better pre-pared.

'You guess rightly, Hetty. We occupy separate beds.'

'But Sophy —'

'His physician insisted. Mr Zedland is a very light sleeper.'

The room which 'does' Edmund for a bedchamber is at the other end of the corridor. Hetty surveys the new bed with its fresh hangings, the wardrobe, the gilded mirror, the writing table and lamp. She looks down at the pink carpet, patterned with song-birds, on which the ladies are standing.

'I'm surprised he didn't have the room painted and papered,' she says at last. 'Before the furniture was put in.'

'It can be moved elsewhere when we paint.'

'There are some good pieces.'

'A little *passé*, don't you think? Edmund barely notices, but for myself, I want the latest things.' She listens to her own lies as they tumble out. All her life she has feared and despised mendacity, has scorned to practise it, and yet, put to the test, she is as slick and proficient as Edmund himself. Drawing Hetty away from the comfort of Edmund's chamber she adds, 'The place was sadly neglected, you know. Old Mr Zedland let it furnished.'

The study is a relief to her. This sterile cell represents nothing a wife might covet, save the right to close the door on household nuisances. She wonders how close Hetty has come to guessing the truth, namely that Edmund's bedroom furniture was pillaged from the marital chamber. Taking her cousin's hand in hers, she bestows on it an encouraging little pat. 'You mustn't worry because our arrangements aren't yours, my love. They suit me well enough.'

'Do they, Sophy?' Hetty perches on the edge of the desk. Inside the top drawer, concealed by a mere quarter-inch of mahogany, lies evidence of spectacular debaucheries – *a pair of sisters* – that Hetty's guesses, no matter how sympathetic, can never come near. Without warning, Sophia is flooded with perverse satisfaction. Hetty has made the good marriage, the marriage of hearts, minds and purses. In the eyes of society, she holds all the aces. But has she ever felt for Josiah Letcher what Sophia felt for Edmund Zedland? How extraordinary, to know one's husband no better than a highwayman, to fear him, even, as a dealer of disease and death, and yet to recall an intimate, headlong exhilaration – could the worthy Josiah Letcher inspire such violence of loving? Never. Never.

Should Hetty hear these thoughts, she would take no offence. Sophia imagines her perplexed musings: *Darling Sophy is grown irrational. She must not be quarrelled with, but bled and carefully watched.*

She is not such a fool as to claim a bad husband as a distinction: *rational*, Sophia is still. But she has discovered a depth in herself, a source upon which Hetty (kind, generous Hetty, living on the surface, in the sunlight) will never draw. Then again, Hetty might say, 'To be thus attached to a bad fellow, my darling, is not

298

strength, but weakness. You must get free of him. Ask your papa to negotiate a separation.' But Hetty would have misunderstood. Her love for Edmund was indeed a weakness, a sickness: Sophia sees this plainly enough. But *what it takes to survive such sickness –* of *that* she is proud. In Hetty's presence she feels herself unutterably the older woman, experienced beyond imagining: an ancient, wizened sibyl. And with this realisation comes the knowledge, irrevocable, that this is why she has not confided in Hetty, and will not, and cannot. Even to Mama she has complained only of Edmund's dishonesty and the low company he keeps. Of the most intimate wounds he has inflicted, not a word.

So struck is Sophia by this view of affairs that the room fades from her consciousness. In another moment she becomes aware that Hetty has her by the elbow and is mouthing something, which proves to be, 'Sophy? Are you well?'

Not until she has recovered herself, breathing as deeply as her stays permit, can she lead the now pensive Hetty to the guest rooms, macabre in dustsheets (the attics, where the servants sleep, being unworthy of attention), then the dining room, the offices and the square of garden at the back of the house. In the scullery (for Hetty wishes to see how it is laid out) they discover Titus, grey and listless, scraping at the burnt bottom of a pot. Mrs Launey and the maidservants, surprised in the kitchen, are caught in mid-bicker, dropping the bone of contention as they drop their curtseys, ready to pounce and worry it directly the mistress has gone.

'I shall dine out today,' says Sophia. 'You may heat up the beef and serve it for supper.'

Mrs Launey looks bilious. I haven't given her much notice, Sophia thinks, but surely she can manage that.

'If you're not wanting me, Madam, may I take a walk? For my constitution. I find I'm not quite myself.'

'As long as the maids are fed,' says Sophia.

When Mrs Launey has thanked her, the ladies withdraw to the breakfast room, which despite its sallow décor retains a faded charm. It is also out of hearing of both Mr Letcher and *les domestiques*.

'You don't have the boy answer the door?'

'Sometimes. He's unsatisfactory.' She really must deal with Titus, who will never learn to speak like a Christian and whose demeanour evidently disgusted Mrs Howell, for that lady never returned. Unlatching a shutter, she beckons Hetty to a window. 'What do you think of the view from here? It isn't St James, of course.'

Hetty steps forward and studies the throng of passers-by. 'Do you know, when I'm in London I always feel I could be jostled off the pavement at any moment.'

'Yes. Such a press of people and often so ill bred. Are we your first call since you arrived?'

'Not quite. After our foul mutton we went to supper with Mr Letcher's sister at Chelsea. I don't think she cares for me much.'

'No?'

'I serve merely to make up a card table. What about you, Sophy? With whom do you visit?'

'Oh, we live in a very retired way. My life revolves around Mr Zedland. You know how it is when a wife —'

'But my dear, you haven't any children.'

Sophia laughs. 'I should be sorry to be in the straw so soon!'

'Quite.' Hetty's expression is one Sophia recognises from childhood: thus did she look just before pushing a naughty boy, found tormenting a swan, into Statue Lake. 'Have you cast us in the roles of Rosencrantz and Guildenstern, my dear? We weren't sent as spies. We weren't *sent* at all.'

'Of course not, Hetty, I never —'

'Then why this reserve? You wound me, Sophy.'

'Wound you?'

'One doesn't keep a dear friend at arm's length.'

'You aren't a dear friend, Hetty, you're my dearest friend – apart, that is, from Edmund. Some ladies become more reserved upon marriage.' She can't resist adding, 'We may have our reasons, you know.'

'Do I? It's all I *do* know. I've so looked forward to this visit, Sophy. To meet as brides —! I was sure we should open our hearts to one another.'

'Please, Hetty dear, let's not quarrel. What earthly reason could I have for wounding you?'

'I don't know.' Hetty bites her lip and Sophia can see what her cousin will be at forty, pouchy about the chin. 'Mr Zedland must be handsome indeed.'

'Let's not quarrel,' Sophia repeats. 'Believe me, Hetty, you are always the object of my tenderest esteem. Now, shall we rejoin Mr Letcher and take a turn in Marylebone?'

In the past the cousins would have strolled together, too well bred not to include a third party in their talk but always more interested in each other's sayings and doings than in those of anyone else. Today, however, they arrange themselves on either side of Josiah Letcher.

Hetty's blameless husband, thus accompanied, presents a faint resemblance to a *man of honour* swaggering out, a mistress on either side. Sophia, who has recently begun to observe such swaggerers with interest, finds herself unconcerned. Anybody approaching near enough to recognise her could not fail to see how chastely Mr Letcher supports her arm. Besides, nobody knows her – she has given up hoping that anyone in London, apart from these two and Edmund, ever will – and where one is not known, one ceases, for all practical purposes, to exist.

301

But what *is* she thinking? She trembles, almost stumbles, at the direction in which her unchecked reflections have been leading, so that the attentive Mr Letcher turns in concern. Not known, when her most secret thought is open to One whose worth infinitely outweighs that of mere human society? Not known, when the Benign Lawgiver, the Tender Father is ever present, though unseen? She is under a loving protection that constitutes Man's chief comfort – though its contemplation, for some reason Sophia is unable to fathom, only deepens the oppression of her spirits.

The sky is all of one colour, a featureless expanse of steel-grey cloud beneath which Marylebone Gardens, shorn of their summer gaiety, show trivial and uninviting. Of course the place is not equal to Ranelagh, she is not so unreasonable as to expect it, but she privately resolves that when Hetty next visits they shall go to the theatre or the menagerie, anywhere likely to provide food for conversation. For what is there to talk of, here? Hedges, bowling greens and gravel walks? Sophia had all of these things at her parents' home, and peacocks to boot. As a girl she disliked their continual skirling but now, as Mr Letcher solicits her admiration for yet another oak tree, she would gladly be interrupted by an entire ostentation of peacocks, rending the air with their harpy screams. Perhaps it is the memory of those parading birds, perhaps the strolling in company, but she is curiously reminded of Bath: strange, when that vulgar, promiscuous, provincial city so entranced her, that she can take no pleasure in this scene of innocent English amusement. *Consider how much our modern elegance owes to their inspiration.* Who said that? Ah yes, she remembers now: Edmund championed the imitators of the classical, while she upheld the native English style. She pictures, as from a great distance, their boat suspended upon the glittering surface of the lake: the rower and the woman watching him, August raging all around them, unmeasured depths beneath. Her own face, which at the time she could only glimpse by leaning over the water, now comes close, poignantly open to her and transfigured by guileless adoration, while Edmund's is blurred.

O, for the innocence of that day! It seems that since then she has almost come to prefer the artful and the dishonest; no doubt if they went to Ranelagh she would scorn the honest English songs and give ear only to the warbling *bel canto*.

'Moving the cardoons was just such a whim,' Mr Letcher is complaining to Hetty. 'When a man has served as long as Tichborne, he should be left to his business.' Sophia is at a loss until she grasps that Mr Letcher's mother and her interference in the garden are again under discussion. She directs her gaze at the ground, half-listening to the conversation of her companions: how Mama is full of ill-judged projects that only serve to give the domestics extra work and how she fancies herself a second Mrs Delany, with none of the ability of that celebrated lady.

'She lacks occupation since the death of your papa,' Hetty murmurs.

'Indeed. There's something pitiable, I always think, in the spectacle of a wife without a husband. Ivy with no supporting tree.'

There follows a sound like the clearing of a throat. Sophia can picture Hetty's exasperated frown.

'Shall we turn in at the Rose?' suggests Mr Letcher with unabashed cheerfulness. 'Something warm would be a welcome restorative.'

'Is it respectable?' Sophia wants to know.

'Lord, Sophy, he wouldn't take us there otherwise!'

Sophia blushes. 'No, of course not.'

'In a place of resort one can never be sure of one's company,' Mr Letcher concedes with more honesty than power to reassure. 'Not even at Ranelagh. But I believe Marylebone is generally considered respectable.'

'The middling sort,' Hetty warns, in case Sophia should expect people of fashion.

The Rose of Normandy, towards which the three are now advancing, is the oldest part and the very rootstock of the garden, from which all the rest has sprung: the bowling greens first of all, then the gravel walks, the paths between the trees and the Great Room and orchestra. No architect, evidently, had any hand in the design of the Rose, but its thick walls and small windows present a stout defence against cold weather. Despite her misgivings, Sophia's heart lifts at the sight of smoke billowing from its chimney.

Behind the front door there is a flagged passageway. The room into which it leads them is also flagged, and completely empty.

Hetty laughs. 'We shan't be troubled by unruly companions, at any rate.'

'Perhaps they are not open for business.' Sophia watches as Mr Letcher goes to the counter and pulls on a rope, setting off a bell somewhere in the depths of the tavern.

The room is furnished with oak tables, benches and settles of the antique English pattern: this place certainly aims no higher than the middling sort, if so high. It appears clean, however, and the prospect of a warming glass is a powerful attraction after such a cold, damp walk. They make their way towards the inglenook in the furthest wall, where a faint gleam lingers among the cinders, and settle themselves at a table close by, Sophia and Hetty commanding a view of the empty tables and Mr Letcher, less careful of his complexion, facing the fire.

'How perfectly Gothick,' Hetty says.

Sophia expects the host to appear from behind the counter like an actor making an entrance upon his accustomed stage. Instead, he arrives via a heavy door at the opposite end of the room, through which issues, during the few seconds that it stands open, a faint hum of conversation.

'It seems all your company is through there,' Mr Letcher says pleasantly as the man approaches. 'Is this part of the inn shut up?'

'Not at all, Sir, and it is the most comfortable apartment for ladies.'

'Then kindly bring us more coals,' replies Mr Letcher. The landlord looks as if he thinks the room is quite warm enough, but his expression changes to one of gratified complaisance when they order hot bishop, a dish of stewed pigeons and some almond cheesecake.

'By *comfortable* I suppose he means not full of rowdies,' whispers Hetty as the man departs. 'What comfort can one find on a wooden bench?'

'A cushion, perhaps,' suggests Sophia. 'What sort of company is in the back room, I wonder? What do you think, Mr Letcher?'

'Some clubmen, I fancy. Not bad fellows, you know, but they like to have a place to themselves.'

'I hope they won't come through here.'

'O no, why should they? Don't be nervous, Mrs Zedland. They'll be drinking long after we've quitted the premises.'

'It's my cousin's nature to be nervous. Do you remember, Sophy, when Radley first put you on Diamond? I thought you'd faint.'

'Did I really look as afraid as that?'

'O, my dear! I told him you'd never learn and Aunt heard me. She said, *I'll have you know, young lady, that Sophia Buller unfailingly performs her duty.* I laughed – insufferable chit I must've been – but you learned, just as she said. I've often thought one can't be truly brave without fear.'

'Condemned out of your own mouth, my love,' remarks Mr Letcher, 'for I've never seen you afraid of anything.'

Sophia smiles to show that she has long forgiven Hetty's superiority – not difficult, since she has no recollection of her cousin's presence. What she recalls is the discomfort of perching sideways on the saddle, her terror of sliding off, the treacherous dip and sway of the pony. Radley led the beast forward, insisting on its gentleness. She suffered untold humiliation from his impatience; he had the terrible briskness, the ill-concealed contempt of all strong and practical people obliged to serve weaklings. What was she learning all those years ago? To overcome her fear of the animal, or to perfect her obedience to her mother? Boys are taught how to strike off shackles, girls how best to bear them.

But this is dreadful: she has begun to think like a bluestocking, or is it a libertine? She doesn't know; she doesn't know what she thinks. She is so over-tired, these days, and so unsettled: *nervous* hardly covers it.

The bishop is brought and she drains a glass almost at once. There seems to be fresh company inside the back room: laughter swells until it washes under the door.

'I wonder who they can be,' says Mr Letcher. 'What sort of club.'

Hetty purses her lips. 'Evidently one for noisy people.'

'I might just look in.'

'You said they wanted the place to themselves.'

'They won't grudge me one peep.'

'I wish you wouldn't, Letcher. Suppose they should be quarrelsome?'

'Come, my dear, they seem a very good-natured company.' Mr Letcher, with the courage taught to boys, takes up his glass of bishop and strides down the room to disappear through the far door, leaving his womenfolk alone.

'If they bring the meat,' grumbles Hetty, '*I* shan't go in there and call him out.'

'I'm sure he'll be back directly.'

Left alone with Hetty, she cannot help recalling their recent *tête-à-tête* in the house. Sophia hopes her cousin is no longer offended. It would be a great comfort to be reassured of this by Hetty herself, but how should she reopen the conversation? An ill-chosen word might suggest to Hetty that she is willing, on consideration, to sacrifice the secrets of the marriage bed on the altar of feminine friendship, and then there would be the whole awkwardness to go through again. Perhaps if she —

Hetty breaks into her thoughts. 'What's the matter with your black?'

'Titus?'

'You said he was unsatisfactory.'

'He talks oddly.'

'O, they all do that. Unless they are bred over here.'

'I know, but Titus's speech makes him ridiculous.'

'A pity. He looks well.'

'You think me extravagant,' Sophia observes.

'Not at all, but I confess myself puzzled. You live in a modest way, and then – this boy!'

'I had nothing to do with his coming into the house.'

'Ah,' says Hetty knowingly. 'Could you employ a master to correct him?'

'I doubt Mr Zedland would consent to the expense. Besides, instruction wouldn't precisely answer the case. There's an insolence about Titus.'

'Does he answer back?'

'I can't quite explain to you what I mean. One feels a lack of respect.'

'Hum! There are graver faults, no doubt, but dumb insolence is the most infuriating.'

'I don't know that I should prefer the pert variety. I'd gladly be rid of him but my husband defends Titus and the boy trades on it.'

'Gentlemen shouldn't meddle in these things. Once a servant perceives —'

'I've taken steps, however. I won't be braved in my own house.'

'By Titus, or by Mr Zedland?'

'Titus, of course. Gracious, Hetty, you make me sound a perfect virago!' The cousins appear to be undergoing a transmutation of souls, for Hetty is in earnest while Sophia meets her cousin's gaze with the prettiest and most inconsequential of laughs.

'But why does your husband defend this boy?'

Sophia hesitates. 'I don't know that he's ever witnessed – I mean, Titus conducts himself tolerably well when Mr Zedland is present, in fact — '

'In fact, you suspect Mr Zedland of putting him up to it.'

Hetty had always this unnerving trick of leaping at things, Sophia recalls. Perceptions at which others arrive only after prolonged mental labour are hers in an instant. Her mother used to refer to Cousin Hetty's *intuition*, but that word is at present too delicate-sounding for what Sophia experiences as a grave failure of politeness. While meaning no harm, Hetty lays bare what one would prefer to leave hidden. In one so amiable, it is an unamiable quality.

A faint masculine roar escapes from the inner room.

'Here come the refreshments.' Sophia resolutely directs her gaze towards the opening door. The landlord, accompanied by a pleasant young woman (who, judging by her features, must surely be his daughter), sets before them a dish of pigeons, one of stewed dried peas, a plate of sliced bread and something resembling buttered cabbage. The daughter refills their glasses with smoking bishop, curtseys and returns through the door, letting in another burst of merriment.

'O, I can't eat garden thrash,' says Hetty, eyeing the cabbage. 'I simply can't bear it.'

'Your mother was too indulgent. Thanks to my famed obedience and courage, *I* can eat anything green provided there's melted butter.' Sophia's manner is sprightly: no husband of hers would set a servant to bait her, nor could any friend imagine such a thing. 'Shall we wait for Mr Letcher?'

'What do *you* say, Sophy? Consult our comfort and convenience, or sit while the food grows cold?' For a second Hetty seems about to return to their earlier conversation. 'Wait for him by all means, if you wish. I shan't.' Yet she makes no move to help herself but sits sulkily twining her fingers in her lap. Sophia wonders at her. Such a very mild trial of Hetty's patience, yet how she frets under it!

It would appear that the landlord has dropped a word in Mr Letcher's ear, for the erring spouse reappears directly, flushed and smiling.

'I trust you entertained yourselves while I was away?'

Hetty raises her eyebrows. 'We can always entertain ourselves. But you did wrong, Letcher, to leave us. Only fancy if some of those clubmen had come in and found us alone! They might have mistaken us for quite another kind of female.'

'I am sure nobody could make such a mistake,' says Mr Letcher, seating himself at the table. 'Your air, your manner must surely prevent it.'

'Even if they were drunk? No, Sir, you should have remained to protect us.'

'Some of those unhappy creatures are so elegantly turned out,' Sophia puts in, 'that they are taken for ladies.'

The other two stare at her. 'Well!' says Hetty. 'It seems you are *au fait* with some London ways, at least.'

'I read the newspapers like anyone else. And I have seen women in carriages, very grand carriages, who did not appear respectable.'

'Some of the highest in the land are not respectable in your sense of the word,' observes Mr Letcher, spearing a juicy morsel of pigeon. 'I could name a duchess or two.'

'Of whom we do not choose to speak,' retorts his wife. 'What of your clubmen? Are they as jolly as you hoped when you abandoned our society for theirs?'

'They are indeed, but not everybody present is a clubman. There is yet another room within that one, with a bank, and tables.'

'Gaming?'

'Aye, and deadly serious.'

'Did you stake anything?'

'My love, I merely looked over the company. I hope that is permitted.'

'Of course. I only question whether it is agreeable.'

'What should offend me? The stock in trade of the professional gamester, Mrs Zedland, is to pass for a gentleman. Most of the time, he's ignorant as a savage – engage him in a discussion of politics or law, and he's lost. Look no further than dress and manner, however, and he's the most charming creature in the world.'

Hetty snorts. 'Like certain duchesses.'

'Of whom we do not choose to speak.'

Sophia could scold them for bickering. They were so affectionate earlier; can they not conduct themselves better, and permit her to order her thoughts in peace? Their talk of gamesters is exquisitely distressing to her. She would gladly leave the inn as soon as manners permit and, in order to achieve this end, attacks her pigeon with an appetite she is very far from feeling.

'Uncle Buller says the age is corrupt,' Hetty says, pushing bone and gristle to the side of her plate, 'but I wonder, were our forefathers always so very virtuous? What do you think, Sophy?'

'I don't know, I'm sure,' she says, hoping that by closing down the conversation, she will induce them to eat. Mr Letcher turns towards her, an earnest light in his eye.

'For myself, I believe our time to be peculiarly adapted to deceptions.'

'Your proof?' says Hetty.

'I speak merely of opinion. I have a notion, Mrs Zedland, that our society is more promiscuous than formerly. You need only consider the easy, natural air which is so admired. Such an air can be acquired by any man of capacity, not irredeemably vulgar, if he will only take pains over it. Everywhere one goes, one sees men of the middling kind conversing with gentlemen.'

'But surely not on equal terms,' Sophia objects.

'Some of the wealthier ones come very near it. It's not unknown for the heiress to a city fortune, or perhaps a coal mine, to marry into an old family.'

'Birth isn't forgotten, Sophy, but the differences are less marked,' Hetty agrees. 'You must have seen for yourself at Bath, such a mingling —'

Mr Letcher nods. 'Quite so, my love. I don't wish to be misunderstood – men of low birth who raise themselves by honest means are an asset to the nation – but what enables them to flourish also gives an opening to countless clever humbugs.'

'Those we've always had,' says Sophia. 'Do you remember, Hetty, what Mama told us? About the woman who gave birth to rabbits?'

'Lord, yes! Mary somebody.'

There is a little silence. Sophia imagines that all three of them must surely have the same picture in mind: that of a man-midwife groping under a woman's skirts, pulling out torn gobbets of fur and flesh. It is an image unspeakably disgusting, especially if one cannot help, as Sophia cannot, speculating as to how the dead rabbits came to be where they were found. She is annoyed with herself for having mentioned the business at all: it has only served to distract them, once more, from the meal. Though perhaps, with such a picture in mind, it is as well not to study one's plate too closely.

Mr Letcher says, 'Such a crude sham as that, exhibiting a supposed monstrosity, might've happened in Shakespeare's day. For an instance of modern charlatanry, look no further than Psalmanazar – have you read Psalmanazar's memoirs, Mrs Zedland?'

'Not yet.'

'Meretricious. He crawls along the ground, lickspittle, repenting on every page, and at the same time takes care to show himself a prodigy and throw blame upon his schoolteachers. If everyone who suffered at school took it into his head to peddle such inventions, well — !' Mr Letcher shrugs, as if to say the result would be beyond even the invention of Psalmanazar himself.

'He must've been clever, to gull so many people,' Hetty remarks. 'Had he not confessed, I wonder how long it would've continued?'

'He had the makings of a scholar, or perhaps, with his fertile fancy, a poet. Such brilliant unscrupulous fellows are dangerous. Is the meat tender enough for you, Mrs Zedland?'

'O, yes, excellent.'

'And yours, my love?'

'Tough,' is Hetty's opinion.

'Mine also,' remarks Mr Letcher, as Sophia wills him to cease chattering and address himself to his food. 'Mrs Zedland has perhaps a younger bird.'

'I miss our cook. Since we came away from home we've never had meat done half so well, have we, Letcher?'

'Hardly surprising, when you think about it. Domestics have every opportunity to study the foibles of their employers, whereas it's ten to one if we ever come here again. There are so many places of public resort in London.'

Let us eat the things and be done, Sophia prays. Hetty, who was never much interested in the topic under discussion despite having started it, imperfectly conceals a yawn.

A woman enters from the flagged passageway and settles at a bench about halfway down the room, her back to the company. Hetty purses her lips.

'We should have gone to the Great Room. One can eat there.'

'It was further to walk in the cold,' says Mr Letcher. 'And we are perhaps too late for refreshments.'

'I'm sure the company would have been more respectable. No, Letcher, don't stare.'

The stranger folds down her hood. Mr Letcher, already studying the newcomer in defiance of his wife's instructions, turns back towards Hetty and Sophia. 'Virtuous ladies have this one fault, that in their spotless chastity they are inclined to judge the rest of the Sex too harshly. May she not be waiting for her companions – as you yourselves waited for me?'

His wife raises an eyebrow. 'You're fond of teasing, Sir.'

'Quite serious, I assure you.'

'No, you're not. You can't possibly think so. What's your opinion, Sophy? Can that person be respectable?'

Sophia strains for a better view of the woman's features. The stranger has dark hair and a brownish complexion. As she shifts about on the bench, arranging her gown, something gleams along the side of her neck: some bauble dangling there.

'I would say . . . not.' Her voice is clear and controlled, yet there is a roaring in her ears. When she looks back at the Letchers they seem pale and far away, as if seen through a pane of green glass.

The landlord enters and approaches the woman. He bends down, insinuating himself towards her so as to speak without being overheard. Even so, the woman is offended. She turns to call him back and thus displays her full profile, including a large earring of black pearls.

It *is* that creature: Edmund's creature. Her face is again obscured, this time by the landlord's coat as he closes with her, and Sophia catches the words, 'Aye, to be sure, but my money's sound.' The voice comes as a shock to Sophia: not the clipped city speech she anticipated but a soft burr. *Surrrre.* The whore is, or was, a countrywoman.

The landlord glances round at Sophia and Hetty, whose eyelids lower at once. Something more is said *sotto voce*.

'What is it?' hisses Mr Letcher. 'I can't hear as well as you.'

Sophia raises her eyes in time to see Hetty pinch him. The landlord seems to be expostulating with the woman. He takes her by the arm, attempting to raise her from the bench, only to have his hand violently flung off. From where Sophia sits the woman's protest can be heard without difficulty: 'Damn you, Robert, a few minutes!'

The landlord again glances towards Sophia's party, evidently weighing which will be more troublesome, forcing this woman out of the door or letting her remain. At last he says in something like a normal voice, 'Then what will you take?'

'Lightning, hot.' She fumbles for a coin. 'And strong. The last was like drinking from the pump. And tell him Betsy's here.' The last word sounds like *yur*. In just that way do the village people speak in the hamlets around Buller Hall.

'Charming company,' murmurs Hetty. 'Let us have our cheesecake and be gone.'

Sophia nods, blessing Hetty and at the same time repressing a fierce desire to reproach her: *You assured me the place was respectable.* Mr Letcher has adopted that benevolent masculine smile by which gentlemen hint that they are inclined to find the Sex too timid and prudish.

'With all due respect, my love, she need not trouble us. One must mix a little in gardens of resort.'

'Mix!'

'I take back the word. We are not mixing at all, merely sitting some yards away. Did you know,' he grins at them both, 'that a lady strolling on the green here was once seized and embraced by a stranger? When she protested, the fellow said to her, *You may now boast you have been kissed by Dick Turpin.*'

'I shouldn't think she boasted of it,' sniffs Hetty.

'Oh come! It's a distinction among such people.'

'I thought you spoke of a lady.'

'Mr Letcher,' says Sophia, 'will you be so kind as to go and enquire after the cheesecake?' It is as much as she can do not to abandon her place and flee. As it is, and since Hetty and Mr Letcher have invited her, she sits, the prisoner of politeness.

Mr Letcher springs up. 'I shall indeed.'

'You seem not quite yourself,' observes Hetty as soon as her husband is out of earshot. 'Do you have your flowers, is that it?'

Sophia shakes her head. 'O dear, Hetty, am I so very dull?'

'Or perhaps *we* have unsettled you. Pay no attention to Letcher and me. We're like two old pug dogs, we enjoy snapping at one another.' Sophia sees Mr Letcher take up a bell from the counter: a brisk ringing summons the landlord. 'What's the use of being married if one mayn't growl a little?' Hetty continues. 'Mama and Papa certainly made the most of it and I see no reason not to follow suit.'

'And your mother-in-law? Is she also of the pug-dog persuasion?'

'Only in appearance. But beware, Sophy, of mentioning her before Mr Letcher,' Hetty lowers her voice to a thrilling dramatic hiss, 'or we shall hear more of *Tichborne's cardoons*.'

Despite everything, Sophia begins to giggle and then stops, as if slapped, as the door at the far end opens. The landlord brings through a steaming jug and tumbler to the solitary woman, then crosses to the counter to inform Mr Letcher that cheesecake will be served up directly.

'As soon as you may,' says that gentleman.

The landlord nods. 'I beg your pardon, Sir. I was not aware of your being hurried.'

Sophia feels she could expound, as a Biblical text, the meaning of being 'beside oneself'. She could start from the bench, leap out of her skin, yet she continues to sit, fists gripped beneath the table, forcing herself to keep still. She has at least the advantage of observing without being observed, but suppose the woman should

315

turn, and look at her? In a minute or so, she surely will; if not before he enters, then after. She cannot imagine what else might follow upon his entrance: her mind refuses to contemplate the possibilities, except for the terrible certainty that the Letchers will be witness to all. Pug dogs! Now, Hetty, here is the Marital Quarrel Proper. What beast can you find, actual or mythical, that can reduce its clawing combats to a witty figure of speech?

The cheesecakes are at last brought to the table. Sophia partakes mechanically, unable to taste hers. Still the wretched woman sits there, sipping what looks like a glass of water. She commences twisting her fingers in her hair, evidently as impatient for the arrival of her friend as Sophia is filled with dread. Possibly (now comes a choking sensation in her throat and chest: is this hysteria?) the woman is not accustomed, any more than Hetty, to being kept waiting.

The door shudders as if about to open. Without her volition, a faint cry escapes Sophia's lips. She endeavours to mask it by staring ahead of her, but Hetty is too observant.

'What is it, my love?'

Sophia, transfixed by the still-opening door, can neither speak nor look at her.

'My cousin isn't herself, Letcher. We should take her home.'

Mr Letcher, impeccably bred, at once pushes away his plate. 'My dear Mrs Zedland, I'm at your service. Shall I ask the landlord to send for a chair, or would a walk be of more benefit to you?'

It is too late for either. Disaster is upon them: Edmund stands poised in the doorway, smiling towards the woman who now rises to greet him.

'One of your *gentry*, Letcher,' Hetty whispers, causing her husband to glance round.

'Well, and has he not a genteel air —? Now, my dear Mrs Zedland, do you feel that some fresh air might revive you? We can come in again directly.'

Sophia can only shake her head. Edmund has seen her: his hand flies to his neck as if he, too, is threatened with asphyxiation.

'Handsome, I allow,' says Hetty. 'Well, my love? Are you able to walk home, do you think?'

The choking obstruction in her own throat is going down, for Edmund also appears confounded, caught so thoroughly off guard that his expression alters with the fluidity of quicksilver. She could, without difficulty, reproduce and annotate the contortions of his features: *Plate the first*, the arrogant smirk of the expectant man of pleasure; *Plate the second,* the start upon finding himself observed. *Plate the third (in colour)* affords some inadequate notion of the flush briefly exhibited by the gentleman in question (O, Edmund! — so *very* briefly, given the shameful situation in which you find yourself) while *Plate the fourth* admirably sets forth the harrowed expression of a man who must greet one woman and cut another and is having the Deuce of a time choosing, not least because he cannot be certain – given the company in which he finds her and the damnably tall and solid whore standing plump between them – that his wife wishes to acknowledge *him*.

This last insight inspires Sophia to an action deceptive in its simplicity: she stands and waves, her face brightening with innocent happiness. All happens so quickly that she scarcely knows how; as when playing a familiar piece of music, she holds to what she must do, and does it. 'Why,' she exclaims, 'here's Mr Zedland!'

Edmund favours her with a look of unmixed loathing, immediately dissolved in a smile of such sweetness that Sophia can almost feel Hetty's astonishment. *See* it, she dare not: exchanging glances with Hetty is out of the question. She is acutely conscious of herself as one of three women, each studying her husband's advance from the far doorway towards the chimney. The stranger is still standing, however, her back turned to the onlookers, and as Edmund approaches she moves into his path.

The crisis is come: how will he meet it?

Edmund glares at the woman, defying her to approach any nearer. His presence of mind, once regained, is astonishing. Sophia understands, as the stranger surely must, that his affronted stare is a warning, but what casual onlooker could see it in its true colours: not the disdain with which respectability turns from encroaching vice, but the signal of an accomplice? The woman stops, plucking at her hood in a gesture of confusion. At that instant Sophia recognises that her own greeting, apparently so innocent, was intended to shield not only herself but Edmund. Without giving conscious thought to the matter – there was not time for that – she has shown her husband a way out that can be seized upon only by sacrificing the other.

Edmund does seize upon it. He becomes a gentleman affronted by vulgar impertinence, swerving round the creature as he might sidestep some nastiness upon the pavement. His face, now somewhat pale, conveys his habitual *sang-froid* as he approaches the company with an easy, gentlemanlike air, greets Sophia and is presented to the Letchers, to whom he extends his hand.

Sophia scarcely need watch him work his charm upon them. It seems Hetty now considers him well enough bred, for her cheeks have turned the prettiest rose-pink conceivable. Possibly she is trying to recall what cutting remarks she passed upon him before he was introduced as her relative by marriage; Sophia cannot give Hetty's pinkness her full attention, however, while the rejected woman, her face once more concealed, stands at the tavern table as if, like Lot's wife, she has been turned to salt.

Unlike that Biblical lady, the stranger has refused, until now, to look behind. Upon hearing Edmund's genteel murmur, she turns her neck a little. Her eye, set in a face hot with humiliation, catches Sophia's. *Why,* Sophia thinks, perceiving unfeigned misery, *she loves him!* The coarse lips are twisting in a fashion that she knows only too well: the creature is on the brink of tears. *Go*

318

then, Sophia silently urges her. *What can you do by remaining here?* It seems her rival has reached the same conclusion, since she takes one last swig from the glass and leaves the room via the passageway. Sophia is filled with a sensation rather like that experienced on narrowly missing a smash-up in a coach: relief mingled with a curious disappointment.

'. . . invited by a friend in the course of business,' Edmund is saying.

'A game or two sharpens the mind,' offers Mr Letcher.

Edmund nods. 'Indeed.'

'Though the dissipations of London being what they are, I imagine one must be on guard, and take care always to play with honest persons.'

'I see you thoroughly understand the matter, Sir,' says Edmund, quietly amused. 'For myself, I never engage with any other kind of player.'

The three of them appear in excellent humour: already Edmund has turned the Letchers outside in.

'Who was that person?' Sophia interrupts.

'Person, my love?'

'That woman at the table there. She looked as if she knew you, I thought.'

Edmund shrugs. 'Did she? I paid no attention.'

'She quite stared at you, Edmund.'

Again that flash of hatred. It vanishes away as soon as seen and Edmund exchanges a glance with Mr Letcher. 'My dear,' he explains as if to a child, 'she was doubtless one of those females who haunt public places in search of prey. Any man with a coat to his back is considered in the light of a potential protector.'

'Had she known of your marriage, my dear, and the warm affection in which you hold your spouse,' Sophia cannot forbear replying, 'she would be persuaded of the futility of any such hope.'

There is a stricken pause in the conversation. Edmund seems

319

considering how he might give a complimentary turn to this last speech, perhaps something about his known loyalty and uxoriousness, but before he can make the attempt Hetty exclaims, 'Such a pity we are too late in the year for Ranelagh! But there, fashion rules everything these days.'

Mr Letcher comes to her aid. 'You know very well, my dear, that it always has. I confess that, in this instance, I think fashion and common sense are in accord. We have not the climate for outdoor entertainments so late in the year.'

'I agree, Letcher. This room is certainly warmer than the Rotunda would be. And we should not see the *ton*, even in season, for they scarcely appear until ten. Such a ridiculous habit, Sophy, do you not think so?'

'Not more ridiculous than many farces acted in Town,' answers Edmund, before Sophia can speak. 'Both in the theatres and out of them.'

The four of them search one another's faces and, finding no inspiration there, sit down to make the best of it.

39

Betsy-Ann runs through the gardens blubbing, until a pain in her side forces her to slow to a walk. It's a warning to her – a mercy – she could give him the trick, nothing'd come of it – he'd give nothing, not he – not a smile. To look at her like that! – cast his lot with his autem mort – with his ma – he'd as soon set her up as, as —

O, to be a man!

How she'd mill him! Punch out his lights!

She can hardly breathe for crying but she hurries on as best she can, wiping her face against her sleeve. Then, as the crying fit spends itself, a voice starts up within her, whining and pleading:

Sure he's sorry for it now. What could he do, but go to her?

Where does it come from, this feeble voice? It's as if some gentry-mort, all meekness, stands wringing her pitiful hands: *O,* she whimpers, *be kind! Never stoop to revenge! O, he loves you best! He suffers as you do!* She knows it now: it's the voice of one Betsy Nobody (since she was never known, even amongst the sisterhood, as Betsy Hartry), bilked of her Spanish trick, not a gown or a greyhound to show for her pains. But Betsy-Ann Blore, termagant sister of Harry Blore, rounds on her, whip in hand, and with a stamp of her foot she drives away the simpering bitch: *Madam, he's known for it.*

She turns out of the park entrance and into the thoroughfare, around another corner and into the street where he lives. The house is halfway up, on the right. Betsy-Ann goes straight up the steps and yanks on the bell rope.

A maid, fair, plump and pert, stands gawping at her.

'Here,' gasps Betsy-Ann. She feels for her right earring, tears it off and flings it over the creature's shoulder into the darkness of the hallway. 'And here —' The other earring skitters away along the polished floor. She kicks off her satin shoes, put on fresh this morning in a spirit of holiday but soiled now with the earth of the gardens, and sends them after the earrings.

The maid screams, 'Fan! Quick!' but, perhaps hoping more baubles will fly her way, doesn't close the door.

'Know me?' Betsy-Ann pants. 'Your master's whore, that's who I am, and these are his gifts.'

'My master —?' Behind the maid, in the deep shadow of the hallway, Betsy-Ann can make out two gleaming dots that swim in the air, and below them a peculiar shape like a knot of linen. 'Is it Mr Zedland you mean? Am I to give them to him?'

'To *Mrs* Zedland. From her husband's whore.'

The dots vanish and return, like eyes blinking. They *are* eyes, she realises: the great dark ogles of the blackbird. He's got up like a mourner and standing well back, only now becoming visible as her sight adjusts to the dim light inside. What she took for linen is just that, tied under his chin.

The blonde is seized by giggles. 'La! Madam! I can't use such language to Mrs Zedland!'

'What words you will, sweetheart, only be sure to say it.'

There is a sound of heels striking on floorboards: another maid. A pale gown and apron surge forward into the light. The girl inside them elbows first the boy, then the first maid aside. She stands framed in the doorway an instant, her coral-coloured mouth fallen open, before wordlessly slamming the door.

Betsy-Ann stands there on her exposed feet, the cold of the pavement striking up through her heels. A faint tittering leaks from within the house and a glance at the window to her left shows her both maids peering out from between the shutters. She's fumbled it. She should have said nothing about whoring, only *Take all this to your mistress*, so the autem mort would be sure to see them.

She'll see them anyway. Let's see what Mister Edmund Zed-land can find to say about the earrings. If those sly bitches don't pocket them.

She walks away from the house, her stupid head held high. Now she's done it. She'll have to walk the rest of the way to Sam's ken with only thread stockings between her flesh and the pavement: nothing for it but to make herself as hard as the paving stones. Her feet will be cut, what of that? All the more excuse to lie down and rest, but not yet: for the time being keep moving, keep moving.

After three roads, her toes that were cold are warm. After five they are stinging. Another road. Halfway now. Her skin feels as if it's being scraped off inch by inch; more and more often she has to stop, but when she does, she can't rub her torn feet because of the filth sticking to them. Such tender soles. Time was, she could walk over rocks and snow. She didn't know what it was to have a shoe on her foot.

This is nothing. Soon be there. Another road. The ken is waiting with a hot fire – only think of that, girl, coal in the grate – and a bowl of water to bathe her blisters.

Standing waiting at a crossroads, she feels something touching the ends of her toes. Stained with mud and blood, her stockings seem part of the street dirt, but she can make out something else there: a clot of fur, shit-coloured, run over so many times that the meat of the animal is long gone, the bones ground under the wheels of carriages. Only this scrap of pelt remains, so tattered that she can't tell whether it was once a dog or a cat. She nearly trod in its soft uncleanness. Were she wearing shoes, she would have done so, and gone on regardless. As it is, she steps round the horrible pitiful thing, not liking to touch it, and as she does so the tears start up again.

Shiner's at home, hugging the fire. There he was all the time, sitting behind the golden windows of domestic happiness, but somehow she left him out of the cheery picture, thinking only of her bowl of warm water. He looks up as she enters and she sees he's mending his stinking coat.

'I'll do that for you,' says Betsy-Ann.

He lets the coat slide off his knee onto the floor. He's staring at her: at her face and neck, at her stockings stained brown and red and grey.

'What the Deuce — ?' He stops, noticing her knotting-bag. She should've thrown it away. 'Where are your shoes?'

Her soles feel as if they have stones embedded in them. Possibly they have. With a groan that she couldn't hold back to save her life, she hobbles to a chair. He comes over to her, kneels and cups one of her heels in each hand, raising them to peer underneath.

'Christ, Betsy, you're flayed! Where are your —'

'Nabbed.'

Shiner lays down her feet on the boards, causing her to wince. 'Did he chivvy you?'

'Eh?'

'There's blood —' He puts up a hand to lift her hair, and grimaces. 'Your ears are slit.'

Betsy-Ann looks longingly at the fire, where a kettle is warming. 'Put me some of that water in a bowl, will you?'

He leaves his questioning for the moment so he can stand nurse to her, first wiping her swollen eyes, then sponging the blood off her earlobes. Betsy-Ann paddles her feet in the bowl, waiting for the remains of the stockings to soak off.

'He never took your bag.'

She was waiting for that. 'I fell on top of it.'

'Easy put off, wasn't he?'

'Someone was coming.'

He pushes up her gown to unroll her stockings. 'Everything

you lost,' says Shiner, 'you got from Hartry.'

He's a noticing sort of man when sober. Betsy-Ann bites her lip.

'Why'd you sport *his* things, when you've duds and trinkets I bought you?'

'Because I had them. You saw my trunk when I came.'

'You could've been arse-naked, Betsy, I'd have clothed you.'

It comes to her that she's thrown away all her favourites, all but the fawney and that only because it wasn't on her finger. She raises one foot in the bowl. The stocking is about ready to come off. She peels it with care, cursing under her breath as water trickles along her calf and drops into the basin.

Shiner says, 'Your keepsakes didn't bring you much luck.'

He's right. 'Look at that. Like beef. I'm walking on beefsteaks.'

'I've news for you, Betsy.'

'Fetch me something to bind them, will you?'

'It's important. Sit and listen for once.' He catches hold of her wrists. 'Are you listening?'

'Yes, yes,' says Betsy-Ann. 'Only let me bandage my feet.'

'They can wait. Let 'em wash a bit.' He rises and goes to a chair a little further off. Betsy-Ann sits facing him, hands clasped to show attention.

'I've gone back to Harry,' he says, as if expecting praise.

'I thought you would, when you considered of it.'

'Welcomed me like a brother.'

She snorts. 'He's never had a brother. You just remember Flash Tom Ball.'

'No fear. I keep sober as a Methodist's dog.'

She is impressed despite herself. 'How can you? Don't it make you want to heave up?'

'I could heave up just thinking of 'em – all maggotty – where's these bandages you keep moaning about?'

'Use wipers.' The minute she says it she could tear herself, but Shiner walks into the Eye natural enough and doesn't linger. He comes out with two big silk ones, a green and a blue, tossing them towards her so that they unfurl.

'The King of England ain't got silk bandages,' says Betsy-Ann, swiping them out of the air.

'Told you that, did he?' He lifts the bowl of water out of her way, upending it out of the window. She hears the contents crash onto the stones below. 'But you've perhaps been in company with him, you and Hartry. I never mixed with the Quality, on account of *my* ma not being a whore.'

She is at once on her guard. 'Forget Ned, can't you? Cheer me up a bit, I'm half crippled here.'

'Hold your peace, I'm not finished.'

His eyes have got that sticky look: something nasty coming. She rests her throbbing toes on a towel and waits.

'I notice you're busy lately. Goings out, comings in.' He taps the side of his nose.

Betsy-Ann laughs. 'You sound like the Excise.'

'And *you* look like a mort that's seen bad company.'

'Queer notion of company you've got – being knocked down!'

'And losing his gifts. Unfortunate, *most* unfortunate.'

She's not going to answer that. Frowning, she dries off her feet and ties one up in the blue wiper. The green silk is larger, so she folds it over for comfort.

'Listen,' Sam says as she ties the ends of the green one together. 'What'd you say to his fams?'

'Ned's?'

'You know who I mean. Delicate, with an elegant motion, wouldn't you say?'

'Anybody would.'

'Well,' says Shiner, 'on account of those nimble fingers of his, I 'prenticed him to another trade.' He grins to see her start. 'He never told you, eh?'

'Ned, a trade? What trade?'

'He got pretty cunning, too – not a patch on me, but tolerable. Now, Betsy, you're a game bird. Ten pounds says you can't name Ned Hartry's other trade.'

Never has he talked to her like this. There's more in it than jealousy: she expected him to throw Harry's spying, and what he saw, in her face, but he seems to be taking a different tack entirely, leading her sideways towards something. Some trap?

'You had him beat to nothing, you say.' She pretends to consider. 'That'll be boozing, I reckon.'

'O, you're sharp, Mrs Betsy! Watch you don't cut yourself. Now tell me how it was that Dimber Ned went penniless to Bath and came back spliced. Did he live on air?'

'Gaming, he said.'

Shiner raises his eyebrows. 'With nothing to stake?'

'Then he had a bit put by. How would *I* know?'

'No, how would you?' He lets that sink in. 'Let's say his new papa wants to see mortgages, deeds. Papers. How'd he come by those?'

'Had 'em drawn up by a faytour, like anybody else. I wish you'd lay off, Sam. I want to lie down, rest my legs.'

'He needed a trusty to back him.'

'You helped him to a faytour.'

'I said you was sharp. When he wanted papers, he knew where to come.' He holds up his damaged hand, flexing the fingers before her eyes.

Betsy-Ann sits bolt upright. '*You're* the faytour?'

'Even now I can draw. As you may recall.'

'So where's your kit?' She stares round the room before turning triumphantly back to him. 'You liar! You never had any.'

'Now there, gents, we see the weakness of the Sex. Goes upon appearances.' He comes up and pushes his face into hers so that Betsy-Ann is forced to drop her eyes. 'I've no kit *now* and nothing was kept *here*. More than that, you're not in a position to know.'

She stares down at her bound feet, seeing not the blue and green bandages but the portrait he made and destroyed. 'Are you still a faytour?'

He shakes his head. 'Takes more than a lump of coal.'

'Why didn't Ned draw up the papers himself?'

'He'd nothing ready. And he hadn't my ability.'

No doubting him now. To think of the pair of them working together for the marriage, and she never once suspecting.

'Damnably stupid, your Zedlanders,' he remarks, as if reading her mind. 'I'd barely time to dry the ink. I warned Ned, if they so much as sniffed at it, he'd have to toddle.'

'They didn't sniff?'

A satisfied smile. 'Swallowed it down like melted butter.'

'Did he pay you out of her fortune?'

'Not entirely.' He gives the queerest look, of cruelty and pity mixed. 'You always did wonder how I won you, eh? How I beat the great Ned Hartry.'

Betsy-Ann leaps upright but Sam also rises and flings her backwards so that she falls against the table, crying out as her torn soles scrabble on the floorboards. She manages to pull herself back into the chair, drawing up her arms and knees for protection.

'Now, don't run away, Betsy.'

'Not another word!' she yells. 'Not a word!' and covers her ears. Shiner seizes her fingers, bending them backwards so that she is forced to let go.

'Sharps playing sharps,' he murmurs. 'What a fancy!'

'You forced him into it.'

'We had an understanding. Though I shouldn't say he agreed to the conditions.' He leans forward, his expression gleeful, and drags down her hands until they are resting in her lap. 'He proposed 'em. His notion entirely.'

Her mouth is too dry to spit at him.

'He was that sick of you,' Shiner goes on. 'But we know our

Ned, don't we? Liable to come sniffing round again. He swore his solemn oath to keep away.'

'He foxed you there,' she retorts.

'We both foxed *you*, Betsy. Did you never wonder how I beat him?'

'Ned was in his cups. You couldn't touch him otherwise, he's a prince to you.'

His mouth twitches: that hit home, all right. But he masters himself as befits a sharp and says, 'Don't flatter yourself, girl. We settled it long before. Your prince was for handing you over like a breeding sow. It was *I* proposed the sham wager – by way of a kindness.'

If he did feel kindness towards her, he's run through his stock long since. But O, it fits, it all fits: how long did she go on like a daisy, lamenting Ned's bad luck?

Sam snorts. 'You may thank your stars I'm a patient man. Haddock's, if you please!'

For a moment she's silent. Her insides are empty: she could be one of Sam's cadavers, scooped out on the slab of some doctor. It won't last, she knows: soon the pain will start up, like coming back to life with the knife already in her. While she can still think, and while Sam's in gloating mood, she must ask more.

'Why'd Harry peach on me?'

His eyes gleam. '*You* just chanced to be there. Didn't Prince Ned explain? Harry advanced him the readies, at interest, to get started in Bath.'

'He hasn't paid?'

'Cursed clever of His Highness,' Sam says with bitter contempt. 'If he lives to boast of it.'

And there she was, flinging an earring or two through his door. She needn't have bothered. A stink of death, a swaggering, grinning vengeance, dogs him through the streets, sends him dodging into alleyways.

How, in the face of all this, could he pick up with her again? She can scarcely believe it. Surely this story's lies after all, nothing but Sam Shiner's spite?

No. It's of a piece: Ned shies away from Harry. He won't come near this place: that, she's seen for herself. Events shift about, slippery, as she tries to join them up. What *is* Ned's situation? He spoke of creditors – claimed to need the Spanish trick before he could set her up – but he also told her he'd pocketed the dowry. If that's true, and he cares nothing for the autem mort, what need of his play-acting in the Rose of Normandy?

Where he chose to cut her.

Like Shiner, she can't fathom why Ned would shower blunt on her, treat her to the bagnio, rather than settle with such a creditor as Harry – unless it was in the nature of bait, setting a sprat to catch a mackerel.

Such a promising start she'd thought it, as good as a declaration. The ratafia, the chair ride, the pleasures of the long night. He was tender: he played her, flattered her, watching his chance. Did he even enjoy the debauch? She winces at that thought. But yes, he relished it – as a man might relish a syllabub, no sooner consumed than forgotten. Even then she should've seen the way things were going: he told her to get from under Sam Shiner, but *he* wasn't having any, O no! And if she hadn't weakened, hadn't half-promised the trick? She wouldn't have seen Ned again.

So far they've come no further than talk: a ken far from Sam and Harry's haunts, where she could feel safe. Her life in keeping resumed, with the only keeper she's ever desired . . . She was ready to give up her last trump card, hoping for much in return: aye, so much gammon and moonshine!

She bites down hard on her lip: Shiner won't have the pleasure of watching her cry. This is how the world works, why did she ever think otherwise?

Besides, she's seen something she never glimpsed before: for

Ned, half the zest of the thing lies in baiting other men. Parading her before Shiner, then handing her over only to return and cuckold his old partner. As for his dealings with Harry – paying back the brother by cheating the sister, what a bite! He makes it his sport to tease them, dangling just beyond their reach, as he dangles beyond the reach of his autem mort.

And beyond hers. Her cheeks flush at the thought. She's never been in the pillory but she fancies it might feel like this: stripped to the waist, bucks in the crowd laughing and pointing. Fear and pain and perhaps pissing yourself in full view of the crowd. Not a friendly face in sight but mouths agape, eager to lap up your suffering and shame.

She bites down harder still, telling herself she's not in such a plight as that, nor so foolish neither. No woman has Ned's heart. To each he tells a different story. He's either too deep to fathom or so shallow there's nothing in him: a man cut from paper. The autem mort, though, gave him everything she had.

Not so Betsy-Ann Blore.

With a mean little smile, Sam says, 'Harry'll settle it, never fear.'

Thinks himself top dog now, doesn't he just! She keeps her eyes lowered to hide the hatred in them, gazing down at her feet where the wipers are already blotched with blood.

40

The Nuns

There live some nuns in Romeville town
And they are wondrous merry,
There's one cries Up and one cries Down
And one cries Kiss me Jerry.
Darkmans they work, O, O, O, O,
Darkmans they work and do not shirk.

They kiss the rod and ply the birch
They're full of burning fire,
To give their love to all mankind
It is their one desire.
Darkmans they work &c.

There's Tabitha and sulky Jane
And dimber little Kessie,
And tallest of them all, them all,
O that is black-eyed Bessy.
Darkmans she works, &c.

Now Bessy had a lover true
A man of noble fame,
That plied the tables night and day
And never lost a game.
Darkmans he works, &c.

One day the Abbess comes to her
Says, 'Where's your own flash kiddey?'
Says Bessy, 'Why?' The bawd replies,
'You must not be so giddy.'
Darkmans you'll work, &c.

Says Bessy, 'I'm no slave to you
And never shall I be.
Although for blunt I sell my c——t
My heart I hope is free.'
Darkmans I work, &c.

But pride it comes before a fall
The bawd was good and ready
For Ned was sold, without his gold
His hand was not so steady.
Darkmans she works &c.

I've twenty pretty roses
All planted in my beds,
Leave Bessy and they shall be yours
To pluck their maidenheads.
Darkmans they work, &c.

And so Black Bessy's lost her cull
And Ned has lost his doe.
The moral of my story
Is one you all do know:
Old Harry works, &c.

41

Breeding can compensate for much, Sophia reflects as she and her party are returning home. In a gesture of mutual friendship and esteem, each gentleman offers an arm to the other's wife, Hetty exchanging small talk with Edmund as if she believed him the most virtuous of men. Mr Letcher, likewise, has the air of one who suspects little and questions less. Though he was seated facing the fire and some elements of the scene played out in the Rose of Normandy presumably eluded him, he must have felt surprise, to say the least, on discovering his absent host gaming in another part of the inn.

Did Hetty understand the look that passed between Edmund and the creature? At the time, Sophia thought it impossible, but she had no opportunity to observe. Whatever Hetty concludes, she will of course make known to Mr Letcher as soon as they find themselves alone. Sophia can already fancy her anxious hiss: *About to accost him in our sight! Plainly acquainted – poor Sophy – no use her denying – intolerable!*

Nothing can be said in present company, for which Sophia is thankful. She could not endure to be questioned by Hetty as to what she intends to do, whether Papa should speak to Mr Zedland or what might be the nature of the settlements signed before marriage. As to advice on wifely submission and resignation, Sophia has served it up to herself by the plateful during these last weeks and found it lacking in sustenance, *damn thin tack* as Radley would put it. Indeed, the wife of Edmund Zedland subsists on such thin tack that her very soul is emaciated.

That another's neglect of duty does not absolve one of one's own is a tenet she absorbed long ago. No Christian could think otherwise. Sophia hopes *she* is a good Christian, yet this shrunken soul of hers affords not a drop of generous sentiment, no longing either to forgive Edmund or to reclaim him. She shrivels at the prospect of explanations, dreading to hear more lies. She has stumbled into an assignation between her husband and that woman whose shadow made an unbidden third at their table, in their walks and conversations and in their bed. What, in these circumstances, can he find to say?

Little wonder, she broods, that he has behaved with such unkindness, depriving her of visits and outings, the lawful pleasures of the newly married lady. Spinning his webs under cover of darkness, he takes good care to remain concealed. It has served his purposes to cut her off, not only from his secret life but also from people of birth, education and respectability. In a city famed for its parks, walks, routs, ridottos, gardens, balls, theatres, she lives half-stifled, in a district so disagreeable that she fears even to walk the pavements for fear of being misunderstood.

Her train of thought moves more rapidly, a train of fireworks laid by a master artificer, each taking life from its predecessor until illumination stands in the sky like day. She has married a libertine addicted to self-indulgence who has taken her fortune and – ah, the illumination fades – what? Wasted it? She cannot be sure even of that much: Edmund may well retain the money in his possession. He has certainly wrested the purse-strings from his wife's grasp – barely a crown has he laid out upon her since they fled Bath – and upended the purse into another woman's lap.

Even that is not the worst. Wives have undergone such horrors before, and have battled them with clear-eyed integrity and dignity. Sophia is robbed even of these weapons: her enemy has fastened upon her person, her sentiments and her intellect. No sooner does she glimpse his true nature than she is plunged into a sea of conflicting impulses: loving him, hating, indignant, shamed and, after all the insults he has inflicted, willing to come to his defence. She is compromised, contaminated, crazed as a soap bubble; in the very moment of grasping all this, she wonders how long she can hold fast to the knowledge. *Sophy is rational!* O, Mama!

'You are quiet, Mrs Zedland.' She starts at being addressed by Josiah Letcher, who is gesturing towards a comfortless-looking arbour with a rustic seat beneath. 'Should you like to rest?'

'Thank you, I am stronger than before.'

'Your colour is improved. A little more exercise may restore you entirely.'

How kind he is, with his mild, brown-eyed smile. Though Hetty did right to rebuke him in the inn, he is devoid of malice. With such a man there could be no headlong dive into love, but there would be security in one's husband and one's household. As the wife of this benign and upright gentleman, Hetty is supported by him and surrounded by friends. She commands respect; she contemplates with pleasure the prospect of returning home.

What could have possessed Sophia, earlier, to put herself above Hetty, even for an instant? Passion ennobles only if its object is itself noble. At fourteen she knew this, having studied a sermon upon the subject which laid out the different heads of the topic with all the clarity of the passionless. Since then she has sunk: she is one of those who fall by the wayside, departing from what they know to be good and right. She pictures herself as in a Bible engraving: a broken, black-and-white figure left tumbled in the dust, ignored even by the Good Samaritan.

'Shall we meet again tomorrow?' asks Letcher. 'We're entirely at your disposal. Mrs Letcher thought you might wish to attend the opera.'

Should she go? That creature will not be there, she imagines, but who knows what domestic misery will have descended by then? 'My health may not permit it. I should be sorry if you purchased tickets and I was then too unwell to accompany you.'

He waves a hand, dismissing such cares. 'A trifle. Never give it another thought. Perhaps Mr Zedland would care to —'

'No,' she cries before recollecting herself. 'That is, I believe he's engaged upon business concerning the estate.'

'Men of business must be beaten from their quarters sometimes. All work and no play, you know.' Mr Letcher's eyes are twinkling. It is impossible to know whether he intends a general pleasantry at the expense of the over-industrious, or a stab at a man whose work turns out to be play.

Hetty and Edmund have paused some way ahead and are waiting for them to catch up. Mr Letcher calls to his wife: 'What do you say, my dear, to the opera tomorrow evening? If Mr and Mrs Zedland are free to accompany us?'

'Pray excuse me,' Edmund calls back before Hetty can respond. Mr Letcher, seeming not to notice his rudenesss, continues: 'Or should Mrs Zedland care to attend a ridotto? I can introduce you to Mrs Cornelys, should it be necessary, and her entertainments are always delightful. You have heard of the celebrated Mrs Cornelys?'

'O, yes, indeed,' is all Sophia can say, overwhelmed by the mere suggestion. Mrs Cornelys! This is stepping from the chimney corner up into the fashionable world, with a vengeance.

'All the world knows Mrs Cornelys, Sir,' Edmund replies. 'We are much obliged to you, but I have a great many papers to look over at that time.'

'Mr Zedland is quite a martyr to his papers,' says Sophia as the four of them move off together. 'His correspondence isn't hastily dashed off before bedtime, but the product of consummate art.'

Hetty bursts out laughing at such praise and Edmund, his eyes needle-sharp, joins in the laughter. 'Lord, Sophy! One would think my letters the work of Samuel Richardson.'

'I think their contents might impress even him,' Sophia replies. 'Your style certainly cannot be described as plain.'

'Prettily said, by God!' Mr Letcher makes her an exaggerated bow. 'The good opinion of a lady is always worth having.'

'Even when undeserved?' Hetty rallies.

'Then most especially. We men are a sorry lot, eh, Zedland? We appear to best advantage when reflected in the candid eyes of the Sex.'

'You never spoke a truer word,' agrees his wife. 'Suppose, Mr Zedland, we were to return directly afterwards? Would you then have time for your papers?'

'Mrs Letcher can command me to anything she wishes, except neglect of business. I leave my wife entirely at liberty. She shall tell me all about it.'

'There, Sophy! You can't refuse us now.'

Sophia smiles, too distracted to reply. A late firework has burst, showering sparks throughout her mind. The study table floats suspended in the air before her, its drawer crammed with incriminating documents.

Why should Edmund forge correspondence? In marriage, the wife's property passes to the husband. Why, therefore, should he swivel and contrive in order to obtain what according to law is already his? Quite unable to supply an answer, she trots along on Mr Letcher's arm towards her shabby, disappointing home which, as she draws closer, begins to cast a shade over her spirits sufficient to distract her. O, to walk past instead of going in – to walk past and never return!

Careful not to tire her, Mr Letcher has set a moderate pace. Sophia is therefore surprised to realise, as they turn the corner into her street, that Edmund, with Hetty on his arm, is falling behind. Mr Letcher turns to enquire if his spouse is fatigued and Hetty replies, in a voice seasoned with a dash of irritation, that she is quite well. *If you wish to know why we are taking such an eternity,* says that tone, delicately sharpened to a pitch where only ladies can catch its acerbity, *you must ask Mr Zedland.*

338

Sophia is about to remark that they will soon be there, when her attention is arrested by the scene outside her house. Lounging against the railings, as if he owned the place, is a ruffianly-looking individual, evidently a 'follower'.

So this is what the maids get up to if she so much as goes for a walk. Sophia, who has forbidden 'followers', eyes the fellow with indignation. His features are singularly disagreeable, but Mother Nature has compensated by endowing him with exceptional stature and a powerful physique. His coat might once have belonged to a gentleman, but nothing else about him suggests breeding. Approaching more closely, she perceives that he has his foot inside the door and that Fan, who stands within, is so far from flirting with him that she is trying, in vain, to force him out. Just as Sophia realises this, the intruder looks round, recognises the Zedlands (for Edmund, too, has now rounded the corner) and steps back in order to face them. Fan, watching her chance and unaware of the approaching party, slams the door to. The stranger waits, arms folded, quite at his ease.

'Are you acquainted with this visitor, Mrs Zedland?' asks Josiah Letcher in a low voice.

'Not at all.'

'Your maidservant was having some difficulty with him, I thought.'

'Fan has a head on her shoulders,' Edmund cuts in, for all the world as if he were eavesdropping. 'Go into the house, love, and take our guests with you. I'll find out the person's business and send him on his way.'

'Let the ladies enter by all means,' says Mr Letcher. 'For myself, I should feel easier if I remained with you.'

'You are too kind, but it won't be necessary.'

'Do accept Mr Letcher's offer, Edmund. One never knows with these people.'

'Kindly refrain from interfering, Sophia, and go inside.'

339

His voice is so harsh that Sophia turns in surprise. Her husband's features are drained of blood and covered over with a sickly sheen of perspiration. She represses the exclamation that rises to her lips, saying only, 'For God's sake, Edmund, be prudent.'

'Your faith in me is touching. I believe I'm equal to speaking to a fellow on a doorstep.'

They are now almost at the house and Edmund steps up to the ferocious-looking individual. 'If your business is with Edmund Zedland, I'm afraid you must come another time.'

The visitor shows open amusement at this. 'Mr *Zedland*, is it?'

Sophia hears Hetty whisper, 'Stick to him, Letcher.'

'I'm not at liberty to speak with you, Sir. If you would be so kind as to come back —'

The huge head shakes. Sophia thinks of a beast, a bear perhaps, tormented by a fly. With the rudeness typical of the low-bred, he replies, 'Another time ain't convenient.'

Edmund sighs. 'You must at least wait while my friends go in.'

'Then they'd best look sharp.' The man turns his eyes – hooded, dissolute – on Sophia and spits fatly onto the pavement.

'Manners, Sir,' says Mr Letcher. The man only laughs. Sophia dodges behind Edmund, takes out her key and lets herself and Hetty into the entrance hall. Mr Letcher remains outside.

'Did you *smell* him?' cries Hetty as they stand in the darkness. 'Thank God Letcher is there.'

Sophia shudders. 'I'm utterly at a loss.'

'I've no doubt *you* are, my sweet.' Hetty places a finger on her cousin's lips. 'Now keep quiet, and we may —'

'No!' Sophia pulls away from her. 'No, Hetty, on no account.' She drags the unwilling Hetty along the passageway, calling to the maid meanwhile. 'Fan! Fa–a–an!'

Fan emerges from the kitchen, her ironical eye disquieted for once. 'O, Madam! Don't be angry with me, Madam, he pushed so, I couldn't close the door. Sir, says I, the master's away, I can't bring him where he isn't. If you hadn't come along, I do believe he'd have forced his way in. He said he'd —'

'That will do, Fan. Bring tea to the Blue Room.'

The girl stares, drops a curtsey and disappears again down the corridor.

'Go and listen, you little goose,' Hetty urges, gesturing towards the entrance.

Sophia at once begins to walk in the opposite direction. 'Listen to what? Coarse language?'

'You know full well what I mean. What's the matter with you, Sophy? You seem determined to go around blind and deaf.'

'I refuse to listen behind doors. Only servants do that.'

'Sometimes I could shake you. "Only servants listen behind doors" – I never heard such poppycock!'

'What need to spy, when your husband's out there?'

'Letcher isn't spying!' Hetty's face darkens with temper. 'He stayed through pure kindness!'

'I never said —' She stops and puts a hand to her forehead, recollecting herself. 'Forgive me, Hetty. I meant only that he'll naturally witness – what occurs, and can tell you all, should you so wish.'

'Don't *you* wish?'

Sophia opens the door of the Blue Room and stands back, giving Hetty the precedence. Her cousin no sooner enters than she whirls round, evidently exasperated at receiving no reply.

'Sophy!'

'You needn't shout,' says Sophia, closing the door behind her.

'Is that all you care about, my shouting?'

'No, of course not. Only don't be angry with me.'

Hetty's eyes are 'snapping sparks', as Mama used to say, but she holds herself motionless, as if to win the trust of some wild, shy creature. 'To think there was always such trust between us, Sophy. We never kept secrets from one another.'

We had none to keep, thinks Sophia. She watches Hetty's bosom rise and fall, the only part of her cousin to betray emotion until suddenly Hetty's fingers curl themselves up into fists.

'For God's sake, Sophy!'

'It's no use, Hetty, I can't.'

'You mean he won't let you.' Without waiting to be asked, Hetty flings herself into a chair on one side of the fireplace. Sophia seats herself opposite. The silence that follows is one of the most uncomfortable of Sophia's life, her early disagreements with Edmund not excluded.

Hetty's lip has begun to quiver.

'If you but knew what a comfort you are,' Sophia cries, only to be interrupted by Fan bearing a tray. She shoos the girl out and makes tea for Hetty, the saucer rattling as she passes it over. The front door slams. Footsteps are heard mounting the stairs; just as Sophia reaches the Blue Room door and opens it, Mr Letcher falls in from the other side, almost knocking her headlong.

'Oh, I beg your pardon, Mrs Zedland!' A flush overspreads his face at the boorish entrance he has made.

'Your haste does you credit,' she reassures him. 'Where's my husband?'

Mr Letcher recollects himself sufficiently to hear the question. 'Upstairs. He's upstairs.'

'Isn't he joining us?'

'I'm afraid he's taken a knock or two.'

'What!' cries Hetty. 'Did that person attack him – strike him?'

'I'm afraid he went so far as to strike both of us. Don't be alarmed, Mrs Zedland. No bones broken.'

Hetty rises and approaches him. 'But where did he hit you? I don't see any marks.'

Mr Letcher ruefully indicates his chest and side. 'I endeavoured to pour oil on troubled water but,' he shrugs, 'it didn't do. Didn't do at all.'

'What did he want?' Hetty asks.

Her husband only clears his throat.

'Well,' says Hetty, 'the brute should be taken before the magistrates.'

'No doubt, my dear. I'd like to see the man who could take him.'

Sophia remembers to speak. 'I'm so grateful for your assistance, Mr Letcher. Should I have bandages brought – ointments — ?'

He shakes his head. 'Not for me, Mrs Zedland. I've nothing worse than the odd bruise.'

'Then if I may,' she edges around him on trembling legs, 'I'd better speak with Mr Zedland. Pray excuse me. Don't hesitate to ring for the maid should there be any need.'

As she moves away along the corridor she hears the low urgent questioning of Hetty and Letcher's muttered response: 'I should say so. Yes.'

Her husband's chamber door is standing open but Sophia knocks anyway.

'Edmund? Are you hurt?'

After a blow to the head, men have been known to rise, walk and dine in high good spirits, only to die later from swelling in the brain. Mama was acquainted with a young gentleman who died in precisely that way after a fall from his hunter.

'Edmund?'

Perhaps he is in his closet, applying cold water. She gives a warning cough, then, still hearing nothing, pushes aside the alcove curtain. The basin is empty; Edmund's soap lies dry and unused beside it.

Puzzled, Sophia moves away. Has he perhaps gone to the necessary house? No: she would have heard him come downstairs. She next tries the study. Though her knock brings no response, the door is bolted on the inside. She can hear him striding about the room, careless of noise: there is the thwack and slither of papers falling, spreading out across the floor.

'Edmund? Mr Letcher says that fellow hurt you.'

He does not reply.

'Will you kindly answer me, Edmund!'

His voice, when it comes, is muffled and sullen. 'Leave me alone. I'm not in want of coddling.'

'I will, if you unlock the door. Suppose you collapsed?'

'Then I'd die in peace.'

There is a groaning, splintering sound. She flinches away before realising it comes from deeper inside the room: he is breaking up the furniture. Before Sophia realises what she is doing, her ear is pressed to the door panel. Fortunately, Hetty is not present to witness it.

'If you don't stop,' she cries, 'I shall fetch Mr Letcher.'

The bolt shoots with a fierce *chack*. Edmund rushes out, seizes her shoulders and pushes her away. She is sent staggering backwards, trips on her gown and falls. Her husband's face, as she stares up at him, is misshapen, as if someone has been kneading it. The skin around his mouth has begun to darken. He says, 'Now get back to your booby friends before I throw you downstairs.'

On the staircase she is overcome by a positive ague of shaking, so intense that she almost falls without any aid from Edmund. Reaching the turn of the stairwell, where there is a wedge-shaped step, she sinks down and tries to lower her head between her knees, only to find that her stays render it impossible. It is thus, clinging to the banister as to faith's anchor, that she hears the swish-swash of a gown hurrying up the stairs towards her.

'Madam?'

Sophia lifts her head. The girl, what's her name? Frances. Fan.

'O *dear*, Madam! Have you fainted?'

She shakes her head.

'Shall I fetch Eliza? Or a doctor?'

'No. Bring me the hartshorn. By the bed.'

'I could unlace you, Madam.'

Sophia waves her away. 'Hartshorn.' This is no time for lying down and complaining of vapours.

The hartshorn is brought. She fears and desires it, having never understood how an odour, that most frail and bodiless of phenomena, can so assault the senses. Sophia steadies herself, grasps the bottle and sniffs.

'Good *God*!'

The cry is involuntary. Fan catches the bottle as it slips from her fingers.

'Help me up,' Sophia says, the hartshorn still throbbing in her nose and eyes.

'Madam, there's something I should tell you.'

'I have guests.'

The girl is persistent. 'Best tell you now, Madam. It concerns Mr Zedland.'

Sophia laughs, causing Fan's eyes to widen in surprise. 'I suppose it's a secret, is it? Something of that sort?' She waits for Fan to cry, *O, Madam*, since that seems to follow next in the script.

'Yes, I believe it is,' says Fan, unsmiling. 'I shouldn't wish to be overheard.'

Sophia glances upwards, to the banisters and the concealed area of the landing, and lays a finger across her lips.

Medicinal drops: one, two. She tilts back her head and lets them run the length of her tongue.

'Don't draw the curtain, Fan.'

She gestures to the girl to sit down, then seats herself at the toilet table with its flasks of cream, its powders and lotions, their mingled perfumes redolent of comfort. Since all the Cotterstone women (even when translated into Bullers, Zedlands or Letchers) share common notions as to cosmetics and how they should be made, each female member of the family bears a certain olfactory resemblance to the rest. Sometimes, upon her first entering this closet of a morning, it seems to Sophia as if Mama and Hetty are invisibly present.

Her mirror reflects something new: maid and mistress both seated, their heads on a level.

'I can still draw it if you wish,' Fan whispers. 'Nobody could open the chamber door without my hearing.'

'I mustn't neglect my guests. Tell me quickly.'

'Then, Madam, Mr Zedland had *two* visitors today.'

'This brute just now – he was the second?'

The girl nods.

'And the first?'

Fan catches her mistress's eye in the mirror. As she does so, she puts a hand into her bosom and brings out an earring of black pearl.

Sophia starts as if slapped. Once, reading of a secret society in which any member falling from grace was sent a token, by which the society announced that Open Season was declared upon him and his, she speculated as to the prey's sensations upon opening the fatal message. Something like hers at this instant, perhaps. She takes the jewel from Fan as if handling poison; the pearls, little drops of wickedness, glow darkly in her palm.

'To whom does this belong?'

'A *person* came to the door. We didn't let her in, Madam, we know better than that.'

'Why didn't you return it to her?'

Fan takes a deep breath. 'It's not precisely lost, Madam. She threw it at us. And her shoes.'

'Where are they?'

'In the kitchen. The other earring broke. I've got it in a teacup.'

'And she went away without shoes? She sounds like a fugitive from Bedlam.'

346

'I think she belongs to another kind of house, Madam.'

Her eyes meet Sophia's in the mirror. There can only be one reason why jewels should be returned here. Sophia wonders whose money purchased them, Edmund's or her own.

'You did right not to admit her. Did she ask for Mr Zedland?'

'I don't recall that she did. She seemed to know he was out. But she said,' the porcelain of Fan's cheeks is darkening, 'that she was a very particular friend.'

'Indeed.'

'Only she didn't put it in quite those words.'

'Has anybody informed Mr Zedland of this?'

'Not I, Madam, and I'd take my Bible oath not Eliza.'

'Good girl.'

Fan bows her head, her expression not so much submissive as relieved. 'Shall I fetch you the other things?'

'Not now.' Sophia hands the earring back to her. 'I must return to my guests.'

'O, I forgot!' the girl cries. Sophia, half-risen from her chair, sits down again. 'The man who came here. I believe he's – connected.'

'Do you mean that beast is her husband?'

'I mean there's a resemblance.'

Sophia is astonished. 'Was she so very ugly?' Perhaps, after all, this is some other mistress of Edmund's. The one in the Rose of Normandy, though coarse and vulgar, was comparatively well favoured.

'O, no, Madam, she's a handsome woman – in her way,' Fan adds hurriedly. 'But there's a likeness. And she's tall. Her feet are big as a soldier's, you may see that from the shoes.'

Sophia considers. Yes: the woman in the tavern was something of an Amazon. She failed to notice it previously, perhaps because no other female was standing nearby.

'Brother and sister, perhaps.'

'That was *my* thought, Madam.'

'What a very noticing girl you are, my dear.'

The maid flushes with what looks like honest pleasure. I have been a fool, thinks Sophia. Had I taken the trouble to win her good opinion earlier, what might I have discovered? I distrusted her prettiness. And with a pang of sorrow: I am what Edmund has made me.

'They might be in with a crew,' Fan volunteers. 'House-breakers, perhaps. It's the first thing you think, isn't it? That they've come to rob the house?'

Sophia almost laughs at the idea of robbing this dismal place. What could they carry off? The carpet in Edmund's chamber?

'But throwing her pearls away,' Fan continues, '*that* I don't see the sense of.'

'It gives her an excuse to return. For false pearls!'

'O, no, Madam, they're real. I tried them.'

Fan does indeed have a head on her shoulders. 'You've done me excellent service,' Sophia says. 'We shall talk later, but for now keep the items safe. I must return to Mr and Mrs Letcher.'

Alas, this astonishing new intelligence joins the great many topics she cannot enter upon with her friends. She begins to devise excuses for the extraordinary time she has been upstairs; so urgent is the need for a convincing lie that the smell of burning paper, as she passes the study door, fails to attract her attention.

42

When the front door rattled in its frame, Fortunate knew what was on the other side. He tried to hold back Fan from answering, but she shook him off with a cry of impatience and opened it: a gust of air entered and on it a smell of death, spreading infection through the house.

Fortunate backed away before the thing could see him, stumbling up the stairs and into a first-floor room where a bed for visitors was kept in readiness but never used. He eased the window open a crack. Fan's voice floated upwards to him, a little shriller than usual because she was ill at ease, but no more than that: she seemed not to recognise the Spirit. Now it answered with ferocious laughter, like a roar deep in its throat. It was not a pleasant sound.

At this moment Dog Eye and the Wife appeared, with the people he had seen earlier on. Fortunate was in agony: should he go down, where the Spirit was, or stay here and run the risk of being called for? He heard the front door close, then open again. For a terrible moment he thought it had entered, but when he dared to peep down again it was still on the pavement: the men had stayed to speak with it while their womenfolk went inside. *Don't speak*, Fortunate whispered, *run away*, but they could not hear him. The Spirit threw them and their words about as dogs throw rats and went away laughing.

Sick with confusion and dread, he stood back from the window. Was it indeed a spirit, or a man? Others could see it. It had no fear of the master. It came nearer each time; perhaps one day it would enter, whether man or spirit, and hunt him through the house.

He told himself it was not in the house now, and stayed there, unmoving, as his terror went down and his breathing quietened and no longer filled the room.

Now he could distinguish sounds: the voices of Dog Eye and the Wife. They were outside the study, quarrelling as usual. Relief washed through him, leaving him limp as grass in wind. The study door slammed. The Wife came along the landing towards the stairs: he knew her step as he knew everybody's in the household. She began to descend. Then the sounds changed to a faint rustling and stopped. He opened the door a crack: she was slumped on the corner stair, her face in her hands. He had no desire to go to her and be found fault with. Closing the door, he waited for her to move off.

She was there for what seemed a long time, but at last he heard Fan coming upstairs. She whispered with the mistress, went away, came back. More talk, and they returned upstairs and went along the landing.

He was glad he had chosen this room to hide in. He waited for the Wife's chamber door to close – she was enraged whenever servants left doors open – but failed to catch the sound. At last he decided he must take his chance. Tip-toeing across the landing, he gained the stairs and crept softly down them to the ground floor.

'La, Titus!' Eliza turns from her pile of carrots as he enters the kitchen. 'You're a ghost.'

'A ghost?'

'Grey, sweetheart. You're grey.'

He follows her gaze down to his hands and catches her meaning: he has neglected to oil his skin. The maid fetches him a spoonful of butter and watches him rub it over his fingers. Mrs Launey wanted him to use lard, it being cheaper, but the Wife said he would smell. It seems to Fortunate he could hardly smell worse: he passes his days stinking of rancid butter.

'I don't know where she got these carrots,' Eliza remarks, holding one up. 'Soft as an old man's sugar stick.'

Soft, a sugar stick? One of his tasks is to grind the sugar loaf and that is hard enough for anybody: it is a strange thing to say. But then, Eliza is a strange young woman. She once told him that she came with the house. He was struck by this and thought perhaps there were such things as English slaves, but then the next day she told him that she could leave whenever she wished and find work elsewhere. She said, 'I'll see life before I'm done, believe me.' He is not sure what she meant by this. Does not everybody see life? He smooths his buttered hands over his face to oil the skin there.

Eliza grins. 'That's better.'

He nods: speech is full of traps. Whenever he answers a question, Mrs Dog Eye corrects him – 'Now repeat! Repeat!' – though mostly he is unable to perceive the difference. It is there, however, since others also react: with laughter, with frowns of perplexity, with contempt.

Eliza says, 'I s'pose you heard them milling out there?'

'Milling?'

'Beating, fighting.' She raises her fists as if to box with him. 'I've seen *him* hanging round before. Ten to one he's a dun.'

'Done?'

'It's loss of breath talking to you, Blackbird. A dun comes looking for money.'

'A poor man. A beggar.'

Eliza laughs. 'A devil, more like. When you borrow, Titus, and you don't pay it back —' She breaks off as Fan enters. 'Did you tell her about the woman?'

Fan looks towards Fortunate and frowns. 'Little pitchers, Liza. Tell-tale tits.'

351

Fortunate says, 'A dun is a devil?'

'Hear that?' Eliza answers, not to him but to Fan. 'Innocent as a babe unborn.'

'Later.' Fan picks up a carrot, wrinkling her nose. 'Are these the best you could find?'

'Launey bought 'em. She must be riding the market man. Time she was back, if you ask me —'

There is a loud slam: the front door.

'Talk of the devil,' Fan exclaims, causing Fortunate's stomach to turn over. She and Eliza become very busy peeling and chopping, but no Mrs Launey appears. 'I'm not losing my wits, am I?' Fan demands of her heap of carrots. 'It *was* the door I heard?'

It was. The dun-devil has entered. It is in the passageway even now, snuffling its way towards him.

'Unless it was the mistress going out,' Eliza suggests.

'Can't be, those Lechery people are still here.'

Eliza goes to the kitchen door. 'Come on, Titus. Let's have a look.' She catches hold of his sleeve and pulls him towards the corridor.

'Scream out directly if you meet a robber,' Fan calls.

'I've got Titus to protect me.'

He would rather Eliza protected him, so he keeps to the rear, listening out for the snarl of the Spirit. All he hears, however, is a murmur of conversation from behind the Blue Room door, proving Fan correct: the visitors are still within the house. Fortunate and Eliza go from room to room, searching behind curtains and sofas and inside wall cupboards.

Taking up a candle, Eliza suggests they should check the cellar. Down they go, Fortunate sweating like an overdriven horse, into a darkness smelling of cesspits where he is forced to breathe through his mouth. Eliza holds out the candle to each corner of the brick vault in turn.

'Nobody here. Let's try upstairs.'

As they mount to the first floor, he is comforted by the knowledge that he was able to hide his fear from the maid. He has not disgraced himself. Eliza goes to the mistress's room and searches there while Fortunate, bolder now, knocks at the door of the study and when Dog Eye does not respond, pushes it open.

'Eliza!'

The girl hurries to him. 'You're not fooling me, are you?'

It is no foolery. The desk is torn like a deer after the kill. A leg has been ripped off and the drawers dragged from its belly, one thrown against a wall, another lying charred near the hearth. In the grate lies a grey feathery nest of burnt papers. Eliza, like Fortunate, stops at the doorway, her eyes wide.

'Dear God,' she says. 'Dear God.'

She whirls about and runs along the corridor to the master's chamber. Fortunate has a happy inspiration. He goes to the box of pistols, sets the safety catches and slips one of them into each of his pockets. They are just concealed. There is a smaller box of powder and one of lead balls. These, too, he takes before following Eliza, his belly tight with anticipation.

Clothes are flung about the bedchamber; the master's razor and other personal items have vanished from the closet. There is a sharp stink on the air. Eliza looks round, lifts the lid of the commode and lowers it with a grimace of disgust.

'He's heaved up in there. Nice job for somebody, and don't I know who!'

'Dun,' Fortunate suggests. 'Afraid of Devil Dun.'

'Could be.' She flops onto the bed and sits there, gnawing at her thumb. A disrespectful action. She would not dare if the master were present.

'He'd a soft spot for *you*,' she says with a sly look at him. 'Did he never drop a hint?'

He shakes his head.

'You know what this means, don't you? He's gone.'

'To Romeville?'

Despite everything, she laughs. 'Who taught you that word?'

'Him.'

'And he didn't teach you what it was? We're in Romeville now, you simpkin. But you can't call it that in respectable company. You must say, *London.*'

She's teasing him. This dreary house, with its sour mistress, is London. He hasn't forgotten Romeville: a savage, marvellous place, where the people live by night.

'I wouldn't be in your shoes,' Eliza says, her face softening. He knows this saying about shoes: in the kitchen, it means a cake is sunken or a sauce curdled. 'She'll get rid of you now, you may depend upon it.'

She begins a story about a housekeeper she once knew, dismissed by the mistress of the house while the master was away in Italy but Fortunate, plunged in misery, barely hears her.

Dog Eye has abandoned him.

43

The Pinched Wife stands a long time staring at the ashes. Before fetching her Eliza hurried to Fan, who now stands at the door, fingers twisted in her apron. All three women are the colour of watered milk.

The Wife murmurs something. Fortunate is unable to understand what she is saying, and perhaps the maids also, since they exchange furtive glances.

'If I may speak, Madam.' For once, Eliza is solemn enough.

'Yes?' The Wife does not look at her.

'The drawer's been sticking lately. Something wrong in the lock. I heard the master pulling at it yesterday.'

'I see,' the Wife says, looking not at the desk but at the ashes.

Fortunate says, 'He's taken his pistols, Madam.'

The Wife says, 'They're on the shelf.'

'The case is, Madam, but it's empty.'

'Why would he leave the case?' The Wife goes to it and opens it up. Folding back the lid, she stands a moment with her hands on the leather, staring out from the study window. To Fortunate she looks as if she is trying to foresee what will come of this. Only now does it come to him that the missing pistols change everything. They mean a duel. He should have held his tongue.

'Tell Mr and Mrs Letcher I'm indisposed and must beg to be excused. Offer them more refreshment before their journey. Fan, I shall want you. Come to me in half an hour.'

Within her closet Sophia takes out her favourite writing paper, a gift from Mama. Extraordinary, the comfort afforded by such an inert and flimsy substance, and at such a time – in those very moments when one might fancy it beneath notice. The inkstand she brought with her from Buller Hall, her rose-scented sealing wax: each speaks to her as a friend, reassuring her that present troubles represent an eruption of anarchy soon to be repressed, after which life will continue to conduct itself *comme il faut*. The very curves of the inkstand insist upon it.

And yet, *comme il faut* is precisely what her life has never been. Always there have been spots of rottenness, maggots deep in the core: Papa's vanity, her 'little weakness', the dishonesty of her parents in concealing it before the marriage, her craven, reprehensible feelings for Edmund. Perhaps misery and uncertainty are, after all, the way of the world and everything else mere surface.

What would a poor woman say? Surely if anyone understands trials and tribulations it is a widow without means. Could she but find some decent but penniless creature, spotless in her person (since otherwise Sophia could not endure to sit with her), she would have someone to consult with. 'Speak frankly,' she would say. 'Do you consider our existence to be made up entirely of suffering?'

The conversation can never take place; her acquaintance does not extend to paupers. Nor could she bear to uncover her own wounds, to respond to questions probing, lancet-like, into the inflamed and infected body of her marriage. Thank God she sent Hetty away! – and yet, she realises, her husband's departure is a development of which her cousin must be told. She may require the assistance and protection of Hetty's husband: who knows what debts, what secrets, what crimes Edmund has left behind him? Suppose that degraded hulk of a man should return in search of him, force the door and find Sophia unprotected?

If only it were possible to quit this house. Mama always maintained that a wife who 'bolts' puts herself entirely and irrevocably in the wrong, but may not a woman flee when her husband has

356

already done so? In what sense does this leaking ship of souls – four females and a black boy – constitute a marital home?

The closet surprises her by its warmth. She pulls the curtain aside – no risk of Edmund spying on her now – and wipes her brow, the skin of which is unpleasantly greasy. *Dearest Hetty*, she imagines writing. What follows? *You are doubtless wondering —*

Supposing she writes her letter now. Will there be another, a worse one, to write tomorrow? On the face of it, a duel seems inconceivable: what honour can Edmund possibly imagine himself obliged to defend? Yet every day men take up arms, knowing themselves in the wrong. Even so, it is difficult to imagine Edmund so engaged. He takes far too good a care of himself.

Best write now. She pictures the words on her fine paper, sealed with the pink wax. This letter will require some delicacy of phrasing. Really, how warm the closet is for this time of year! More than warm, it is stuffy, quite intolerably so —

Something strikes her nose, filling her eyes with water. There is a voice, flat and toneless: 'Madam.'

Then a scratching sensation in her fingers. Another voice, toneless likewise: 'Told you.'

Sophia is unable to distinguish the words that follow. Her closed eyelids appear to her as blood-coloured curtains. The sensation in her hand softens, is now a patting, while the jumble of speech swells, gathers depth and nuance and becomes recognisable at last as the familiar voice of Fan, saying, 'There, you see?'

Sophia raises the red curtains of her eyes on a puzzling scene: the two maids standing over her, one on either side.

'What's the matter?'

'You asked me to come for a letter, Madam.' Fan's manner, calm and respectful, suggests there is nothing in the world the matter. Sophia, recalling the blow to her nose and the shock of

357

pain that resulted, is about to ask what happened when she observes her vial of hartshorn lying upon the toilet table.

Fan says, 'Mr and Mrs Letcher left word they'd be back tomorrow.'

The dead weight Sophia escaped in unconsciousness promptly rolls over her again, crushing her: Edmund, gone. She sits motionless. Everything that suggests itself to her, even rising from the chair, strikes her as futile.

'You fainted, Madam. Shall I help you to bed?' Fan suggests at last.

'I meant to write to Mrs Letcher.'

'Your delicate health . . .' Eliza allows her voice to trail off insinuatingly.

Indignation lends Sophia strength enough to snap, 'I wasn't aware I'd discussed my health with you.'

For all that she bows her head, the girl's face is sly rather than humbled. She is a coarse creature, and has the insolence one might expect in a household where servants are told more than the wife.

Fan tries to soften the thing down. 'Pray excuse the impertinence, Madam. Eliza meant well.' Yet she, too, has a curious way of looking at Sophia, as if she has glimpsed new lights in her. Without a master, the household has begun to dissolve: Sophia senses its dissolution as she might a physical, palpable process.

'Eliza,' she says, 'go to the kitchen.'

To mark the punishment, Fan, the favoured, may remain. She regards her employer with such an expression of preparedness, of faith in her own abilities, that it is a comfort in itself.

'Does Mrs Launey know Mr Zedland is out?'

'I can't say, Madam.'

'Then tell her to keep something hot for him.'

'What I mean, Madam, is that she went out after dinner and hasn't come back.'

'After dinner?'

'About three o'clock. I pray God she hasn't met with thieves. She has a gold brooch, and other things.'

Sophia considers this. 'Could we send Titus to ask?'

'Ask who, Madam?'

'The watchmen, of course.'

'The Charleys won't have seen anything.' Fan is emphatic. 'They never do.'

'Well. Let us hope she soon returns. In her absence, do you think you and that silly wench could put together a cold supper?'

'Of course.' The maid goes to the door, hesitates, and turns back. 'If I may ask, Madam. When you are finished, might we also serve ourselves?'

'Certainly,' Sophia answers. 'Take whatever you wish.'

Left alone, she stares into the mirror, a sibyl intent on divination. Does she detect a sickliness – a pallor? Could a woman of her complexion conceivably look any paler?

Eliza's mention of delicate health has struck terror into her. Mama has told her, more than once, of the faintness that comes from being *enceinte*, how Mama herself was prone to it, and how Aunt Phoebe's swoonings were notorious. Once, when four months gone with Hetty, Phoebe was admiring a bed of roses when she toppled headlong into it. The gentlemen ran to lift her out; finding her face barely scratched, everyone cried out upon her good fortune and said it was a mercy she hadn't lost an eye.

Sophia's flowers are overdue, and now she has fainted.

Anything more precise than 'overdue' is beyond her unless she first consults her diary. Since the first faint stainings at the age of fifteen, her visitations have been irregular. She lives resigned to this inconvenience, believing it connected in some way with her weakness, a deficiency of one kind balanced by a superfluity of another: in her bodily make-up, anything to do with vessels and liquids can be relied upon to go wrong. As Dr Brunt told Mama so long ago, such difficulties are exacerbated by anxiety and of late Sophia has been nothing if not anxious.

She runs her hands down the swell of flesh at the base of her stays. She will leave off tight lacing, if it is so. Surely it is *not* so? Yet as she sits, folded in upon herself, it seems that minute by minute an indefinable change comes upon her, a change so subtle that no figure of speech could convey its nature. There are no words for this consciousness, which cannot even be located; all she knows is that, until very recently, her bodily sensations were otherwise.

Perhaps, then, it *is* so.

At once her mind swarms. Edmund, a father: how she would once have welcomed this! How she might have blushed, inform-ing him —!

There they are, all three of them, afloat upon the flaming sur-face of the Statue Lake. The little boy, clapping and crowing, is tenderly supported upon his mama's knee. Mama holds up her head and looks about her with zest, blithe as a milkmaid in this fresh access of married happiness. Papa, bound to wife and child by the silken ropes of affection, rows with practised control to-wards the jetty and every so often fixes his black eyes, full of longing, gratitude, *desire*, upon the woman who has given him this precious jewel: a son.

Perhaps he has other sons.

The child's busy hands, the seething glitter of sun upon waves and Edmund's languishing, subjugated gaze vanish like a soap-bubble that, wavering prettily here and there, is drawn into a candle flame and so comes to grief.

It is dusk. Sophia stands at her chamber window, watching the in-habitants of that other world which is so strange to her, so familiar to *him*. This street is not reliably lit: flickers of torchlight show where an occasional passer-by has hired a link-boy, but most of those below either have no need of light or prefer not to be seen too clearly.

Across the way another woman stands in a window much like hers, but where Sophia is concealed by darkness, the window opposite is illuminated by a well-trimmed lamp. Its occupant continually lets down her curls, brushes them and fastens them up again. She is a slovenly *coiffeuse*, but Sophia understands the artifice: as a means of displaying her hair, and suggesting the intimacies of the bedchamber, it could scarcely be bettered. When bored with this occupation, the woman heaves up the sash, leans out and scouts the pavement, occasionally greeting some person she recognises below. Withdrawing, she seems to lose interest in her hair and grows almost as motionless as Sophia herself, a still life whose frame is the window. Sophia has never before seen this woman, who appears to exist only by night.

How different from her imaginings of married life in the capital, and how strange to think that Hetty was in Town only a few months earlier, staying with wealthy friends. What a delightful picture she painted! Even in May the city was abuzz, she wrote, with everything that could amuse and edify. Mr Garrick, returned from his travels, was once more in command at Drury Lane and Londoners looked forward eagerly to new productions. Hetty danced at balls, splendid in French silk; wearing her warmest pelisse, she attended a musical service at the Foundling Hospital. When not visiting or engaged in some party of pleasure (which pastimes seemed, to the dazzled Sophia, to fill up Hetty's every hour) she found entertainment in reading those same memoirs of Mr Psalmanazar which her husband condemns as meretricious. *Imagine*, Sophia remembers her writing, *the intellectual labour required to invent an entire language, alphabet and all! Had he been honest, what might he not have achieved?* Sophia agreed: it was astounding that one so capable should have thrown away his brilliance upon the construction of a sham, which, directly it was known, must bring him into contempt.

Her opinion has altered since then. She believes there are men whose souls compel them to deceit, whose genius finds its fullest flowering in the elaborate workings of betrayal.

Instead of watching a slut comb her hair, Sophia should be exploring the waxworks and the Tower, dancing at Mrs Cornelys's house and perhaps hearing the Mozart boy and his sister. She should be patronising public lectures, attending plays and operas, reading fashionable memoirs, visiting respectable families. In short, moving in good society.

Is that the front door? Mrs Launey, returned home to explain herself at last? But no, the noise must have come from a neighbouring house, for a silhouette now detaches itself from the pavement on Sophia's side and crosses towards the building opposite. The woman at once bends to throw up the sash, but Sophia, straining her eyes, can distinguish nothing more than a patch of shade. It flits a few more yards and dissolves, swallowed up into the gloom.

'Am I to understand that Mrs Launey and Titus have run off together?'

Her own lamps are now lit, so that Fan and Eliza throw goblin shadows on the chamber walls. Predictably, Eliza fails to conceal a smirk at the notion of Mrs Launey's absconding with the boy. The maids, thinks Sophia, are a study in contrasts. When she first came here, she thought them much the same, a misapprehension which it pains her to remember. She adds, 'I was not aware that I had implied any indecency,' but Eliza's expression does not change. The girl is an imbecile.

'What do you think, Fan?' she demands, despairing of rational discourse with Eliza. 'Could they be in league?'

The maid looks doubtful. 'They were never thick with one another.'

'Then why should both of them leave? Is anything missing downstairs?'

'Not as we can see, Madam.'

'Can see? You mean you haven't searched?'

'For what, Madam? And it's poor work searching at night.'

She has a point. Sophia rubs her eyes, wishing she had gone to bed when Fan first suggested it: she would dearly like to sink down onto the closet table, pillow her head on her arms and sleep. 'Did Titus ever talk of running away?'

'Never.'

'What about the man who came here? Could Titus be in league with him?'

'Oh, no, Madam.' Fan is more emphatic on this head than any other. 'He was frightened of him. I noticed it particularly.'

Yet fear means nothing, Sophia realises: one scarcely imagines criminal association to be motivated purely by affection. Still, Titus seldom leaves the house. There seems no reason to think him connected with that brute: her mind clutched at an idea, that was all.

'He's cut up with the master leaving,' Eliza says.

'We do not know that the master has left.'

To this both maids return a perfect silence. It is a disagreeable moment, broken by Fan's saying, 'Perhaps, Madam, I might bring you Mrs Launey's book.'

'Help her find it, Eliza.' Not that there should be much finding involved, but it is imperative to get Eliza out of the way, Sophia realises, before she succumbs to overwhelming temptation and administers to that face, glistening with prurient excitement, a good sharp slap.

Alone, Sophia gives herself over to wild imaginings. Perhaps

Fan and Eliza are even now packing their boxes and at a signal from the street, a soft whistle, a pebble on the attic window, they will slip out of the house and rejoin their master, leaving only the deserted wife to drift about the place, a living ghost.

Some time later Fan returns alone to announce that the book is gone from its usual place.

'Did you look in her chamber?'

'Yes, Madam. She's taken her things.'

So they have seen the last of Mrs Launey. Evidently Edmund was not the only one with something to hide, Sophia muses with growing bitterness: since the creature has taken pains to cover her tracks, doubtless she levied duties on their every joint of mutton, on their candles, flour, butter, coals. Now she has sniffed the air and found a taint. The household is going off and the stink will be unmerciful, so away scuttles Mrs Launey, intent on finding another pantry to pillage.

'She's a wicked, disloyal, dishonest woman,' Sophia complains. The words seem inadequate even to her; she wonders what they call Mrs Launey downstairs, where language is freer. 'Didn't you notice she was lining her pocket?'

'Maids can't question the cook's doings.' Fan's mouth has taken an obstinate little turn. Of course, Sophia thinks, servants detest tale-bearing. Had Launey not deserted, then Fan, decent as she is, would scarcely have said so much. 'But it's my opinion, Madam – if you won't think it impertinent in me —'

Sophia braces herself. 'Yes?'

Fan lowers her eyes. 'The thing is – if you will permit – it's my belief that Mrs Launey couldn't have known the master would be away.' She clears her throat: a tiny, discreet sound.

'That must be obvious, surely,' Sophia replies. 'When Mrs Launey left, Edmund was still here. I don't understand the application of your remark —' and then she does understand, and stops dead. Fan means there will be gossip: it will be whispered that a tender understanding existed between Edmund and a woman with the shape, complexion and perspiring wetness of a boiled beetroot. Her husband and Peg Launey! And Fan, if you please, talks not of knowledge to the contrary but of *belief*! Evidently some shred of wifely pride remains in Sophia despite the humiliations piled upon her by Edmund, for Fan's hint, though kindly meant, stings like vinegar.

Sophia's head bows in misery as she blames herself: I should have gone into everything, no matter what he said. It was my business to go into it.

But Edmund had insisted that things were already upon a well-established footing, an arrangement set up during those years when there was no such person as Mrs Zedland. Looking back, she realises that each time she attempted to investigate the servants' doings, he at once moved to thwart her: you have not the experience, they know their duties very well without you. 'But they must at least answer to me,' she protested, to which he replied, 'And so they do! What more could you wish?'

'The house has never suited me,' she says aloud. 'I should prefer another.'

'I'm sure he'll release you, Madam, if you don't dispute the remainder.'

Sophia can make nothing of this information, delivered in a manner so respectful as to rule out any sly reference to Edmund. Before she can request clarification, Fan cries out, 'Beg pardon, Madam. I forgot my instructions.'

'Instructions?'

'Mr Zedland's. Your sentiments, you know, on the subject of,' Fan's voice lowers as if to utter some unavoidable indecency, 'renting.'

'What *can* you mean?' Sophia exclaims. 'What sentiments?'

'The master said,' the maid falters, 'we were never to speak of it. That you considered it – vulgar.'

365

'But some of the best families rent for the Season.'

Fan casts down her eyes like a saint in a painting. Hers is a very speaking sort of silence: to misinterpret it, one would have to be blind as well as deaf.

'Let us understand one another,' Sophia says at last. 'You, and the other servants, were told by Mr Zedland that on no account was the tenancy to be mentioned in my presence, and that he wished the house always to be spoken of as belonging to him.'

'Yes, Madam.'

'But it does not.'

This time the answer is longer in coming. 'No—o,' Fan says, as if only now realising the significance of her own words. Raising her head, she gazes, helpless, at Sophia. 'It belongs to Mr Moore.'

Sophia gazes back, watching Fan's pretty mouth compress to a bloodless incision. She forces herself to take deep and regular breaths, imposing a control she does not feel. This must be how soldiers face fire and shot, she thinks: one keeps putting one leg in front of the other, though suffering unspeakably from anticip-ation, until the last unlucky step. *Then* one fathoms the depths in an instant.

'So we're the tenants of this – Mr Moore. And who may he be?'

'He owns all these houses, Madam. He built the street.'

'A builder and speculator, then.'

'Madam, we believed you knew, we did indeed —'

The girl shakes and weeps. Sophia pictures the scene: the cand-our and good humour with which the master of the house ex-plained his wife's little whims. O, the tenderness of his regard for her! The pain he suffered if her wishes were crossed in the slightest! His earnest desire that the servants should do everything necessary to her happiness, and of course the eyes, the eyes speak-ing more than all of this together. What woman could fail to envy his wife?

She wonders that he did not, after all, ruin Fan. Had he given himself over to the work of seduction he must surely have met with success but perhaps, thinks Sophia, it suited him not to foul his nest at home. He had, in any case, interests elsewhere.

'*You* are not to blame,' she says now, pitying the girl's mottled cheeks – for Fan is like herself, an ugly weeper. 'When you said someone would release me, I take it you meant Mr Moore. Are you acquainted with him?'

'He put us in here. First me, then Eliza and Mrs Launey.'

'Am I to understand that you came with the house, like the chairs?'

'Mr Moore's business is with people coming to town at short notice. He prefers to have his own servants in place, says things are better looked to. Though Launey's wiped his eye this time.'

'Have your wages been paid?'

'His man brings them last day of the month.' Fan dabs at her eyes. 'It's not often you find a master so open-handed.'

'Indeed.' Mama's servants are paid after half a year, which at least discourages them from vanishing into the night. 'So, if I should leave this house, you'll be turned off?'

'No, Madam. If nobody takes this place, he'll put me into another. I've worked for him three years now and he finds me satisfactory.'

Does he approve likewise of Eliza and Mrs Launey? At the thought of the latter a faint and not disagreeable sensation, of which she has been aware for some time, becomes more insistent and announces itself as hunger.

'Did you find anything for supper?'

'There's cold beef.'

'Bring it up here, with some wine.'

'It'll do you good, Madam, I'm sure I hope so,' and Fan is off to retail the latest horrors to Eliza. Every word of their conversation will be repeated downstairs, as Sophia well knows. Still, there remains gratitude for Fan's kindness. Miss Sophia Buller that was, grateful for the kindness of a servant! Had Edmund been a little kinder, what might she not have grown to tolerate, in the end? Degraded, yet doting: an ignoble fate, not uncommon among women. Would it, all things considered, have involved more suffering than her own?

Not Fan, but Eliza (unable, Sophia supposes, to resist this chance of witnessing her humiliation) arrives bearing cold beef, some slimy green stuff in a dish, bread and fruitcake and a jug of wine. The beef resembles leather. There is something to be said for even the most unscrupulous cook, provided she is handy at her work. Mrs Launey would have taken one look at the coarse, dry chunks and cut them fine to be heated through in a good gravy.

Having dismissed the girl, Sophia contemplates the unappetising mess before her and imagines Hetty's verdict, particularly on the 'garden thrash'. What will she do for a cook? Since all such hiring is the responsibility of Mr Moore, she assumes she has not the right to advertise.

How much better to choose one's own staff, in one's own home, with one's loving husband, children, relatives and friends: all the accoutrements of feminine happiness which this female has so signally failed to acquire.

She sniffs at the jug. Surely even Eliza knows that a gentlewoman does not sit and drink alone. 'Mrs Buller,' guests would solicit her mother, 'will you take wine with me?' – a charming courtesy which gave pleasure to all concerned. *That* is how life is meant to be: improved, polished, refined. To take it in the rough is to take a raw onion and bite into its stinking, stinging core: a primitive sensation, disgusting to the refined palate. For civilised people there is the long apprenticeship of education, morality, taste: the daily endeavour to haul up from the mud our fallen human nature.

With a blush, she remembers: she herself asked for wine. She meant as a restorative, but Eliza has brought her sufficient for inebriation. Perhaps it is intended, in the crude well-meaning way of such people, as a kindness. Sophia takes a sip. Surely this was broached days ago. Yet she sips again, in a silent toast to the life upon which she is about to embark, a life in which wine of any description may prove a rarity. She grinds, a dutiful child, at the leathery beef. The vegetables (leeks, apparently) have congealed in their butter dressing, but she eats them all. At least the fruit-cake is palatable. She pours herself another glass of stale wine, pushes the tray away from her and sits back to think.

Now what? Now what. She must make a list of everything requiring attention, must write to Mr Moore, to Hetty. To Mama and Papa? What will they say, she wonders, upon discovering that her husband has bolted? Will they admit that Sophia was right all along, and Edmund a practised deceiver and yes, a forger? Though he has destroyed the contents of the desk, the maids and Hetty can attest to the arrival of Edmund's 'friend', no longer a suspicion but a living, breathing animal in satin shoes. After Mama's unfeeling reassurances, there is a grim satisfaction in contemplating that aspect of her domestic catastrophe.

Should Edmund not return, and she hardly expects him to, she and her parents must take measures to seek him out. They will come to some arrangement, she supposes: beat Edmund away from his prey, pay him to sign a deed of separation. Will he pocket his 'winnings' with those elegant fingers of his, smiling a vulpine smile, or will he claw and bite? Until this moment, Sophia realises, she has been picturing him as fled to Wixham. Does that place even exist, or is it like this one, a convenient fable?

There is a knock at the door.

'Yes?'

Fan enters in more of a flutter than Sophia has ever seen her before. 'Madam, that woman's here.'

Sophia is past pretending not to understand. 'The one with the earrings? Get rid of her.'

'We were about to, Madam, but she claims to know something to your advantage. Very much so, she said.'

If only Hetty were present. What would she advise? 'She can't come in here. I won't have her in here.'

'Of course not, Madam. She won't be let out of our sight. Should you wish to see her, I'll tell Eliza to go with her into the Blue Room until you arrive. Be so kind as to hold still, one second —' Fan reaches out and pins back a lock of her mistress's hair.

'Is Eliza with her now?'

'Yes, Madam. She's strong is Eliza, well able to hold the door.'

'Good,' says Sophia. 'I should hate to lose the plate as well as Mrs Launey.'

And the master, she can feel the maid thinking. Certainly this is an unfortunate house.

44

In the Blue Room the person stands quite at ease, apparently accustomed to scrutiny. Accepting the implied permission, Sophia studies her in a manner unthinkable with a polite visitor. She sees a tall female with some faint, bedraggled relics of elegance, not unlike an out-of-work lady's maid. She notes the woman's height, her large, capable hands and the toes (shod today in red leather) protruding from beneath her gown. Yes, this person could have filled the satin shoes. Her complexion is brown, her lips (as Sophia has previously noted) full and coarse. By candle-light the eyes and brows are inky, not unlike Edmund's. Why, they could be sister and brother! Are *all* these people related? Will that dirty brute who came to the door turn out to be one of her in-laws?

One thing is certain: Sophia herself is Odd Man Out. She says, 'I believe you have something to tell me.'

The woman's voice is a fortune-teller's wheedle. 'Everything, Madam. Everything you wish to know.'

'I wonder.' This creature could not begin to comprehend all that the wife of Edmund Zedland wishes to know, still less what she would shrink from knowing. 'You would presumably require some payment?'

'No, by God! And I shan't accept any.'

For the first time Sophia glimpses her appeal: a self-possession that owes nothing to the dancing-master's deportment. With a certain dryness she replies, 'Pray excuse my ignorance. If there is an etiquette for such meetings as this, I confess it does not spring to mind.'

The visitor's mouth turns up just a hair's breadth as if she, too,

perceives the absurdity of their situation. 'We could have introductions,' she suggests. 'And tea.'

'Introductions and tea! This is indeed the Age of Gentility,'
says Sophia. 'Let me ask you one thing before we "have introductions", as you put it. Have you come from Mr Zedland?'

On hearing his name, the woman turns and spits into the fire.

She's been thrown over, Sophia thinks. She seeks revenge, and
I – good God! – I am to be the means.

It was folly to allow her over the doorstep. Sophia rings the bell
without further ado, intending to have her visitor shown out. But
as Eliza bustles in, eager for raised voices and pulled hair, Sophia
seems to hear Hetty's words: *little goose. Blind and deaf.* All very
well for Hetty, who objected to sitting in a public room with this
same person. Still, what does it matter, now, if the woman stays?
Chaos is already come. She tells Eliza to fetch some tea.

The woman says, 'I take mine with French Cream.'

Sophia, to whom the expression is unfamiliar, is rescued by Eliza's 'Brandy, Madam.'

'There's nothing of that sort to be had. I'm afraid our cook has
absconded with the cellar key.'

The visitor throws her an insolent look but Sophia is adamant:
if she wishes to get drunk, she must do it elsewhere. Fan is rung
for, arrives with suspicious speed and is instructed to take Eliza's
place outside the door, where she has probably been listening
already. Wife and mistress are alone in the Blue Room, where
the mistress seats herself without waiting for an invitation. Sophia
takes the chair opposite and proceeds to 'having introductions'.

'You know me, I think, as Mrs Zedland. What am I to call you?'

'Betsy-Ann Blore, also known as Mrs Samuel Shiner, though
that's not rightly my name.' She gives a sudden bark of laughter.

'Pray, what's so amusing?'

'O, queer names. Mrs Shiner, Mrs Zedland,' the woman
prattles as if speaking with an equal. At the notion of addressing

her as 'Mrs Shiner', Sophia shudders inwardly.

'I should be obliged, Betsy-Ann, if you'd come to the point. Say what you have to say.'

'Well, *you* know who *I* am, I suppose,' Betsy-Ann Blore retorts. 'What I am to you, I mean. I'm here to tell you, Mrs Zedland, that you've been shabbily abused. And you might not believe it, but knowing the party as I do, I pity you from my heart.'

Sophia bites her lip: to be pitied, by the likes of this! Mere cant, of course. Such people patter off a sentimental rigmarole, devoid of true feeling.

'You are too kind,' she says frigidly, 'though I doubt whether you can enter into my feelings, our situations being so different. You were never married to my husband —' here she breaks off, stricken by an appalling possibility. Suppose Edmund deceived her in that also, and has entered into some earlier contract with this child of the streets?

'Never married,' says Betsy-Ann Blore, if that is indeed her name. 'But near enough.'

'As far as I'm aware one is either married or one isn't.'

'Call it love, then.' The dark eyes are big and hot with resentment; then they relax, and their expression grows sly. 'After Ned you're spoiled for any other man, you'll be aware of *that*.'

Edmund has discussed her with this woman. Her bridal innocence, her humiliating weakness, all doubtless afforded them merriment. Had he painted her naked and posturing upon a brothel wall she could hardly feel more degraded, but she holds herself all the straighter as she says, 'What you call love strikes me as somewhat acquisitive.'

'A what?'

'Mercenary. For money.'

The woman laughs. 'I don't suppose you married on half a loaf. You had your settlements and all the rest of it, eh? But I haven't come here to quarrel.'

'Then be brief. You cannot imagine your presence is welcome.'

Her visitor's manner grows confidential. 'He's played us both a filthy trick. I can't get back at him in law, but *you* can.'

'I hope you don't imagine I'll serve your turn, or act for you against my husband.'

'You might feel different when you know. Where's the blowen – the girl, I mean? I don't want her walking in on us.'

'She'll stay outside.'

As if expressly to create confusion, Eliza knocks and enters with the tray.

'Did you find any French Cream, sweetheart?' the woman asks.

'It's all gone, Madam,' Eliza answers with much artificial flutter. She is a hopeless liar: Sophia wonders how she can have failed to notice this before.

'Eliza, wait outside with Fan.' She is not going to be dictated to by this woman: both maids will remain for protection, even though it means they will listen at the door. She moves to the table and pours the tea herself.

'That's right,' says the visitor, 'you stand bitch.'

The teaspoon drops from Sophia's fingers and bounces off the table leg. The woman bends down and picks it from the carpet, meekly enough; she seems surprised. Is it possible that no insult was intended? At least she holds her cup with a degree of grace and does not, as Sophia feared, slop tea from the saucer.

'You're in a tight spot,' she begins as Sophia settles herself back in her chair. 'He's got hold of the blun – the money, eh?'

'Are you speaking of Mr Zedland?'

'Aye, damned sharp that he is.'

'All gentlemen game occasionally,' says Sophia, conscious of turning aside from the main thrust.

'Your sharp swivels the other players. He *lives* by it, Mrs Zedland.'

'Fortunately Mr Zedland has more resources.'

'In Essex, I hear. And you'll have visited, eh?'

'During the Season one stays in Town.'

'But you've seen the place?'

'These are very particular questions. Kindly state your business.'

Betsy-Ann Blore shrugs. 'What I intend to tell you, that's also very particular. You won't regret humouring me, Mrs Zedland.'

'I've yet to visit Wixham,' says Sophia, resigned. 'And now I hope you're satisfied.'

Betsy-Ann Blore sits back in her chair, biting at some ragged skin on her forefinger. 'Your man of law,' she says. 'Would he know a faytour's work?'

'Fater?'

'A faytour makes queer papers. Forgeries.'

'Mr Scrope is honest and extremely diligent.'

'Diligent, my arse! Is he fly? I mean, is he a knowing sort of man?'

'Papa's very satisfied with him.'

'Oh, well, if Papa's satisfied! Only I'll stake my eyes there's no property, not as much as you could put in this teacup.'

'Mr Zedland's there now.'

Betsy-Ann Blore shakes her head with relish. 'That's just where he isn't. I can tell you where he is this minute. Shall I? Only say the word.'

This minute. Is she able to endure whatever *this minute* might bring in its train? The clock ticks as if thinking for her: Yes. No. Yes. No. Yes. No.

Yes.

'Very well. Where do you imagine him to be?'

'Cosgrove's.' Betsy-Ann Blore puts down the name like a gold coin. There is a pause while Sophia attempts to divine what response she should make, for plainly *Cosgrove's* demands one.

'You don't know it, I perceive,' says Betsy-Ann. 'And why should you? Never mind, I'll show you where it is. We'll go right up to the window.'

'I'm not accustomed to prowling about, peeping through windows.'

'Who said anything about prowling? Lord, you don't think it's a secret, do you?'

Sophia stares.

'It's a gaming club, Mrs Zedland, open day and night. The shutters are left open on purpose.'

'I shouldn't care to enter such a place.'

'They wouldn't let you in. But they like people to look on, and admire.' The woman holds out her cup to be refilled. 'What'll you do, then? You'll have to shape yourself.'

The meaning of this last piece of Greek is clear enough. 'I hardly think that's your business,' Sophia says.

'You don't know your own business yet. That's what I've come to tell you, if you'll hear. There's not another woman in Ro— . . . in London, can tell you what I can.'

'The question is, whether there's any truth in it.'

'That's for you to find out. Your papa'll help you, and your Mr Scrope. All I can do is lay information.'

'Since you are so very – *informative* – I can only conclude you had a hand in it.'

'No hand in anything to do with you. That was all in the country.'

'But a part of the country that you know,' Sophia insists. 'You *are* from Somersetshire, are you not?'

'I'm not from anywhere. Though we lived some time in Zed —'

She breaks off. Sophia pounces: 'On Mr Zedland's property, you were about to say?' For the first time the woman appears confused. 'Did you, or did you not, live with my husband in the country?'

'*Zedland* is the St Giles, Madam. The lingo, the cant. What you might call a slang term —'

'I should certainly call it a slang term.'

'— for Somersetshire.'

Sophia is conscious of a superior power of analysis. 'My husband's name is Mr Somersetshire? Come, you can do better than that. You began to say that you lived with him in the country. Don't deny it, I distinctly heard you.'

Betsy-Ann Blore bites her lip. 'I'll have to go back a long way. I want that agreed before I begin,' she says, raising her hand, 'agreed that you'll hear me out and let me speak free.'

'Very well. And *I* want it agreed that I don't undertake to believe a word.'

'I'll need a flash of lightning, to bear me up.' She sees Sophia once more at a loss. 'A glass of gin, Madam. Just one will do my business.'

'We haven't —'

'There's a stall at the end of the street, by the horse-trough.'

Sophia can no longer hold out against curiosity. She goes to the door and gives the necessary instructions to Fan.

'Much appreciated,' Miss Blore says. 'And since you've been so handsome about it, I'll tell you first the most important thing, and show how all this came about. Your husband's name isn't Zedland.'

'I beg your pardon, but it is. I was married to Mr Edmund Zedland.'

The woman holds up a finger. 'You agreed to let me speak. He went under the name of Zedland while travelling — in Zedland.'

'This is perfect gibberish.'

'It is to you, Mrs Zedland, because you're a daisy. You know what cant is, I suppose?'

'I've read of it in the newspapers. A kind of secret language between felons, is it not?'

'Well, in the cant, Somersetshire goes under the name of Zed-land. Now, when a sharp moves off his own ward and goes where he isn't known, he takes a name so that his brother sharps may avoid him, d'you see? Sharps playing sharps, that's a poor show. You follow me?'

'So far, yes.'

'Well, his was Zedland. He said it was suited to sheep-shearing.'

Sophia always thought it an unusual name. More, she found it charmingly romantic and *Sophia Zedland* full of music, so much sweeter to the ear than *Hetty Letcher*. But even that sweetness, it seems, was illusory. With a pang she recalls the drunken young fool bubbled at Bath. It hangs together . . . she can no longer keep up her pretence of coolness, she must know all. 'What's his true name? Can you tell me?'

'That I can swear to. I know his ma.'

Sophia trembles. 'Not his father? He's a natural son?'

'Of a lord, it's said. He's Ned Hartry, son of Kitty Hartry, of the Cun — of a house near Covent Garden.'

'Hartry! I've heard that name.'

Betsy-Ann Blore looks doubtful. 'He'd take good care you shouldn't.'

'Or seen it. *Hartry* . . .' One of his papers, she is sure. But which? Had this person only called yesterday, before everything was reduced to ashes! She groans and puts her hands over her eyes, overwhelmed by the repeated shocks she has sustained: not only this crowning detail of Edmund's duplicity but his flight, the destruction of the documents, the loss of the servants and the real-isation that she is liable to be turned out of the house.

There is a knock at the door; Sophia straightens. Fan brings in a tray with two glasses on it, two jugs, lemons and sugar. She sets them down on a table near the fire, glancing as she does so toward Betsy-Ann Blore, as if to check she has not yet stolen anything. Sophia nods to indicate the girl may go.

'Now *I'll* stand bitch,' says Betsy-Ann when they are alone, 'and show you how it's done.'

'I shan't have any.'

'She's brought you a glass.'

'I'm aware of that, but I won't drink gin.'

'Gammon! It's the best drink in the world, if you just put enough sugar and lemon to it.'

'To mask the taste? Of the best drink?'

'Aye, well,' and the woman laughs at herself so that Sophia almost likes her, 'I meant the most stiffening, only you have to swallow it first.' She pours some gin into each glass, adds sugar and lemon and a splash of hot water and nods encouragingly towards Sophia.

The mixture is unspeakable. Sophia adds as much water again and ventures another sip: it is dismal as ever.

'Now,' says Betsy-Ann Blore after a greedy swig at her own glass, 'shall I tell you his history?'

'I'm not sure I wish to hear it.'

'That's not the spirit. If I'm to do you good, you *must* hear. Your Mr Zedland is the only son of Kitty Hartry, and heir to a fortune.'

'His father acknowledges him, then?'

'He may do, but I meant his mother's fortune. She keeps her own establishment.'

'Gaming?'

'It's a bawdy-house, Mrs Zedland.'

Hearing this, Sophia is somehow not as surprised as she ought to be, even as certain puzzling incongruities present themselves.

'You're thinking he's too genteel? Kitty wanted him genteel. She sent him to school, and to the university. He went abroad, even, to pick up the manner.'

A poor kind of gentility, thinks Sophia; yet Edmund fooled her well enough, as long as he continued the effort. If nothing else, she owes her self-respect one last attempt to refute the

379

tale. 'Why should a reputable school admit the child of such a woman?'

Betsy-Ann Blore looks pityingly at her. 'Depends who his papa is. There's many a fine lord's "nephew" there, from what I heard.'

'Is that the case with my husband?'

'Who knows?' Betsy-Ann gives a shrug. 'Kitty's a shocking liar.'

So that is the explanation. Sophia's husband is a statue of inferior make, given a high finish to deceive the undiscerning. He passed with her parents – also with herself – though she cannot for the life of her see why he should take the trouble.

'What took him to Bath?' A hateful possibility suggests itself. 'Was it his health?'

'O, no. He and Kitty fell out, on account of him springing one of her whores from the House.'

Sophia considers this in astonishment. 'Do you mean he effected a rescue? Enabled her to live a virtuous —'

'As I said, Mrs Zedland, you're a daisy. He set her up for his private use.'

'So his mother lost an asset,' says Sophia, to show she is not quite a daisy. She begins to comprehend the mentality of such people. One need not be especially clever, and certainly not well educated. The essential thing is to conduct one's life as war: everything is permitted except compassion. 'Was this girl so difficult to replace?'

'Bless you, Madam, there's no shortage of flesh in Romeville. The thing is, Kitty can't bear to be crossed. She offered him the pick of her stock if he'd only give me up.'

Sophia gasps.

'Yes, *me*, and he defied her.' Betsy-Ann Blore's eyes gleam with a mixture of pride and gin, but Sophia's gasp is not for her. K. Hartry! *Kitty* Hartry, the brothel-keeper: now it comes to her, that terrible letter bent upon debauching and enslaving a young man already far gone in indulgence. Never could she have imagined that the writer might prove to be a female and a mother, and the recipient her own husband. Had the woman before her announced that her legs were carved of marble, and pulled up her gown to demonstrate the fact, it could not have run more contrary to Sophia's notions of the world.

'Kitty wasn't having any,' Betsy-Ann continues. 'She cut off the funds sharpish and after a bit we found ourselves in Queer Street. He'd no notion of economy, or hog-grubbing as he called it, since he'd lived out of his ma's purse, and I was nearly as bad, so he sold me to a friend of his, a Mr Shiner.'

'Sold! You can't sell a woman in England!'

This remark is received with an indulgent smile. 'For the pleasure of scratching a certain itch he had, Sam Shiner settled Ned's debts – most of 'em – and they cooked up a lie, that I'd been staked at cards and lost, and it was a debt of honour, and I had to go. So like a halfwit I went. But Kitty smelt a rat, and still wasn't satisfied. So Ned toddled up to Bath, where he wasn't known, and there he met with you. The papers he showed your Mr Gingumbob —'

'Mr Scrope —'

'— were counterfeit.'

'But why? Why me?'

'He thought marrying a gentry-mort would win over his ma. You had a bit of blunt, of course, and you fell in his way.'

The casual sting of this last statement compels Sophia to retort, 'I was never acquainted with Mr Zedland at Bath. He called upon my father at home, and it was there that he asked for my hand in marriage. Our courtship was conducted in quite the usual fashion.'

'I daresay. I wouldn't know, myself, how it's done among the gentry, only he said your people wanted you married.'

So Betsy-Ann Blore has indeed been told about the *weakness*.

There is no private matter concerning his wife that Edmund has not sacrificed to this woman – whom he has also sacrificed, so little does he —

Sophia has read of the choke-pear, a device in vogue among extortionists who lie in wait, overpower a victim, force the instrument into his mouth and expand it by turning a key. She feels at this moment as if just such a pear has been jammed into her throat, and her flesh is closing round it.

'O, now!' says Betsy-Ann Blore. That shrivelling pity: Sophia steels herself, swallows down the choke-pear and wipes her eyes on the heel of her hand. Her voice is almost steady as she says, 'And then he picked up with you again.'

'I didn't know I'd been sold, then. D'you think I'd go back to him after that?'

How should Sophia have an opinion? A woman who consents to be won at cards, then returns to the man who gambled her away, knowing him married: what might that woman not accept?

'You'll want to talk the business over with your friends,' Miss Blore suggests. 'A lady like you always has friends.'

'I shall tell them what you've told me, but you've given me no proof. Can you prove any of it? In such a way that it would persuade a court?'

'Papers, you mean?' Betsy-Ann Blore shakes her head. 'The canting crew don't live as you do. If a record's kept of us, it mostly means we're in Queer Street. And his ma won't oblige me, not for a thousand pounds.'

'Could *I* go to her?' The woman raises her eyes to Heaven. Sophia ignores the rudeness. 'The counterfeiter, then! Would *he* help us?' It occurs to her in speaking that the counterfeiter and the mysterious Mr Shiner may be one and the same individual. The name Shiner appeared among the burnt papers, surely? Some sort of bill, or chit, in an exquisite, delicate script. 'Could you talk with him – ask him?'

'I don't know him,' says Miss Blore with an emphasis that betrays the lie. 'And besides, it's hanging.' She looks straight at Sophia, holding the look, as she says, 'The shover hangs with him.'

'Who's the —'

'The one that passes it on. Ned Hartry.'

The choke-pear, cold and obstructive, is now doing untold damage down in Sophia's stomach. 'It wasn't *coining*,' she protests. 'They were papers – documents.'

'It's hanging right enough – not about to faint, are you?'

'No.'

'You look it.' Miss Blore crosses to her and picks up the barely touched cup of gin. 'Here. It's cold, but coldness don't signify.'

Meekly Sophia takes the cup and sips.

'That's medicine for you,' says Miss Blore, going to the table and helping herself to another dose. 'You don't want him scragged, that's only natural. Nor more do I.'

What does she want, then, if not vengeance? Is it possible that Sophia guessed right at first, and the creature is in league with Edmund – that all this visit is mere play-acting, with the aim of – of *what*? Some of what she says must be true: it tallies with Sophia's own discoveries, and since those discoveries show Edmund in such a damning light, surely no emissary of his would be so stupid as even to hint at them? And now Miss Blore sits coolly holding her gin and saying, 'He needn't come within spitting distance, if you only keep ahold of things.'

'Keep ahold?'

'Don't let your Mr Gingumbob get carried away. He'll want to, they always do with the likes of Ned, but the threat'll be enough.'

'What threat?'

'Of swinging, what else? Your man writes to him at his ma's, setting out your terms, only he writes to Ned Hartry, not Mr Zedland. Once Ned sees that, you've got a rope round his neck and a stick between his teeth. Manage him right, and you'll saddle and ride him.'

She has the certainty of Radley himself. And suppose, Sophia thinks, we go further and hang him? But she knows I should hate that. O, she's managed it nicely!

'Tell me something,' she says, remembering. 'Your Mr Shiner's been here, hasn't he? To talk with my husband?'

The effect of these words is electrifying: the woman starts and spills gin onto her gown. 'Shiner?' she says, scrubbing at the wet place with her fingers. 'What makes you think so?'

'*Someone* was here. What kind of man is Mr Shiner? In person, I mean.'

'You mean to give a description to the officers.'

'No, I —'

'Pernickety when sober, sweaty when drunk,' says Miss Blore, looking stubborn.

'A man came here, very tall and thickset. The maidservant said,' Sophia summons her courage, 'he resembled you.'

The woman seems to be weighing her answer. At last she says, 'Could be my brother.'

'Why should he come here?'

'Ned owes him. He'll pay double if Harry catches him alone, won't he just!'

'Then your brother's also a sharp?'

'Bless you, Mrs Zedland, Harry's got hands like spades! He was a pugilist.'

'Was? He's retired, then?'

'In another line of work. Supplying carcasses to butchers.'

'Now you mention it,' says Sophia, into whose memory Harry's pungent personal atmosphere has soaked to saturation, 'I thought he was something of the kind.'

'Stinks, eh?' Miss Blore wrinkles her nose. 'I believe there was money lent, to go to Bath.'

'You'll have to repeat what you've told me, Betsy-Ann, and have it written down as a statement. Are you willing to do that?'

'Wouldn't come here otherwise. Can't you get a better man than your Mr Gimgumbob?'

'Mr Scrope.'

'Ned's had him once already.'

'I can't see Papa trusting anyone else.'

'Then he'll have to do.' Betsy-Ann spits into her palm. 'Shake on it? You spit first,' she complains when Sophia fails to copy her actions. 'Otherwise there's no luck.'

Sophia lets a drop of spittle fall into her palm and presses it against Betsy-Ann Blore's.

Sophia is rational.

'Soft as a child's,' says Betsy-Ann Blore, examining her fingers.

Had Hetty made this remark, Sophia would have resented it. One gentlewoman no more congratulates another upon her well-kept hands than upon her being clean, or having enough to eat. To this woman, of course, a fine hand must seem extraordinary. And yet Betsy-Ann Blore's clasp, though coarser than her own, did not feel calloused.

'I should like to ask you something, Mrs Zedland.'

'Pray ask.' She wonders what the woman can want: a promise of protection afterwards?

'Have you any notion how your husband earns his bread? If you like, I can show you.'

'O, no! I never game.'

'Don't call it gaming. A demonstration pure and simple, only I must have a flat to my sharp.'

'A loser, you mean? I must endeavour to lose?'

'You won't be able to help yourself. I'm telling you that fair and square, no money riding on it. Not a farthing.'

Sophia is sorely tempted. Here, at last, is intimacy, of a kind: if not Edmund's love, at least his secrets.

385

Miss Blore grins. 'Come, the wickedness won't rub off on you.' She commences pulling and twisting at her own fingers as if to work them loose in their sockets. 'You might even call it edifying. That's what Sam used to say.'

'And how, pray, can it be that?'

'It's as well to know how the traps are laid.'

Wise as serpents but harmless as doves. Were it impossible, the Lord would not have enjoined it upon his followers: Sophia's resistance shivers to pieces in an instant.

'We have cards somewhere,' she says, rising to ring the bell.

'No need. Look here.' Miss Blore produces from her knotting-bag a small packet which proves to be a deck bound in a silk handkerchief.

'Those are marked, I suppose?'

'First, a shuffle.' She snaps the pack into two halves between her thumbs, then reunites them, two streams flowing into one, in a motion so flawless and compelling that it suggests to Sophia (may God forgive her the comparison) the Red Sea parting for the Children of Israel then surging back together, to the destruction of the Heathen.

'You see I know my business,' says Betsy-Ann Blore. She commences a different kind of shuffle, taking a section of the pack each time and passing it from back to front, the cards chopping into one another.

'Not so clever as your first,' says Sophia. 'I myself can do this one.'

'Can you? If you'll be so kind as to remove the things from the table —' Miss Blore spreads the cards there, each of the four suits in turn and every card in its proper rank. 'And do they come out like this?'

Sophia is filled with an unreasoning, childlike delight. 'No, indeed! Is that Edmund's trick?'

'Anybody can learn it. You see the rig?'

'Is that a card?'

'The rig is the trick, the profit. In plain English, the use of it.'

Sophia nods. 'Should you deal now, you'd know everyone's hand.'

'Not bad – for a daisy. And I can bestow the royalty where I like.' She folds up the pack again and clears her throat.

Sophia says, 'I see no marks. *Are* they marked?'

'Naturally. I should like to show you my particular favourite, only I'm out of practice.'

'Could you try?'

'A miss is as good as a mile, with this one. If it don't come off, it's nothing.' She hesitates, weighing the pack in one hand, then sits back in her chair, moving her shoulders up and down as if weighing them also. A change comes over her, a gravity that Sophia has never before seen on a female face. It is, she realises, the air of someone for whom things have passed beyond play. So must the great lord look whose entire estate rests on the turn of a card, or the athlete whose fame calls for a *tour de force* greater than anything previously achieved.

Betsy-Ann tenses her fingers. The cards seem to crouch in her palm, then spring, arcing through the air into her opposite hand, a moving bridge, nowhere joined yet with all the appearance of it. The entire pack having made the crossing, she pins it down with her thumb.

Both women exhale in the same instant, Betsy-Ann's features relaxing into complacency. 'Ned can't do that. He hasn't the control.'

'He wouldn't anyway. Would he?'

On hearing this, Betsy-Ann Blore looks oddly like Sophia's old governess, when some question of her pupil piqued her interest – which, admittedly, was not often. 'And why's that, Mrs Zedland?'

Sophia is excited by her own perceptiveness. 'Were *I* a sharp, I should take care to appear clumsy and unpractised —'

387

She breaks off, recalling a long-past day in Bath. Its events now appear in quite a different light: Mr and Mrs Chase, such a name, but how was she to know? And how was it that they, in their turn, failed to note *Zedland*? But now she recalls that Mrs Chase tracked her for days beforehand, until satisfied that she was indeed the innocent she appeared. The Chases were, she supposes, mere beginners in the gentle art of fleecing. Edmund's more powerful shears must have left them stinging for days afterwards: what a scalping he gave them, and how little she realised the game being played out! Her own life seems to her almost the stuff of mythology, frequently recounted yet imperfectly understood. Was he, she wonders, merely securing the prey to himself? Was there ever the least affection in his heart?

'Is something troubling you, Mrs Zedland?'

'I was thinking of that last trick. Such skill, and no use to it. It seems a pity.'

'Lord, Mrs Zedland, you talk like a sharp!' Sophia stiffens before realising the woman is rallying her. 'It serves to entertain.' She half-smiles at Sophia, as if gauging whether *she* is sufficiently entertained. 'Let me tell you something,' she adds. 'I've been making observation of your fams.'

'My what?'

'These.' She indicates Sophia's hands. 'Made for the books. Should you like to learn?'

Betsy-Ann holds out the pack of cards. As a child, Sophia had constantly impressed upon her the danger of accepting any object from the lower sort, with their dirty and disgusting habits, but what does that matter now, when she and this woman have sealed their bargain by shaking upon a gob of spittle? Besides, the deck looks as fresh as any Sophia played with as a girl. Uppermost lies the Knave of Hearts, his profile at once melancholy and debauched.

Sophia says, 'He has the wrong hair colour.'

'Not at all. It's always yellow.'

'I've known it black.'

'Black!'

There's something unsettling in the gaze of Betsy-Ann Blore as she stares at Sophia: the eyes are so very like *his*. She seems about to say something of importance, but evidently thinks better of it, for she lowers her eyes to the cards and the momentary frisson is past.

Sophia thinks: They are unutterably a pair. Further than that she cannot go; beyond she senses a bleak shadow-perspective in which she, and not this woman, figures as the interloper upon a marriage intended by nature. Who can say what fruit Edmund's natural gifts might have borne, had he been provided in childhood with the means, material and spiritual, of an upright life? The sins of the fathers, and mothers, are visited upon the children. He himself has not had justice. Nor has this woman.

Libertine thoughts, again. That the world is unjust does not excuse human wickedness, which is the root of much of the world's injustice, and so the sins and excuses go round in a self-perpetuating circle. She takes the cards, moves the Knave to the bottom of the pack and begins to shuffle, accustoming herself to their texture and weight.

45

For two nights he has walked without direction, turning away if anyone should approach. The Pinched Wife has probably advertised a reward for his capture: Eliza told him, once, about the money that is offered. So he hides away during daylight, resting his feet on which the shoes, good enough for padding around Dog Eye's house, have raised scalding welts.

Even in the dark he is not safe. Last night he passed through a gate and into a grassy place with a sour, foamy smell: the smell of rotten apples, of an orchard. He was about to drop to his knees and feel about him for the fruit when a man stepped out of the darkness and pulled him towards the orchard wall. Fortunate screamed and kicked out. He ran on his blistered feet perhaps a hundred steps before he heard a cry behind him – 'You shall have a guinea!' – and realised the man had not given chase. After that, he took off his neck-linen, so as to melt more completely into the darkness, and limped on, through other scents: roast chicken, the sour odour of mould, smoke and hops belching from tavern doors, cesspits. This is surely Romeville, with its fierce, dirty, exuberant people: a place of danger as well as joy. If he can once get to Dog Eye, and be taken back into his service, he will be safe enough. And where would Dog Eye be, if not Romeville?

After escaping the man he strolled listlessly about, stopping once to buy hot meat and bread in a dish. It did not satisfy him, but he knew he must not spend more. He continued walking until towards dawn he slipped, exhausted, between two bent railings and into a churchyard. His first thought was to lie among the stones, but a bad person might enter and be upon him before he could wake. Next to the church he found a better place: a flight of steps leading down into the ground. At the bottom of these steps he crouches throughout the day, coming out only to relieve himself – seldom necessary, since he seldom eats – or to scoop rainwater from a marble pot on a nearby grave.

Mr Watson did not believe in baptising his slaves. Fortunate went once or twice with the Wife to church, where the blank-eyed statues filled him with dread. When he learned that corpses lay beneath the earth, both inside and out, he felt the full terror of the place. This hole in which he hides seems as if it would go down to the world of the dead, but it is stopped at the bottom and the ghosts contained by a stout wooden door, against which Fortunate rests his back.

He does not regret leaving the house. The Spirit has already brought bad luck upon it. Dog Eye was the first to go, then Mrs Launey, a person of some consequence, also vanished and Fortunate felt panic spread among the rest of the inhabitants. And yet he is not safe here, either. Once his money runs out, hunger lies in wait; indeed, it has already begun to tickle him with its claws. It occurs to him to go back to the orchard and try to pick up with the man, but perhaps it was a trick and he will not be given a guinea, but beaten and robbed. It is some comfort that he has weapons, but they cannot work themselves: he must not become too weak and confused. He must find a roof to lie under, and food to eat.

The cemetery is surrounded by stiff dark trees and twining shrubs that throw themselves over the railings. Sounds from the streets wash across its green shadows: unseen horses trotting and whinnying, wheels on cobbles, people arguing or laughing and the occasional shrill squeal of a child at play. Fortunate dreams of being shouted at by the Wife, of beef pie, smoking hot, of the dead coming up out of the ground, and once, of strange animals, purple-coloured, lying peaceful in burrows. He is woken by people scuffling and panting together in the grass. He creeps to the top of the steps but can distinguish nothing more than a rolling, swaying mass between two of the stones. After a while a woman's voice says, 'My arse is frozen,' and if Fortunate were less frightened he would laugh.

He soon learns that certain sounds return each night: a hubbub of voices, the whine of a violin, tuneless singing, the occasional shout, and along with these the chink of plates and a hot thick scent of gravy that brings the spit to his mouth. A tavern of some kind, just along the street. He wonders how he can turn this to account. Should he step in and offer to sell his neck linen, or the crippling shoes, or ask for some work? There are evil men in those places. He fears for his stock of money, obtained by raiding one of the kitchen jars. Should he meet with robbers in the darkness he will lose it all.

On the fifth morning he weeps while trying to straighten his arms. The cold, and hugging himself all the night, have tied him in knots; he understands that he must find a warmer bed or die. He takes a knife he brought with him from the house and scoops out a hole directly under the church wall, slots most of his coins into the exposed earth, presses them down and pulls the grass across. Nobody would notice the wounded place but for good measure he covers it with a scrap of brick. Now he has in his pocket a few pence, no more. He lies back and dozes awhile, intending to go to the tavern as soon as it is night.

He wakes with a start: the church bell is tolling, a dreary, insistent sound. Fortunate rubs his eyes and stares up into the sky overhead: it is a pale grey, lit but not warmed by the pallid sunshine of this country. He creeps up the stairs until he can just see over the top. Tugging a child by the hand, a woman hurries through the tombstones. Beyond her, men are carrying a coffin along the churchyard path followed by a procession of men and women holding cloths to their eyes.

Hoping nobody chooses to walk near these steps, Fortunate waits until everyone has gone inside the church before rising and rapidly circling the graveyard. He finds the pit on the same side of the church as his flight of steps, but some way off: the mourners will not come near his hiding place. He wonders that in his cold, cramped sleep he did not hear it being dug.

He returns to the door at the bottom of the steps and after what seems a long time, hears people coming out from the building. A man is speaking near the grave. Then they begin to come away. Footsteps pass, more closely than he expected, and he stiffens with fear. At last there is no more sound, only the usual overflow from the street.

He allows himself to sleep.

When he next wakes, the sun has gone behind the church tower. Fortunate puts up his head, an animal sniffing the air. He climbs stiffly out of his burrow and goes over to the place where the hole was. It has grown upwards into a mound of thin brown earth, with flowers laid across it and to one side, almost hidden by leaves, a thing he has never seen before: a kind of metal tooth.

He does not like the look of this tooth. He goes to one of the prickly shrubs planted there and breaks off a branch; then, standing well back from the mound, he uses the branch to brush away the earth around the metal. He then goes to the other side of the mound and tries there, and so works his way round. At last he can see what the thing is: a grinning steel mouth stretches over the grave, as if to eat the corpse.

A trap has been set.

Perhaps the person in this grave was especially wicked, and this was done to prevent him coming out. But what if he should climb halfway and be cut in pieces? He hugs himself, shivering with disgust. In the distance, cheerful and insolent, comes the opening skirl of the tavern fiddle.

46

Palpable genius! Can anything be so entrancing? Sophia deals again and again, aspiring to the practised motion which deceives the eye and, from a swift river of passing images, hooks out the critical card. One must learn to *love* the cards: not merely in their ideal aspect, their suits and significations — anyone who can play understands that much — but physically. It is a marriage: hand in hand, will wooing inconstancy. One must allow for youth and inexperience in a fresh pack, search out the slackening and dissolution, the give, in an old one. She slides her thumb down the edge of the pack and finds, as expected, His Majesty the King of Diamonds.

'It tickles me, Madam,' says Betsy-Ann Blore, 'how you've taken to the books.'

Sophia fans out the cards into a circle, then snaps them shut. 'I shall at least have the means of supporting myself.'

'No word from Ned, then.'

'No. Papa's been talking with Mr Scrope.'

'And what'll Mr Scrope do?'

'He has yet to decide.'

'Lord, what a time he takes,' grumbles Miss Blore.

Does she suspect she is being deceived? If nothing else, the events of the past few months have tutored Sophia in prudence. She no longer doubts that Betsy-Ann Blore hates Edmund *now*, but reconciliation must always remain a possibility. Such things have happened before.

In fact Mr Scrope's plans are already drawn up, and despite his not being *au fait* with all the facts of the case, demonstrate a certain force of mind. No letter to 'Ned Hartry' will be despatched to

Mrs Hartry's bawdy-house or any other address. For fear of Papa's rushing and bungling, Sophia chose not to reveal Edmund's alias. Instead, she told Mr Scrope that private papers, now unfortunately destroyed, linked Edmund with the house of one Kitty Hartry, a woman of bad reputation, and asked was it worth writing to him there. Mr Scrope's opinion (though not in so many words) was that such a letter (far from restraining Edmund, as was Betsy-Ann's notion) might spur him to bolt – if indeed he should be there at all. Then Papa was very much in favour of advertisements, and it was with great difficulty that Mr Scrope persuaded him against them, arguing that such measures tend to produce fraudulent sightings. The end of all this sound and fury is that a letter has been despatched to Mr Fielding at Bow Street with a view to obtaining the services of a discreet and courageous officer. Only when Sophia has met with this man and found him satisfactory will she reveal the identity of her husband, if husband he is.

Nor has Titus been advertised for: Sophia has not time, energy or inclination to pursue him. Since he has proved so unsatisfactory and ungrateful, let him try his fortunes elsewhere.

'Do say you'll come,' urges Hetty. 'Letcher is as fretted about it as I am. He says a woman ought not to be left alone at such a time.'

'You're too kind,' says Sophia, 'but I really think it unnecessary. There's nowhere I'm less likely to be troubled by Edmund than here.'

'And to think I fancied you biddable.' Hetty rolls her eyes. 'Really, Sophy, you might give in this once. I promised your mama we should take you in.'

'Then tell her you've done so.'

'Lie to her?'

'Not in so many words, then. Say nothing to bring her here.'

Hetty looks pained. 'But Sophy – your *mama* —'

'When I begged her help I got none. I don't want her here now, telling everyone what a tender mother she's been and how she never would've thought it of Edmund.'

'Well – no. But what of that brute of a fellow – suppose he should return?'

'The maids open to nobody without first looking out of the window.'

'They'll forget.'

'I think not. Fan found him very disagreeable.' She can only hope Fan has sufficiently impressed his disagreeableness upon stupid Eliza.

The sight of Hetty seated, her hands folded in her lap, recalls to Sophia her own visits to the sick around Buller. A measureless chasm divides Mrs Edmund Zedland from the girl she then was: so very sure of herself! The people she visited said little except, 'Yes, Miss,' and she was satisfied. It never occurred to her that they might have private opinions.

'Sophy? Can you be quite sure, Sophy,' Hetty touches her arm, recalling her to the present, 'that Mr Zedland has absconded?'

'He isn't hiding in the cellar, Hetty, if that's what you mean.'

'Indeed I don't. He kept bad company – he may have come to harm.'

Despite her bluntness, Hetty's expression reveals such kind concern that Sophia rises and kisses her on the brow. 'I believe he meant to go. Beyond that, how should I know? He told me nothing of his life.'

Her voice trembles on the last few words; Hetty's touch becomes a squeeze.

'O my dear, don't give way.'

'I shan't. But you, Hetty, with your kind husband – you can scarcely imagine my feelings. So little thought of, that I'm not to know whether he's alive or dead!'

'We shall find him out.'

'Perhaps.'

Sophia's gaze wanders over the Blue Room. Hetty evidently longs to rescue her from this shabby lodging which, strangely, no longer gives her the least pain. The coming struggle with Edmund absorbs most of her mental energy: as long as she can eat and sleep, papers and hangings seem of little importance.

Hetty clears her throat. 'If you're determined not to come to us, will you accept another kind of help? I imagine your affairs are left in some disorder. Letcher says you are to have whatever you ask for.' She smiles. 'I mean *money*, Sophy.'

'He's too good – you both are. Some money of my own, just for a while, would be of the utmost assistance.'

Hetty says, 'Then name the sum, my dear.'

'Perhaps a hundred.'

'Take more. Don't fear to pinch him, he's too well padded for that.'

'Then two hundred, if you would be so kind. We may owe something to Mr Moore.'

'Mr Moore?'

'The landlord. It seems this house is rented.'

'Not yours? – no matter, no matter,' Hetty says, failing to conceal her shock. 'As long as we're here, you shan't sink. But I should sleep more soundly if you came to us.'

'There's no need, my dear. I know I'm welcome.'

'Indeed you are!' cries Hetty, embracing her. Sophia breathes Cotterstone face cream: scents of iris and of vanilla. Edmund must have smelt something similar on her own skin when first they bedded together. She wonders if he took pleasure in it. The odours of his bodily life once they came to London, of tobacco and liquor and the perspiration of – of Betsy-Ann Blore, she supposes – were harsh and insistent, repugnant to her nostrils.

Sophia perfectly understands that Hetty would like to bind her and carry her away, a captive under guard. Today's call, for instance, is typical, in that her cousin's carriage drew up without warning: Hetty visits frequently these days and at the oddest hours. She pushes to the limit the relative's privilege of informality and has taken to speaking on the slightest pretext of *encroaching persons*, *unhealthy fascinations* and the bosom of one's own family as the surest protection against *insinuation*. At first Sophia understood all these hints as referring to Edmund, until a chance remark from Hetty enlightened her. It can only be that one of the servants has dropped a hint: Sophia suspects Fan, whose features have developed an oblique, closed-off cast. Should Sophia ring the bell while Betsy-Ann is on the premises, the servant to answer is invariably Eliza. *She* arrives eagerly enough, with popping eyes, as if hoping to find her mistress and the whore tearing at one another, her disappointment so ill concealed at the calm of the Blue Room that Sophia can hardly restrain a giggle as she despatches the girl for refreshments. The tea is brought with a knowing look, and since Betsy-Ann is now openly received by the mistress, a jug of 'French Cream' placed beside the milk.

Fan may, of course, be distracted by her new responsibilities. In the absence of Mrs Launey – Mr Moore has not yet engaged a substitute – she contrives to produce simple dishes, such as she and Eliza might make for themselves: fried beef and cabbage, a bread pudding. Yet this, in itself, cannot explain her awkward manner. Evidently she is pained at recent developments, either at the lack of propriety or because she perceives in Betsy-Ann a dangerous intruder. How can Sophia blame her for sentiments so eminently proper? She does not insist upon Fan's bringing refreshments to Betsy-Ann, making do instead with the irritating Eliza.

Though she would willingly wound neither Hetty's feelings nor Fan's, they must not be permitted to meddle. Betsy-Ann Blore may have encroached upon her, but Sophia tolerates her visits for good reason. Miss Blore's knowledge renders her a uniquely valuable witness, one it would be folly not to attach. She has not yet given evidence, but has promised it: should she perform that promise and make a statement to Mr Scrope, she may turn the key of Sophia's marital prison. For (Sophia actually cried out aloud when first this thought burst upon her) it would appear she is married to a non-existent personage, that is, not married at all: possibly Ned Hartry has no rights upon her person or her property. In order to unmask him she requires the help of Betsy-Ann Blore, whom she is very far from trusting entirely, and whom Hetty must not be allowed to drive away before the delicate negotiations can be concluded. Papa would go crashing in likewise, so for the moment she has told neither of these people of Betsy-Ann's existence, or that of Mr Ned Hartry. To them the gentleman remains Edmund Zedland, Sophia's lawful if wilful spouse.

She starts at finding Hetty speaking to her, asking, 'Have you thought what you'll do?'

'Do?'

'If he fails to return. I mean, what will Uncle do? Has he taken advice?'

'I believe the plan is to write to Mr Fielding at Westminster.'

'In your place I should try for a separation.'

'I shall. I shall have to endure Mama's hysterics, of course. The scandal and so on. *She* doesn't have to live with him.'

Hetty says sadly, 'Either way, the wife comes off worse.'

It is galling to realise that even should the marriage be declared void and her fortune wrested from Edmund's grasp (a circumstance unlikely in itself) he has irrevocably blighted her life. No silly wench seduced on a sofa, no society matron taken *in flagrante* with the footman has worse marital prospects. Possibly there is a certain justice in that, she thinks with a pang. In the eyes of the world she entered discreetly and soberly into matrimony, but the world's eyes were deceived: she fell headlong. To break this melancholy train of thought she rises and proposes a replenishment of the tea-table.

'He must be brought to terms,' Hetty says as Sophia rings for the maid. 'Everything watertight, or you can never rebuild your establishment. He'll return, whenever he chooses, and take every stick.'

'That's what Scrope says. One can be reduced to rags.'

'Well, *you* shan't be. Here, Sophy, Letcher and I agree on this absolutely.' From her purse she counts out banknotes to the value of two hundred pounds and passes them over to Sophia.

'God bless you, Hetty! You and Mr Letcher both.'

'Thank us by keeping it secret, Sophy, or you won't have it long.'

But is it legally Edmund's? This is the Great Question. Sophia supposes he would have preferred to marry under his real name, to make all sure, but having introduced himself as Mr Zedland, he was obliged to go through with the sham. If it now appears that he has no claim upon her fortune, he will surely *wish* to be rid of her. Should he demand money in return for supporting an annulment, she will gladly compound for whatever she can afford.

Fan brings tea and bread-and-butter but Hetty, generally so ready to eat upon all occasions, appears lacking in appetite.

'I should be getting back,' she says after half a cup of tea. 'Letcher will worry. He wanted to come with me but I said I should be quite safe in the carriage. Some subjects are better discussed without gentlemen present.'

'There can't be many, Hetty, with such an excellent husband. I'm sincerely grateful for his help, and yours.'

On the doorstep Hetty turns, holding Sophia by the hands and studying her at arm's length. 'This business has had an effect on you,' she says.

Sophia shrugs. 'Of course.'

'But not as much as I feared. I thought you would be quite broken down.'

'I'm *comme il faut*, just as broken down as I ought to be.'

The cousins exchange smiles. Hetty says, 'My love, your courage is admirable but don't overdo it. Remember our door is always open. O, I nearly forgot! I brought something for you – it's still in the carriage, I believe —'

Her manservant, obedient to his cue, opens the door and brings out a small parcel wrapped in white paper and tied in ribbon.

'I thank you,' says Sophia, beginning to pick at the ribbon.

'Open it later.' Hetty lays a gloved hand on hers. The man helps her into the carriage and she is gone, the blinds pulled down against impertinent stares.

Sophia carries her gift back into the house and sits at a table in the Blue Room. The ribbon does not resist her long and she is able to unfold the paper, which is finely made, without tearing. Inside is a volume, finely bound: *The Memoirs of George Psalmanazar.*

Left alone, she takes up the cards once more and shuffles, endeavouring to keep an ace at the top. Easy to understand, the move requires practice to render it invisible: it seems to Sophia that nothing she was ever taught called for such a pitch of concentration. What a paltry schooling hers must have been!

Sometimes, her attention flagging, she allows herself to dream a little: dressed as a gentleman, she strolls idly between the tables of a gaming club. Beneath a chandelier gleaming with wicked fire she spies Edmund, sly as the wolf in the fable, his mouth slavering as he sizes up some wealthy booby. Sophia steps up to his table, thus cutting out the booby – who, not recognising his saviour, is pettishly offended, but what of that, he must do as he pleases – and asks Edmund would he care to join her in a friendly wager, shall we say two thousand? Edmund shakes her hand. His eyes are fixed upon her so intently that the boat – no, the table – seems to rock as she takes her seat, but she boldly returns his scrutiny and snaps her fingers for fresh cards.

'You remind me cursedly of someone I once knew,' says Edmund, his tone softening just sufficiently to hint at memories not altogether contemptible. 'Tell me, were you ever acquainted with a Miss Sophia Buller?' And then, and then —

Beyond that, fancy refuses to carry her. Granted that the Wolf-Husband has failed to recognise her in her male attire – impossible though she knows it to be – how could she engage him in such a conversation? She might, of course, feign dumbness, have herself introduced in a whisper as, 'A Young Gentleman newly come to Town, a *mute*, but perfectly understands the rules of play,' or 'A Young Gentleman maimed at birth and obliged, ever since, to wear a mask in public so as not to distress the gentle hearts of the Sex,' or even 'A Young Gentleman of such delicate make that he might pass for a Lady' —

It is of no use. Notwithstanding that Sophia has read her Shakespeare, a man with whom one has shared a bed is not to be fooled by hats, wigs, breeches or even a mask: her manner of sitting down, the make of her hands, her very breathing would betray her. There will be no handful of trumps laid fanwise on the table, to the universal astonishment of the company; no cry of rage as it dawns upon Edmund that the game is at an end, the Biter Bit, *et cetera*. Instead, things will be managed dully, according to the law of the land. But O, how she would have relished her triumph!

47

Fortunate is in the hold, listening to the groans of the man next to him whose chains have rubbed the skin from his ankles. A man's strength is of no use, here. Better to have the fine bones of youth. With an effort, he raises his head: a seabird is picking its way along the rows of slaves, hopping from one to the next as if they were stones on a beach. A sunbeam, a good omen, follows wherever it goes, the rest of the hold remaining dark.

Then he sees that the bird's beak is stained with blood. He cries out, 'Turn your heads, turn away from it,' but his voice is too parched to be heard. He can only only whisper to the man beside him, 'Look there, look there,' and the man replies, in English, that he's a whoreson fool.

He jerks awake, shivering, a pain in his head and eyes as if the bird has already blinded him. A fearful pain: it recalls the only time he ever joined Dog Eye in drinking punch, when his master woke at noon the following day, calling for more drink, and Fortunate crawled moaning from his truckle bed to fetch it. The stabbing spreads into his shoulders; he wonders if he has injured himself while asleep. He swivels his neck in an attempt to ease it, turning his face this way and that, and as he does so he sees a gleam cross the church wall above his head, a fugitive, quivering light as if reflected from water.

'Is that your notion of a glim?' hisses a male voice a few feet away. 'Kill it before I kill you.'

The light vanishes with a snapping sound.

Fortunate's body shrills and jangles with shock; a tiny squeak escapes him, adding to his terror. He crams his hand into his mouth, biting down hard, and to keep from shaking he presses his body into the bank of earth alongside the steps, straining his eyes upwards to the place where he saw the light. All is dark now, and there is no further cursing, but he can feel the vibration of feet passing near him. One man. Two. A confused scuffling: perhaps two more. Something soft is dragged along the grass. He hears a man grunt as it catches, and there is a faint snigger from further off.

He stays like that for many minutes, his heart painful. Were he a dog, he thinks, his ears would stand so high on his head a woman could sew them together. A clink. A laugh, followed by a growled command to mind what they are about. Everything comes to him with unnatural distinctness: the sea of sound that usually laps this grass island has drained away, meaning it is deep in the night.

When his heart has gone down a little he raises himself on cramped legs and looks out. Something white is hovering near the newly dug grave: he grimaces in terror, then remembers the dragging noise he heard: someone pulling a cloth. In another moment he sees the cloth partly raised from the ground and a dim streak of light thrown upon it from the other side, forming a screen on which the coat-tails and legs of men appear briefly in silhouette before passing out of the beam. The quivering light, he now realises, was a dark lantern not properly closed.

'Well, lads,' says one in a hoarse whisper, 'it seems they left us a present. A mighty queer one.'

Another man says, 'Not covered up. I never seen that before.' They keep their voices low, but the sound carries across the quiet graveyard to Fortunate in his burrow.

'It's a decoy, I reckon. The right one is underneath.'

'Hop in, then.'

Suppressed laughter. There follows a rustling, tussling sound as if someone is fighting a bush. The outline of a broken branch appears, then the screen vanishes as the cloth drops to the ground.

404

He can now make out four men, two facing him across the grave, two standing on the near side.

'Go on, Sam.'

There is a sound like an axe cleaving wood, followed by a gasp.

'Fuck that for a decoy!'

'I see how it is,' says the hoarse man. 'Another crew's been here, and didn't fancy the job.'

'No more do I.'

'Here, Sam. Davey.'

Fortunate's breathing has slowed, and his shuddering almost ceased: he can hear the pop of lips and faint gasp that tells him they are passing round a bottle. A man laughs. 'Shiner's turned Methodist.'

Someone else says, 'Not so deep as it looks, I reckon.'

Does he mean the metal jaw, or the corpse beneath? These men must be enemies of the dead man's family, or perhaps magicians. Suppose they should perform some ceremony, and walk about the graveyard, and look down these steps?

He must get out onto the street. No use trying for the main exit, a wooden gate with a small roof over it, since the men are directly in the way. There remains another gate, a smaller one, some way behind him. If he can once get round the angle of the church wall, he will be hidden from them and can take his time seeking it in the darkness, but first he must leave his hiding place. It is a risk: were this daylight, he would be in full view as soon as he came up the steps. He reaches out towards the church wall and finds the scrap of plant-pot that marks his buried store. Never taking his eyes from the men, he gropes in the softened dirt until a finger stubs against a coin. One. Two . . . five.

He slides the money into his coat pockets where the pistols are, one in each. His fingers are slippery against the mother-of-pearl handles. Were he put to using them, would they work? Dog Eye told him they must be kept dry.

There are grunts and soft, ugly sounds like blows being struck. The sliver of light from the shuttered lantern picks out something shining that moves up and down. Fortunate's eyes are clearing now, and he can make out the men themselves, bending, growing upright.

They are digging.

Magicians or not, they are about to commit a terrible crime. He must not be present. Now is the moment, while their ears and eyes are occupied.

As he rises the blood surges in his own ears so that he is half deaf. If they should look this way! Clinging to the stones, he moves silently round the angle of the church and half-collapses against the wall, trembling, while he looks for his way out of the churchyard.

The gate is a few yards off, next to a yew. Fortunate can just distinguish the tree, a thickening mass in the darkness, and beside it a paler patch: the gable wall of the house opposite. He pads across to the gate, feels for the top spikes, and eases it open without any creak or squeak.

He has used this gate before. It is one of a pair, facing each other across a metal pen: the gates are so devised that any stray animal attempting to enter the churchyard would find itself trapped. Fortunate pushes it open, enters the pen and softly releases the gate, taking care to make no noise. He is about to pass through the second gate when a man's voice whispers, 'Davey?'

Fortunate turns and flees the pen, back to the side of the church. Behind him he hears the gate crash. The far gate opens and closes, then the one nearest him. The man has entered the churchyard.

'Who's there?'

The man waits. Fortunate holds his breath: it seems the slamming of the gates drowned out his footsteps over the grass and back to the church wall, so that the man cannot yet place him. If he should come in search, moving away from the pen, Fortunate can perhaps dodge past him in the dark and get through it unhindered. But now the man whistles long and low.

It will be a hunt.

Where to go? If he makes for the trees, twigs will crack underfoot. He is conscious of a sweating coldness about his head and neck. Then he sees a faint gleam reflected from a gravestone at the side of the church. Someone is coming that way. If he doesn't move now, he'll be trapped between the two of them.

He remembers the bent railings where he first found his way in. They lie somewhere along the darkest side, away from the men. Willing all his strength into his trembling legs, he breaks from the wall and runs for it, tripping on stone ledges, staggering on the uneven ground.

'Ware hawk!' someone shouts. 'There he goes!'

He is through the bushes and at the wall. This is the wrong place: the railings here are sound, the bent ones further off. Sobbing with terror, he tears through brambles, their thorns lashing his face as he feels for the rail. The man with the lantern comes round the side of the church, making straight for him.

At last he finds the place and tries to squeeze himself through. The pistol in his right pocket catches on the railing and holds him there; he wails with terror but at last falls headlong on the pavement, a tearing pain in his side where the metal crushed into him. He scrabbles upright and runs on, expecting to be pulled down. There comes a roar. When he looks back, the man with the lantern is at the railing, too big to get through. Fortunate sees the great furnace mouth and cruel eyes of the Spirit. At the same time, a gate clangs: the other man, the unseen one, is out now and on the street, but some distance away. Fortunate pushes himself on, on, until rounding a corner he comes to an alleyway. The nearest door opens to him: saved by the carelessness of a servant. He drags himself through and fumbles for the bolt, scraping his fingers. At last his hand falls on it and drives it home.

At first he can see nothing, owing to a flaring and flashing inside his eyelids. When his eyes clear, he finds himself in a yard of some kind, even darker than the churchyard and with a stale, sourish smell. From the roadway comes the pounding of feet, the gasping of his pursuers. With the desperate effort of one whose life hangs on it, Fortunate pinches his lips together and stills his breathing. The suppressed breath beats inside his skull and the darkness swarms, blinding him afresh as he takes the defender from his pocket. It is loaded: his fingers slip on the metal as he releases the catch. The pursuers have stopped near the entrance to the alley; he pictures them looking round, seeing lanes, gates, doors on every side where he might have let himself in. So close, so close, surely they can smell him out.

'That was no trap.'

'Best make him easy, *I* say.'

There is a moment during which he hears nothing, a silence thick with terror. Are they creeping down the alley, closing in? Then he hears them walking away, moving slowly. One of them says, 'I had a bad feeling about this job,' and that is the last of them apart from their retreating footsteps.

He expels the breath he has been holding and is about to put away the pistol in his pocket when he realises he is squeezing the trigger. So the thing was damp, as he feared. He sinks forward, thinking he will vomit, but nothing comes into his mouth; instead, his knees give way and he drops on all fours. With immense effort he turns and wedges himself into the corner, his back propped against the wall. After many jerks and starts when he thinks he hears them pushing open the yard door, he loses consciousness.

My darling girl,

You cannot imagine my distress upon learning from Hetty that Edmund is still not returned. Papa swears he will see him gibbeted. Mr Fielding has suggested a suitable person to assist us; we are to come to London in order to meet with him.

As you see, all is in motion, but why, Sophy, why do you not write? Hetty has hinted that perhaps I was insufficiently sympathetic on an earlier occasion. Try if you can, my love, to understand my position. Young wives frequently (I would say, invariably) find themselves disappointed in some respect: a respectable female is so innocent, and her hopes correspondingly high. I was sure Edmund must fall short of expectation, not because I believed him to be a bad fellow but because I perceived how very tenderly you were attached to him; if I may be pardoned for saying so, you were in a fair way to becoming a idolater. Papa, of course, thought you as rational as ever, but your mama, though she said nothing, saw it all. It is the usual way with us women: if we can but find a man half worthy, our love has always an admixture of worship in it, and who is to say it should be otherwise? If the marriage is a happy one, such wifely worship contributes not a little to our happiness. But if we find our idol has feet of clay, what then?

Our son-in-law is a careless fellow, I said to myself when you wrote of his behaviour. Poor Sophy will have her work cut out. Later it was: Edmund is not quite the gentleman we thought him, our daughter must take care. I had no inkling, however, of the reality of the situation.

What can I say to that, Mama, except: Why did you not know it? I informed you in the plainest possible language.

I am quite at a loss how to broach my next subject, yet I must. Pray bear with me and remember I am dependent upon Hetty

409

for intelligence. I will state the case plainly: you are said to re-
ceive into your house a degraded creature known to Edmund. I
should scorn such a report from anyone else but coming from
Hetty, as it does, I dare not set it aside. Is it true? My dearest
girl, what can you be thinking?

O Hetty, you traitor! Is this how you keep them from the door?
Presumably you had already written when you gave your promise, but could you not have warned me?

No matter how charitable your motive, such a person can never
be fit society for you. And what of her motives? Who is to say
she is not in communication with Edmund? Can you not see
how, in all these ways, her acquaintance must inevitably com-
promise you? At present, you cannot afford the least breath of
scandal. This consideration should outweigh all others, and I
sincerely trust the person will speedily begin to find you not at
home.

We intend to be with you shortly. I hope you will not be
hasty, Sophy, or too implacable in your resentment. If we can
induce Edmund to return, that will be a start, and perhaps you
may yet make the best of it: a wife deprived of her husband's
countenance and support can hope for little happiness in life. If
Edmund cannot be found, or cannot be prevailed upon to re-
turn, we shall bring you home to dear old Buller, where you
will be looked after as befits the daughter of a gentleman, but
this can never be my fondest hope. I had rather see you recon-
ciled with Edmund and the mother of a thriving brood.

Papa this morning sent 200L to Mr Letcher. You may there-
fore keep the money Hetty lent you and trouble yourself no
more about it.

My dear child, I pray the Lord may guide you and keep you
safe from all harm. I could wish a better man had offered for

you, but it is of no use to think about that now. Until I can be
by your side, believe me your most loving
    Mama

How wise she is after the event, Sophia thinks, flicking the letter aside. The 200L is more of a comfort than anything else Mama is likely to offer.

Libertine thoughts, again. What of them? A deserted wife not intending to go through the world as a victim must develop a species of double nature, both masculine and feminine, and even bring herself, at times, to think brutally. If only she had a brother who would carry some of the burden for her! The protection of a brother must be a comfort indeed. But *her* brother might have been as complacent as Mama, as fond of prosing after the event: in short, intolerable.

She goes to the window. This morning, which dawned in a sparkle of frozen fog, continues bitter. Eliza the Incompetent is in this as in everything, and cannot for the life of her build a brisk fire. For the sake of warmth Sophia would condescend to manage the fire herself, though she has never become accustomed to the use of coal. What would she not give for some sweet-smelling logs, instead of this foul smoke and gritty dust! Coal seems determined not to take unless a maid kneels in the grate, working the bellows. But then, she is probably being supplied with the poorest quality: a cheat, like everything else in the house.

What, what, *what* is she to do? Mama's letter on the table has the ominous quality of a *memento mori*. Rescue means an end to these miseries, yes, but also the start of fresh ones: growing old with Papa and Mama, listening to stale chit-chat about the villagers, the servants' illnesses, what is to be done about the mould in the stable and perhaps, once in a while, a visit from James Samuels and his wife from Little Buller, eager to boast of their son's travels in Italy. Damn that blameless young man, double damn him. She has no desire to listen to his adventures and exclaim over his prospects while sitting in the Yellow Room embroidering a pincushion.

Or to marry again, a sorry provincial woman with a dribbling bladder, a reduced fortune and a scandalous past: what husband worth marrying would stoop to *that*? Only an idiot would propose because she can make small talk, and holds her shoulders well. Or perhaps some ancient debauchee, now past performance —

There is a knock at the door. 'Miss Blore, Madam.'

'Show her in.' Sophia flips Mama's letter into the fire, where it produces a brilliant though brief flare. How brightly the light must have danced in Edmund's study while he was disposing of his past life.

Betsy-Ann Blore is pink-cheeked from the cold, the first time Sophia has seen her look anything but sallow. Now, why is she here? What has she to say for herself? Sophia muses, for though she will not be dictated to by either Hetty or Mama, she has enough sense to weigh their warnings.

The first thing out of Betsy-Ann's mouth is: 'Lord, Mrs Zedland, what a shabby fire!' Without further ado she seizes the scuttle and pours fresh coal into the grate, then pushes and prods with the poker and finally, as her *pièce de résistance*, applies herself to the bellows until the flames fairly shoot up the chimney.

'Now you may warm yourself,' puffs Betsy-Ann, as if the house were hers. Hetty is right: the woman encroaches. Sophia says coolly, 'Pray be seated, Betsy-Ann. Have you brought news?'

'Of Ned? No. Are you expecting any?'

'I hardly know *what* to expect.'

'Nor me, to be sure.' Betsy-Ann Blore tips her head towards the fire. 'I love to see flames,' she confides. 'I can watch a fire an hour together.'

'Indeed? But that isn't why you came to see me, I'm sure.'

'Well, no. The thing is, I've given some thought to what a body might call your situation.'

Despite her irritation, Sophia cannot help laughing at this turn of phrase. 'Yes, a body might call it that.'

'And there's no one can help you like I can.'

With a certain dryness, Sophia replies, 'I believe you've said so before.'

Betsy-Ann seems not to notice her tone. 'Listen. I can undo Ned Hartry.' She is quite breathy with excitement. Sophia, who has not seen her in this mood before, reminds herself of the need for discretion.

'I've a trick,' Betsy-Ann explains. 'Worth a fortune to a man in Ned's line.'

'I take it you mean a card trick.'

'He asked me many a time,' she is positively exultant now, 'but I *never* told him. I didn't choose that he should have it.'

What an extraordinary world is hers, thinks Sophia. A woman permits a man the last freedom, submits to be passed to another fellow, but denies him a card trick! If that is indeed how things stand.

'You didn't choose? Why not?'

'To keep something for myself.' The exuberance has vanished as rapidly as it came. 'And I couldn't give it to a Hartry.'

'Why not, when you were such good friends?' Sophia is proud of that phrase. *Good friends*: no accusation in it, even from the lips of a wife. Well, perhaps just a little.

'It wasn't a thing I thought to give to anybody. Mam left it me, you might say. But I might've let him have it, if not for his ma. There's gaming at her house, see. I couldn't stand for Kitty to get it – I'd have to cut her throat.'

Sophia recoils. 'I know you dislike her, because she —'

'Split me and Ned?' Betsy-Ann snaps her fingers in dismissal. 'That's nothing, Madam. Kitty Hartry killed my sister.'

'O, no. That I refuse to believe —'

'Not believe it!' Betsy-Ann swells like a toad. She is about to plunge into details when Sophia cries out, 'No! I beg of you —'

She covers her eyes, overwhelmed. She must not – she cannot —

'What is it?' Betsy-Ann asks, seemingly astonished.

'I can't listen to it. Don't you understand? She's my mother-in-law. My family.'

There is a silence. She thinks she hears a faint *hem* of astonishment: such vaporings, at something so obvious! It is, of course, not the bare fact of the alliance that thus seizes upon Sophia. She grasped its implications from the first, the degradation and disgust that must attend such a connection. Anything that reminds her of *that letter* is at once pushed from her mind, so acute is the mental suffering it produces, but to find oneself intimately connected with murder, a crime abhorred by the meanest and most brutal of human beings, is to enter a still deeper gallery of Hell. The very thought of it paralyses. She uncovers her eyes but only to sit motionless, unable to speak.

Betsy-Ann Blore, when she comes into focus, has a sullen offended look about her. 'Very well, you needn't hear,' she says, gathering herself together as if to leave. Sophia realises she is about to lose her witness. With an effort, she reaches out to place a hand on the woman's sleeve.

'Don't go. I was – shocked, that's all.'

'Then you'll hear me out?'

'Yes, if I'm able. Did you give evidence against her?'

Betsy-Ann bites her lip. Naturally she did not. Once more Sophia has failed to grasp how things stand in that other, subterranean world. She is to Betsy-Ann Blore as Mama is to herself: three-quarters blind. In her most encouraging voice she says, 'Will you tell me what happened?'

'It was Kitty made me a whore, Madam. Before that I barely knew the meaning of the word.'

'You were respectably raised?'

'Not like you, like gentry. But fair people and travelling people are strict about sweethearts. I never had one, I wasn't allowed.'

'Were your people gypsies?'

'No, but we was often alongside of them. We worked where we could find it – fairs, farms.'

'You and your sister?'

'Four of us. Me, Ma, Keshlie and Harry – you've seen him. He was first to come to Romeville.'

'Romeville?'

'This city, Madam. The rest of us followed on, but Mam wasn't long for this world. She died soon after we arrived.'

'So you were dependent upon your brother.'

Betsy-Ann snorts. 'That's a good one. Keshlie and me was nabbed by Kitty Hartry.'

'I'm afraid I don't quite – surely you don't mean she snatched you from the pavement?'

'We was engaged as servants. Once you're in the house, and the door locked —' Betsy-Ann gives an expressive shrug.

'But that's trepanning! She could be hanged!'

'Happens all the time. Ever notice a kind of creeping female, hanging round the coaching inns?'

'I can't say I have.'

'You will, now I've told you. They watch for country wenches. It's all, *Lord, sweetheart, all alone in this terrible city?* Until the poor bitch is terrified. Then it's, *I can offer you a respectable place and a bed.* There's a bed, all right.' Betsy-Ann rises and gives a vicious poke at the fire, sending sparks roaring. There is an actual, corporeal pain in the region of Sophia's heart, a tearing pity at this picture of innocence ensnared.

'Why are these people tolerated? Does nobody take them before the justice?'

'Who's to do it, Madam? Before the girl arrives at the place, there's no proof. Once she's there, nobody interferes.'

'And this is done by women!' Sophia murmurs. 'But aren't there enough unfortunates in town to stock any number of – houses?'

'And many that'd be glad of it,' is Betsy-Ann's chilling reply. 'There's worse places than Kitty Hartry's.'

'What need, then, to trepan the innocent? When there are already so many engaged in the trade?'

'Aren't there enough hand-me-down gowns to be bought, Mrs Zedland?'

Sophia stares.

'New sells dearer than used,' says Betsy-Ann. 'Stands to reason.'

'Men require – variety.'

'More than that. Breaking in a wench is said to cure the pox. That's what happened to my sister, Madam. So little she was flat-chested, but she nabbed the worst dose ever seen in that place.'

Intolerable images crowd Sophia's brain. The words *flat-chested* are particularly distressing, suggesting as they do the puny ribcage of a child.

'Kitty's safe enough,' Betsy-Ann adds, looking as if she would like to flay the woman. 'She's friends very able to help her.'

'Yes. Of course.'

'You see it now. You've learnt something,' says Betsy-Ann with an air of triumph that grates upon Sophia: it is almost as if the woman would have every other female deprived of innocence. She says, 'Perhaps I was ignorant, but my parents did right to protect me. They could hardly reveal the truth.'

'Not to a respectable young girl,' Betsy-Ann puts in with what might or might not be satire.

'But men – if this were known to men of standing and reputation, who could prevent —'

'*Known?*' Betsy-Ann flares up. 'It's known, all right! Who do you think goes to these places? It's not your chimney-sweeper that can afford Hartry's!'

Sophia is silenced. The nightmare of that many-headed monster snarling and snapping just beneath the surface of polite society is hideous enough. How much more hideous to realise that Edmund is not unique in his descents to it, that faces dear to her – Papa? Mr Letcher? – may also, at times, be known there, may number themselves among its inmates and familiars. She recalls her dream of running along the London rooftops, abysses opening up at every stride. Inwardly trembling, she says, 'I should like to ask you a question, if I may.'

'About Kitty?'

'About you. Did you, were you able to keep yourself . . .' She is at a loss for the word.

'Clean?' Betsy-Ann sits back and looks her straight in the eye.

'You didn't —'

'I had a little trouble that way.' Her mouth twitches as she adds, with unmistakable emphasis, '*You* look well, Madam.'

Sophia has brought this upon herself. She put the question and the woman answered it, but she cannot, must not, continue with a topic which threatens to hurl her from the rooftop once and for all. And yet she is seized by the most tormenting curiosity. What of Edmund? She closes her eyes: later! She can consider matters later, when she is alone. Steeling herself, she remarks, 'I imagine you often lacked occupation. Was it there that you learned your card tricks?'

Betsy-Ann Blore can take a hint. 'Ma showed me first,' she says, reaching into her bag and bringing out her deck. 'When I remember how Ned used to beg!' She begins to shuffle. 'He thought to worm it out of me. He's sly, is Ned, but so am I. A regular slyboots.' And she winks, actually winks: after her excruciating history she is capable of winking. Sophia feels shame. She has always thought of herself as compassionate towards the poor, yet she was unable even to hear to the end what Miss Blore had suffered. Who has ever heard the woman out – surely not Edmund?

'Your life has been a most unfortunate one. I hardly know what to say.'

'Most respectable folk say a deal too much.'

'There are foundations to help women – the Magdalene House. Would you consider the Magdalene House? I'm told it's managed upon the most enlightened lines.'

'With a brown uniform.'

'Yes. Very modest and simple, I thought.'

'Would *you* wear that uniform?'

Sophia feels the refusal like a slap. 'Do you speak in earnest? You would reject such a chance, purely because —'

'I'm too old for the Magdalene House, Mrs Zedland. They like to catch 'em young. And what'd be the use of it, after all?'

'I should've thought that was obvious.'

'Magdalene girls go into service. I shan't scour jerries for a living, not while I've something put by.'

'You have something now, perhaps. But what if you're tempted back into keeping?'

'Not likely. Seen too much of it. A little shop is what *I* want.' She holds Sophia's gaze an instant before turning back to the cards.

'I understand you. I think Papa might find it in him to help, if things go as he hopes.'

'You've all been rascally abused.'

Sophia can't help smiling at this: it comes so pat. 'I quite see the charm of independence. Would that I could attain it.'

'You would, if Ned died,' says Betsy-Ann without the slightest restraining delicacy. 'Provided you're snug, widowhood's a blessed condition – men bowing and scraping, you sitting there, taking your pick.'

'And if you don't marry again?'

'Then you're mistress of what's yours. Now, look.' She has divided the cards into four piles. 'See what's in here.'

Sophia examines them. Each pile is a suit, unmixed, from deuce to ace. 'Now put them together, one on top of another.' She takes the reassembled pack from Sophia. 'You put down every one in order, right?'

Sophia nods.

'I'll shuffle and deal, same as before.' The cards chop back and forth between her hands, Sophia on the watch for juggling. Betsy-Ann again divides them into four piles and Sophia turns over each in turn: one of court cards, one all eights, nines and tens, one of lower cards from seven down to five, ones of threes, fours and deuces.

'Where are the aces?'

'Here.' Betsy-Ann fans out the heap of court cards to display them. 'Can't range 'em quite like that, of course, it'd be noticed directly.'

'Can't any sharp meddle with the deck?'

'This is faster. Ned would give his teeth to know how it's done.'

Sophia sees Edmund toothless, his jaws fallen in.

I shall return to Buller, she thinks, as Betsy-Ann, with a satisfied expression, lays down the cards. While I sit over my embroidery you'll be serving up tobacco, or perhaps lace. In a year or two I'll look back on this London misadventure as I might a delirium.

I shall be the terror of the card table.

'There's something else I want to ask. About Mrs Hartry's establishment. What did Edmund, Ned, know of it?'

Betsy-Ann looks puzzled. 'There was nothing kept from him.'

You were better prenticed to my trade – is that how it went? 'Was he familiar with how *you* came to be there?'

'He knows how the world wags, Mrs Zedland. He stands to

419

inherit the business. Here, take the books. Let me see you deal for Faro.'

'What's your game, friend?'

A sharp pain in his side: Fortunate starts awake to find two youths standing over him. It is an instant before he realises that one of them has just kicked him in the ribs.

'Perhaps he don't talk English.'

'I do, I do,' he mumbles, drawing up his arms and knees for protection.

'Who put you over the wall?'

'A man chases me.'

'That door, Snowball, was shut and bolted.'

'I came here, I wouldn't sleep if —' the English words refuse to come to him. 'If doing bad things.'

'Nothing's gone from the house,' says the other youth, who seems to be of a more kindly disposition.

'Runaway, then,' says the one he suspects of kicking him. 'Up, up, Blacky,' and before Fortunate can protest he has been hauled upright and his arms dragged behind him.

'Easy, Matt. He's not fighting you.'

'I am Titus.'

'Sure he's not fighting, I've got a hold. Search his pockets.'

'No,' Fortunate cries, but the lad is already drawing out a pistol.

'Not a thief?' Matt jeers. 'With a barking-iron!'

'Broken.'

'Take a look, Jim. Is it loaded?'

Jim examines the pistol and nods his head.

Matt steps forward and seizes it. 'Now,' he says, 'tell us who was with you.'

'Nobody.'

'Very well.' He raises the pistol level with Fortunate's head. 'You heard him say it was broken, Jim?'

'Put it down,' Jim pleads.

'The man says it's broken.'

'For Christ's sake, Matt —' Jim reaches for the pistol, but Matt at once aims it straight into his face. Jim backs off, though continuing to protest: 'There's money in runaways! You want to think of that!'

Fortunate hopes the dampness of his pockets will save him. It seems hardly to matter any more: life is so wretched, so relentless and terrifying, it would be a relief to end it. In his exhausted, shocked condition nothing seems real. At the same time, some instinct not yet befuddled warns him not to seem afraid of the pistol, and he stands as if calm.

'Dying game, are we? Your last chance now. Who put you over?'

Fortunate spits at him.

The pistol clicks. Jim screams and lunges at his fellow servant. The pistol skitters across the cobbles of the yard: Fortunate stoops for it, unbolts the door and is gone while the two of them are struggling. Life and energy re-entered his body the moment the youth tried to kill him: his feet pound the pavement as if to make holes in it. There is a strange noise and after a while he realises that it is himself, wailing aloud as he goes.

Some time later, exhaustion having returned and closed on him like a fist, he enters a tavern. Here people find food and drink, and perhaps a bed: things of which he is in desperate need. He can barely see the faces of the people inside, the room is so dark and his eyes so unwilling to stay open, but he knows without looking that some of those within are staring at him with cold dislike, some leering, some with a milder curiosity. He is aware of fingers on his back, even on his neck: people walking up quite coolly and touching him for luck. They used to do it when he lived with Dog Eye. For reassurance he puts his hand to the pistol. After leaving Matt and Jim, his first action was to search for the other one. His fingers encountered a tear in the bottom of his pocket, through which the weapon had slipped into the lining of his coat. It is still there, resting against his leg.

The woman serving drink takes his money and pours him a tankard of beer. She also asks him if he is a slave. He says no, and wonders how she would feel, if he should ask the same question of her. Fortunate's father was wealthy and kept slaves of his own: what would he say, seeing his son so insulted? But here it is not the dignity of the man or his position in life that matters but the colour of the skin.

'You were freed, then.'

'Freed. Yes.'

'Down on your luck, are you?' She seems friendly enough but his eyes are closing in his head and his tongue feels shackled. With an immense effort he manages to ask if there is a room he can have.

'It's a shilling,' the woman says.

'I pay. Please some food.' The press of bodies, the starers, some mimicking his manner of saying *pay* and *please*: it is all loathsome to him just now, even more than at other times. They allow nothing for his condition. They make no allowances ever. If his weapons were not damp, he would be tempted to shoot one of them and see the rest scatter.

'There's . . . .' the woman says. He cannot catch the words but says, 'Please. Take me room now.' He is conscious of sounding stupid. It is the tiredness of many nights, rolled into one: his tongue is too thick to speak.

She comes out from behind the bar, calling, 'Clem!' as she does so. A tall fair-haired man separates himself from the customers and comes to take her place as the woman leads Fortunate, clutching his beer, upstairs to a small shabby room with a servant's bed, not unlike the one he had in the New Buildings, but dirtier. He waits for her to leave, then slumps on the bed to finish his drink.

When the woman returns Fortunate is in a doze, still holding the tankard on his lap. He starts, spilling a little, as she sets down his food on the counterpane: a plate of boiled bacon, of the coarsest, toughest kind, and slimy cabbage greens. He sees now that the chamber has a fireplace, and a door that can be bolted.

'Fire, please.'

She pulls a face as if to say: You don't want much, do you?

'Pay.'

She gives him a shrewd look, but fetches a coal scuttle. When she has lit the fire and gone away, Fortunate bolts the door. Fighting the urge to sleep, he lays his pistols in front of the fire, not too close. The box of powder he retrieves from his coat lining. He opens it and pushes the contents about with his finger: they feel dry, but he warms the box anyway, a little further from the fire, with its top covered in case of spitting coals.

Then he gorges on the cabbage and bacon, the stringy flesh catching in his throat more than once and almost choking him. With the help of the beer he gets it down. He lies on the bed fully dressed and the world disappears.

48

'Best front pair in the house,' Mrs Ledley says, holding back the door. Betsy-Ann looks round. Not bad: wallpaper stained but not peeling, a hearth, a bed and a few other sticks of furniture, not up to her rooms in Covent Garden but then nothing is. The usual chamber fug of sweat, spunk, fannies, pisspots, drains. The bed must have been especially stinky: someone, Ledley probably, has been dousing it in Cologne water.

'Who had it before?'

'A Miss Roberts, very genteel.' The woman's moist, bulging eyes put Betsy-Ann in mind of a pug dog.

'Where's she gone then, this genteel Miss Roberts?'

'She found herself a friend.' Mrs Ledley looks coy. 'The district is noted for good company and good cheer.'

Betsy-Ann knows what it's noted for. 'Are there many church-yards round about?'

'Churchyards, my dear?'

'I've a horror of skulls and bones and graves. Been like it since I was a girl.'

'There's churchyards everywhere.' Mrs Ledley looks doubtful, then brightens. 'But you won't be troubled here. The church in this street is end-to-end with the houses, brick to brick. You couldn't bury a mouse.'

There is a commode in the room but the woman shows her the necessary house, which is as foul as any she has seen.

'I've a cart and a few knick-knacks to sell before I can move in,' says Betsy-Ann.

Mrs Ledley doesn't miss a trick. 'I was hoping to let it directly. There's a lady coming to see —'

'O, that needn't stand in our way. Suppose I paid you a quarter's rent, straight off, and took the key? Would you be so kind as fill the scuttle for me?'

'Of course,' the woman simpers. You needn't think you'll be let to bilk me every time I want a few coals, Betsy-Ann silently retorts. To secure the chamber, though, it's worth it this once. She hands over a quarter's rent, retrieved from under Sam's floorboards.

'O, Mrs Ledley,' she says when they have shaken hands. 'Are you able to write the direction for me, nice and plain, so I can give it my friend? My lady friend,' she adds, as if Ledley cares.

Mrs Ledley can read but not write. However, Mrs Sutton from the back pair is quite a scholar and always obliging provided there's no ribbon tied to her door handle – that is, no intimate 'conversation' taking place within. Mrs Sutton comes to the door frowzy and bored, seemingly glad of distraction, and invites Betsy-Ann (though not Mrs Ledley, who goes sniffily downstairs) to step into her rooms.

The air within is every bit as stale as in Betsy-Ann's own place. There's the usual greasy bed, one leg missing and its absence supplied by a rough length of timber, plus a jerry and a bowl for bathing, should visitors be particular. Over the mantelpiece Mrs Sutton has pinned a piece of paper covered in print. The last time Betsy-Ann saw something of this kind, she was told it was a prayer.

'What's that?' she enquires, nervous lest she should have misjudged her company.

'O, nothing of importance.' Mrs Sutton reaches down the gin from a shelf. 'A gentleman gave me the *Bath Chronicle* – he'd just come back from taking the waters – and that part entertained me, so I cut it out and kept it.' She hands Betsy-Ann a full glass. 'To health and happiness.'

'To health and happiness,' Betsy-Ann echoes as they clink and smile. 'Would you be so kind as to read your – chronicle – to me?'

'Of course.' She goes over to the mantelpiece and peers. *'Mail from Flanders and Stockholm. A few days ago a small hound was brought here from Angermansland, and shown by one Garney, a book-keeper, which has been taught to speak.'*

'To speak!'

'The hound, not the book-keeper. *He not only utters whole words, but whole sentences one after the other, in the French and Swedish languages, and among other expressions, he speaks plain, Vive le Roi.'*

'Veevla?'

'God Save the King, in English.'

Though Mrs Sutton's mouth and cheeks are dimpling up, Betsy-Ann is unsure whether to be astonished or amused. 'Can a dog really do that?'

'No, no!' cries Mrs Sutton, openly laughing now as if delighted at the question. 'Some sham or other.'

'I wonder how it was worked.'

'How should I know? I fancy he pinched it, made it cry out.'

'Poor little cur.'

'Aye – out of luck, like others I could mention!' Herself for a start, Betsy-Ann thinks. The way Mrs Sutton holds up her head, her speech, her broad, creamy features, her pleasure in a scrap saved from the newspaper – all these suggest a life begun in comfort and respectability.

'I see I've made you curious,' Mrs Sutton observes. 'I'm quite the usual thing, I assure you. A promise of marriage – he's in India, now, and the child in the Foundling.'

'And your family?'

'Cut me off.' She shrugs dismissively. 'When I first came on the Town, I wasn't well known. But Mr Derrick puffed me in *Harris's* – *a fine witty wench, eminently well adapted to a man of solid parts*, it said – and after that I was more in request.'

Dirty Sam Derrick! For all Betsy-Ann knows, he might have

written that very report of the Talking Hound. She says, 'Do you know Kitty Hartry?'

'I've heard of her.'

'A bitch,' says Betsy-Ann.

It is almost like old times.

She has her work cut out all that week, keeping Sam Shiner in ignorance. Plainly he expects some sort of revenge – as well he might, the filthy bastard – but though suspicion stinks up the place like that infernal coat of his, he can't be resurrecting and spying at the same time. She's managed to clear every last bit of gold, leaving untouched the buckets of umbrellas, the shoes, anything bulky and deceiving.

It's a wonder he hasn't set a nose on her. She's been on the lookout, same as him: peeping round corners, turning without warning, but there's nobody skulking about. Meanwhile, the stock in the Eye's dwindled almost to nothing.

Loading and selling the cart has to come last: it's a job that takes time and can't be hidden. She could, she supposes, make the journey by night, but it's not something she fancies: too many blades about and she'd be banging and bawling for the Uncle when she got there, drawing attention to herself. Best wait for a morning when Shiner's been out and failed to come back, when he's finally answered the call of the booze. With luck it won't be too long. Between the foggy weather and the dark of the moon coming on, he goes out regular now.

There comes a night black as Hell's arse, and Harry sends word. She's not supposed to hear so she goes into the bedchamber until the boy has skipped away downstairs.

Shiner's cursing like a damned soul.

'What is it, Sammy?' she says in the lying voice she still uses with him.

'Three at Bart's. Smalls.'

At once she's hopeful. He had a kinchin himself, once, and by all accounts was a fond father: he can't abide the smalls. Directly he's gone she undresses for bed where she lies wide-eyed, listening out for the tolling of the hours.

Sure enough, at four he's still not back. She pictures him slung across the back of a drayhorse, sliding head first into a hogshead. By five she's at work, stripping from the Eye every last bottle and boot that might turn a penny, prising up the floorboard to pocket her sweet stash.

She pushes one sovereign, wrapped in paper, under Liz's door for luck.

At last the cart is loaded up and Betsy-Ann behind it, pushing away like a whore with a slow cully. The Uncle's fly: he's been warned to expect an early call, one of these days. Before eight she's ringing his bell, and while Mr Shiner snores away the morning, to wake somewhere with a bear's head and temper, she disposes of all Mrs Shiner's earthly goods, cart and all. As for Mrs Shiner herself, that lady is as dead as any other flesh Sam might have trafficked in. Mrs Ledley's new tenant is Mrs Talbot, a very different creature.

49

'It's impossible,' says Sophia. 'I have no acquaintance here to speak of, certainly not the kind that would be required. Mr and Mrs Letcher aren't London people.'

'You give up too soon, Mrs Zedland. Your Mr Letcher will have friends, sporting gents.'

'If he does, I don't know them. And how could I ask? No, I absolutely refuse.' Sophia sits up a little straighter. The shared fantasy of fleecing Edmund has provided not a little pleasure, but Miss Blore appears to have got the bit between her teeth in earnest: she must be 'pulled up sharpish', as Radley used to say. 'It's needless, don't you see? Our best chance is to stick with the evidence.' She is about to add, by way of encouragement, that Mr Scrope's Bow Street agent is on the track of the young person *bubbled* at Bath, but prudence bids her hold her tongue.

Betsy-Ann Blore says nothing, but looks distinctly mutinous.

'Are you afraid to give evidence, Betsy-Ann, is that it?'

'I thought *you* liked the idea of biting him.'

Sophia laughs. 'Talking of it, yes. But to do it in earnest — !'

'Then I misunderstood you,' says Betsy-Ann Blore.

'If you run any risk in the business, Papa will make sure you're protected.'

Miss Blore's mouth twists into an odd shape, her expression somewhere between the anxious and the mocking. Perhaps it is the word *protect*, with all its shades of meaning: this can't be the first time she's been offered protection. 'You mean well, I'm sure,' she says civilly enough. 'But it's hard to keep a body safe, once she's peached. He could pay a man to make me easy, if he don't care for the job himself.'

'Easy?'

'So easy, nothing'll ever trouble me again.'

'You won't appear in court, Betsy-Ann. We're seeking a private settlement. And surely you don't think he'd —'

'I don't think him inclined to it, no. But if it was himself or me, well!' Betsy-Ann shrugs.

Sophia thought this day might come. Betsy-Ann's sort shrink from any dealings with lawyers: her fear was driven out, for a while, by her violent hunger for vengeance, but now that's on the wane. During the last week she's spoken constantly of games, disguises, tricks: anything but the process of law.

'We may not even need to use your evidence. And if necessary, we can send you into the country.'

Betsy-Ann seems less than delighted at this prospect. 'Begging your pardon, Mrs Zedland, but I shouldn't like that. A new name, and a shop, that'll do me – if he settles.'

'He will, no question. The facts are plain as day.'

'Nothing's plain. He'll get himself men of straw —'

'Of straw?'

'Tame witnesses. They'll swear anything he likes against you.'

'Against *me*? What on earth could they swear to?'

Betsy-Ann shrugs. 'That the pair of you was in it together, to cozen your papa and mama.'

'But that's absurd,' cries Sophia, laughing. 'Why should I do anything so foolish – so wicked?'

'Because he *said* to. So as not to *lose* him,' says Betsy-Ann, with an air of stating the obvious.

'Nobody would believe it.'

'They hear of such things every day, Mrs Zedland. Is your man up to all that?'

'He's experienced,' says Sophia, her confidence somewhat diluted by these revelations.

'I hear Ned's quite the gent at Cosgrove's. He's plenty of palm-

430

grease – yours, Harry's, Sam's, his winnings – if he kicks back, you'll have to go before the Beak.'

'That's enough!' Sophia raps out. She rises, rings for the maid and throws herself back into the chair. The women sit in silence a minute, eyeing one another.

'Come to Cosgrove's,' Betsy-Ann says at last. 'See for yourself.'

Sophia shudders. 'I couldn't.'

'I don't intend that he should meet with you, nor me neither. But you should see the cut of him, Mrs Zedland. By God, it's a good thing Harry can't go into those places! If he met Ned looking such a peacock, he'd tear him limb from limb!'

'How do you know all this? Do you go spying on Edmund?'

'Of course,' Betsy-Ann replies. 'Be a fool not to.' She feels in her stays. 'Here, I almost forgot.'

Gingerly Sophia takes the paper, which is damp from Betsy-Ann's skin, and reads: *First floor front, Denman's Buildings, The Strand.*

'My new lodgings, should you need to know,' explains Betsy-Ann. 'Don't go there. It's not a place for you.'

'Am I to write, then?'

'I can't read. If you want me, send a letter with nothing inside. I'll know what that means.'

'I see. Thank you.'

'So, we'll go to Cosgrove's?'

'I don't think it would —'

'Just a peep, Mrs Zedland. Anyone may take a peep.'

'Well.' She considers. 'I might, perhaps, but not today. I've things to attend to.'

The food, for instance. This morning's breakfast was eggs and grilled bone in congealed fat: even now, at the thought of those gelid yolks, her stomach turns. Without warning, a sour fluid rises in Sophia's mouth. She clutches a handkerchief to her lips and hurries from the Blue Room to her closet where she retches into the commode. Wiping her lips, she reflects that her recent troubles have affected her digestion. She has been prone to sickness lately, and to sudden revulsions.

When she returns, Betsy-Ann Blore appears not to have moved. It did occur to Sophia, while she was helplessly vomiting, that her guest had now the opportunity to steal any tempting little *bibelot* that might catch her eye. She is half ashamed of having entertained such suspicions, but only half: a Greek cup was once removed from Papa's collection at Buller by a trusted guest, the son of a visiting gentleman. The young man had ample funds, and could easily have purchased what he had stolen: how much more tempting must such things appear to the likes of Betsy-Ann Blore! Perhaps she might be drawn by the marble Cupid on the mantelpiece, a present from Aunt Phoebe. Sophia finds its puffy cheeks, the half-moon chinks of its eyes, downright sinister and would gladly be rid of it.

'Are you well now, Mrs Zedland?' Betsy-Ann is studying her, making no attempt to disguise the fact.

'Thank you, I'm quite well.'

'You lace pretty tight, considering. I always think that's right. A woman likes to keep her shape as long as possible.' Betsy-Ann's features have assumed the impudent smirk of a midwife, as if she expects Mrs Zedland to continue the intimate revelations that Mr Zedland began. Sophia stares at the leering, baby-faced Cupid. It would be a relief to her feelings if she could take it up and fling it at Betsy-Ann's head. Instead she says, 'My mama was a great believer in narrow lacing. She thought it essential to good posture.'

'I'm quite of her opinion,' says Betsy-Ann Blore.

Fortunate wakes to the boom and crash of rolling barrels. The ship is taking on fresh water. Then he sees a plastered ceiling above him, stained with damp. He stretches out on the bed, cold and stiff from lying in his clothes. In the yard below men are cursing as they struggle to unload the dray; the horse curses along with them, whinnying fretfully as they call to one another.

With difficulty he rises and goes to the window. There is Clem, the man he saw yesterday, wiping his hands on his apron while others do the heavy work: a person of authority. Clem looks upwards, as if knowing himself observed. Fortunate steps back, out of sight. He studies the sky. It is so even a grey that the sun might be anywhere.

His guineas are still in place, tucked into the wadding next to his breast. He removes one and checks the others are secure. The king's head is darkly picked out, as if inked. That is the churchyard soil, filling in the gaps. He shivers at the memory of the Spirit, hoping it is now far away, but he has no way of knowing: in his panic after leaving Matt and Jim he ran blindly, perhaps in the direction of the church, perhaps away from it. And those other shadows in the churchyard, what were they? Names come back to him: Sam, Pete. Davey. Men's names. Though they seemed to be men, they carried the smell of decay.

He takes up the pistols, tips out the powder into his palm and replaces it with fresh dry powder from the box. Then he slides both weapons into one pocket and shrugs on his coat.

Downstairs the tavern is almost empty. Last night's revellers are at home, nursing their heads. Clem can be heard outside the window, telling someone to leave that one on the side.

The woman sits behind the counter, heeling a man's sock. It is a strange choice of task, when all around her the room is dusty and stained, and the serving-bar, as he can see from where he stands, is sticky with spills.

She looks up as he approaches. All he observed of her last night was her seeming good will. Now he notices her hair, which is as dark as his own. Its natural form seems to be straight, but it is piled up on top of her head, stiff and dull, and fixed in place with pins. She has a pale, pleasant face, not distinctive in any way but mild and womanly. As soon as she smiles, the effect is ruined by a mouthful of brown, jagged teeth. Fortunate keeps his distance, wary of her breath.

'I trust you slept well.' She looks as if she might laugh, after saying that. 'Will you be staying on another night?'

She might mean only to tease him for sleeping late, but it strikes Fortunate as a good idea. He needs another day of rest and food to make him strong.

'Another night, yes.'

'I'll trouble you to pay for the two of 'em now. And will you want feeding? Breakfast, dinner?'

'Yes. Please.'

He is embarrassed, at first, about bringing out the coin from his pocket, until it strikes him that his embarrassment is pointless. He must carry the money somewhere about him. If these people intend to steal it they will find a way.

'My!' she says, seeing the gold. As she is giving him his change, Clem enters and nods.

'Here's our young gent back,' says the woman, as if she had not seen her husband's greeting. Clem understands something by this, for he turns and looks Fortunate up and down.

'Too small,' he says, shaking his head.

'But a draw. Trust me.'

Plainly these two have discussed him while he slept. He wonders if they have advertised him, and if the Pinched Wife is already on her way.

Perhaps he is to be robbed and murdered. The tavern is in the familiar style: he must be in Romeville, now, where a man with

434

money is surrounded by false friends. He should have thought of this before.

The woman says, 'You look to me like a good-natured lad. And an honest one.'

'I am honest, Madam.'

'I hope you are, 'cause I'm about to make you an offer.'

'To buy something from me?' he says, the shoes pressing on his flayed heels.

'Am I right when I say you've been in service?'

'Yes.'

'There you are, Clem! Knew it by the clothes.'

'I have good shoes,' he says hopefully.

'Are you in a place now?'

He shakes his head.

'Are you in search of one, then? Clem and me was wondering.'

Somehow he does not think Clem wants him. He says, 'To work?'

'Naturally to work. And live in. You're lucky, see.'

How can she know that his name, in his own language, means just that? Then he realises: she means he'll fetch in the customers.

'Mornings and afternoons, it's mostly dead.' She waves towards the empty benches. 'Evenings we're as full as we can handle, you'll have to be nippy. Know the trade?'

He shakes his head.

'It's only serving food and drink.' She grins, showing her horrible teeth. 'I'll show you what to do. If you want the situation. *Do* you want it? Don't say much, do you?'

She hasn't given him a chance. 'I shall work for you, Madam, if – if I have something.'

Her eyes narrow. 'I hope you ain't one of these saucy blacks, Mr Lucky.'

With care he slides off a shoe and shows her one of his heels.

435

His stocking is worn through, showing tortured flesh bright and angry with pain. The woman whistles. She bends and picks up the shoe he has taken off, sees the bloodstains and says, 'Sweet Christ.'

'They hurt me.'

'Aye! They would! Well, I know a woman who'll fetch you something.'

'Shall I work without shoes?' He asks knowing that London people set great store by these things but she shrugs, as if to say it's of no importance. What matters, he concludes, is his complexion.

'What shall I call you, Madam?'

'Keep with *Madam*. That'll do. My name is Mrs Harbottle.'

'You are married to Mr Clem.'

'Lord, no! What gave you that idea?' she giggles. 'Mr *Harbottle* was my dear dead husband.'

Fortunate sees how it is. She believes that if the words are not used, the thing will not be known.

'And you? What's yours?'

He is about to say *Titus*, but why help the Pinched Wife to find him? 'Lucky is a good name. Shall I start today, Madam, and not pay my shilling?'

Again she favours him with her dreadful smile. 'It's after four, did you know that? Come down to the kitchen.'

After breakfast, if food eaten in the afternoon may be so called, she takes Fortunate back to the bar to teach him his new trade. Demand is mostly for gin, but he will also be asked for wine, port wine, rum, beer, brandy, ale or porter. Some people, says Mrs Harbottle, can't drink like Christians but must invent 'such nasty slop as you couldn't pay me to swallow'. The nasty slop she has in mind is huckle-my-buff, which turns out to be hot beer with eggs and brandy.

'But there,' she says, winking, 'I let the world go by.' He understands that the mixture is profitable. 'Anything you don't know, you've only to shout out.'

It is well for him that business is slack and his mistress easy-going, for he is sorely tested. It is not that he is too small, as Clem feared. He is quick on his feet – once the shoes are off – and quite strong enough for the work, but there is one thing he cannot help: he is a person not used to drinking.

Each time someone places an order there is immediate silence, followed by cheers and groans and the sound of coins being swept up from the table.

'Not know swizzle!' somebody cries. 'Sure the man in the moon knows swizzle!'

It seems they are laying money on him. A few times he surprises them: once, with French Cream, because he heard Eliza and Fan talking about it, and again with Bristol Milk, or sherry-wine, because some of Dog Eye's women drank it, long ago. Most of the time he is at a loss, and they bait him with their hotpot, stitchback and callibogus, their stewed quaker and red fustian, their kill-devil, bishop and bub, besides many more names heard and forgotten as he scuttles about behind the bar. He fumbles, spilling the drink, while Mrs Harbottle stands by laughing.

When they have gone it is a different story. 'Mixtures is one thing,' she says, 'but not to know heart's ease! You'll have to do better than that, my lad. And I showed you how to do three threads, and no sooner was it done than you asked me again!'

'I am sorry,' he says, humiliated that in his hurry and confusion he forgot the recipe. To her this space behind the bar is home, easy and familiar. To him it is rows of casks and bottles covered in strange markings, hard to remember even without men betting on the outcome.

'I thought you was in service?' She looks now as if she repents of hiring him. At the thought of being thrown onto the streets, tears prick his eyes.

'All right,' she says, more gently. 'You shall have law.' She hands him a glass of Bristol Milk. He sips, a mouthful of sadness: it takes him back to Dog Eye's lodgings, before the marriage. That time will never come again, he thinks, and then: No, I will find him.

'You know it, eh? Was you ever on a Bristol slaver?'

If the woman but knew what she is asking! He arrived in Annapolis so stupefied, he would scarcely have noticed had he stepped in a fire: how should he concern himself with the name of a port in England? He says, 'I knew no English then.'

'Nor much now,' she answers pertly, as if expecting him to laugh. 'Well, Mr Lucky, I shall have to drill you. We'll start with gin and the rest can come after. And you needn't fill the jugs so full – see here.' She takes one and shows how far the drink should come up the sides.

Some bucks enter, already swaggering drunk. One calls for kill-priest and gages, and Mrs Harbottle serves him. She waits until the men are settled and drinking toasts – *To Mother Hartry and her chicks! To the best cunt in Christendom!* – before telling Fortunate, 'I won't put you on tonight. You're not up to the game.'

He is indignant. 'I can learn, Madam! It's when the men lay wagers —'

'Don't get your back up. Who are you, Tender Parnell?'

'Who is that, please?'

She rolls her eyes. 'Tender *Parnell*, that broke her finger in a posset drink!'

'I never heard of this lady.'

'She's nothing, she's – O, never mind! The thing is, you mustn't mind their sport. You can go now.'

'I must leave?'

'I'm giving you time off, simpkin. Stay in the chamber, go out, whatever you please. Tomorrow you start in earnest.'

'Thank you.'

'And wash your hands and face before you come down, and comb that wool of yours. You'll feel a sight better for it, and Lord knows I shall.'

After these few hours, who knows when he will next be free to walk about? There is always the chance of finding his master, even in an hour.

Once outside, he studies the front of the tavern so as to know it again. Its sign shows an important-looking metal tube floating amid moon and stars, with faded gilt lettering underneath.

'Prithee, friend,' he hails a man on the other side of the way, 'what is this?'

'The Spyglass.' The fellow clears his throat, about to say something more, but Fortunate thanks him and hurries away, not wishing to be delayed by questions about what brings him here or where he was born. His purpose is to walk as far as possible and he is on the watch for details that might guide him back to the inn: a humped railing like the top of a bridge, a shutter hanging loose from one hinge.

The Spyglass has not a good situation: the further he travels, the more prosperous the houses. A very little distance and they have gardens in front, with railings to keep out such as himself – but then he remembers he is no longer a beggar, and has a bed to go to.

No shoes, however. He looks down at his feet, the toes caked with greyish dirt. There is nothing disgraceful, at home, in going barefoot. Nobody, not the most important man of the village, would think of desiring such foolish things as wigs and shoes, yet Fortunate has learnt to be ashamed without them. Even his feet have made peace with the things: since he took off that last torturing pair his flesh feels exposed.

If he were to go home now, would his little sister know him? Has his voice become foreign? He turns over the old words in his head, not daring to say them aloud. They seem thin and flat, the strength gone out of them. They have been pushed aside, crowded out by words unworthy of attention: kill-priest, gage, nantz. Tender Parnell.

Does he see Dog Eye that day? His feelings, as well as his thoughts, are so stirred, perplexed and muddied afterwards that he cannot be sure.

He is pushing along on his miserable feet that can never be contented, either in shoes or out of them, and looking for a place, not too dusty, where he may sit and rest. At length he comes upon a disused horse trough, drained of its water by a spreading crack along the bottom. It stands where a lane branches off towards some fields, and here he seats himself, swinging his legs in the air.

The bushes along the lane have been cut back, perhaps to discourage robbers. In the distance he can make out what must be another inn, and in front of it, despite the time of year, men playing bowls. Comfortable men: men not obliged to work, who can afford the time to stand in a garden throwing a wooden ball. Men with warm coats and well-broken-in shoes. Blissful men!

Though the lane is deserted – he supposes not many people wish to go that way – a carriage is rattling along the main road in the direction of the Spyglass. It pulls up just past the entry to the lane. The coachman glances at Fortunate, half-lying in the trough, and looks away again as if the sight pains him.

The blind is lowered. 'Go back, Tufts!' a man cries. *'That's* the place the gentleman said. Turn off there.'

'He did indeed, Sir. But it's out of our road.'

The master groans. 'Why the Deuce didn't you say so before?'

'Begging your pardon, Sir, I wasn't aware, not precisely.'

'Not precisely! You've lost us again, you boneheaded booby!'

The driver mutters under his breath. Fortunate thinks it would give the man great pleasure to lose carriage, master and all.

'Is there no fingerpost?' a voice enquires from within.

'Not unless you consider a drunken blackbird as one,' the man replies drily, 'which for my part I don't.'

'A drunken blackbird!'

The carriage tilts as both occupants press to the window. Fortunate can see only the near one, a jolly fat fellow with a double chin, but he is caught by the sound of the other voice, which resembles Dog Eye's. The fat man cries out, 'As I live and breathe, sitting in a trough in the middle of nowhere!'

'What, sousing himself in this weather!' comes the voice from within.

The first man shakes his head. 'No water in it. I say, fellow,' he calls down from the window, 'you've been going it, haven't you?'

'Sir?'

'He doesn't understand me, you see,' says the man.

'He's drunk the trough dry at any rate,' comes the other voice, sounding so like Dog Eye that Fortunate must see for himself. He scrabbles out of the trough onto the verge of the road, but can see only the first man and beside him, a dark shape.

'It's Titus, Sir!' he calls. 'Your servant, Titus!'

'Titus,' says the fat man, raising an eyebrow as if surprised he has a name at all. 'Had you a servant of that name?'

Fortunate strains his ears but catches nothing of the reply. A gloved hand is put out of the carriage window. 'Here, my fine fellow, and my advice gratis – leave off idleness.'

A penny drops onto the verge. It is followed by a gold coin that soars, spinning, out of the window and into the trough. The fat man turns to his unseen companion.

'My word, you're free with it!'

'O, blackbirds are luck,' murmurs the other.

'The gentleman is kind,' Fortunate cries. 'May I thank him?'

'He's heard your thanks,' says the man, waving him away. 'Tufts, take us along the lane and ask at the inn.'

Fortunate stands as if in submission, watching the carriage pull round so that the unseen man is now on the near side. As the vehicle approaches he springs forward and runs along next to it, panting through the window, 'Don't leave me – take me with you —'

The man has moved back from the window and is trying to close the blind, his long fingers groping for the tassel. Fortunate reaches upwards but the hand is snatched away.

'I beg of you!' Fortunate wails.

The coachman's whip comes down on his arm and he flinches away. The blind snaps shut. He is left hugging himself where the lash caught him as the carriage rolls on towards the inn.

In tears, he collapses onto the verge. The penny, worn so thin as to be almost invisible between the blades of grass, lies near his ankle. *That* is a beggar's portion. No man in his wits ever gave so much as a guinea to an unknown beggar. The man who did, knew him: that man was Dog Eye.

Having settled it in his mind, he at once begins to doubt. A gentleman may do anything for a frolic, may give a beggar his estate, should he choose. This man spoke like his master, had hands something like his. That is all.

Yet this man, though not willing to bring him into the carriage, evidently wished to be kind to him in some way. He folds his fingers round the guinea. Perhaps Dog Eye (if the man was indeed Dog Eye) could not speak freely. Suppose they were to meet alone! Then he might embrace Fortunate as a brother.

If he is Dog Eye.

Fortunate gets to his feet. He has no wish to walk any further; he will return to the Spyglass and lie down, and rub his stinging arm. After a while he glances back at the carriage. It has stopped at the inn, taking directions; he watches as it once more turns round and comes back towards him. There is a moment of wild, throbbing hope: they have repented, they will stop and take him up, carry him away. He stands clasping his hands in supplication. As the carriage comes nearer, Tufts whips up the horses. They pass at a gallop, but not so fast that Fortunate cannot see the master laughing.

'My friend's brought you something,' says Mrs Harbottle. 'Upstairs.'

He hardly cares what her friend has brought, but murmurs his thanks. In his chamber he finds a couple of shirts, stockings, breeches. Beside the folded garments lie a wooden comb, a clothes brush and a pair of shoes, dull and scuffed from long wearing.

Someone has left a jug of water on the windowsill. He smooths some over his head and tries to dress his hair, but the teeth of the comb are too tightly packed: they splinter and break off.

Perhaps she will send him to the barber.

He lies down on the bed, pushing his face into the bolster that smells of other people's skin.

What a fool he must have looked, standing there with hands clasped. How that man laughed! The scene plays over and over in his mind like the song of a spiteful bird.

After a while he is woken by Mrs Harbottle, who has entered the chamber without knocking. Afraid he must appear disrespectful, Fortunate scrambles to his feet still half asleep.

She stands with her back to the window, eyeing him. 'The stockings look well. Is that the shirt?'

He nods.

'You take it very coolly, I declare! I'm sure if anyone found *me* in clothes I should be cock-a-hoop.'

443

He says, 'I thank you, Madam,' even though the shirt is tucked in tightly to disguise how he swims in it. Does he owe her anything? She has taken away his old shoes, with their fine-cut buckles: worth as much, probably, as all this lot together.

'Madam, will you give me some butter?'

She blinks at him. 'Butter?'

'For my skin.'

'Butter, in this house, is for Christians to eat. If you must grease yourself, there's the dripping pot.' She touches his head. 'Have you combed your hair?'

'I was not able.' He can hardly tell her why, or where he has slept these past few days. 'A barber —'

'Aye, and then a tailor, and then a man to carry you on his back,' she retorts, but it seems she is not really angry, only fond of this sharp way of speaking, since she then says, 'If you pay him yourself, I'll fetch Toby to you.'

Fortunate bows his head in agreement.

'You didn't stay out long,' the woman says. He wishes she would go.

'I should like to visit my friend Mr Hartry, if I can find his house.'

'You can visit the devil provided you're back in good time. Once Clem's locked up and gone to bed —' she shrugs.

Fortunate has his own ideas as to Clem's unwillingness to get out of bed but he repeats, 'In good time.'

'Tell your Mr Hearty to come here and bring his friends.'

When she's gone he lies down again, drawing up his knees to his chest. She must have got a good price for his buckles. She has gained by him already, or she would hardly let him out in the new clothes: suppose he were to run off? But no, she has put a string around the leg of her blackbird and is sure of him.

He stares hungrily at the hearth. Last night he was a guest: he had a fire and when he went downstairs there was some coal left in the scuttle. Now coal and scuttle have disappeared.

Fortunate does not care for these people, though Mrs Harbottle seems an easier mistress than the Pinched Wife, more in the style of a maid or a cook, perhaps. The Wife lived locked up in herself, barely moving except for that one time she lashed out. Compared with her, there is something free, almost mannish, about Mrs Harbottle. If *she* loses her temper, he'll know about it. But she seems good-natured, on the whole, and he'd sooner have a beating than the cold spite of Mrs Dog Eye.

But the carriage, the carriage! It was out of its way and will never come back: if he stays, he must not expect to see his master again.

Towards the inn. They were to ask directions at the inn.

He must be quick. In no time he is on his feet, his coat buttoned, the pistols carefully wrapped and smuggled into his pocket.

As Sophia picks her way over the wet pavements she has the curious impression of observing her own progress: in her mind's eye a tiny female, an anonymous and inconspicuous ant, moves at a determined pace through the seething ant-hill that is London.

The chair-men agreed to take her as far as Hyde Park 'and then see how matters stand'. They were as good as their word, but at Hyde Park matters stood quite still, as did the men, saying they must have a *damper*. She rather feared they might urinate in her presence but the *damper* proved to be bread and meat, followed by a pull at a flask. After this she thought they would continue, but the front man then shook his head and said that to go on directly was more than flesh and blood could support. At first she thought he was angling for more pay, and showed him a coin, but he shook his head. She bade the men farewell and climbed down, whereupon a youth leaped into the chair she had just vacated. The chair-man's 'If you please, Sir,' was followed by 'We ain't for hire,' and finally, as Sophia moved off in search of a fresh team, by an exasperated, 'Then sit there and rot, you —', followed by a perfect deluge of foul language which nobody except herself appeared to notice, let alone resent.

Evidently demand for chairs outstrips supply. Having been elbowed aside a few times by other pedestrians – both men and women abominably rude – she has no option but to continue on foot. So off she trots, this determined little ant woman of Sophia's imagination, taking care to keep to the centre of the pavement for fear of jostlings or worse.

She is dressed, as far as possible, according to Betsy-Ann Blore's instructions: 'None of your ruffles. Plain, serviceable stuffs.' That the advice was sound she has no doubt. To a certain cast of mind, any elegant female constitutes a walking provocation. There are circumstances, however, in which simplicity proves more difficult of attainment than the most artificial contrivance. Such is the case here, for Sophia's delight lies all in delicate shades, in silvery greys, pinks and creams. Her search eventually produced a gown made up at Buller, for the purposes of visiting the afflicted: it is simple enough in style, though anyone who felt it between finger and thumb would know it at once for silk. Over this she wears a dark pelisse borrowed, without permission, from Fan, but her shoes have no such protection and are already soaked, since, without the maid's help, she was unable to find her pattens.

An intrigue, she thinks as she hurries along, Fan's hood pulled over her hair and a veil flapping across her face. The veil is especially trying, adding as it does an additional layer of darkness to the gloomy, slippery pavements. At least the drizzle has stopped. She stepped into her chair disagreeably damp but emerged into a drier, colder air.

St Mary le Strand is the appointed meeting place, chosen by

Betsy-Ann for ease of identification, and because 'they meet there in the evenings, Madam, so you could go in, should anyone trouble you'. As it turns out, the protection of St Mary's congregation is not required. Thanks to her dull garments and rapid walk, she reaches the Strand with no more nuisance than an occasional lip-smacking noise out of the darkness. Once in the Strand it is a simple matter to find St Mary's and there is Betsy-Ann by the gate, her hand raised in greeting.

'Bitter cold,' she calls as Sophia crosses the road.

Sophia supposes it is, though her journey has left her short of breath and with a sticky back.

When Betsy-Ann extends an arm Sophia hesitates, not wishing to be so intimately coupled. Is that not what the unfortunate women do, stroll arm in arm? From inside the church she can hear what sounds like a psalm: she pictures rows of worshippers, decent people with orderly lives, safely stored in pews.

'It's not far.' Betsy-Ann again extends her arm. 'Come on, link me.'

'What for?'

'O, don't then! If you'd rather be pushed over.'

'Pushed? Why should anyone do that?'

'Did you never fall over as a little girl?'

'Naturally I —'

'And didn't your mama ever say to you, *Watch out, Missy, or you'll show your money*? Well, that's what the bloods want. To see your money.'

'Mama would never have said anything so vulgar.' On reflection, however, Sophia takes her companion's arm.

'Cosgrove's? Where is that, if you please?'

The boy, thin and drooping like a plant starved of water, only shrugs. Another boy, of a livelier make, says, 'I'll fetch the master to you, Sir,' and goes out. His companion continues to sweep up, so cack-handedly that Fortunate itches to seize the broom and do the job himself.

The landlord, when he arrives, seems of a different race to the drooping boy: a tall, shiny red-faced man packed with fat. Once more Fortunate explains his errand.

'Somewhere near the Oxford Road, I believe,' the man says, eyeing his shabby clothes. 'I was never there myself. Are you of the household?'

'Not now, Sir.'

'Hoping to get back into service?'

He nods. 'To find the Oxford Road, Sir?'

'Know the Spyglass Inn? Yes? Past there, then keep to the road until you reach a church. Then ask again.'

As he goes to the door, the sickly boy says to the other one, 'Queer do, leaving him behind like that,' as if Fortunate cannot hear it.

Coming up to the Spyglass sinks his spirits a little: he has spent a deal of time only to return to the same place. However, the land-lord thought that by walking briskly he might arrive at the Oxford Road within an hour. It seems Cosgrove's is a place known far and wide, even to people who have never seen it. Once arrived at the Oxford Road, he is sure to find it out.

The church is only a couple of miles. After that, on the advice of a beggar-woman, he branches off towards the south, onto a road where the houses soon become more frequent and, after a while, more elegant also. The road is better kept, making for easier walking, and when he first sees a number of spires in the distance his mood soars in sympathy. He lengthens his stride and picks up his pace.

It is not one but two hours before he arrives at the square where the great building is, to stand wet and hungry and contemplate his own foolishness. He pictured himself in a street, touching Dog Eye's sleeve, but at Cosgrove's nobody arrives at the door on foot. The entrance is fenced off from the square, the space inside the palings guarded by liveried servants. Guests are borne inside in sedan chairs, invisible until they appear at the windows.

Fortunate clenches his fists.

He has no alternative but to wait, perhaps wait so long that he loses his bed at the Spyglass and still does not find Dog Eye. Glancing around the square, he tries to judge how safe it is. The people seem peaceable for the most part but incoherent shouts warn him of the presence of roughs who will grow more boisterous as the hours pass. On his way here, he was rushed by such a man and knocked against a wall: it was a marvel that the pistols did not go off. The man stole nothing from him and Fortunate can only assume the brute took a dislike to his complexion. It has happened before.

Inside Cosgrove's, manservants are going about with tapers, bringing the chandeliers into bloom. The great room is finer even than Mr Watson's apartments in Maryland. Fortunate tries not to think about how warm it must be within.

More and more lights appear in the windows, as if to imitate day, and Fortunate notices people pushing forward to the palings. He has missed his chance. All the places along the front are already taken and he is not tall enough to look over their heads; he could stand further off in the square, but that would not help him.

Cosgrove's occupies one entire side of the square. At the right of it lies the entrance to a narrow street, now sunk in shadow, but Fortunate knows it is there, having entered the square from that side. The street bridges the gap between Cosgrove's and another terrace, forming a right angle with the club, the two terraces,

449

between them, making up half the square. This second line of houses has a garden at one end, forming a squarish gap between the two terraces, and in that garden stands a tree.

Fortunate studies the tree with interest. Though its trunk is concealed behind a wall, the branches spread wide onto the square and must surely offer a view of the lighted windows. Better still, it is one of those prickly trees that keep their leaves. If he slips away now, between the houses, and finds a way into the garden, he can get into the tree and sit concealed until Dog Eye appears.

He has taken only a few steps in that direction when he is pulled up short by the sight of a tall, shabby-looking woman who seems familiar. Has he seen her before? Perhaps she has been sent by the Wife. He hurries away from her, towards the road.

It is not until he has dropped down inside the garden wall that he remembers she used to visit the house. He was wise to avoid her. The maids said she was a spy and a person of no reputation.

Despite having formed no clear notion of Cosgrove's, Sophia is astonished by her first view of it: upon turning a corner she is confronted by a façade so commanding she cannot help but be impressed. The women approach in silence, Sophia admiring, though much against her will, the marriage of comfort, convenience and taste here represented. Nothing is left to be guessed at: the immense and speckless ground-floor windows – their panes must be polished every day – are left unshuttered, blazing into the dusk in such a way as to make a public stage of the interior. She gazes, ravished, upon the papered walls of the great salon (gold and green, one of her favourite combinations), its vast and lofty ceiling, its stucco frieze and its profusion of exquisite chandeliers. Not even the Assembly Rooms at Bath, until now her notion of a splendid gathering place, come anywhere near it.

Against this magnificent set the actors strut about, very much at their ease. The company is of a distinguished sort: gentlemen, naturally, but there is also perceptible an inner circle whose superlative tailoring marks them out as nobility. Some sit at cards or dice, while others look on, promenade about the room or engage in conversation. In all this, even from such a distance, Sophia perceives that grace of manner that distinguishes those of noble birth. She sees it in their very beckonings to the liveried manservants. The whole presents a delicious spectacle at which there is no shortage of lookers-on, frankly agape – as well they might be. For many of these people, spying into Cosgrove's is no doubt a regular entertainment.

'Are ladies ever admitted?'

When no answer comes she glances round to find her companion staring at the passers-by.

'Betsy-Ann? Are ladies ever admitted?'

Betsy-Ann turns towards her. 'No. Fairly knocks you back, eh? Cosgrove can keep watch on three games at once.'

'He must be a mathematical prodigy,' says Sophia, not entirely convinced.

'And rich.' Betsy-Ann whistles. 'He could buy half the gents in there. With their own gold.'

'You're acquainted with him?'

'Lord, no! It's the common talk, everyone knows Cosgrove, only,' a half-smile, 'I thought *you* might not. They say his manners are vulgar. Much he cares, I'm sure!'

'I suppose he's one of the marvels of the Age,' Sophia sniffs. She is examining the people within, as well as she can when they keep shifting about. Such company must play very deep: deeper, perhaps, than even Edmund would dare. 'What makes you think my husband might be here?'

'Seen him. Step away a minute – this way.'

A clutch of females is approaching, some of them linking arms. There is a trailing, languishing quality to their gait which Sophia notices even before she observes the familiar twitched-up gowns.

'Surely you can't think they'd mistake *me* for a rival?'

'They're in liquor,' says Betsy-Ann with a little air of patience. The women pass through the square and out again, doing no more than glance at the gamblers. They do well, thinks Sophia, not to attempt men ensnared by such potent distractions.

'They'll be back later,' Betsy-Ann says, 'when it's played out.'

'Is that very late?'

'Could be morning.'

'I can't stay until then!'

'No need. He generally comes to the window after a bit, to take the air.'

'Won't he recognise me?'

Betsy-Ann laughs. 'In the dark, with a veil? And what if he did? I know who'd be more frightened.' Evidently Edmund has never hit Betsy-Ann Blore. 'He'll neither see you nor hurt you. But keep an eye out for foysters – nothing they like better than to find everyone staring, nobody with a mind to his purse – no, don't feel for it, you daisy!'

Stamping her feet to warm them, Sophia studies the knots of people engaged in spying on Cosgrove's, to see if anyone is standing suspiciously close. Each group is lit along one edge, their faces gilded by the blazing windows of the club, their backs lost to view. She notices with concern an elderly man leaning on a stick, perilously close to some wizened children who are just of a height to slip their hands into his pockets. There is also a sprinkling of discreetly clad individuals, perhaps small traders taking the air before bedtime. She wonders if they envy the pleasures of their betters.

'Mister Stick there,' whispers Betsy-Ann. 'He's an old hand. Empty your pocket as soon as cough.'

'But he looks so respectable.'

'Good foysters can afford good togs.'

The square is starting to fill with loiterers. Hucksters thread their way among them, offering gin and evil-smelling meat pies. From time to time chairs arrive, bearing their occupants through the lower orders and inside the doors of the club. As each one passes under the lintel, Sophia wonders if Edmund is within and her heart beats a little faster at being so close to him, unseen.

Betsy-Ann makes a hissing sound. 'Sweet Christ!'

'What?' Again Sophia surveys the company within the gaming-house. 'Is he there?'

'Listen to me and don't look round.' Betsy-Ann's voice has sunk to an urgent whisper. 'We're being watched. Hold still and look through the windows like you're doing.'

'Who is it? Edmund?'

Betsy-Ann's only answer is to pull the hood of her cloak as far forward as it will go.

'Shall we go away?'

'Let me think,' her companion mutters. 'Hold still, God damn you —'

But Sophia has already turned. She moves back smartly to her previous position, having glimpsed nothing – unless it was the hem of a coat, the back of a leg, vanishing into a group of people. More than that, she is unable to distinguish. Those in the square are now so numerous that they might be referred to as a crowd, and her eyes, from having stared for so long at the lit windows, are ill adapted to shade.

'Can't you tell me what it is?'

There is a pause before Betsy-Ann whispers, 'We have to toddle. Watch where I go, count twenty and follow. If you lose me, or see me in company, go home directly.' Her hood still tight around her face, she moves off, as if for a stroll, towards one of the roads leading out of the square.

Despite her best efforts, Sophia loses sight of her almost at once. Turning back to Cosgrove's, she perceives a male figure, not behind the great windows but standing at a smaller, though equally bright, aperture on the first floor. He appears to be waiting while one of the liveried servants attempts to raise the sash. Agitated, she squints through her veil, trying at one and the same time to pick out Betsy-Ann and study the fellow at the window.

The sash is up —

Yes.

How handsome he is, in a coat of dark blue. How he must relish his privileged position, looking down upon all these gapers! Vice triumphing over virtue? Hardly. Some of those below are plainly marked with ignorance, cruelty and vice: made privy to the detestable fraud of her marriage, they might well side with the gentleman, considering him a species of Marital Highwayman and a regular blade.

Yet there must also be among the onlookers some honest citizens. What do *they* make of Edmund? It is hard to know what she herself makes of him; hard, through the gauze of the veil, even to distinguish his expression, but she thinks she can detect an amused air, as if Edmund is saying to himself, 'Well, my good people, there you are in the cold and here am I among India carpets, chandeliers and champagne. I suppose you'll own that I've bested you?'

But you shan't best everybody. She steps forward, intending to find Betsy-Ann, when she is seized by the wrist.

Whirling around, she finds herself confronted by Harry Blore.

She has always imagined that if seized by a bully she would cry in a ringing voice, 'How dare you, Sir! Release me directly!' Now the moment is come, and Sophia surrounded by persons unknown, courage fails her and it is Blore who speaks.

'Shape yourself.'

That is all: just those two words. He pushes her in the direction

454

of Cosgrove's, marching her at such a pace that she has to trot to keep up, turning her face aside from the foul odour he exudes. When she trips on the cobbles, about to tumble headlong, he grasps her arm so that she merely sinks to her knees. But the rescue comes at a price: a hideous wrenching at her shoulderblade, so painful that it forces a cry.

'Get up, you bitch,' he says, jiggling her sore arm and piercing her shoulder with white-hot skewers.

Despite the menace, his voice is flat and business-like: she is an object to him, a means. Trembling, she scrambles to her feet, seeking an indignant countenance among the onlookers. She meets only averted eyes, blank stares or (most terrible of all) amusement. No rescue will come from these people. Like a tethered lamb she walks alongside her captor towards the great windows.

At first she thinks Edmund has recognised them, since he seems to be looking in their direction. Then she realises he has merely observed the stir caused by their pushing forward; from where he stands, even Blore's conspicuous stature would scarcely be noticeable and besides, Edmund is looking from a brilliantly lighted room onto darkness. In a moment he glances away again. Seen closer to, he appears not amused but abstracted: a man above common care.

Blore halts, breathing brandy into Sophia's face. 'Now. See what I have here?'

She looks down, since that seems to be his meaning, and perceives a metallic gleam.

'Know what that is?' Her throat dry, Sophia nods, though in truth she is not sure. 'Now, should you take a fancy to cry out, or run off, or queer my pitch any way whatsoever, you shall have a taste.'

He takes hold of her torn shoulder for emphasis, causing her to gasp. Suppose he should wrench at her? Would she be able to suppress a scream?

'Pray Sir,' she manages to whisper. 'My arm. Don't pull on it, I beg of you, or I may cry out unawares.'

'Then you'll nab it unawares.'

She has to grit her teeth against the pain, but it is only a few more steps before he stops and flings up his massive head.

'Hartry!' he bellows.

This one word apparently suffices for Edmund to recognise the speaker. He makes as if to move back from the window, then halts.

'Now, Ned, don't be shy! Here's your Mrs Sophy,' Blore tugs at her hood and veil, 'a-keeping me company!'

With the raising of the veil, Sophia observes a fleeting expression cross Edmund's face: horror, at once masked by his customary *sang-froid*. He has not yet found them in the crowd, as evidenced by the turnings of his head, but he knows and dreads that voice.

Blore chuckles to himself. Sophia realises what she might have realised before, had she been less terrified: the man is intoxicated. It occurs to her that he may sway, clutch at her torn muscle and force from her the shriek that will end her life. Or does he intend to murder her in any case, as a proxy for Edmund?

'I've been looking for you, Ned!' Blore is bawling. 'Come down and talk, man to man.'

At last Edmund seems to distinguish Harry Blore's height and bulk. She wonders what he makes of the spectacle of Blore and herself together, and how he imagines they have come there.

Whatever his conclusions, he evidently decides to brazen things out. He makes a show of flicking some dust from his sleeve before calling in a languid, mocking tone, 'I wish you joy of the lady,' a sentiment which is greeted with a huzzah from some person behind her and hisses from others.

'What, Ned! Your own dear lady wife?' The emphasis with which Blore speaks these last words renders them obscene. 'Don't

456

be shabby, man. Be a sportsman, come down.'

Edmund looks as if he could be so much a sportsman as to tear Blore in pieces, had he only the strength. Somebody in the crowd screams, 'Go to your wife, you dunghill!' and is answered by a voice further back:

'He ain't dunghill, he's game – come down, mate!'

There are inarticulate cries, jeers, whistles. A shrill female urges Sophia to go into Cosgrove's and fetch out the erring spouse. The cry is taken up by other women in the crowd. Edmund steps back from the window and bangs down the sash.

'Don't you stir a finger,' growls Blore.

Sophia can hear a braying voice, further back, referring to her as *the whore*. She is filled with an unspeakable nausea, as if her body were corrupting from the inside out. Once before, as a girl, she experienced such a sensation: it was the prelude to a faint. Will she faint now? Not even Blore can prevent it: but how appalling to be unconscious and in the power of such a man! And where is Betsy-Ann? Where the square is not illuminated by the blazing windows of Cosgrove's, its shade is impenetrable: Betsy-Ann might be twenty feet away or scurrying through the night streets, leaving Sophia to fend for herself.

Sophia's terror is absolute. Has she been decoyed here by Betsy-Ann, in order to serve Harry? Is she nothing but a *flat*, as these people say, a decoy with which brother and sister hope to ensnare Edmund?

On the ground floor of Cosgrove's, gentlemen have come to the window and are shading their eyes against the lighted glass. Outside, knots of onlookers are being swallowed up into the larger crowd, swelling it by the minute: there is shoving, boorish laughter, an atmosphere of excited anticipation. Once more it is borne in upon Sophia how alone she is. Among gentlemen she might appeal to bystanders for protection, but what help can she expect here? Blore is one of their own.

457

Insufferably arrogant and blind, to ignore the advice of Mama, and of Hetty. With sickening horror she sees it all: she has allowed Betsy-Ann to insinuate herself – abject folly! – and this is her reward, and who knows how it will end?

The door of Cosgrove's opens and Edmund strolls out, accompanied by two well-set men in livery. A second brace of liveried fellows guards the entrance. Edmund frowns, studying the crowd; it is a moment before he again locates Blore and Sophia, after which he moves towards them, taking care, however, to keep behind the railings that separate him from the onlookers.

'Come along, Madam,' he calls, beckoning to Sophia. 'Come away from that brute. You have leave from Mr Cosgrove to enter the premises.'

Her mouth is disagreeably full of saliva, so that she has to swallow before she can whisper to Blore, 'May I speak with him?'

Blore does not answer. Some of the bystanders are calling out, 'Come along! Come along, Madam!' in high facetious voices.

Dear God –

Her belly contracts and urges, propelling a sour, viscous brew onto the cobbles. Sophia hangs her head, panting. Fan's pelisse has caught a splash or two, but nobody else was within range of the vileness: where Blore goes, others give room. Dreading a sudden yank upon her arm, she straightens herself, striving to keep pace with her captor.

Blore ignores her plight, if he is even aware of it, and raises his voice again: 'I see you daren't come alone, Ned.' The onlookers are laughing: some at Edmund, and a smaller number, close by, at Sophia's clumsy attempts to wipe her mouth on her sleeve. Blore has never stopped moving forwards. He is now only a few yards from Edmund, continuing to bawl at the top of his lungs, rallying the mob to his side.

Edmund's face is frigid. 'You're detaining that lady against her will.'

'You're her husband, ain't you? Come and rescue her! Step up!'

Some fool is screeching, 'Form a ring! Fair fight!'

Frowning and biting a fingernail as the catcalls increase, Edmund moves back. He is plainly unsettled: at a loss how to deal. In all that perplexity, vanity and fear, is there, Sophia wonders, the smallest admixture of care for herself?

At any rate, he appears to have reached a decision: his shoulders sit lower, his mouth twitches as if at a pungent witticism. When he raises his arms to the crowd, he might be Mr Garrick calming the pit at Drury Lane.

'Friends! In the interests of fair play – dear to the heart of every Englishman – hear me out!'

They are unsure what to make of him, Sophia can see: some of these people take a delight in pelting with filth anyone so finely clothed. But Edmund is Edmund, and possessed of all the charm that implies.

'Let him talk,' from the crowd.

Blore sneers, 'Why don't you meet me, man to man?' but Edmund has succeeded in catching the interest of those around. They may stamp him into the ground, thinks Sophia, but they'll hear him out first.

'He's a regular sport, eh, ladies and gents? A fine fellow, because he takes advantage of his size to insult me, and insult the lady. But you're deceived. Take another look at him – he's a man you won't often see by day.'

Blore shouts, 'Mind your tongue, whoreson.'

'He's a night bird – a resurrectionist! He digs up pretty wenches and brides just married, aye, and your infants at the breast, little angels, and sells 'em to be ottomised.'

At once Sophia is conscious of a new sound issuing from the onlookers, a kind of spiteful hum. Even the most degraded wretches loathe the resurrectionists: Betsy-Ann told her that. Sure enough, a woman screams: 'Shame on him! Shame!'

'Scrag him!'

Blore's huge head swivels from side to side, weighing up the odds. With the prize-fighter's sense of when to strike, he flings away Sophia's hand and makes a rush at Edmund, the crowd leaping back. Edmund no longer seems to be enjoying his moment: he turns to flee but trips and sprawls on the flagstones just within the railings. Blore hurls himself over them, lands heavily on the other side, stumbles in his turn and falls beside Edmund.

Sophia's throat, which has been paralysed by shock, now opens up, enabling her to cry, 'He's armed! He's armed!'

The liveried servants run forward, seize hold of Blore and manage to pull him upright, upon which one of them is kicked and left doubled up on the cobbles. The other plucks at the back of Blore's coat, trying to restrain him, and is flung off as a bull might fling off a terrier. By this time Edmund is likewise upright, but not escaped; Blore catches hold of his arm and the pair of them whirl round in a clumsy dance. The spectators close on them, presenting Sophia with a view of their backs. She stands helpless, clenching her hands.

There is a sudden loud report, followed by screams, including Sophia's. With a roar, the crowd fractures, some pushing this way, some that. Does she hear the sound again? So many women are screaming that she cannot tell. Everywhere men are forcing their way through the crush, dealing with their neighbours as they might with so many senseless blocks. Sophia is knocked off balance, whirled among them like a bobbing cork: it is as much as she can do to avoid being pulled down and trampled.

Someone is tugging at her bad arm. 'He followed me,' pants Betsy-Ann Blore. 'Quick, come this way.'

'What happened? Did you see?'

'This way!'

'Is Edmund hurt?'

'For the love of Christ! I don't know. Come, will you?'

There is nothing to do but follow. Betsy-Ann leads her along the edge of the crowd, skirts the rear and travels by a circuitous route by three sides of the square before turning back towards Cosgrove's. By the time they once more approach the railings the crush is greatly thinned. Even so, the scene outside that celebrated establishment now resembles a public performance, the lower sort flattened against the railings in their eagerness to miss nothing of the action while the gentler spectators, raised above the stage, have actually mounted their chairs for a better view, their faces pressed so tightly to the glass that they appear stacked row upon row. As a result, much of the light from the interior is blocked. Of Edmund and Blore nothing is visible: try as she may, Sophia is unable to see past the hats of those in front.

'Let us through, *if* you please!' bawls Betsy-Ann. Her strong arms and stronger voice make way through the packed bodies so that Sophia, following in her footsteps, feels she has exchanged captors, Blore brother for Blore sister. When they finally reach the entrance the remaining spectators are loath to give place. Betsy-Ann stations herself at the gap between the railings, surveys those nearby and lights on a small, dowdy woman. This person she shoves aside, ignoring her curses, and wedges herself into the place thus created, at the same time dragging Sophia in front of her, much as she might a child.

From here Sophia can see her husband and Harry Blore stretched on the ground, so close together that Blore's massive head, bloody and misshapen, rests in the crook of Edmund's arm. Three liveried servants stand between her and the fallen men, blocking the way in case the mob should start to spill in there; three more are keeping a wary eye out for anyone who might vault the railings. One man is squatting, feeling Edmund's neck.

'His wife!' Betsy-Ann shouts for the benefit of the servants. 'Let her through.'

At once those around them turn and gape. Sophia has the

impression that they had forgotten that part of the story, and are glad to go on with it. The servants stay where they are, but one of them calls, 'Is that correct, Madam? You are married to this gentleman?'

'To Mr Zedland.'

The man hesitates. 'The gentleman who jumped the rails?'

'The other. In the blue coat.'

'That's Mr Hartry,' says the servant.

'It's the same man.' She sees his distrust: who can blame him? She has given the wrong name, her plain clothing makes a poor show against Edmund's fine coat and the servant perhaps witnessed her approach alongside Blore. She holds up her head and speaks in her most genteel manner.

'This woman is the sister of the other —' No, she cannot call Blore a gentleman. 'I'm aware that we hardly seem – all will be explained, but please, *please* may I go to my husband? I beg of you —'

She moves towards Edmund but the man at once blocks her. 'I must ask you to stay back, Madam. The gentlemen are our responsibility.'

'Has a surgeon been sent for?' asks Betsy-Ann.

The man nods. 'I believe so.'

Sophia clasps her hands in supplication. 'Then for pity's sake take him inside, before the cold kills him.' A boy has arrived with lanterns and she can see a glistening dark stain spreading from beneath Edmund's right armpit down the side of his coat.

Another manservant, hearing this, proves more conciliatory: he assures her that both combatants are to be taken indoors as soon as hurdles can be procured. The ladies can rest assured that the greatest conceivable care will be taken, and he will personally enquire of Mr Cosgrove if they themselves may be admitted.

'Tell Mr Cosgrove I'm Mrs Hartry,' calls Sophia as he walks

away. She watches the servant disappear into the house as if he were the one remaining hope of her life.

'That's the last we'll see of him,' mutters Betsy-Ann. He returns directly, however, to inform Sophia that she and 'the other lady' may accompany the injured gent and must give what information they can.

Under the servant's watchful eyes, Sophia is permitted to approach. She sinks down and takes Edmund's head in her lap, turning up his face towards her own.

For Blore, nothing can be done. A ball shattered his skull: it seems that life departed his frame even before he hit the flagstones. His huge corpse, rolled onto a hurdle carried by two grunting men, is taken into the house and an expressionless Betsy-Ann informed that until matters have been 'looked into' it cannot be fetched away.

Blore thus disposed of, a hurdle is fetched for Edmund who, limp and bloodied, is brought inside the club. Greedy for scandal, gamesters pour out of the salon into the lobby: Sophia has a confused impression of stumbling between two long lines of faces. Not until she has gained the landing do the men drift back into the salon to resume play.

In a private chamber on the first floor Mr Cosgrove, an undistinguished individual with red hands, receives her with courtesy and even kindness, begging her to make herself at home. He takes Betsy-Ann to one side, conferring with her briefly before returning to assure Sophia that help is on its way. In the meantime, the ladies are to have everything they need. Sure enough, servants arrive bearing port wine, and cordial, and biscuits, and spirit of hartshorn, and tea: an endless succession of futile comforts. So unobservant has misery rendered Sophia that she sees nothing in this but common humanity. It falls to Betsy-Ann to point out that Cosgrove's attentions, though acceptable in themselves, are managed in such a way that Mrs Hartry and Miss Blore are never left alone with the victim.

Their spying is of no consequence to Sophia. She arranges herself beside her husband, now laid on a truckle bed, and attempts to staunch his bleeding by pressing a pad of linen to his side. Though a maid has offered to take over this duty, Sophia refuses to let her. Already a heap of stained clouts is forming at her feet: the sight fills her with both dread and hope, for as long as he continues to bleed, Edmund's heart still beats.

Betsy-Ann is seated nearby, sipping at a glass of port wine. She has not spoken a word for some time, seeming wrapped up in contemplation.

'What will you do about your brother?' Sophia asks at last. 'The funeral.'

'He can go in with Keshlie.'

'In your sister's grave? Where is that?'

'The poor's pit.'

Sophia winces.

'You surely didn't think I'd pay.' Betsy-Ann drains the glass and sets it down with an air of defiance.

Sophia wets a clean scrap of linen and begins to sponge Edmund's temples. Her words, when they come, are calm and measured. 'To forgive such a man as your brother must be difficult. But he can do you no wrong now, and has need of your prayers.'

'He's no need of anything where he's gone.'

Sophia lays down the linen. 'How can you talk so,' she exclaims, 'when God hears your every word? Only think, your brother has gone before God guilty of self-slaughter.'

Betsy-Ann starts. 'He shot himself? You *saw* that?'

'I saw the weapon.' She shudders at the recollection. 'He shot Edmund and then himself.'

'What's he done with the pistol then?' Betsy-Ann is regarding her in a most peculiar manner. 'They can't find it. Not on the flags, not on Harry's body.'

'How do you know?'

'Cosgrove said, when first we came in.'

'But your brother showed it me.'

'Then you'll have to give your evidence,' says Betsy-Ann. She rises and comes to feel Edmund's hand. 'He's cursed cold. Don't you think he's cold?'

Sophia is trying to remember precisely what she saw in the dark: a faint metallic gleam.

'It could have been a knife,' she says. But Betsy-Ann gestures towards Edmund's wound and shakes her head.

Despite the linen pad, the blood continues to flow. Sophia stands in order to press down more firmly. She holds out the linen to Betsy-Ann, thinking she might want to take a turn, but the other woman backs off, saying only, 'He may yet come through it.'

'If only he would, for just a few seconds! I could tell him I forgive him.'

Betsy-Ann's voice cracks like a whiplash. 'And if he lives?'

'If he lives?'

'You'll have him riding the three-legged mare, you and your Mr Gingumbob. Forgive him then hang him, isn't that the plan?'

Sophia stands astonished at the injustice of this, and at the naked animosity in Betsy-Ann's sloe eyes. 'But I told you,' she said. 'The plan was – is, to negotiate a separation. You were in agreement. Why, it was you that told me who he was!'

'*I* wanted him bitten. That was my way.'

'Not at first —' But seeing the other woman's expression, she realises there can be no reasoning with her, and is forced to change tack. 'Look how reduced he is,' she says softly. 'We can both forgive him.'

'Not I,' says Betsy-Ann. 'And I'm not a-going to hang over him

465

pretending. Though I could talk as soft as you, too, with a Mr Gingumbob to tie the noose for me.'

To this Sophia can find no reply. She could do very well, at the moment, without the company of Betsy-Ann Blore.

The surgeon is a man of middling age, whose florid and corpulent person attests to a thriving practice. Rubbing his hands together to warm them, he approaches the truckle bed.

'May I present myself? Mr Wilson, Madam, come to be of assistance to Mr Hartry.'

As Sophia stands to greet him, blood drops from the cloth she is holding onto the carpet. 'I am Mrs Hartry. This lady is Miss Blore.'

The surgeon looks from one shabby woman to the other. 'Indeed,' he says. 'Well. Let us lose no time.'

He feels for Edmund's pulse.

'Will he recover?' Sophia asks. 'Will he know me?'

'Shhh —!'

They are obliged to wait in silence. Letting Edmund's wrist drop back on the bed, the surgeon frowns. He proceeds to thumb open each eyelid, peering close as if to read inside Edmund's brain. To Sophia there is something nightmarish about the eyes thus exposed: glaring and blind as the rolled-up eyeballs of a poisoned dog Radley once showed her. She is relieved when the eyelids are thumbed down again.

'You didn't think to take off his coat and shirt?'

'I was afraid of hurting him. Of doing harm, I mean.'

'He was insensible, then, at first?'

'I believe so.'

'Has the bleeding decreased at all since he came in?'

'I can't tell —' Her voice cracks. 'I've tried to staunch it.'

'You've done no harm, Mrs Hartry, and may have done good,' says the surgeon, relenting. With a pair of silver scissors he commences snipping at Edmund's coat, pausing only to order the maids to bring in more coals. 'He must not be allowed to lose vital warmth.'

'I said he was cold,' observes Betsy-Ann.

Edmund's coat and shirt are cut away at the front. Taking a fresh clout, the surgeon cleans the wound with deft swabbing movements.

'If you would be so good as to help me turn the patient.'

'I'm not sure I'm able to.' Sophia blushes at her uselessness. 'My shoulder —'

'Here,' says Betsy-Ann Blore. She holds Edmund up so that the surgeon can cut away more of his clothing. Seeing the sheet beneath soaked in gore, Sophia gasps.

'Just keep him there, miss,' says the surgeon.

Despite welling blood, the injury to Edmund's breast is small, even neat. Now Sophia utters a cry of incredulous horror: the flesh of his back is torn open, scarlet and ragged as beef. She thought she was helping, dabbing at what now seems the merest scratch, while all the time —

'Dear God!' she wails.

Betsy-Ann has turned her face aside.

'It's a nasty one, right enough,' Mr Wilson says coolly, as if examining a sprain.

'Is it?' A stupid question, but her voice has grown so feeble and husky at the sight of Edmund's insides obscenely exposed to the air that perhaps the surgeon did not catch it.

'The ball flattens, you see.' He indicates the wound in Edmund's chest. 'He was shot from front to back.'

'Will he have to be cut, Sir?' Betsy-Ann's voice is hardened by the strain of supporting Edmund's torso upright.

The surgeon continues to dab and wipe. At last he is finished, and gives the signal for the patient to be returned to his original position. As Betsy-Ann lets him down, Edmund utters a peculiar groan.

'Is he in pain?'

'Only in a manner of speaking, Mrs, er —'

'Hartry.'

'Mrs Hartry. Your husband is like a man asleep. Sensation is faint, as in a dream, and passes in an instant.' He holds up his hand for silence. 'There. You perceive he has ceased groaning.'

Betsy-Ann Blore looks as if she has heard such comfort before, and found it barren. She repeats, 'Will he have to be cut?'

'The ball's already out. But there's splintered bone – a tricky business – and bleeding in the lungs.'

'Is that very dangerous?' Sophia asks.

'Few things are more so.' He speaks with a grave emphasis, his eyes turned full upon her. 'It would be wicked of me to pretend otherwise.'

'Is there any chance of his knowing me?'

He lays his hand upon hers: a fatherly gesture, intended to impart endurance.

'My dear Madam, what am I to say? You naturally desire your husband to regain consciousness. Try to bear in mind that insensibility can be an instance of Divine Mercy. Were he conscious, his suffering would be intolerable.'

It comes to Sophia that the man talks only of suffering or lack of it.

'You don't expect him to live.'

'He *may*,' Wilson quietly corrects her, 'but I think it unlikely. I shall do my utmost, but my best advice is to prepare yourself. Pray for him, and leave the rest to Heaven.'

'Edmund would laugh at prayer.' The wretched tears, that have never gone quite away, are pricking now in her eyes and throat. 'He has lived a very – *imperfect* life. How, in his present state, can he make his peace with God?'

'That, I'm afraid, is a question I cannot answer,' replies the surgeon. 'But consider: how can we know what might be passing in your husband's soul, even as we speak? To God all things are possible.' He gives her hand one final pat and moves away to rummage in his bag.

Edmund is again raised in the strong arms of Betsy-Ann Blore, turned and laid on his side. The blood around the smaller wound is beginning to congeal.

Sophia stands aside, forcing herself to watch as Edmund is probed for splinters, then stitched up, his breath coming with an ominous wheeze. The spring before her marriage, Papa's hunter, Blaze, impaled himself on a fence. Radley told Mama that the horse bubbled bloody foam at the mouth: will Edmund do that? Perhaps he *is* conscious, paralysed, speechless, suffering unimaginably as his flesh is gathered and crimped under the needle.

Or perhaps he dreams himself safe, strolling amid pleasant gardens, when he was never more in danger: his soul, the immortal part of him, hangs upon the brink of the abyss.

Nothing, she thinks, is more important than such moments. We know it as we sit by a sickbed or kneel by a grave. Then we arise, and go about the world's business, and forget.

'Sir,' Betsy-Ann Blore is saying. Sophia becomes aware that Edmund's breathing has changed, the wheeze grown shallower and more ragged.

The surgeon shakes his head.

'What's happening to him, Sir?'

'It's as I thought, the internal bleeding.' He cuts the thread with which he has pulled Edmund together like so much cloth. 'If we keep him propped up, Miss, it will help him to breathe. You,' he beckons to one of Cosgrove's spying maids, 'get cushions for his back.'

Edmund moans. Sophia is on her knees directly, crying into his ear: 'Repent, Edmund! God will forgive you —' so that the surgeon is obliged to edge her aside in order to continue propping the patient. Straightening, she sees Betsy-Ann's sleeves rolled up, her naked forearms bloodied and trembling with the effort of holding Edmund's torso upright.

'He's going,' the maid says, as if seeing a tradesman off the premises. Since it is his privilege to pronounce upon the patient's condition, the surgeon does not reply. He again takes up Edmund's wrist, feeling for the pulse, then lays it down with a gentleness that tells Sophia everything she dreads to know. With a cry of exhaustion Betsy-Ann gives way, allowing Edmund to sink back.

Sophia kneels once more by the side of the bed, clasping Edmund's hand between her own. It is in this manner that she sees her husband die, insensible of either wife or mistress. His breathing ceases abruptly, without any marked change beforehand; his eyes remain closed but his mouth falls a little open. The maid, with a knowing look, pinches it shut. Sophia watches Edmund's face grow pale, as if the skull is working its way up to the surface of his skin. His mortal flesh is now a death mask; the immortal Edmund is fled, gone to stand before the Judgement Seat. What can he find to say there, after such a life! Yet God is Love and has Eternity to hear his creature's plea and consider it, perhaps to forgive.

'A very sad business, a dreadful business,' the surgeon murmurs. Sophia realises that her torn shoulder is pincered with pain. She does not move away; it seems as if she and Edmund are suffering together, even though he is no longer here. 'Altogether shocking. Such a fine fellow' (will he never hold his tongue?) 'should have lived to see seventy.'

Even the heartless maid is now gazing on Edmund. Around the bed, the living are fixed, fascinated by death, until Sophia has to swallow down a hysterical urge to laugh.

It is not until the sheet is pulled over Edmund's face that Sophia realises she has not the wherewithal to pay the surgeon. She stammers out an apology but the man assures her this is quite unnecessary. Nor will he call at her house: it is already agreed that Mr Cosgrove will settle the account.

'Let him, since he wants to,' whispers Betsy-Ann. 'Takes off some of the scandal.'

Sophia has not sufficient strength for contention. She submits, asking only what she should do about the body.

'That will depend upon your personal arrangements,' replies the surgeon. 'You may send someone to bring him away. I'm sure Mr Cosgrove will help, so far as it lies within his power.'

'He is too kind.' How does one arrange a funeral in this city? For that matter, she has no very clear idea of how it would be done at Buller, but supposes Papa would speak with the minister and the carpenter, who between them would engage everyone else. Here she has nobody to whom she can apply. So very private has her religion become that even the habit of churchgoing has fallen away.

It occurs to her that collecting the remains is only the beginning of her perplexities. Should Edmund be interred in the chapel at Buller Hall? How intolerable to pray there, with his memorial in full view! Besides, he was never of the place, and despised everything it stood for; had he become master, he would have pillaged the estate. And then the business of the inscription: Mr Zedland, or Mr Hartry?

Was the man lying on the bed ever her husband at all?

Downstairs a man in a greasy wig is writing in a notebook. Cosgrove presents him as an officer, come to take statements about the night's dreadful events, and asks if Mrs Hartry is equal to answering his questions. Mrs Hartry replies that she is. She explains that she had not seen her husband for some days, and fearing his taste for gaming had got the better of him, had come to the club to see if he was there. While waiting in the crowd she was attacked and threatened by Harry Blore, to whom Mr Hartry owed money. A humiliating scene ensued, followed by Blore's assault upon her husband.

'Did you see Mr Blore fire the fatal shot?'

471

'I heard it. He showed me the pistol earlier.'

The man, a skilled scribe, notes her answers almost as quickly as she can produce them. When he looks up his eyes are shrewd.

'And the other lady? What is her part in all this?'

Sophia is at a loss.

'Harry Blore was my brother,' says Betsy-Ann. 'My name is Betsy-Ann Blore.'

'Did you know Mrs Hartry before tonight?'

'Miss Blore was a friend of my husband,' Sophia replies, having by now worked out that the flimsiest investigation will reveal Betsy-Ann's visits to the house. 'I'm not familiar with London and I wished to see Cosgrove's. She offered to accompany me.'

'Very obliging, I'm sure,' says the man, sitting back and putting the quill between his teeth. He's letting her see that he's noticed the garments. 'And you disguised yourself? Made something of a . . . a prank of it?'

'I wished not to be recognised.'

'And why was that, Mrs Hartry?'

'So my husband shouldn't think I was spying on him.' *Although I was.* It rings so loudly in Sophia's ears that surely the man can hear it.

'It's fortunate for you, Mrs Hartry, that you were standing where you were. A number of witnesses have confirmed that you were placed almost opposite the door when the shot was fired.'

'Do you mean it might have hit me?'

'I mean you could been under suspicion. We found no pistol on Mr Blore or anywhere near his body. Several persons report the shots as coming from further off, from a tree at the edge of the square. We believe there may have been an assassin concealed amid its branches. The first shot hit Mr Hartry, the second Mr Blore.'

'Someone in a *tree*?'

'That's my information. Are you quite sure, Mrs Hartry, that Mr Blore showed you a pistol?'

'I saw something shiny. He said I'd get a taste of it.'

'Something shiny,' the man repeats. 'Not necessarily a pistol.'

'He carried a shiv,' says Betsy-Ann.

'Is that so?' He reaches into his pocket and brings out a brutal-looking knife. 'And is this the one?' The haft is of some dull grey metal, the blade about eight inches long.

Betsy-Ann nods. 'Could be.'

'I doubt he meant to use this on Mr Hartry,' the officer tells her. 'Too many witnesses. He wanted the satisfaction of milling him, that's all. Someone else had different ideas.'

'But he *was* holding the knife?' Sophia asks.

'We found it between the flagstones. It's my opinion that he lost it as he fell.'

They are ushered into Mr Cosgrove's personal carriage with assurances of continuing assistance. The man has been kind far beyond what was expedient: at the memory of her earlier contempt, Sophia's face floods with shame.

As they are driven away she cannot help but look back. Behind the great windows the players continue unabashed, no doubt stimulated by the frisson of passion and scandal attaching to tonight's events. Rain has begun to fall. Night air and drizzle are sucked into the carriage but she lacks the energy to shut them out: it is Betsy-Ann who leans forward and closes the blind. 'What will you do now, Madam? Go back to Zedland?'

For an instant Sophia thinks it is Edmund she means. 'I expect so,' she says. Her future existence rises before her in pitiless detail: that poor dupe Sophy Buller, the talk of every tea party, her life a blend of ennui and humiliation.

'It'll be hard for you after Town,' says Betsy-Ann, who seems to have forgotten her earlier fury. 'Unless you leave your papa's house, you know.'

'Marry, you mean?' She can barely restrain a laugh: Edmund

not yet in the ground, and his mistress matchmaking on his wife's behalf! She toys with the idea of informing Betsy-Ann that – Edmund having squandered her modest portion, partly on Betsy-Ann herself – she has nothing with which to attract a suitor.

'All men aren't alike,' says Betsy-Ann.

'Thank God.'

'Once you're over this, you'll be right enough. Comfortable.'

If Sophia were not so beaten down she would order the woman to stop prattling. Comfortable! Possibly this is for Betsy-Ann a mode of begging, of hinting that her own prospects are unappealing, but the truth of the matter is that at present, Sophia cannot care about Betsy-Ann Blore. Her sentiments are desiccated, hard, parched: in a nutshell, used up. Even the thought of her parents produces only a sullen dread. They will want to preach and moralise when the sole thing she craves is privacy, the better to grieve. For the grief has barely started: she has seen enough mourners to know that.

'I could perhaps work for a chaunter cull,' says Betsy-Ann. 'I make up songs in my head but I can't write 'em. I reckon he could put me to use.'

'Indeed,' says Sophia.

She insists that the driver go first to Betsy-Ann's lodging. By the time they arrive, the moon has come out from behind the clouds and Sophia has sufficient curiosity about this place, which she has so long imagined, to exert herself and raise the window blind. There stands Miss Blore, ghostly on the house steps, her face turned back towards the carriage while she fumbles for her key and the driver, instructed by Cosgrove, waits to see her safely inside. Sophia also waits, with a sense that some part of her life is ending, unwitnessed, in this obscure street. At last the key is produced. As Betsy-Ann puts it to the lock and enters, a glimmering candle appears at a top-floor window: the landlady, Sophia

474

supposes, curious to see what company her lodger keeps.

She feigns not to see Betsy-Ann's wave of farewell. Instead, she sits back in the shadowed interior as the vehicle pulls away. Afterwards she remembers: the lodging was not the one she wanted to see, the one where Betsy-Ann was installed by Edmund. She was mistaken in that, as in so many things.

At her own house she happens to glance upwards in alighting. There are chinks of light between the first-floor shutters. The candles should all be snuffed, and the servants in bed: evidently they are profiting by her absence. She hands the driver the shilling she had saved for a chair on the way home.

The bell brings a sound of footsteps within but to her surprise, no extinguishing of the lights upstairs, which have evidently been forgotten. What does it matter? She will soon be rid of the entire household.

A faint rustle announces the arrival of a maid at the door.

'Who is it?' Fan's voice is anxious.

'Mrs Zedland.'

'Mrs Zedland, Madam — !' The bolt shoots and there at last is Fan, candle in hand.

Sophia wonders what the driver makes of Mrs Zedland who is also Mrs Hartry, but he is already moving off. She steps inside, fatigue sucking at her. Fan helps her off with the pelisse: if she recognises it, she gives no sign.

'Forgive my asking, Madam, but is anything amiss? We thought you'd had an accident, or you were lost —'

'You see I'm not.'

'— and you have company, you see —'

Company, at this hour? She starts as a man's step is heard descending the stair.

'Mr Letcher?'

'Sophy? Is that you?'

'Papa!' For Papa it is, holding out a lamp, and behind him,

beyond its dim circle of light, an indistinct figure in a night wrapper: Mama.

Instead of coming directly to embrace her, Papa holds the lamp aloft and studies his daughter. Once more, Sophia is aware that her shoes are damp and disagreeable, her entire appearance bedraggled in the extreme. Papa exclaims in disgust. 'What's that smell?'

'Vomit,' Sophia murmurs. 'Blood.'

'*Blood?* What the Deuce —?'

Mama hurries forward. 'O, my darling, are you hurt? Shall we send for help? Who did this to you – Edmund?'

50

O I am one loves company
Drink up
With drink and dancing night and day
Drink up drink up
Give me a man with an open purse
A merry heart, a mighty tarse
Who'll love and never count it loss
Drink up drink up drink up

Damn parsons they're but buzzing flies
Drink up
That fill men's heads with canting lies
Drink up drink up
Gay company's the thing my boys
With kisses and with pretty toys
To find the way to sweetest joys
Drink up drink up drink up

I gave my love my heart to hold
Drink up
Put in his pocket with his gold
Drink up drink up
I kissed him and his ring I wore
He turned me then from out his door
And took up with a richer whore
Drink up drink up drink up

I beat him when his back was turned
Drink up
I said Take that 'tis fairly earned
Drink up drink up
He said My love pray do not scold
I must have her for truth be told
She has a hundred pounds in gold
Drink up drink up drink up

I took from him my diamond ring
Drink up
I took from him most everything
Drink up drink up
There's nothing so becomes a whore
As does the keeping of a score
And chalking it upon the door
Drink up drink up drink up

His quittance I have fairly signed
Drink up
It's out of sight and out of mind
Drink up drink up
And I must find another one
To kiss my lips and plump my bum
Now my old cully's dead and gone,
Drink up drink up drink up

51

The drove lies between flooded fields and he is walking before her, talking with Keshlie, Keshlie skipping, holding his hand. The back of Keshlie's gown comes undone and begins to drop away from her, Betsy-Ann fussing along behind, gathering up the stuff, tying it anyhow, hoping nobody will notice, until her sister is naked but still skipping, seemingly unaware, such a daisy she is, and Ned turns and winks at Betsy-Ann, and turns Keshlie to face her and the child is smeared with something, some dust from the roadside where she has fallen. Ned says, 'What a dirty little thing,' and takes off his hat – his finest, with the gold brocade – and makes to put it over Keshlie's head, but instead it goes over Betsy-Ann's, and she struggles in darkness, and by the time she gets the hat off they are far away in the field, the child still skipping, water splashing up round her feet and her white body twinkling.

Rolled in her old quilt, she lies stretched before the hearth. A sullen light oozes, rather than shines, into the room; a faint wisp of yellow-grey smoke shows that the fire is not quite out. On her hands and knees Betsy-Ann drags herself to the coal scuttle, and pours some slack over the embers. She kneels there with the bellows, breathing life into it, Romeville's familiar waking noises all around her. Somewhere kegs are being loaded onto a dray. A woman down the street is crying hot rolls. She thinks of her Eye, in Shiner's place, lying open now and ransacked.

Blind Eye.

She hugs her knees, hoping to still a queasy curdling that she knows comes from drink. Last night when she came home, O, didn't she go it! A week's worth down her throat: laughing and crying together, and screaming, and rolling on the floor.

The fire begins to pick up. She stays a long time unmoving, watching the smoke. No sneaking about with Ned now, of any description: he's secured, the property of his autem mort.

When she saw the black boy, she thought nothing of it. Not such a fashion, now, as they used to be, but still you see them. He was out of livery and might have been anybody's. Shockingly turned out, in fact, his shoes hanging off his heels: what could Ned be playing at, not to find him in better togs? The boy was already backing off, heading towards the tree. She supposed he was too shabby to enter, and was there to see the Quality go in and out while he waited for his master.

Later, as the shrieks started and the charging about, she saw a flash hang in the tree like a star. That'd be the second shot, the one that dropped Harry. If the boy was up there, he'd have leaped from the branches and been away almost before the star faded.

Ned said the boy was entirely his. Why, then? Unless it was Harry he wanted dead. Harry was known at the house. It comes to her that the boy meant to defend Ned, and his first shot was a bungle. If anyone has him strung up for that, it won't be Betsy-Ann Blore.

His master's just as dead, though. O Ned, clever Ned! To die of a bungle!

Can't you forgive him, Mrs Zedland said.

No, she can't. She loved him to the bone. Can't hang over him like you do, repent, repent. She peached on him, couldn't sit forgiving him for very shame, though you're no better, sitting there blubbering with your Mr Gingumbob primed and ready to go off, shame indeed, do you know the meaning of the word?

What sort of funeral will they give for Dimber Ned? *She* won't be invited. Suppose Kitty Hartry turns up? Rum doings, if she does! Good as a hanging! She manages half a smile before the pains start up inside her throat, and the tears.

'I told her you'd be trouble,' says Clem.

Fortunate stands grey and forlorn, bent and aching from the hours passed in the porch of the Spyglass.

'Where you been, then?'

'In Town.'

'Don't give me your lip. In Town!'

'I can't say the place.'

'Don't suppose you saw much of it,' says Clem. 'I hear you got a gentleman friend. Well, whatever else your *friend* pays for, he don't pay your wages here.'

'I will stay now. Stay inside.'

'If you're allowed to, which I sincerely hope you ain't. I got my eye on you.' At last Clem moves aside to allow Fortunate to enter, though his voice pursues him along the passageway: 'Beats anything for impudence. *One day* in the house —'

Dog Eye falls.

Fortunate runs up the stairs to his chamber, stumbling, crying out as he bangs his knees on the steps.

Alone, he wets the comb and applies it to his head, persisting this time though it pulls out his hair by the roots. He rubs water over his face. His eyes are swollen: he bathes them, begins to weep again, rubs them on his sleeve, weeps. Dog Eye falls.

Dog Eye falls.

Papa and Mama have travelled with Rixam, who is despatched

the following morning to Cosgrove's to reassure the proprietor that he will not be left with a dead man on his hands, while Papa accompanies Sophia to the nearest church. Should the funeral be that of Mr Zedland or Mr Hartry? Mama thinks Zedland less mortifying for Sophia, though Papa, with his strong legal brain, points out that if the marriage is to be proved void, it would be as well to bury a Hartry. Sophia, for her part, is nervous that an interment under that name may attract the *K. Hartry* whose letter remains engraved on her memory as the quintessence of filth. She wonders how many other names Edmund has gone by, and for what ends.

The minister is not eager to have Edmund, whether Hartry or Zedland, interred in his churchyard. He begins to explain about parish settlements but Papa, though not a native of London, carries a panacea in his pocket. Soon the man is in possession of a generous donation and of his Christian charity prepared to preside over the burial of a murdered stranger.

'After which,' says Mama when they are all together again, 'you shall come home to Buller and endeavour to be cheerful. Hetty is to visit, and we plan an excursion when the weather improves.'

Sophia cannot exert herself sufficiently to feign gratitude. Her feelings, raw, ragged and muddied, absorb her entirely. At times she experiences a dreadful, corrosive pleasure of which she had not thought herself capable: *he is dead, I am free*. At others she is choked with grief for her early love, for the time on the lake that can never come again. Self-torturing, she recalls every seductive smile, every affectionate gesture: there is no coldness, no cruelty in the Edmund whose charmed ghost stalks her memories, only misunderstanding. She wrings her hands to think that he has gone before his Maker with so stained a soul, and prays the Lord to have mercy on him. Though what use is that? God does not revise his judgments to please the living.

Lastly comes the most terrifying suspicion of all: a sense that with all its misery and wickedness, this episode may yet prove the most vital and engrossing chapter of her life, to which the rest will prove mere epilogue.

With care, Betsy-Ann unwinds the silk wiper from the Tarocco.

She had a pain this morning, a visit from her red-headed friend. First time she's ever been sorry. Mrs Ned has at least that much of him: there, she holds all the aces. What if it's a boy, though, and the boy grows up a Hartry, with his papa's pleasures and pastimes!

How will Mrs Ned like that?

Strange to sit here, doing nothing. Having been bounced, all her life, from one beating to another – bounced by hunger, by lust, by hopes that were nothing but chaff, in the end – she finds herself with no one to fear or depend on. Outside the window the very air is blank, white with frozen mist.

In fact, she's not precisely doing nothing. She's thinking. Not about Sam, or Harry, or Mrs Ned or even Ned himself – though he breaks in all the time, can't be helped – but about Betsy-Ann Blore, with no support but her own two legs. What's to become of her? Fancy – from the wagon to Denman's Buildings, all that long, long road just to find this shabby stopping-place! Though it's quiet enough, and the window frames snug. She can dig in here awhile, alongside of Mrs Sutton, or she can go elsewhere.

She'll be the one to decide. There's no part for her to play, now: her life is as unshaped as all that whiteness hanging in the air. This must be how it feels to be rich. Though even the rich play parts, and fall into traps. Some of them fairly fling themselves in.

Most of her stash is still sewn into her petticoats. Suppose she took the mail coach to Bristol, where the cousins lay up over winter? She'd have her own people around her – and once they'd got their hands on the gold, there'd be precious little meat in the pot, and everyone's nose poked into her business. She hasn't crawled out from under Kitty and Sam, only to be pushed around by the likes of Ben and Davey. You can starve in Bristol, same as here. She's seen them propped against walls, too weak to beg.

Shuffle. A *straight* shuffle, so the cards tell true.

Her gold won't last forever. If she could only settle the business – get behind the counter of a pretty little shop, say – she'd be made. Queen of her premises, showing folk the door, should she choose.

There's no Knave of Hearts in this pack, no Pam neither. Where's he now, Dimber Ned?

Seven-card horseshoe. First up: King of Cups, reversed. One who takes good care of himself, leaving others to sink or swim. Not much to puzzle her there. Next, Five of Batons, also reversed. Lawing, cheating, trickery. No surprise there, either.

She hopes there won't be too many of these reversed cards. They are always unlucky. Still, it's only Past and Present: what matters is Future. She slides her finger under the Future card and turns up . . . two. Two of them! Never in her life has she fumbled the Tarocco like that: is there some special meaning in it? Three of Cups, upright; Four of Cups, reversed. So close together, Three and Four! Had it been Cups and Swords, now, she'd try to read them together, but these might just be a slip of the fingers, two cards stuck together through all the shuffling and come out here. The question is, which is the true card? Not the Three, surely. That means kinchins, and here she sits with her rags on.

So: Four of Cups, Reversed. Too much of a good thing, leading to sickness, weakness, punishment. *Blushing like port wine*, says a sly voice in her head. But this is the future. Ned has no future. It's the first time she's had that thought. She sits motionless a while, taking it in.

Suppose it should be her own sickness, and she like Lina Burch,

484

headed for the Lock? She shudders. Come spring, Lina will be walking carrion, earning her bread by frightening off cullies until some furious whore throws her a shilling. Four of Cups is Lina's card. Though it won't be Betsy-Ann's, not in that way, because she'd kill herself first.

Having two cards queers the reading. She's begun to wish she'd never opened the pack: the future seems shrunken now, gelded of the magic she sensed when looking out of the window.

Never mind, on we go: Five of Coins, ruin but with hope. To hell with hope, better have no ruin, then you don't need the hope. Should she just stop reading – no, get it out, know the worst. Six of Coins, a giver. Last card. Seven of Cups. Chance of great fortune, easily missed. And how in Christ's name is a poor mort to know it when it comes? As if she hasn't spent her life trying. Everyone in Romeville, from Cosgrove to the man with the talking dog, they're all watching for the Great Chance. The Blores came here in search of theirs, and look at them now: she's the only one left above ground.

There was the night at Haddock's. That seemed like it, at the time. Perhaps her chance wasn't Ned but Mrs Ned, all along. Either way, she's missed it. The wind's changed, Mrs Ned won't pay. She heard it in the noise of the carriage, rattling off.

Four of hers have died here: Mam, Keshlie, ugly Harry and Dimber Ned. Shouldn't such things, as much as your birthplace, count as a parish settlement? She's heard that carters pick up young runaways trudging the roads and fetch them into Romeville. The fee is the usual thing, after which the chit is said to be 'made free of the cart'. When you've seen as much as she has, and lain with as many men, you're surely made free of the Town.

Lord, what care my mother takes! Could she but procure herself a Hottentot.

He was Kitty's son, yet he was more besides. He had his moments of kindness, it's only right they should be remembered.

Does The Cunt in the Wall now boast a Hottentot? That Betsy-Ann doesn't know the answer, that she herself escaped the place and will never go back, is owing to him.

She sets down her Tarocco and takes up the deck with the soldiers and the dancing ladies, flicking through until she finds Pamphile. There he is, the little devil, with his melancholy, lascivious phiz. She sets him aside to look at awhile. Then she places him back in the deck and practises shuffling, again and again, turning him this way and that, keeping him always under her eye.

Glossary

This glossary includes cant, slang, archaic words and the French with which elegant speakers peppered their conversation. Expressions still current, such as *memento mori* and *frisson*, have not been glossed.

   The primary source is Grose's *Dictionary of the Vulgar Tongue* but many of the expressions used were current much earlier; some, such as cove and dimber, date back to the seventeenth century or before.

à la mode in the fashion
Abbess bawd
active citizens body lice
au fait knowledgeable
autem bawler parson
autem mort 1) wife 2) female beggar impersonating a desperate wife with small children
autem church

bagnio a cross between a Turkish bath and a sex hotel, extremely expensive
bantling child
baubles testicles
bel canto Italian style of singing
bibelot ornament
bilk cheat
billet-doux love letter
bing avast steal away, clear off
bishop hot drink made from wine, fruit and spices
bitch booby female bumpkin
bite (*noun/verb*) a theft or trick; to steal or trick
blood riotous disorderly fellow

blowen disreputable girl; whore; thief's mistress

blunt money

bob trick, criminal racket

bonnet a decoy who distracts attention away from his cheating partner

books playing cards

boozing-ken drinking den

bubbies breasts

bubble cheat

bubble and squeak beef and cabbage, fried up together

buck notable debauchee

buggeranto sodomist

bullybacks 'bouncers' in places of entertainment

bunter 1) a rag picker 2) the lowest and most desperate kind of prostitute

buttock ball sexual intercourse

cackler preacher

candid generous, ready to think the best of others

cant criminal slang

canting crew criminal fraternity

chaunter cull composer of songs for street musicians

cheese it shut up, keep mum

chivvy cut

clog burden, impediment

closet private space within a bedchamber

comfits sweets

comme il faut as it should be, as one must

Corinth brothel

Corinthian debauchee

cove bloke

Covent Garden Ague syphilis

cracksman safebreaker

crew gang

crib grave, graveyard

cull(y) a prostitute's client, or a woman's dupe

cundum condom

Curse of Scotland the nine of diamonds

Cyprian prostitute

dairyworks breasts

daisy naïve person

damper snack

darby money, cash

darkmans night

dell girl, young woman

déshabille undress/casual dress

de trop superfluous

deuce in cards, the Two of any suit.

Deuce, the the Devil

dimber beautiful/handsome

dinner the time of this varied, but was generally much earlier than
   our modern 'dinner' (see 'supper')

doe mistress

done brown cheated

drab prostitute

drug drag, hindrance

duddering rake lewd, filthy, extreme rake

duds clothes

dummee pocket book, wallet

dun (*noun/verb*) person who collects debts; to collect a debt

enceinte pregnant

ensemble (here) overall effect

entre nous between ourselves

ergo therefore

fam hand

Farmer George George III

fawney ring

faytour counterfeiter, forger

fingerpost parson

fire priggers thieves preying on victims of domestic fires

flash 1) knowing (the opposite of 'flat'). 'To patter flash' = to speak the
   slang of criminals, the 'cant'
   2) a glass of gin ('lightning')

flash house a gathering place for criminals, especially thieves

flash kiddey young thief, often with the sense of ostentatious style

489

flat naïve person, fool
flesh-hound man in search of sex
flowers menstrual period
fly knowing
flyer 'knee-trembler'
follower servant's suitor
foyster pickpocket
frig masturbate
frisk search (a till or a person being robbed)
funk panic

gammon nonsense, rubbish
garden thrash contemptuous term for vegetables
gentry-cove gentleman
gentry-mort gentlewoman
gingumbob thingummy
glim partially concealed lantern, 'dark lantern'
Grand Tour European trip, part of the education of young gentlemen
guinea gold coin worth £1.05

Harris's (List) a catalogue of prostitutes, with their prices and specialit-
ies, anonymously edited by Sam Derrick. From 1761 he took up the
'day job' of Master of Ceremonies at Bath and Tunbridge Wells
while continuing to edit *Harris's*, something that only became public
knowledge after his death.
hartshorn ammonia used as smelling salts
high toby/toby man highwayman
hogo stink
hollow leg man with huge capacity for drinking

in keeping (of a woman) financially supported by a lover
in the straw pregnant

Jack Ketch traditional nickname for the hangman
jerry chamber pot

keeper man supporting a mistress
keeping cully dupe supporting an unfaithful mistress

ken house, dwelling

kiddey *see* flash kiddey

kidney disposition, principles or humour

kinchin child

knotting-bag a workbag, used by some women as a handbag

large, a the corpse of an adult

lay enterprise, pursuit or attempt

les domestiques the servants

letch kink, perversion, particular attraction

lift pickpocket

lightning gin

link-boy boy carrying a torch, or 'link', who could be hired to guide
  pedestrians

Lock Hospital hospital for the treatment of sexually transmitted disease

loobies bumpkins

lush (*noun/verb*) a drinker; to drink

lushy fond of drinking

ma femme my wife

Magdalene House charity which rescued prostitutes

make someone easy kill someone

man of honour libertine

man of spirit debauchee

mantua-maker dressmaker

marrowbones knees

middling sort middle class

mill beat

Miss Laycock a woman's sexual organs

monosyllable, the a woman's sexual organs

mort woman

Mother female brothel keeper

Mr Lushington a drunkard

Mrs Delany a bluestocking known for her interest in gardening as
  well as other aspects of what we might now call 'lifestyle'

muff a woman's sexual organs. Women beginning a new relationship
  or getting married were toasted, 'To the well wearing of your muff.'

Mussulman Muslim

nantz brandy from Nantes

nap/nab catch/get

necessary house lavatory

New Buildings new developments in the area around Marylebone

niaiseries foolishnesses

nose spy

nuns prostitutes in a brothel

ogles eyes

Old Harry the devil

Old Scratch the devil

one of us a prostitute

ottomised dissected (corruption of 'anatomised')

Pam, Pamphile the Knave of Clubs

panney house

parish settlement the right to reside in a parish or to receive parish assistance

partie de plaisir enjoyable outing

peach, to to 'grass someone up'

pelisse type of cloak

perruque earlier version of 'periwig' (modern English, 'wig')

phiz face

pièce de résistance (in this context) finest achievement

pike (off) 'do a runner'

plump currant 'in the pink'

plus ça change the more things change (the more they stay the same)

pomade hair dressing

poor's hole/poor's pit type of communal grave in which the coffins of
the poor were stacked three or four deep

posset drink of alcohol mixed with milk or cream and spices

prad horse

priggers thieves

prink oneself beautify oneself

provocatives aphrodisiacs

pushing academy brothel

put one's finger in one's eye feign grief/force oneself to cry

queer culls sodomites

Queer Street a tricky situation, especially financial

Quel dommage! What a shame!

ragoo ragout

Ranelagh a fashionable pleasure garden

readies ready money

Receiving House early kind of post office, often based at an inn

red-headed friend menstrual period

resurrectionist grave-robber

revenons à nos moutons let's get back to where we started (literally:
   'Let's return to our sheep', an allusion to a fifteenth-century play)

riding St George sex with the woman on top

ridotto gathering with music and dancing

rig fun, game, trick

Romeville London

rose (never blown upon) a virgin

rout fashionable evening party or reception

rum good, fine, desirable

sacque style of dress

sal salivation caused by mercury treatment (for syphilis)

scrag, to hang (a person)

seraglio continental type of brothel, considered more upmarket

Sex, the with a capital 'S', this means 'women'

shiv knife

simpkin simpleton

Sisterhood, the prostitutes

small, a the corpse of a child

sot drunkard

sotto voce spoken so as not to be overheard

Spanish fly cantharides, an aphrodisiac

sparrowgrass asparagus

Spitalfields silk silk of London manufacture, from the parish of Spitalfields

sprain one's ankle become pregnant

squaretoes old-fashioned person

stand bitch act the hostess, pour tea

sugar stick penis

supper evening meal

sweating mercury treatment for syphilis

take the King's Shilling join the army

Tarocco Tarot

tarse penis

tendresses 'tendernesses'. Here, intimate talk and other sounds from the bedroom

three-legged mare the gallows

toby *see* high toby

toddle leave, run away

togs clothes

toilette grooming, self-presentation

ton, **the** the fashionable nobility

touché 'You win that one'

tray in cards, the three of any suit

trepan to kidnap, usually into slavery

(trusty) Trojan trustworthy person, confidante

Uncle pawnbroker

Upright Man gang leader

wap fuck

ware hawk! look sharp!

ware trap watch out for the police

warm(er) (more) sexually explicit/arousing

whelp young man (literally 'puppy')

whipping culls customers seeking flagellation

Wilkes, John republican, political writer and libertine

wiper handkerchief

wolf cancerous tumour

wrapper 1) dress made by winding fabric about the body 2) a dressing-gown

Zedland the West Country

Select bibliography

To acknowledge one's sources is not to present oneself as a historian.

Arnold, Catherine *City of Sin*
Ashton, John *The History of Gambling in England*
Baines, Paul *The Long Eighteenth Century*
Boswell, James *Journals*
Boswell, James *The Life of Johnson*
Brumwell, S. and Speck, W. A. *Cassell's Companion to Eighteenth-Century Britain*
Burnett, John *A History of the Cost of Living*
Cahill, Katherine *Mrs Delany's Menus, Medicines and Manners*
Clarke, Norma *Queen of the Wits*
Cockayne, Emily *Hubbub*
Colquhoun, Kate *Taste*
Cruickshank, Dan *The Secret History of Georgian London*
Cunnington, C. W. and P. C. *Handbook of English Costume in the Eighteenth Century*
Douglas, Alfred *The Tarot*
Equiano, Olaudah *The Interesting Narrative*
George, M Dorothy *London Life in the Eighteenth Century*
Grose, Francis *Dictionary of the Vulgar Tongue*
Harvey, A. D. *Sex in Georgian England*
Horn, Pamela *Flunkeys and Scullions*
Jacobs, Harriet *Incidents in the Life of a Slave Girl*
Moore, Wendy *Wedlock*
Olsen, Kirstin *Daily Life in Eighteenth-Century England*
Peakman, Julie *Lascivious Bodies*
Picard, Liza *Dr Johnson's London*
Porter, Roy *London: A Social History*
Porter, Roy *English Society in the Eighteenth Century*

Rubenhold, Hallie *Harris's List of the Covent Garden Ladies*
Rubenhold, Hallie *The Covent Garden Ladies*
Russell, Gillian 'Faro's Daughters' (article)
Sands, Mollie *Invitation to Ranelagh*
Sitwell, Edith *Bath*
Smith, Virginia *Clean*
Thomas, Hugh *The Slave Trade*
Vickery, Amanda *Behind Closed Doors*
Vickery, Amanda *The Gentleman's Daughter*
Wardroper, John *Lovers, Rakes and Rogues*
Warner, Jessica *Craze*
White, Jerry *London in the Eighteenth Century*
Wroth, W. W. and A. E. *The London Pleasure Gardens of the Eighteenth Century*

The story of Fortunate's capture and enslavement draws upon the account given in Olaudah Equiano's *The Interesting Narrative*. That the word 'fortunate' is one possible translation of 'Olaudah' is pure coincidence, since my character took shape, complete with name, long before I came across that book. The coincidence itself seemed fortunate, so I have left the name as it is.

Betsy-Ann's songs 'Sometime I am a butcher bold' (chapter 4) and 'Moll of the Wood' (chapter 15) are authentic; the other songs are of my own invention.

Acknowledgements

Thanks are due to my agent Annette Green (as ever) and to all at Faber, particularly my editor Sarah Savitt whose clarity has been invaluable.

An earlier incarnation of this book included much more material on both folk music and gambling. I am grateful to C. J. Bearman who patiently answered my queries on Cecil Sharp, and to Professor Gillian Russell of the Australian National University who responded generously to an email from an unknown writer, supplying me with useful materials on eighteenth-century women gamblers. Historical errors and deliberate distortions are of course my own responsibility.

My friends and fellow writers of the RABS group are an unending source of support, encouragement and the occasional bucket of cold water when I need it. My thanks and love to you all.

Lastly I should like to thank Ruth Borthwick of the Arvon Foundation, whose offer of work at a crucial time enabled me to complete this novel. May Arvon go from strength to strength.